The Edge of Darkness

The Chronicles of Ragnorak Book 3

A novel by

Christiano Prime
https://www.facebook.com/profile.php?id=1000333
01249234

Cover Art by Kayla Ginther
https://www.facebook.com/kaylanicoleginther

## Foreword from the author:

This is a work of fiction. All the characters, organizations, and events portrayed in this novel are either products of the author's imagination or used fictitiously.

This book is dedicated to the many teachers and professors who helped foster my mind and cultivate my creativity.

# Chapter 1 Freshmen Weekend

The Omegas of Bay Valley rolled onto campus Friday morning, twenty strong, it was the day freshmen moved into the dorms! Their fraternity set up a table at a prime location, near the freshmen dorms, by a small faculty parking lot, catching new people by the dozens. A group of four brothers manned the table with a large Omega banner across the front, handing out water and flyers for different activities around campus and in the community. Every brother of the Omegas had on their lettered shirts and hoodies, the best kind of advertisement. Virgil Pitcher felt like they were doing a great job of getting Omegas name out to the new faces. Virgil was walking around with his best friends and fraternity brothers, Alec Birdman (whom everyone affectionately referred to as Birdy) Louie V, and Dante. Birdy was a tall and lanky guy, with a bit of an aloof personality that got him a lot of slack from the brothers. He was more reserved, good natured, and always a caring friend. Louie was Vietnamese, with some Chinese and Caucasian. He had a medium to dark complexion, with round pudgy cheeks that mirrored the rest of his body, and his dark hair was buzzed down into a mohawk with the middle dyed a bright blond. He was a crowd favorite for his humor and fun-loving attitude. Dante was slightly under average height with auburn hair, dark eyes and a confident attitude. He was talkative and outgoing, and liked sports. Virgil had been friends with them since around this time last year, when they all joined the Omega fraternity as Omicron class. There was only six of them now, two had died in battle, another fell away from the Chapter shortly thereafter.

Dante and Birdy saw a kid struggling with the bags and boxes he was carrying, so they rushed over, and helped him out, striking up a conversation with him. His name was Zane, he was from Mayville, a village in the Thumb of Michigan. He was built similar to Birdy, but he was more toned and athletic looking. He was nineteen, older than Virgil, with a few tattoos poking out from his clothing. Zane had a chill and laid-back disposition. He was polite and graciously accepted their help in moving the rest of his stuff in. Louie had him cracking up within minutes, and they quickly developed a good rapport. Once they'd finished helping him get all his belongings to his dorm room, Louie invited him to the Omega house party Saturday night. Louie shook hands with Zane afterward, the blue Dreamstone on Louie's silver fraternity ring, lit up.

"Wow," Zane exclaimed letting go of Louie's hand. "Did you guys just see that?"

Virgil shared a knowing look with his pledge brothers, as they said goodbye to Zane, Virgil and Birdy being careful to shake his hand with their non-ring hands. Only someone with the immortal blood of a Judge could make the ring react that way.

"He's definitely Omega material," Dante chuckled as the four friends headed back out to the campus sidewalks to look for more freshmen like Zane.

Virgil had a large grin on his face, Dante was right, and this whole experience brought back so many memories for him. Virgil's fraternity, the Omegas, weren't your average college fraternity. They were a part of the Paladins, an order of Nephilim warriors who had lived on Earth alongside humanity, since before the dawn of civilization. The Paladins recruited other Nephilim by a number of ways but in modern times, one method that had developed with continued results was the Greek system at collegiate establishments around the world. Nephilim were drawn to places of power, and the elite were well educated. The Dreamstone was a special piece of magicite, crystalized spiritual energy, whose function was twofold; it could detect the presence of someone with Nephilim blood, and conceal the person's aura from being detected.

Virgil had always felt different from others that he'd met, though he was what some would call handsome, six feet tall, sapphire-colored eyes, and a nose slightly too large for his face; it wasn't until he pledged the Omegas that he learned how *truly* different he was. Virgil had tattoo like symbols on his hands, a black sickle scythe on his left, and a white shooting star on his right. The day he'd turned eighteen the symbols had formed on his hands. They were his Devil Arms, a gift given to all Nephilim, and any person with Nephilim blood could gain them by going through a short process called the Oath of the Paladin. Virgil was a Pureblood Nephilim, so his Devil Arms came naturally along with his wings. Virgil usually had his wings concealed, Nephilim were able to summon them like the Devil Arms, and then will them back into their flesh. Virgil was the son of Fallen Judge Raphael, the third God General of the Demon King Diablos' army of demons, Nephilim, and Fallen Judges in the Ever After.

Virgil had met his father, Raphael, just a few months earlier. The Tournament of the Chalice had taken place on the Summer Solstice, in the Paladin Capital Alexandros, a floating island about the size of Rhode Island that hovers above Lake Michigan. The Tournament had been a tradition of the Paladins almost since their founding, every five years the strongest Nephilim warriors would gather in a test of strength. The mightiest of their order, was given the Chalice, their reward for winning was to become the new bodyguards and Guardians of the Chalice. The Chalice was what allowed the Paladins to create more of their kind, it was a cup that never emptied, golden ichor, the blood of the immortals bubbled inside. Just a taste was all that was needed to bring out the Nephilim powers in someone with very little Judge blood in their veins. Virgil's fraternity, the Upsilon Delta Chapter, had won the tournament. Right after they'd won Virgil and a handful of his brothers were taken prisoner by the Harbinger, and the Gatekeeper, the leaders of the Death Dealers, the legion of Nephilim allied with Diablos. Virgil's father had visited him in the Death Dealer prison, Hel. In truth Virgil had secretly longed to meet his father, but it had been more painful than expected. They were on opposite sides of this conflict, and neither was willing to budge. Raphael was supposed to bring Virgil over to the Death Dealers. It was revealed during Virgil's first year that he was one of seven Nephilim, The Seven Seraphs, prophesized to bring about the war that will end the world…Ragnorak.

Virgil was the Sixth Seraph, his was the Redeemer, though he preferred his name rather than a title. Virgil was given the power to Redeem Fallen Judges, and had recently discovered, that power could also be used on fellow Nephilim and even Fallen Eidolons. Virgil was rescued from the Ever After by Artreyu, the Avatar and the First Seraphs. Together they'd helped rescue hundreds of fellow prisoners, the cost being they unwillingly helped a Fallen Eidolon into the human world, Tiamat the Mother of Eidolons and Dragons. Artreyu had managed to kill the dangerously insane dragon with the help of Virgil and an unidentified female Battle Maiden. Virgil had come to the conclusion she'd been a Valkyrie, a special kind of Judge who watches over the fates of mortal warriors. After the death of Tiamat, the Omegas had been tasked with bringing home the Chalice of Immortals, to safeguard until the next Tournament. The Chalice had brought significant changes to the Omegas daily living, namely a regimen of Paladin warriors from the Capital, to protect the Omega house and the Bay Valley Campus from any possible Death Dealer attacks. Though their presence hadn't proven to be that intrusive, they were nevertheless under closer watch by Internationals than they were used to.

After hours of helping random people, Virgil and his friends were ready to be done. They walked back to the Omega table for some water. It was well into the afternoon now, and the days could be stifling hot in August, in Michigan. Near the Omega table the Alpha sorority had set up a similar table, they were Paladins as well, and recruited women who were to some degree

Nephilim. Virgil saw one of his other best friends, Blair Nedeau, working her social magic talking to everyone she met near her sorority's table. Virgil walked over to the growing group of over a dozen brothers and sorority sisters, the move-in process had begun slowing down.

"Virgil Pitcher!" he heard his name being shouted out and turned. TK and Selene came over to him to give him a hug. They were both sorority sisters of the Alphas, TK was Selene's Big Sister, and they were also the girlfriends of brothers in the fraternity, fraters Gabriel and Brody. TK was slightly taller, with a thinner frame; she had a healthy complexion with dark hair, piercing green eyes, and a permanent smile. TK was quirky, loving, outgoing, and extremely fun. Virgil had bonded with her over the past year and she was a good friend. Everyone knew Gabriel was a lucky guy. Though equally lucky was frater Brody, as Selene was on track to hold a major public office, cure a lethal disease, or take over the world, whichever came first. Selene was slightly shorter than TK with raven black hair and a tanned skin tone from being a quarter Native American. She had a pretty face with chocolate brown eyes. Selene was President of Student Association, a member of the community service co-ed fraternity, and an Alpha sorority sister, on top of several other organizations she'd joined in her four years at Bay Valley. Selene was graduating with a Master's in Occupational Therapy in May. She was a humanitarian who gave selflessly to others, and when she put her mind to something, she gave it her all.

"How are things going?" TK asked him.

"Great!" Virgil said with a bright smile, "I think we've met at least thirty guys who had potential," he told them. "I didn't expect for there to be so many Nephilim walking around."

"Not even half of the guys who could join, will come out," Lamar interjected.

"I know," Virgil sighed. Lamar was co-Rush Chairman with Brody, and they were in charge of recruitment week. Lamar was a third year, a large and very loud man, he lived for fun and was usually laughing.

"Hey tramp," Blair said, coming over to Virgil and giving him a hug.

"Hey trouble," Virgil fondly replied, reciprocating her warm embrace.

"Are you done with helping freshmen for the day?" Blair asked him.

"Move in lasts for two more hours," Jace called out, seated at the Omega's table. He wore an Omega shirt, along with his signature baseball cap, and glasses over his one brown eye and one green eye. He was outspoken and opinionated, well respected on campus, and well connected. He could be one of the more serious brothers but enjoyed pranking more than most.

"Yeahhh," Blair drawled out. "I'm passing on that," she laughed.

"Right behind ya," Louie shouted. "Let's get some food and have some fun!"

"Ditching freshmen move in Louie?" Jace reprimanded. "I see where your priorities lie," he said jokingly.

"I've been helping freshmen move in for hours!" Louie snapped. "How many guys have you helped sitting on your butt in the shade?" he asked Jace.

Before the two could start arguing, one of the fraternity Sweethearts, Raven, seated near Jace interjected. "Boys! Let's not argue. If Louie needs a break to get some food he can, we're all volunteering here," she said in a friendly tone.

"Thanks Raven!" Louie called out turning tail and heading straight for the cafeteria.

"Wait up Louie!" Birdy called out heading after him.

Virgil and Blair followed their friends making the short walk over to one of the main campus buildings that held the university cafeteria. The sidewalks were congested with people, college students of all ages were roaming the grounds under the warm August sun. The cafeteria was overflowing with food, seemingly limitless choices, to trick the freshmen into thinking this is how it would always be. Virgil and his friends grabbed several plates and managed to find a small spot in the overcrowded dining hall. As they caught up Blair told them about some freshmen she'd met that seemed legit.

"Blair? Blair Nedeau?" a guy called out.

"What?" Blair asked looking around. "Brett! You dirty bastard!" Blair laughed. "I was wondering when I'd run into you, didn't think it'd be on your first day," she remarked.

Brett got up and came over to stand near where they were seated. His roommate, Nigel, came with him. Brett struck up an awkward but friendly chat with Blair, they knew each other obviously, but Birdy, Louie and Virgil were not clued into who he was.

"Sorry guys," Blair said to them, "Brett these are the Omega boys I told you about. This is Brett, he's kind of like my little brother," she smirked.

"He's your little brother!" Louie exclaimed, "Well why the hell didn't you say so earlier?" he asked getting up to hug Brett.

"Well, I said kind of," Blair said, "His dad is dating my mom, they've been together for a couple years now," she added.

"Oh," Louie said awkwardly half into hugging Brett.

"It's okay big guy, I'll still take a hug," Brett joked his face growing red holding out his arms like a good sport.

Louie gave him a half hug, half handshake, Louie's Dreamstone lighting up once his skin touched Brett's. Virgil's eyebrows raised, Brett was a Nephilim, interesting. Brett didn't notice the ring react and was none the wiser, he didn't have Devil Arms symbols on his hands, Virgil was guessing he couldn't see theirs. Blair, Birdy, and Louie all had unique Devil Arms symbols, he didn't like to brag, though he did feel his friends were some of the stronger Nephilim he'd met. Brett introduced his roommate Nigel, an overly friendly, if somewhat eager to please youth. His social awkwardness made Louie crack up.

"You should come hang out with us sometime," Birdy offered Brett. "Any friend of Blair's is more than welcome around our fraternity house."

"Thanks man," Brett replied with a bright grin.

"I'd love to come to one of your frat parties!" Nigel shouted a little too loudly. "You guys seem like the shit, I'd want to get down with y'all!" He exclaimed with a large grin, smacking the gum he was chewing.

"Geez dude!" Louie laughed, "Ease up. You're both welcome to come, but don't call it a 'frat party' frat is usually perceived with negative connotation," Louie said. "We're an elite fraternity, a brotherhood. It's a party at the Omegas, or just a little get together, but not a frat," he told him.

"Didn't mean to step on your toes dawg," Nigel nodded.

"No worries," Birdy told him. "We're cool."

"I'll probably have a get together tonight," Blair told Brett, "I'll text you later, if you're looking for a place to have some fun," she said with a wink.

"Nice meeting you guys," Brett said to them and they walked back to their own table.

"You didn't tell us you had a Nephilim little brother," Louie quipped once Brett was out of ear shot.

"Well he's not really my little brother, but I have been talking to him about you boys all summer. He didn't know where he was going until really late, so I didn't want to hype him up, then have him not come here," Blair told them.

"You think he is Omega material?" Virgil asked her.

"I'm not sure," she said looking down, "I think he's a good guy, a little goofy and airheaded. Honestly, he's definitely got some growing up to do, but I think he'd be a good fit for Omega," she thought out loud looking up at Virgil.

"I like him," Birdy shrugged his shoulders. "We should hang out with him."

"Any family of Blair's is welcome in our group," Dante said warmly.

"His roommate is a total klutz!" Louie cracked himself up laughing like a hyena.

"Let's have a get together at my place tonight," Blair suggested. "You boys are having a party tomorrow night, and Sunday is the night before classes."

"That sounds fun to me," Birdy nodded getting on his phone, starting to send out a wave of text messages inviting people over to Blair's that night.

"You guys going over to the Student Life event?" Virgil asked once they'd all finished eating and were sitting around talking. "Omega is hosting it," he pointed out.

"I'm all Rushed out for the day," Louie yawned patting his full belly, "I might head home for a nap, so I'm at full steam tonight."

"I'm going to head home too," Blair said stretching as she slowly got up, "I have to get prepared for tonight."

"I'll go with you," Birdy offered Virgil. They split off from Louie and Blair, heading to the freshmen courtyard. A couple hundred students were standing around the large square, the campus mascot was present, and music was playing. Brody, an Omega, a class older than Virgil, was on the megaphone as the MC of the event. Brody was a natural performer, with a goofy and fun-loving persona. Gabriel was helping run the show with fellow Omegas Vahn, Rowan, and Tarek Jeter. They were some of the guys Virgil looked up to, and the more powerful warriors in the fraternity. They had set up a water slide competition, seeing who could do the best slides and stunts. For almost forty-five minutes, dozens of men and a few women ran down the tarps on the grass. It generated a lot of hype attracting several hundred people, making both Student Life and the Omegas look good. Rowan couldn't stop himself from showing off, taking his already skintight designer shirt off, he flexed his chest and toned stomach dancing for the crowd, to the pleasure and dismay alike from the viewers.

"Damn show off," Vahn said casually to Virgil, his Little Brother in Omega.

"Some things never change," Virgil replied nodding. Rowan was a gifted dancer, he was great at a lot of things and one of the best brothers, though he liked to make sure everyone knew that.

The competition ended, the winner jumped over a table and dove into the water, sliding down the wet tarp. He was easily the most handsome new face in the crowd, with deep brown eyes, and a finely trimmed beard. He performed flawlessly for the crowd, taking his shirt off and flexing showing off his six pack. Brody took him to the microphone.

"Congratulations! Man, you are definitely the winner of this slip and slide competition!" Brody declared. "What's your name?"

"I'm Colton Cormier," he panted out into the microphone, still trying to catch his breath. "College freshman, I'm from Frankenmuth, and I'm single," he added at the end smirking into the audience and wiggling his eyebrows to the cheers of the ladies. Brody gave him a thirty-dollar gift card to the campus store. Virgil immediately saw Colton's Devil Arms when he accepted the envelope from Brody. On his right hand, an amethyst symbol in the shape of a large sword. Virgil didn't know its name, or even if Colton could see his Devil Arms, but it was powerful. Virgil was good at gaging a Nephilim's power. Other brothers noticed as well, freshmen with Devil Arms were rare, and a dead giveaway as Nephilim.

Gabriel and Rowan talked with Colton for a little bit after the competition, they were interested in bringing him around the Omegas. Colton seemed interested in the fraternity, he agreed to come check things out and 'hang out' with the brothers. Birdy went with a group of brothers and a few potentials, including Colton. Virgil caught a ride with his Big Brother, Vahn. Vahn was sarcastic, sassy, and sharp...he was one of the most beloved brothers in the Chapter. Vahn was a fourth year at Bay Valley, and in Lambda class, about the same height as Virgil, with mossy brown curly hair he kept short. He had a ruby Devil Arms, Furybrand, a flaming shortsword. Virgil looked up to him as what it took to be a good frater in Omega.

"That was a pretty successful day," Vahn boasted to Virgil as they walked to the parking lot together. "I'd say Rho Class is shaping up to be a great pledge class."

"I hope so," Virgil nodded thinking the same thing, "We could really use the numbers."

"We're always hurting a little at the beginning of the school year," Vahn reassured Virgil. "Once we get a group of candidates at the fifth week of the semester, we'll be stronger, it'll bring the brothers back together. The pledging process has a way of unifying us all."

"Are you coming over to Blair's tonight?" Virgil asked.

"Yes, I already got Birdy's text invite," Vahn chuckled. "Sounds like fun!"

It was a five-minute drive to get to the other side of campus, where Greek Lane held all the Greek housing. The Omega's estate was at the end of the road with a large roundabout before the gated entrance. Red brick walls surrounded the complex, with hundreds of unseen spells cast on their surface, they provided more than one layer of protection. The Omega mansion was several floors, painted cherry with grey paneling. The grounds were open and provided more space than they could need. The back yard was the length of a football field before being consumed by the forest.

The inside of the Omega's home was even better. Virgil remembered how overwhelmed he had felt when he first came here. Cherry and grey were the color schemes, the main living area was on the first floor, with the meeting room, pledge dorms, library, and small secondary living room on the second floor. The brothers lived on the third through the fifth floors and the sixth floor was for administration, namely the Chapter Advisors, and out of town Paladins from the Capital. They had a small group of men stationed on the sixth floor of the house from Alexandros, but the majority were living in rented town house apartments not a mile down the road, across from campus. Upon request they would vacate the premise for an evening but were always hesitant to do so, wanting someone guarding it at all hours. The Chalice was safely hidden, no one had seen it since it had been brought several weeks ago.

The Omega's fraternity manor had become Virgil's home away from his mom. His room was towards the end of a hallway on the third floor. Virgil showered and changed for Blair's. He wore a professional yet sleek and silver button up shirt over a nice pair of jeans, the silver made his sapphire eyes stand out. Virgil hung out with his brothers Nev, short for Nevin, Nolan, and Louie before heading to Blair's. They felt more like his roommates than any of the other brothers, as they shared a small dead-end hallway, and a bathroom.

"I think I'm going to pass on going out tonight," Nolan said as they were getting ready, everyone shared the bathroom, as it had two sinks and three mirrors.

"Aww come on Nolan!" Nev hackled him, "You never want to go out!"

"It's just, we're having a party here tomorrow night," Nolan explained, "So I can drink, and not worry about a ride home. If I go there, I won't drink, and I'll be too nervous to talk to a girl, and just screw things up," he said frustrated.

"You don't need alcohol to be successful, what you need is confidence," Virgil encouraged his friend.

"Nolan," Louie shook his head, "We need to help you find a girl!" Louie exclaimed.

"I agree," Nev laughed, his fair complexion growing rosy red. "If you'd just let us help you, I'm sure between Louie and I, we could work our magic, and help you score a chick!" Nev chucked at his idea, liking it the more he thought about it. "Seriously Nolan, you could use our help."

"Hey!" Nolan cried out.

"I'm not saying that to criticize you," Nev defended with his hands raised up in a show of no aggression. "I'm just pointing out, okay for example your outfit makes you look like you're a ten-year-old boy, who still lets his mother dress him up, and style his hair."

"He's got a point," Louie added.

"You dicks!" Nolan laughed. Nolan looked at himself in the mirror and sighed, "I'm never going to catch a girl's attention looking like this," he said sadly.

"Dude, you're going to be a major catch for some lucky lady," Virgil jumped in. "What you need is a little make over," he encouraged, "A polishing of the goods, to grab some attention."

"Maybe," Nolan nodded.

"Yup," Virgil, Louie, and Nev said leaning in the mirror behind Nolan.

"Maybe another time," Nolan shrugged, and he went to his room and closed his door.

"Did we hurt his feelings?" Virgil asked.

"Naw, I think we're good," Louie shrugged.

"He'll come around," Nev nodded, finishing up and straightening his shirt. "When he wants it bad enough, he'll come to us for help Louie," Nev grinned devilishly and the two friends shared a manly laugh.

The three of them carpooled with Birdy and Virgil quickly volunteered to drive, much to everyone's relief. It was only a few miles down from campus into the outskirts of Bay City into Kawkawlin. There were already over fifty people when they arrived. Helene was Blair's roommate, and best friend since junior high, she was also frater Landon's younger sister. She was softer and bubblier than Blair and played hostess well with her friendly and upbeat personality. Blair was in the basement running the flip cup table with Gabriel, Vahn, TK, and Rowan. Colton, the Nephilim from the slip and slide, was on the other team with a group of freshmen. There was a good mix of returning friends and new acquaintances.

"Finally, you guys show up!" Blair exaggerated with a grin greeting Virgil and the others.

"Virgil you've met Brett, and these are his roommates, Nigel and Cameron," Blair said.

"Haven't met you before Cameron," Virgil said shaking his hand. Virgil's Dreamstone lit up. Cameron looked like a surfer dude, with long thick wavy brown hair, and a really relaxed demeanor. Birdy and Cameron clicked instantly, the two started talking and their conversation just kept going. Brett was shy and kind of quiet, but Tarek Jeter was present and his over the top outgoing nature was able to bring Brett out of his shell.

Saturday night the Omegas had a party at their home, opening it up to campus. There were so many new women walking around, each more seemingly appealing then the last, Virgil felt a little intimidated to start conversations. He'd never been good at meeting new people, something the fraternity had helped him with, but he still wasn't a natural.

Virgil made eye contact with this pretty brunette, punk girl, who looked him over a few times. He approached her and struck up the normal awkward party pleasantries. After a few minutes the conversation died, they'd run out of things to say and she went to find her friend.

Virgil went to get a drink and after several more strike outs, he decided to talk with people he knew instead. Girls were more complicated than anything Virgil had encountered, and he couldn't make something out of nothing, he just had to be open to it when it happened.

Sunday's meeting was the first of the semester, nineteen of the twenty-three actives were present. Zender, the Chapter Pylortes, had warded the door once Magnus, the Chapter Prytanis, had called the meeting to order. Now none of the Paladins from the Capital could hear what they were saying.

"The slip and slide event was awesome!" Brody declared. "We had a great turnout, and we may have recruited one of Rho class' top members. We definitely shined at the event," he laughed, his big round cheeks getting rosy.

"Same thing with our welcome back party!" Abe said excitedly. "There were a lot of guys interested in us last night."

"What matters is if they are still interested in us when its Rush," Lamar retorted.

"Right," Jace added strongly, "I don't want guys in Omega who only come around for the party."

"Enough!" Magnus cut in hitting his gavel to gain authority over the room. "The Rush chairs still have the floor; they should be the only one talking. Sheesh," Magnus sighed rolling his eyes. "Like a bunch of sixth graders in here," he chuckled.

"We yield," Brody and Lamar declared.

"Good," Magnus nodded, "That leaves my report, then open, and the meeting is done," he said stretching and getting up. "Alright guys, something big has come up," he told the room drawing the immediate focus of the group. Virgil was sitting between Louie and Nev, the three of them leaned in, listening intently. "The Omegas from Upsilon Chapter are carrying out an operation in Flint this coming weekend. They've requested our aid as well as the other Paladin Chapters in the surrounding area," Magnus told them. "As you may know, the crime rates and demonic presence within that area have exponentially increased over the past month."

"It's been in the news," Birdy interjected. "That area has been struggling since the decline of the middle class, then the water incident hit the people hard," he pointed out.

"Their Prytanis believes an Arch Demon has burrowed into the city, and in response the demons have multiplied in that area. They have begun spreading to other cities for more feeding ground," Magnus explained. "Clio is already being affected, it won't be long before it starts affecting Saginaw, then us," Magnus paused and looked out at the brothers. "We need to help our brothers try to bring a solution to this...plague that has been allowed to run rampant. We have to help eliminate the threat there, before it gets a stronger foothold here," Magnus ended. "Thoughts?" he asked the group. Louie raised his hand. "Speak Louie," Magnus commanded.

"So basically, the Omegas at University of Michigan want us to go into Flint, at night, looking for a powerful Arch Demon that could fry our asses," Louie paused his expression was priceless, his eyes bulging from his head, his mouth aghast. "That sounds like the Saginaw operation all over again! Are you for real man?"

"Yes Louie, this is *for real!*" Magnus emphasized. "Saturday night, we're meeting at the U of M campus in Flint, they've reserved a room where we'll be debriefed on the specifics," Magnus clarified for them. "I'm passing around a signup sheet, anyone interested in going on the operation, write your name down so I have a figure of how many men we can pledge." Magnus passed the paper to Landon, who skipped putting his name down and passed it to Jace seated next to him. "Let's move into open and finish this meeting," Magnus said. "Does anyone have anything for open?" he asked.

There was a knock at the meeting room door, the Chapter turned its attention to Zender who stood up and approached the door, looking through the eyehole. "Oh!" Zender exclaimed and opened the door, the charm that had been in place as a sound barrier dissolved in the process.

A thin man came into the room, he had a beany on his head covering a mop of messy brown hair. He had a big nose, and bright eyes. Virgil could tell that he was a little different, in all the best ways, as he could tell that this man was a brother.

"Frater Spencer!" Zender said embracing him and welcoming him into the room. Zender then turned his attention back to spelling and guarding the door. Spencer came into the room, Gabriel and Vahn immediately got up and greeted Spencer with hugs, followed closely by Landon.

"Fraters, this is Spencer, our pledge brother," Magnus told the room.

"A long-lost Lambda!" Louie exclaimed. "Those things gotta be worth a fortune!" The room burst into laughter.

"Louie, shut up," Dante said making Virgil laugh. Dante didn't live at the fraternity house, he was staying with his parents in Clio, going to community college. Even while going to a different school, he was still around more than some brothers who lived at the house.

"Seriously people, imagine how powerful he must be to be a part of *their* class," Louie bobbed his head excitedly.

"We'll move right into closing," Magnus told the room, "When you take the gavel in your hand, feel for that minute the responsibility, and weight, to lead and carry this Chapter forward," he passed his gavel onto the brothers.

Landon was up first, "I just want to say how happy I am with this Chapter right now. We've done a great job this weekend of making Omega look great, and I'm proud of you guys. I'd like to end with, saying how touched I am to have you back in this room Spencer," Landon choked up getting teary eyed. "It honestly feels like our family, Lambda is whole again, and it means a lot to have you here, I miss you frater," Landon spoke passionately, passing the gavel.

"Well, there's no way I can follow something like that," Jace laughed nervously getting red. "So go Omegas, and it is good to see you again Spencer!" Jace said passing it on.

Eventually it was Spencer's turn to speak, "Fraters, I just want to say, how moving it is, to hear only praise upon coming back, even after being gone for so long," he said looking down.

"We love ya!" Landon laughed, "We don't care about that."

"I'm proud to say I'm taking classes at Bay Valley this Fall semester," Spencer smiled adding, "and I'm moving back into the Omega house," which earned a chorus of cheers. "I plan on being around more, there are a lot of new faces here that I don't recognize, and a lot of brothers gone that I hoped would still be here," Spencer said with a forlorn expression. "I'm looking forward to being a part of the Omegas again, and helping out this brotherhood," Spencer smiled, finishing on a high note. That night the brothers had a small celebration, to honor Spencer's return to their brotherhood. Having him at the Omega house was like getting a new family member overnight.

# Chapter 2 Operation Flint!

Virgil's first week of the Fall semester was thrilling, the start of the new year brought renewed energy to everyone. Saturday was the big operation in Flint. Virgil and a dozen of his brothers went to U of M, Flint campus. Over a hundred men and women were present from Paladin fraternities and sororities all over Michigan. The ones running the show were Omegas from the oldest Chapter in the state, the University of Michigan. Demon activity had spiked since the Tournament of the Chalice. Flint had been hit hard, more recently the city had been ravaged by an unexplained spike in crime…demons. Demons took advantage of the suffering locals, by swarming the area, and feeding off the auras, or spiritual energy, of humans. The demonic presence in the area had become so overpopulated, the demons were migrating like parasites in search of fresh hosts. The large group of Nephilim were meeting in hopes of stemming the flow of evil that had putrefied the area, rapidly spreading its tainted rot.

Virgil's brothers were getting a lot of attention, due to being the Guardians of the Chalice of Immortals. It was the highest honor that could be awarded to any fraternity or sorority in their order, and overnight Upsilon Delta had been put on the map in their world. The Prytanis of the Omegas from U of M, Donnell, called the room to order.

"The demon attacks have been more coordinated," Donnell announced, "Uncommon of demons left to their own whims. We have gathered everyone here for a simple solution; clean house. Hit the streets in large groups and comb through the city. If we can clean out the demon population, crime rates are sure to return to normal levels. Each group has a specific zone of the city they'll cover, and no group will have more than three members from their Chapter. We encourage you to mingle and begin forming groups, we'll help as needed."

The room slowly broke into conversation, people got up from their seats, first talking with their own Chapters to see which of their members were going to stick together. Virgil turned to his brothers and friends.

"Hey Louie, do you want to be in the same group?" Virgil asked. Louie looked around sheepishly, avoiding eye contact with Virgil. "Louie!" Virgil snapped, and Louie turned innocently to meet Virgil's gaze. "Do you want to be in the same group?" Virgil asked again.

"Well, uh," Louie stumbled to find the right words scratching the back of his head with one hand, "Don't take this the wrong way or nothing man, but I was kind of thinking about joining, you know…a safe group."

"A safe group?" Virgil repeated his eyebrows knitting close together in anger.

"Well yeah," Louie laughed nervously, "I go with you I'm bound to run into that ugly suckin' Arch Demon!" Louie cried out. "I think I should be a part of the group guarding this building. How else are we supposed to use the secret room in the basement to teleport back home?"

Virgil's stare grew intense, his eyes never leaving Louie. "You're telling me you don't want to be in the same group because you think I'm a danger magnet?" Virgil asked not happy.

"Well you do have a habit of running into big baddies," Louie shuddered.

Blair and Helene came over to Virgil, "Hey Virgil, want to join us?" Blair asked him.

"Sure," Virgil smiled happy someone wanted him in their group.

"Who is with you?" Helene asked curious.

"I asked Louie but he's too scared to be in my group," Virgil shrugged.

"Oh, for the love of, Louie!" Blair yelled stomping over to him. "Get your big ass over here! Leaving your best friend hanging like that!"

"Oww!" Louie cried out; Blair yanked him from his spot pulling him over. "Don't be so grabby! I am volunteering to protect our escape route!" Louie explained to Blair.

"There is no need," an Omega from U of M, who overheard Louie, interjected. "Everyone present will be asked to go into the field, we need every able body we can helping to clear the streets."

If Louie's frown could have dropped his face to the floor it would have happened in that moment. Taking small, defeated steps Louie came to stand by Virgil, a look of dread on his face. "I was hoping to be in a safer group," Louie murmured barely audible.

"Well tough titties," Blair snapped, "You're in our group whether you like it or not!" Blair's authoritative tone left no room for disagreement.

"I just know we're going to run into that stinkin' Arch Demon," Louie mumbled, almost like a sob, staring blankly ahead.

"I'll protect you," Virgil told his friend with seriousness. "You have my word Louie; I'll do whatever it takes to keep you safe."

"Ahh shut up, you big whiner!" Blair said swatting Louie on the back of the head. "I hope we do get to fight 'em! I've been hungry for a real challenge lately!" Louie's mouth dropped open as he stared aghast at Blair.

"We need some more people," Virgil said looking around. There were so many men and women in the room he didn't know, Nephilim just like them from colleges across the lower peninsula of Michigan. His eyes came to rest on a familiar face in the crowd, Damian was standing next to one of his brothers, he looked uncomfortable his face slightly flushed as his eyes looked around for people to partner with.

"Let's ask Damian to join our group," Virgil told his friends.

"Damian who?" Helene asked.

"A friend of Virgil's in the Betas at Bay Valley," Louie added.

"I didn't know you were friends with a Beta," Blair asked a little impressed.

"Well truthfully we're more like acquaintances, but I think he'd make a good friend," Virgil rambled nervously.

"He's in," Blair nodded walking over to Damian. Virgil couldn't hear what she had to say, but she nodded towards Virgil and Louie, Damian saw Virgil and his face lit up. Damian followed her back over to them.

They quickly introduced themselves, "I'm Damian," Damian said politely.

"And I'm Trent," Damian's fraternity brother introduced himself. Virgil recognized him from the Tournament, he'd had lunch with Alexa, Damian, and Trent on the first day of the competition.

"We got six peeps, how many more we need?" Louie asked. The group looked around, most people had found groups, but a small number of people were still milling around, a little shy to ask to join. The Omegas from U of M quickly helped those people jump into other groups. Two girls were led over to Virgil's group.

"You guys need two more, can these ladies join you?" The Paladin asked them.

"Of course!" Blair cried out. "Where are you ladies from?" she asked in her usual outgoing and loud manner.

"We're Alphas from Eastern Michigan University. I'm Minerva, and that's Tawania," Minerva introduced them. Minerva was Hispanic with dark hair and features. Tawania was a striking African American with medium skin tone and great bone structure.

"We're in the same sorority!" Blair cried out and the girls quickly grouped together and started speaking in high pitched rapid tones. The guys came together staring at the girls like they were another species.

"Women," Louie sighed. "Damian, Trent, tell me about yourselves. I'm glad we got paired up with you guys, we need stronger ties with the Betas," Louie asserted.

Trent gave Louie a surprised look, the Betas must not be used to hearing that sort of thing, but Damian just laughed and started talking to Louie like they were old friends. Louie had an amazing ability to fit in pretty much anywhere.

"You are good people Louie," Damian nodded at Louie.

"You too," Louie replied in earnest, "Damn Virgil, why didn't you bring Damian around sooner? He's cool as shit!"

"Everyone listen up!" Donnell, the U of M Omega's Prytanis called out. "We have maps we're going to be handing out, your zones are clearly marked. You are to patrol your area and stay there until the order to withdraw has been given. If you get into trouble, send out the distress signal, and the groups closest to your location will move in to assist. We'll send portals for evacuation if needed. We don't need any causalities, let's go in, clean up this city, and get out!"

They received two maps with group #12 written at the top, their part of the map was highlighted, with a spot marking where they'd be dropped off, and a spot marking where they needed to go to get a portal home. It was an area about twenty blocks, it would take them some time to walk through the entire area, especially if they were fighting often. They were led to the basement to a room that was indiscernible to humans. It was a small room with an archway built into the wall straight ahead. There were large gatherings of ley lines, natural currents of energy running through Earth, under the city, and this was one of thousands of gates Paladins used to navigate them.

"Gosh I hope we don't run into hoodlums," Louie said thinking out loud as they waited their turn. "That is the last thing we need, to get shot at while we're fighting demons."

"If any thugs start giving us trouble, we'll put them in their place," Trent said cracking his knuckles.

"Yeah, easy there Rambo," Blair retorted, "Let's try *not* to dodge bullets tonight!"

"You have a little over three hours, be at the extraction point on time!" They were instructed. "We'll hold open the portal for five minutes, then we'll have to move onto getting the next group. If you don't come back, we will send others to that location to begin looking for you!"

The group stepped through the familiar swirling black vortex with blue and purple veins of energy. The portal emptied them out into a residential area. Darkness had descended, it was a warm Autumn night, and a half moon rose in the overcast night sky. Damian and Trent took point, leading their group through the residential streets they were patrolling. The women were in the middle, with Virgil and Louie holding up the back. The girls from Eastern looked slightly on edge, becoming progressively worse as the first few minutes passed, and the cold dark of the night settled in around them.

"Don't worry ladies," Louie proclaimed in his most macho voice to Minerva and Tawania, "I'll protect you both while we're out here!"

Blair attempted to stifle a laugh, almost dying as she lost it walking slightly ahead of the Eastern Alpha girls. "Sure Louie!" Blair blurted out laughing so hard she started to wheeze and cough, the idea of Louie protecting anyone was clearly amusing. Virgil had a grin on his face, and Blair's laughter was contagious making him chuckle.

Louie ignored Blair's response completely, "See my Devil Arms?" Louie said showing off both of his hands, the bright blue Devil Arms symbols starkly standing out.

"Oh wow! You have two!" Minerva exclaimed excitedly. "I've never seen that before!"

"Our hero!" Blair cried out clasping both hands together and batting her eyelashes.

"Yup!" Louie's head bobbed back and forth; a shit eating grin plastered across his face. "My Devil Arms, Shiva's Bow, is an ice bow. And since I'm aligned with water if either of you gets hurt, I can heal your wounds like that!" Louie smiled snapping his fingers. They were impressed.

"But seriously girls," Blair added in having finally caught her breath, "When real trouble comes, Louie will be at the back of the group, maybe by half a mile, probably looking for a car to hide under. Virgil and I are strong enough to protect this squad," Blair told them confidently, "Stick by one of us if things get dicey."

"Hey!" Damian said from the front turning around as he walked. "Don't count me out! You haven't seen me in action yet Blair," he boasted confidently showing off the two Creation Devil Arms symbols on the backs of both of his hands.

"You have two Devil Arms too!" Tawania asked.

"Well, like Louie they're both the same weapon really," Damian shrugged. "I have a pair of Creation gauntlets called Beowulf. But I'm one of the strongest in our Chapter," Damian boasted.

"Sure is," Trent nodded in agreement.

They hadn't seen Virgil's symbols, and he was thankful. Soul Reaver and Ragnorak brought him enough attention, it was good just to be a 'regular' guy in the Nephilim crowd for a change. The group came to a stop and gathered around looking at the map, Louie used the flashlight on his phone so they could see it clearly.

"Alright," Blair said putting her hands on her hips. They'd only been walking for ten minutes, but they needed to chart the best course to cover as much ground as they could, while making the extraction point their main destination. "Let's walk the length of this area, then double back one block up when it's time to turn back," Blair suggested. "At intersections we can look both ways and scan the middle sections that we're passing."

"That'll help us cover more ground, but it won't be as thorough," Trent pointed out.

"Thorough my ass," Blair retorted, "No one is going to be able to cover their areas entirely."

They continued forward with Trent marking street signs on the map. Some demons were likely in people's homes, but they couldn't exactly go knocking door to door. The group moved up to the next street. Louie had started flirting with Tawania, her breathtakingly aesthetic looks had caught his eye. She flirted back, and Virgil and Blair both shared looks with raised eyebrows. Louie's relationship with his past girlfriend had ended over summer vacation. It was hard to maintain a long-distance relationship as they'd both moved home for summer break.

"Should we like summon our Devil Arms to draw out some demons?" Trent asked the group. "At this point I'm thinking we're not doing the city much good just walking around."

Louie's eyes bugged out of his head, like he had just seen someone burning a massive pile of money. "No need to go advertising our location to demons there Trent," Louie insisted talking fast, "I'd be happy if we didn't see a single demon tonight!" Louie declared firmly.

"I bet," Virgil said under his breath.

"You're not scared are you Louie?" Tawania asked seriously not knowing Louie like Blair, Virgil, and Helene.

"Oh nooooo girl!" Louie replied in his most suave tone. "I'm one of the toughest and bravest warriors in my Chapter!" Louie boasted flexing his arms and chest.

"It's getting deep in here," Blair and Virgil whispered at the same time. They shared a knowing look, and quickly looked away from each other before they burst out laughing at their friend's expense.

Helene, who knew nothing of the art of subtly, spoke up, "Really?" Helen asked curious in her high-pitched voice. "I thought all the brothers said you're the biggest chicken to ever join the Omegas," she declared grinning. Louie glared at Helene with a scathing look of betrayal.

"You really think we'll go the whole night without seeing any demons?" Minerva asked the group.

"Don't count on it," Blair said her eyes narrowing. Virgil turned his attention to what she had seen, a pack of demons were just ahead, maybe half a block. They looked like large wolves, walking on four limbs with thick black hair.

"Envy Demons," Damian whispered. "They're shape shifters, be careful guys, these aren't bottom of the barrel wimpy Solider Demons," he warned.

"Shit!" Louie cursed. "I'm okay with the bottom of the barrel!"

"Come on hero!" Blair taunted Louie, "Let's see ya in action!" Blair's grin almost made Virgil lose it, but he quickly regained his composure, things were about to get dangerous.

"I'm going!" Louie complained.

"I'll take the lead," Virgil offered starting to walk to the front.

"No," Damian replied sharply. "You're strong Virgil. Hang back and make sure nothing happens to Minerva and Tawania, there could be more in the shadows."

"There's always more," Louie whispered looking around apprehensively, his voice slightly shaking, like a little kid talking about the monsters in the closet.

A fierce growl rent the night air and the four Envy Demons burst into a sprint racing towards them.

"They've seen us!" Damian cried out. "Beowulf!" His hands burst with light, powerful metallic gauntlets forming to cover both of his hands extending up to his elbows.

"Harmut's Saber!" Trent yelled a sword aligned with earth coming to his hand.

"Flametongue!" Blair commanded her flaming shortsword coming to her left hand.

The three warriors charged the oncoming demons. Louie summoned Shiva's Bow to his right hand, using his left hand he pulled the string of the ice bow back, a glowing blue arrow of energy materializing in the center. The arrow became fully formed and Louie released it, the arrow flew like a bullet passing their allies, sinking into the skull of the Envy Demon at the head of the pack. The demon tumbled across the sidewalk, skidding to a halt, it crumbled into ash. Virgil's thoughts turned to Soul Reaver, the Chaos Devil Arms on his left hand came to life. Virgil summoned the scythe and it materialized its corporeal form, dark flames and shadows appeared before his hand, the scythe snaking into existence. Virgil grabbed the handle of the scythe with his left hand, and the black flames that covered its body flowed up Virgil's left arm.

"Summon your Devil Arms," Virgil encouraged the girls, "You may have to enter the fight at a moment's notice, you must be ready to defend yourselves!"

"Don't worry, he's not dangerous to us!" Louie winked at the girls who were looking at Virgil like he'd sprouted horns. The two girls quickly composed themselves, their Devil Arms symbols producing their soul weapons in a flash of dazzling light.

Blair slashed her sword across a demon's chest that had leapt at her, it was flung down to the sidewalk by the momentum of her blow. The demon quickly got back to its feet. Growling at her the demon stood up on its hind legs, its form shifting, its face losing its canine features, to look more like a warthog, its front legs morphing into hands. The Envy demon had transformed into some pig humanoid hybrid abomination. It opened its arms extending sharp claws from its fingers roaring fiercely! Blair cracked her sword forward like a whip, the blade broke apart connected by a thick band of fire. She smacked the weapon against the ground before her, challenging the demon.

"Come on precious, I don't have all night!" Blair demanded and the demon charged her. As good as Blair was with her sword, she was an artist with her fiery whip. Blair's movements were like a dance, as she battled the demon, lashing it with Flametongue several times, and dodging swipes from its sharp claws.

"Louie!" Helene cried out. More Envy demons appeared from the dark coming at the group from all directions, one charged Louie before he had a chance to aim, it crashed into him sending them both tumbling backwards from the momentum.

"Zephyr's Scepter!" Helene shouted. A small scepter with an emerald adorned on the top, slipped into her fingers appearing from a gentle breeze. Helene began to twirl her Devil Arms in her hand spinning around in place, her long blond hair dancing as the wind she created began to circle her. The emerald on the top came to life with bright light, and a vortex of wind spiraled out. The large tunnel of ferocious wind crashed into three demons, lifting them into the air at blinding speeds, blades of green energy spiraled out, exploding into the demons, ending them.

"Way to go Helene!" Virgil cheered. He'd never seen Landon's little sister in a fight before, he was pleased to see skill ran in the family.

"Virgil!" Louie screamed in full panic. The Envy demon was on top of Louie, pinning him down. It struggled to clamp its jaws onto Louie's throat as he held back the demon with his bow, holding it in front of his face like a shield.

"YAAAA!" Tawania yelled striking the Envy demon that attacked Louie with a type of flail Devil Arms. Minerva quickly followed up stabbing the creature through the back with her small blade, the demon dissolved into ash.

"T-thanks," Louie said as Tawania reached down and helped the big guy to his feet.

"Anytime hero," Tawania replied with a bright smile looking deep into Louie's eyes. Louie blushed sheepishly.

"Yo get your heads in the battle!" Virgil demanded swinging his scythe at an approaching demon, the blade sliced through the demon's mid-section, cutting it cleanly in half. It was ash before it hit the ground.

"Close our ranks!" Damian shouted. "We fight these fiends, back to back, don't let them flank us!" The group closed in their formation, and slowly fought back, working as a team, taking on three more waves of shape shifting foes that became more bizarre and varied. Finally, Blair felled the last Envy demon, that they could see. Their group prevailed suffering minor wounds, mostly Trent and Louie, and were covered in demon grime and ash.

Louie went to heal Trent, "I got this," Virgil offered interrupting his brother. "Cura!" Virgil commanded and three clouds of intense and warm light flowed over to Trent, Damian, and Louie.

Damian looked to Virgil nodding with a smile on his face, "Thank you Virgil," he replied with genuine heart.

"You're like a jack of all trades, aren't you?" Trent asked Virgil.

"I have your back Damien," Virgil said with confidence. "And anyone who chooses to stand with the Paladins, against the Death Dealers and Fallen," Virgil added looking to Trent and smiling.

"Are we done holding hands?" Blair asked. "We have a lot more ground to cover," she snapped and quickly led the group forward. The rest of their walk became much more active. The beguiling and deceitful quiet that had permeated the air, ruptured by waves of demons. Virgil had never encountered opponents on this scale before, it was almost like…they were breeding here. There squad had gained rapport rather quickly, and soon Virgil was fighting with the Betas like they were Omegas. Everyone was getting along great, and their connection carried over into their battles, helping them avoid serious injury. After some time, they'd covered three quarters of their area, and had an hour to get to their extraction point.

"Time to head out," Virgil recommended as they caught their breath from taking down a group of solider demons they found, clinging to the sides of a house, feeding off the people inside. "We can't cover any more ground, and we need to get home."

"Agreed!" Louie nodded. "I'm tired yo!"

"Me too!" Minerva yawned.

Their group quickly decided with their map the quickest route, following the river south. If they wanted to make it on time, they needed to keep a good pace. Their spirits were high as they headed out, back to campus, then back to their own schools, their own lives. Louie and Blair kept the group smiling and laughing, they kept their voices low. Virgil wished the other groups did as well, by the end of the night, the city should be better off for their efforts.

Close to ten minutes from their extraction they noticed the air was getting thicker near the water up ahead, a fog was present just in the distance, and within a minute, was at their feet. Louie became tense, looking around suspiciously. The group's demeanor shifted gears, going from jolly and relaxed, to anxious and alert. Virgil sensed it before he saw it, the power of its presence, its malice, and hatred for all life. Virgil turned in time to see large tentacles reaching out of the water.

"DEMON!" Virgil managed to blurt out. Its first tentacle came crashing down where Trent had been standing two seconds earlier. The creature was moving towards them, out from the water and onto land. The group ran, struggling to gain space between themselves and the gargantuan demon. It looked like a giant squid, with dozens of tentacles on its body. The macabre body was a twisted nightmare of different creatures' bodies and faces, their parts looking like they'd melted onto its skin. Worse yet, upon closer inspection, the parts were actually moving, a head on the demon's chest turned to stare at Virgil, the eyes were human. Virgil felt like he was going to throw up and looked away. It towered over them, standing slightly shorter than the Arch Demon, Abdanon, its presence was just as terrifying, this was one of the Alphas on the enemies' side.

"Judge Spawn," the demon gurgled out of a massive beak at the center of a squid like head.

"What the hell is that!?" Tawania asked her voice shaking with dread.

"It's that damn Arch Demon!" Louie shouted stomping his feet. "I knew it! I KNEW IT!" Louie turned to Virgil his head shaking back and forth his words firing out full of attitude. "This is why I didn't want to come along with your bitch ass!"

"My name is Vagningula, I am the Arch Demon of Envy," the Arch Demon told them proudly. "What brings Judge Spawn into my domain?"

"YOUR domain?" Blair snapped full of fiery anger. "You don't belong in our world."

"I've been here for weeks," the Arch Demon boasted, "Engorging myself on the auras of the race of cattle known as man. I've spawned thousands here, my kin will spread across the land, draining the humans dry, and driving them to madness," the Arch Demon declared proudly.

Virgil nodded, he'd thought there had been an overly high amount of demon activity, this Arch Demon could…birth other demons? "Who sent you here and to what purpose?" Virgil asked the Arch Demon.

"I asked first," the Arch Demon snapped, one of its slimy tentacles snaking in Virgil's direction in response. They edged back slightly.

"We came to quell the demonic presence in the city," Damian defiantly declared. "We've been slaughtering Envy demons all night," he said with a grin.

The Arch Demon cried out, a sound like it was in pain, the heads on the body of the demon opened their mouths and cried out in response. Everyone's face in their group fell, it was one of the most disturbing sounds they'd ever heard. Virgil tasted bile, the acidic sting on his tongue. Virgil's heart began to beat faster in his chest. He was terrified.

"What are those?" Tawania asked aloud.

"Those are the faces of the many mortals I have swallowed whole," the Arch Demon explained happily.

"Act-actually," Louie spoke up nervously, "Mind if we just duck out, and never come back?" he suggested with a shrug of his shoulders inching away from the demon.

"Ignorant Judge Spawn!" the Arch Demon growled at Louie. "Your blood's power will give rise to new, and more powerful spawn!"

"SHIT!" Louie responded his face falling into a heavy frown.

"Run!" Blair shouted. The group turned to flee, and the Arch Demon belched from its beak a thick black tar that landed ahead of the group blocking their path forward. The black substance bubbled on the ground, looking like it was sinking down, dissolving everything underneath.

"We have to fight," Damian said weakly staring up at the large Arch Demon with a heavy heart, his earlier confidence having evaporated. It was easy to talk smack, until the towering monster you were mouthing off to choose to rip you in half.

"No," Virgil said shaking his head. "We don't stand a chance; we need to clear a path to our extraction!" he shouted. "Follow me!" Virgil ran forward leading his shaken friends away from the abomination and the river. The Arch Demon pounced, screeching it lurched forward, swinging its tentacles with tremendous force, they slammed into the ground in front of it, as it came at them. The Arch Demon couldn't move very fast on land, but its large size allowed it to make great strides. A tentacle slammed into the ground near Virgil. A high-pitched scream rent the air, Minerva was being lifted off the ground, wrapped up in a massive tentacle.

"Ragnorak!" Virgil shouted, the white symbol on his right hand that looked like a shooting star, came to life, light shining out from the glowing symbol. His Creation Devil Arms, was the most powerful Devil Arms in existence, the Holy Blade. A bolt of light struck his hand from the heavens, and the golden sword with a glasslike blade stretched out into existence.

Virgil gripped the blade tightly, concentrating on its power, a pulse of energy ripped through, beating in his hand like a heartbeat. Virgil swung Ragnorak at the tentacle, a blast of energy in the shape of a crescent raced from the blade's surface, cutting through the demon's flesh. The severed tentacle fell to the ground, withering and dying quickly, Minerva got to her feet and raced to her friend. She was crying and visibly shaken. There was no more escaping, its arms descended on them, and things became a chaotic nightmare. Virgil summoned Soul Reaver to his left hand, throwing his scythe at an incoming tentacle, and stabbed Ragnorak through another as it touched the golden veil that surrounded him, a protective barrier from his sword. Another tentacle arm came snaking at him, Virgil used Soul Reaver with his mind slicing it downward, severing the arm before it could reach him.

Virgil stole a glance around him while he had the opportunity, his friends were in trouble! "Searing Beam!" Virgil shouted, a ray of fire energy erupting from his left hand cutting down an arm just as it reached to ensnare Damian. Virgil's aura burned; the cost of the powerful spell sucked its power right from his spiritual energy. They were barely keeping themselves free from the powerful suckers on the fleshy undersides of the wet and slimy tentacles. Louie's hands were in constant motion, his ice bow had an unlimited supply of ammunition, and he fought fiercely to keep the girls, and himself free. Louie had grown in skill over the last year, his earlier fear was replaced with steel confidence, and steady arms. Virgil had never felt prouder, watching Louie singularly protecting so many. This did not go unnoticed by the Arch Demon, Louie's weapon had the longest reach, and the best precision. Virgil saw the demon's intent as a large cluster of arms gathered, and he knew his friend was in trouble. His wings burst from his back, his left was black like those aligned with Diablos, and his right was white like those aligned with the Creator. Virgil took flight, Soul Reaver spinning around his body.

An arm shot out at Virgil seeking to stop him, he flung his scythe slicing through the demon's putrid flesh, he kept his pace flying towards his friend. "Louie!" Virgil screamed in panic. Louie realized he was in danger too late, the tentacles descended upon him. Virgil flew straight into the chaos of the twisted arms before they reached Louie, yelling at the top of his lungs, slicing with both Devil Arms.

"Virgil!" Louie cried out in panic, their eyes locked, and Virgil read in his friend's dark eyes just how scared he was. Louie was one of the funniest and most loving people he'd ever known. Virgil cared deeply for him, and he felt guilty in that moment, Louie had been right to not want to partner with him. Virgil prayed if he could get Louie out of this, he'd never ask his friend to tag along with him again. Virgil fought like a madman, cutting through the flesh, and the Arch Demon turned its fury onto Virgil. A tentacle smacked into Virgil's back, and began to grip him tightly. Virgil quickly turned trying to break free but the arm wrapped around him more. Virgil quickly found himself imprisoned between two tentacles, squeezing him so hard he began to suffocate. Virgil's wings snapped, he opened his mouth to scream in pain, but he didn't have any air in his lungs. His Devil Arms faded from his hands; he couldn't hold onto them.

"Virgil!" His friends screamed from below.

The tentacles brought his trapped body up to the Arch Demon's hideous face. The dark red eyes of the demon peered into Virgil's terrified sapphire blue ones. The demon opened its beak of a mouth and began sucking, Virgil felt his aura weaken, as the monster suckled on his energy, drinking it in.

"You taste different," the Arch Demon said excitedly as it savored the first taste of Virgil's aura. "I've never fed on an aura so powerful!" the demon cried out and began sucking more furiously. Virgil could do little more than whimper in pain, as his very life force was being hungrily devoured.

"Leave my friend alone!" Louie screamed out angrier and more fired up than Virgil had ever heard him.

"You'll be next, don't worry," the Arch Demon murmured darkly.

"Virgil hang on!" Blair yelled slashing her fiery whip sword through the Arch Demon, trying to get to Virgil. But the Arch Demon was enormous and bigger than a building, they couldn't cut through it fast enough to free Virgil.

"How do we save him!" Damian shouted, panicking like the others.

"That should be me right now," Louie said to himself, "It was coming for me, when Virgil flew right into its path. He protected me," Louie whispered tears coming to his eyes. "He's always protecting me…I'm sorry my brother," Louie said closing his eyes tight. Wings burst from Louie's back, he propelled himself in the air his bow held fiercely in his hand. "I'm coming Virgil!" Louie screamed flying through the air like an arrow.

"You don't have the power to stop me, mortal!" the Arch Demon cried tentacles shooting out to strike Louie down.

Louie sailed through the air, plucking an arrow of energy along Shiva's Bow, a tentacle lashed out, he released the arrow destroying the upper portion of the arm, which in turn began to slowly regenerate, these things were growing back!  Virgil was growing weak before the Arch

Demon's maw, his aura growing dim, he couldn't do a thing to defend himself, his mind was growing foggy, his limbs weak, the lack of oxygen was making his vision spotty, he wouldn't be conscious much longer.

Louie pulled his bow back, inhaling as he aimed for the open beak of the Arch Demon, he released the arrow praying it would be enough to save his friend. The energy arrow of ice flew true, the Arch Demon moved Virgil to block the attack, one of the tentacles that held him was struck and loosened its grip. Virgil was still held tightly by one thick and powerful arm. The Arch Demon's eyes blazed with fury, a dozen arms rising up before it, taking aim at Louie.

"You're a fat little nothing!" The Arch Demon barked in its deep demonic tone. "You can't save your friend, or any of the others!"

The cries of everyone below filled the air, Blair, Helene, Damian, everyone was tightly coiled in a tentacle now. Only Louie was free, floating on his white wings, his heart beating quickly, sweat upon his brow.

"Virgil's more than a friend," Louie uttered through clenched teeth, "He's my freakin' pledge brother!" Louie's Devil Arms symbols glowed with power. "And I'll be damned, if I let some nasty ass freak of nature, eat him for some munchies and crunchies!" Shiva's Bow, the majestic and beautiful ice bow began to radiate with power, the string of the bow was glowing the same hue as his Devil Arms. The bow began to howl, Louie pulled back on the bow string, the arrow that began to form was unlike any he'd ever created, a thick glowing beam of energy. This arrow radiated power, Louie struggled to pull the arrow into existence, his arm shaking as he took aim. The Arch Demon, Vagningula, launched dozens of tentacles at Louie growling fiercely.

"Diamond Dust!" Louie's voice thundered out and his arrow rocketed from his bow. The beam of ice blue energy shot through the tentacles, every piece of flesh it came close to became frozen solid, the ice spreading along its limbs, freezing it in place. The beam of ice energy flew through the tentacle holding Virgil, straight into the Arch Demon's mouth. The beam exploded into a spray of ice that cut like diamonds, flying out in all directions. The limbs that had become ice shattered, Vagningula fell to the ground. It immediately began limping to the river, dragging its severely wounded body.

"Louie!" Virgil and the others exclaimed getting off the ground where they'd dropped, running over to their friend. Louie landed on the ground and folded his wings in.

"That was incredible!" Virgil shouted unable to contain the excitement of having just cheated death. "Louie you were magnificent! Your bow, it released a Soul Scream!"

"Louie your one brave son of a bitch," Blair said laughing, "No one back home is going to believe this story! Louie saved the day like a badass, staring down the Arch Demon without running!"

"Our hero!" Tawania and Minerva cried out running up to Louie and hugging him tightly.

"Thank you for saving us," Damian said shaking Louie's hand. "I've never seen anything like that!"

"Aww shucks guys," Louie said growing red in the face. "It was nothing."

"You're a great warrior," Virgil said placing his hand on Louie's shoulder, "with one of the biggest hearts of anyone I've known, that isn't nothing. Best friends don't get better than you Louie," Virgil said proudly, feeling overcome by emotion.

"Come here," Louie sighed, and he gave Virgil a quick hug.

Everyone was relieved they'd survived a run in with the Arch Demon, but they were still shaken up. Virgil felt exhausted as they walked towards the exit, he walked close to Louie.

"Whats up?" Louie asked turning to look at him, still elated from saving everyone.

"If you, if you don't want to team up with me anymore on assignments, I'll understand," Virgil smiled softly at his friend. "I shouldn't be putting you in danger."

"Yeah," Louie said drawing out the word, "But if I don't look out for you, who is gonna stop your bitch ass from getting killed, before you're supposed to save the world?" Louie asked with a smile. "Shit gets scary sometimes, but with or without you, it's still the same world. I'd rather be fighting by your side, than someone else's, worrying about you."

Virgil was so touched he didn't know what to say, "Thank you Louie," he said humbly.

"Anytime my brother," Louie nodded. Louie turned his attention to the Betas up ahead walking towards them. "Yo Damian, we should hang out sometime, without the demons!"

Vahn, Gabriel, Tarek, Zender, Lamar, Birdy, and Brody came through a portal as they approached the extraction point. They instantly saw their group and rushed over.

"You guys were late," Gabriel barked, "What kept you?"

Vahn studied Virgil intently. "I've never seen your aura look so damaged," Vahn observed with concern walking over to him. "What happened to you?"

"We ran into some trouble on our way out," Damian put it mildly.

"Could you be more specific?" Gabriel asked impatiently.

"The Arch Demon!" Louie blurted out all animated. "Just like I predicted! Just saying!" Louie bobbed his head with a small grin.

"Chickenwuss bitchin' he'll run into a scary monster," Zender mocked, "Sounds typical."

"Screw you," Louie retorted with his signature attitude.

"Actually, we were all captured by the Arch Demon," Virgil explained loudly wanting Zender to eat his words. "It was powerful, maybe on the same level as Abdanon. It called itself Vagningula."

"It looked like a giant...squid," Tawania explained laughing nervously.

"With hundreds of tentacles, and human faces and bodies melded in its body and mantle," Minerva shuddered remembering, "It was the most frightened I've ever felt in my entire life."

"I'm so sorry for all that you folks have faced tonight," Gabriel replied with a soft empathetic tone.

"How the hell did you all escape an Arch Demon?" Tarek asked. "Did Virgil go super saiyan again and save the day?" Tarek joked.

"It's more like a Limit Break, or Godmode," Vahn theorized sarcastically.

"It's called Ascending, when my immortal spirit and my conscious mind meld forces," Virgil sighed. "And I DID NOT save the day, my aura was being sipped on like a juice box. Louie saved me, he saved all of us!" Virgil exclaimed proudly. Louie had been nothing short of magnificent, and he deserved the glory and accolades that came with it.

"Chickenwuss?" Zender joked.

"Louie unleashed a Soul Scream from his bow," Blair bragged to Zender. "He flew fearlessly, right up to the Arch Demon's face to save Virgil."

"It was the bravest thing I've ever seen," Minerva said breathlessly.

"Me too," Tawania said shyly staring at Louie.

"It wasn't that great," Louie shuffled his feet. "Virgil's stronger."

"But I was trapped like a fool, unable to do a dang thing," Virgil smiled. "That attack, it was one of the strongest I've ever seen. And I've battled two Arch Demons, an Eidolon, and two of the other Seraphs," Virgil boasted. "Louie's up there with the greats!"

"Well no shit Louie!" Tarek exclaimed.

Gabriel embraced Louie in a quick bro hug, "I'm proud of you brother," Gabriel told him.

Louie was flushed with embarrassment, but he loved the attention. The group went through the portal and everyone said their goodbyes. Louie and Tawania swapped numbers. The operation was considered a success, though the fruit of their labor wasn't seen for a few days. They *had* made a difference that night. Unknown to the American citizens, thousands of lives had been saved from the demons. Word spread through the fraternity about Louie's valor in the operation, and he gained a newfound respect with the brothers.

# Chapter 3 Fall Semester

Virgil's second week of classes felt twice as long the first week, the material he had to study was astronomically greater than anything he'd faced thus far. He was taking a 4-credit class Bio 232 Anatomy and Physiology, an important requirement for any science or medical based major, and one of the most difficult. He was only taking 14 credits at Bay Valley, though it felt like 20 credits, this was going to be his most challenging semester yet. The best part of his schedule was Communication 105A, a general ed, a class he shared with Louie, and History 138A, a general ed, a class he shared with Nev. His last class was Math 231B, Bio Stats, which required a lot of homework to keep up.

Friday after work at the campus gym, Virgil drove home, and he found his brothers were already cutting loose. Everyone wanted to have some fun before the stress of Rush and pledging began. There were more candidates in the Fall, and during Fall semester people were more social, parties were bigger, the weather was better, which created unique social opportunities. Virgil said hello to Jace, Mu, Lilly (the newly chosen Sweetheart #5 and Mu's girlfriend) Lamar, and Troy who were in the living room. After touching base with them he went to his room to drop of his things. Birdy came into his room within the first few minutes. He was wearing a hat, his usual style, his phone and constant companion in hand. Virgil clicked with Birdy in a way he didn't with anyone else, they could sit in the quiet together and not have it be awkward. Birdy was so chill, understanding, and a great communicator, one of the best in the fraternity; ironic as he had hearing aids, nearly deaf without them. He was also one of the smart guys, which he didn't get enough credit for, due to not always having the most common sense, which resulted in a lot of Birdy accidents that made people think he wasn't so bright. Virgil valued their friendship, and of all his best friends, he'd begun to spend the most time with him.

"What are you doing tonight?" Birdy asked, sitting in Virgil's desk chair.

"Not sure yet, just got home," Virgil told Birdy, "But my brain is fried! I'm already sick of Anatomy and Physiology, and we're only going on the third week!"

Birdy shuddered, "Yeah that sucks," he chuckled. "I'm dual major in Criminal Justice and Social Work. All I have to do is type papers, they don't make us memorize hundreds of new words and terms every week."

"Maybe I'm in the wrong major," Virgil shrugged his shoulders.

"What do you want to be again?" Birdy asked knitting his eyebrows together trying to remember.

"Well I'm a Pre-Med major, I was thinking of becoming a doctor," Virgil told him.

"Ehh," Birdy recoiled, "That's like twelve years plus of schooling and residency, you want to do all that? You're one of the seven Seraphs anyways, do you even have time to be in school that long?"

Virgil laughed, "Who knows! Making lots of money and being respected and valued to the community sounded good at seventeen. But that was before I knew I was Nephilim, or Seraphim Nephilim, or whatever!" Virgil sighed. "Maybe I should look into changing my major."

"Well you can have a mid-college life crisis another night, tonight we're partying!" Birdy beamed with a huge grin on his face.

Virgil chuckled, "Alright."

"Get yourself ready and come downstairs. The brothers invited a few guys we've been pre-Rushing, as well as some ladies," Birdy wiggled his eyebrows. "The Paladins from the Capital have left for the night, so we have the house all to ourselves. Dante texted me saying he was thinking of coming up this weekend too."

Virgil could always count on Birdy to navigate their way to a good time. Virgil and Birdy shuffled downstairs and began mingling with the brothers, and friends of the fraternity. After an hour a little under a hundred people were there, with more coming through the door every minute. Virgil saw many faces that were starting to become familiar, Brett, Nigel, Cameron, and Colton.

"TK! Selene!" Virgil called out happily.

"Virgil!" They called out ecstatically, barreling up to him for a tight embrace.

"You are both looking lovely this evening. TK did you get a haircut?" Virgil asked noticing her usually waist length hair was barley at her shoulders.

"Aww you are so sweet for noticing," TK winked at Virgil, "You're the first guy to notice," she said flatly looking towards Gabriel across the room.

"It looks great," Virgil smiled brightly, how in the world did Gabriel not notice?

"You are always so complimentary," Selene pointed out. "You always seem to have something nice to say about everyone."

"Virgil's the nicest guy in the Omegas, hands down," TK laughed.

"I wouldn't say that," Virgil shrugged. "But I like being nice to you ladies, you both are my favs!" He laughed.

"You're our favorite too!" TK exclaimed with a bright smile. "I tell Gabriel that all the time. Tell us about your semester, how are classes going? Seeing anyone special?" she asked at the end, and both of them stared intently at Virgil.

"Classes are going fine, a little stressful with A&P but," Virgil didn't get to finish.

Selene's eyes grew big, "Oh my gosh that is one of the hardest classes I've ever had! You're not going to have a life this semester!"

"Thanks," Virgil said sadly.

"You'll be fine, you're smart," TK nudged him with her shoulder. "Anyways, talking to any cute girls?" TK asked again with a big grin.

Virgil laughed, "Well I try, but haven't really made any progress. I think I suck at flirting."

"Nonsense!" Selene waved off Virgil, "You're a perfect gentleman, and you're incredibly sweet. Women should be throwing themselves at you."

"If being sweet was all it took to get a girl, nerds everywhere would be rejoicing," Virgil jested. They shared a laugh, he smiled, he'd missed over the summer break.

"The right one will come along," TK said confidently, "And someone as special as you honey, it's going to take a one of a kind to win your heart. Sometimes there isn't anything you can do but wait for them."

"I'm waiting," Virgil sighed.

"Oh, there's Raven and Terra!" TK told Selene.

"We'll talk more soon," Selene smiled at Virgil and they walked over to greet their sisters. Terra was the President of their sorority for the second year running. She was always professional, with a stern side, but there was also the dedicated, loyal, and loving side that made her beloved by her sisters. Raven was TK's other Little Sister, and the Omegas Sweetheart #4. Raven had been a Sweetheart in Omega a year and a half before she'd joined the Alpha girls. A Sweetheart is an honorary member of the fraternity, a girl who can wear the letters of the fraternity, come to fraternity only functions, and know the secrets. All Sweethearts take the Oath of the Paladin, Virgil had even gone on a mission to clear out a nest of demons with a Sweetheart, Ariel Sweetheart #2. Ariel had graduated in May and moved to Florida for a teaching position. Ariel was so loving, so friendly, she made everyone feel special.

Virgil went over to one of the beer pong tables in operation, Louie was on a team with Nev against…Damian and Trent.

"Damian!?" Virgil exclaimed.

"Hey Virgil!" Damian called back. "Was wondering when we'd see you."

"I invited them over," Louie said nonchalantly, "Figured it'd be good for the brothers to mingle with the Betas a little, we should be closer."

"How's it going Virgil?" Nev barked out in an unusually cocky and arrogant tone, with a flushed face, he was a few drinks in.

"I'm doing okay, not as good as you," Virgil pointed out noticing his swaying stance.

"I've had a couple," Nev announced with a grin, "Louie and I are kicking ass in beer pong! Four wins in a row!"

"This one will make five!" Louie exclaimed bobbing his head. "I'm on fire tonight!"

"Doubt it!" Damian said waving his hands in front of the cup.

"Get your bitch ass outta there son!" Louie called out.

"Virgil!" He heard someone he knew call out. Virgil turned around to see Dante walk up to him with two young guys he'd never met. Dante was fun to be around due to his contagious energy and his great sense of humor.

"Dante!" several brothers called out at once.

"I have so much to catch you up on," Virgil told Dante, "Including an epic story of how Louie saved Blair and me from an," Virgil trailed off looking at the guys behind Dante and those at the beer pong table he didn't know. Dante hadn't been able to go on the operation.

"Louie, saved Blair and you?" Dante asked in disbelief. "Our Louie V? You sure it wasn't some panda that had escaped from the zoo with a dyed Mohawk down its head?"

"Shut up!" Louie called out.

"We'll talk about it later, that's a story I want to hear," Dante laughed. "But first there are two guys I want you to meet, Vinny and Tanner, this is Virgil Pitcher, my pledge brother, and one of the best guys you'll ever meet!"

Virgil rolled his eyes at Dante's comment, "Nice to meet you both," Virgil smiled brightly shaking each of their hands with his fraternity ring hand. The Dreamstone magicite on Virgil's ring reacted to both guys.

"They're from Clio like me," Dante explained excitedly, "We were in football together. Vinny is a freshman at Bay Valley this year, and Tanner is coming here next year."

Vinny was a guy of average height, with messy dark hair, big cheeks like Tarek, a deep voice, and had the personality of a 'good ol' boy.' Tanner was handsome, with light brown hair, a large nose that fit well on his face, and a perpetual quirky smile. Tanner was goofier than Vinny who seemed more serious.

"Awesome," Virgil nodded, "Vinny would you like a beer?"

"I've never had one before," Vinny replied sheepishly.

"You've never drank before!" Louie cried out like it was the biggest deal in the world. "And you are going on your third week of college? Son, what have you been doing these past two weeks?" Louie laughed.

"Learning and going to class!" Vinny responded getting red in the face.

"He sounds like a good kid, nothing wrong with that," Virgil laughed.

"Yeah don't end up like Nev over here," Louie hiccupped as he leaned in close to Vinny, "This guy used to be a lame certified straight A nerd! Before we got a hold of him that is," Louie joked laughing hard.

"Hey now, I still get all A's in my classes," Nev defended himself. "I'm just a little more social."

"How come you never came out to any parties?" Louie asked Vinny.

"I live in Clio with my parents," Vinny told him, "I'm commuting."

"Makes sense," Nev nodded.

Virgil quickly fetched Vinny a drink and handed it to him. Vinny took a big swallow of the beer and almost spit it out.

Vinny made a revolted sound of disgust, "It tastes like piss!"

"How would you know?" Dante retorted rolling his eyes.

"Yup," Virgil laughed, "It's an acquired taste that I'm still acquiring. If you don't like it, you don't have to drink it man, I just thought I'd offer you one so you could see what all the fuss is about," Virgil told him. "You don't have to drink to be cool, I don't drink that often."

Vinny held onto the beer, taking small tiny sips. Vinny and Tanner were quiet, looking around the party. They reminded Virgil of himself at his first college party, out of place and unsure of what to do. Dante ditched them to start hitting on chicks, per usual for him, Virgil felt kind of bad for them as they knew no one but Dante. Virgil realized Dante had introduced them to him so Dante could mingle, knowing Virgil would feel responsible for making sure they had fun. Louie looked over and must have felt the same, so he invited Tanner to take his place at the beer bong table, to make him feel included. Tanner had never played before and Nev's superior attitude from the winning streak, reminiscent of Magnus, (perhaps they were spending too much time together) quickly deflated as they began to lose.

"Vinny, what's your major?" Virgil asked, striking up a conversation.

"Secondary Education, I want to be a teacher," Vinny replied in a very gravelly tone.

"That's a noble profession, teachers don't make half of what they should, it's disgusting what's happening with this country," Virgil gruffly stated.

"I know, but I have to do something, and I like teaching people so," Vinny shrugged, "It's a living."

"How long have you known Dante?" Virgil asked him.

"I've known Dante since middle school. He's a grade above me so I never knew him well till high school, when I joined football," Vinny explained.

"What was he like?" Virgil asked.

"Well," Vinny started laughing and Virgil joined in, that was Dante. "His senior year he was the Capitan of the team, loud, opinionated, and extremely hyper," Vinny started chuckling.

"Sounds like the guy I know," Virgil nodded.

"We were friends but not close or anything. When he moved home in the summer Adam and I reconnected with him. He's been telling me about the Omegas, thinks I should join," Vinny mumbled awkwardly moving his hand on the back of his head.

"Well I'll tell you what I tell everyone, going Greek is one of the best decisions I ever made, and I would recommend it to anyone," Virgil said confidently. "Of course I'm going to say my fraternity is the best, and you should join us," Virgil shrugged. "But honestly the best thing you can do, is meet all the fraternities, meet the guys, and see how you click with them. There might be a group that you fit in with better, and it's a good idea to shop around," Virgil suggested.

"Are you supposed to tell guys that?" Vinny asked surprised, not expecting Virgil to be advertising for the other fraternities.

"What? Check out all the groups before picking one? That just sounds like common sense," Virgil laughed like it was no big deal. "My roommate from freshmen year, Damian, he joined the Betas, he's playing against Louie, the loud and obnoxious Asian guy. You should talk to him about his fraternity too."

"Okay, I'll do that," Vinny nodded smiling at Virgil. "Thanks for the good advice."

"I take it Tanner and you are friends?" Virgil asked.

"Best friends," Vinny said proudly. "Since we were kids."

"That's awesome! I wish I had a best friend like that," Virgil said with envy.

"And what's wrong with the best friend you've got?" A sassy voice asked from behind him. Virgil turned around to see Blair and Helene standing there, Blair with a hand on her hip, a drink in the other, and an intense glare aimed right at Virgil.

"Blair! Helene!" Virgil greeted them enthusiastically. "Vinny, it is an honor to introduce you to my good friends, Blair and Helene. They are in the Alphas, a kind of sister sorority to the Omegas," Virgil told him. "Ladies this is Vinny, he's a freshman at Bay Valley, and a friend of Dante's," Virgil explained.

"I feel for you," Blair jokingly said to Vinny. "And Virgil what the hell is this, 'good friend' crap? Did I get downgraded and miss the email?"

"Sorry!" Virgil sighed. "Vinny this is my bestest, best friend in the whole world! We're practically family!" Virgil said in a very exaggerated excited tone giving Blair a one-armed hug.

"That's better," Blair retorted with a small grin. Virgil rolled his eyes, giving her a real hug anyways.

Vinny and Helene started chatting, and after a few minutes were deeply engrossed in conversation. Their body language spoke leaps and bounds. Virgil hadn't seen Helene like this before, her face was red, she looked nervous. Virgil and Blair shared a look and walked away giving the two some space.

"What are you drinking?" Blair asked stirring her drink with a straw.

"I'm not," Virgil said putting his hands in his pockets.

"Oh merr!" Blair said using her made up sound. "It's the weekend, cut loose for once you uptight preppy boy!"

"I am not uptight!" Virgil said his eyes getting big and his mouth dropping open in a mock aghast expression at her words.

"I'll believe it when I see a drink in your hand," Blair said flicking her hair uncharacteristically like a diva.

"You just want to get me drunk!" Virgil accused her.

"No, no," Blair waved off his accusation, "I just want you to loosen up! You're always taking care of everyone, making sure people are having fun, and policing the drunks. You deserve to have some fun too!"

"I do have fun," Virgil pleaded with her honestly. "I don't mind looking after my brothers, someone's got to be responsible."

"It doesn't always have to be you though," Blair said softly nudging him a little.

"It isn't," Virgil declared firmly, "And if it will make you happy, I will get a drink right this minute!"

"Yay!" Blair raised both hands up as she did a little dance. "I'll escort you, so you don't get lost," she teased looping her arm through his. "I don't want to see you with an empty drink for the rest of the party mister man," Blair firmly told him. Virgil sighed and let Blair lead him to the kitchen.

Sunday's weekly fraternity meeting was extremely busy. They went through their usual agenda, and Vahn handed out Big Brother applications. Afterwards they went into a long overview of Rush, with Lamar and Brody taking center stage. Virgil was seated next to Nev and Birdy, he wrote on his paper he used for notes, *kill me now*, to Nev. Nev laughed softly and wrote back, *you still got those earplugs you made me get you when I was a pledge?* Virgil started laughing and quickly went silent with a strong glare from Brody. The two beat the dead horse into the ground, saying all the same things they'd said a dozen times before. Brody passed around a signup sheet, announcing they'd be hosting an Omega man cave on campus all week in addition to the normal Rush table. Brody explained they'd get more people to the events if they actively engaged students walking by, all day long, and looked like they were having fun. Brody insisted every brother sign up for at least two hours. Virgil had to admit it was a great idea, Brody was the class clown of the room, but the guy had fire in his heart and was creative.

That week felt like the week from hell. Virgil's classes were only getting more intense, and every night there was an Omega event he had to attend. Dante came up to Bay Valley, true to his word, Tuesday, Thursday and Friday to help with Rush. Frater Spencer, the Lamba class pledge brother who came back to Bay Valley, ended up being a big help at Rush. He sat at the Rush table/Omega man cave, on campus every day, putting in more hours than any other brother. Landon and Vahn spent a lot of time with him at the tables, reconnecting and visiting. There was the Lambda class dedication Virgil knew and looked up to. There were dozens of potentials coming to the events. At Info Night on Wednesday, they had eight guys show up, which was impressive considering only serious potentials came to that Rush event.

Vinny showed up and Virgil walked over. "Vinny! What's good man?" Virgil greeted him warmly.

"I'm glad it's finally time for this event, I've been sitting on campus for six hours, since my last class was over, waiting," Vinny confided to Virgil.

"Wow!" Virgil remarked. "That's dedication! Dude why didn't you just come over to the Omega house to hang out?" Virgil asked him.

"I didn't know I could," Vinny remarked getting red in the face, "I didn't want to just show up, and have the brothers be like, who the fuck is this kid?" Vinny laughed.

"Dude, no one in my fraternity would do that…well maybe Lamar, if you were unlucky enough to have him answer the door, but he wouldn't mean it," Virgil smiled.

Colton was there as well, he'd cemented himself during Rush, as the potential that all the brothers liked, by coming to every event, and always bringing a new friend. Virgil hadn't got a great impression from him, he seemed a little too arrogant like Magnus, but without the humbleness of Gabriel. There was only enough room in the world for one Magnus, he could pull off the 'I'm the smartest guy you'll ever meet' attitude, but it didn't feel like it fit right with Colton. Though to be fair, Virgil had only one real conversation with him at the party last weekend. He'd been kind of a douche, but Virgil was willing to get to know him regardless.

Zane showed up, a freshman that Birdy, Louie, and Virgil had helped move-in several weeks ago. He still had the same surfer stoner look, with wavy unkempt light brown hair, strikingly good looks, and a chill demeanor. Louie quickly went to make him feel welcomed.

Flynn, Jeramiah, and Randy were three of the other guys who showed up, they mingled nervously with the brothers. They had been at other Rush events so Virgil remembered their faces. Flynn, a freshmen, was a quiet man from Howell; with blond hair kept buzzed short, kindly blue eyes and a long nose. Flynn was a country guy, he liked hunting and guns, driving his truck, and of course, country music. Jeramiah, from Auburn Hills, was a transfer from Oakland Community College, and was twenty-one. Jeramiah had mossy brown, curly hair, a lot like Vahn, with masculine jaw lines, and piercing eyes. Jeramiah was extremely nervous and timid. Virgil could tell he earnestly wanted to impress everyone but didn't know how or what to say. Randy was a second year at Bay Valley and was interested in getting more involved on campus. Randy was Latino with a fair complexion, dark hair and eyes, and a small moustache. Randy was polite, well spoken, and inquisitive.

Surprisingly, Aidan came in the room a few minutes before the event started. Everyone reacted strongly to his presence. He was Vahn's blood brother, and he'd been a pledge with Virgil in Omicron class the previous year. Gabriel approached Aidan with a gentle smile, and loving eyes that twinkled looking at his first Lil. Aidan was two years younger than Vahn, they looked similar, but Aidan was shorter, more muscular, with a pointer nose.

"Hey buddy," Gabriel cooed, "What brings your cute lil' face around here?"

Aidan laughed getting red in the face. "I was talking to Vahn, and I was thinking," Aidan took off his hat scratching his head, "if you guys would have me, I'd like to come back around, and give this pledging thing another shot," Aidan mumbled nervously. All eyes in the room were on him.

"My friend, it would be an honor," Gabriel told him placing his hand on Aidan's shoulder, "to have you in our brotherhood." There were cheers, whoops, the brothers were excited!

"Thanks, Big," Aidan said getting a little emotional and Gabriel hugged him.

"Of course, but I'm not the Hegemon anymore, so it's really up to Vahn," Gabriel joked.

"Vahn?" Aidan called out to his brother.

"Absolutely not," Vahn said shaking his head, "Get your trailer park trashy ass outta here!" Vahn barked laughing at the end not able to keep a straight face. Everyone else started joining in.

"Whatever, I'm joining whether you like it or not," Aidan shrugged his shoulders.

"That's my Lil!" Gabriel shouted out proudly letting out a loud whoop, a giant smile spread across his face.

"Hey I thought I was your Lil!" Rowan exclaimed, with playful sadness added in, that was half joking, half serious.

"Aidan was my Lil before you joined, in Omicron class, but he had to stop for personal reasons," Gabriel told Rowan. "So technically I was his Big first," Gabriel pointed out. "But I can be both your Bigs," Gabriel told them. "Doesn't mean I'll love either of you less."

"Shut up!" Aidan cried out rolling his eyes. "Too much of that crap!" he said breaking into a laugh.

"Right!" Flynn, one of the potentials, said standing not far off. Aidan and Flynn immediately struck up a conversation, finding they had a lot in common.

Friday night Rush had finally come to an end, and the Omegas threw a Rush Party at their house. The Paladins from Alexandros, staying at the mansion to help guard the Chalice, were not happy with the Omegas and straight out refused to leave. Magnus struck a deal that they could stay, but had to remain on the upper floors for the night. Virgil had met so many new guys it was hard to keep them all straight. At the beer pong table, two freshmen were on a hot winning streak, Homer and Tucker. Rowan and Brody instantly connected with them spending most of the party talking and hanging out with them.

"You guys should join our fraternity!" Brody yelled out to them.

"Sign me up," Homer said enthusiastically. "You guys are awesome!"

Sunday night the fraternity gathered in the meeting room. There were thirty-three guys to vote on. Brody was at the center acting as moderator. Lamar operated the computer pulling up people's social media, so a face could be put to the name. Colton was up first.

"Do we even need to talk about him?" Rowan asked. "Colton was everywhere this week and even helped out at the man cave! He did more work than most brothers!" Rowan laughed.

"It's true," Brody nodded chuckling a little, "Colton was the best Rush tool we had this week, not gonna lie, man's golden," Brody said, making himself chuckle.

"Alright, we have thirty-two more," Gabriel began.

"Oh, sorry I dropped one, its actually thirty-four guys total," Lamar interrupted with a sheepish look like he was going to get hit.

"Thirty-four," Gabriel's words came out distasteful, "of these damn things to go over, let's just call this one to a vote," Gabriel suggested in an irritated tone.

"Agreed," Magnus nodded, "All those who don't want Colton to get a bid, raise your hand." No one raised their hand. "Colton gets a bid," Magnus nodded.

The next few guys went smoothly, with little arguing or debating. Steve, Elmer, Frank, and Flynn all got bids. But the next two names caused some debate, Homer and Tucker. They hadn't gone to any Rush events, they'd showed up at the Rush party and Brody had them fill out Rush forms. But they were both freshmen at Bay Valley, and they'd said they hadn't heard about the fraternity before their friends invited them to the party.

"Alright these two guys are solid as hell!" Brody declared. "Rowan can vouch for them too! I spent most of my night talking to them, these guys want in, and honestly I think they'd make great Omegas."

Landon was called on, he stood up slowly, "I don't want brothers who only come around to party," he said simply. "They didn't come to any Rush events, just our party. We shouldn't be considering them, end of story."

"Bullshit," Vahn said as he began biting his nails.

"I have the floor," Landon retorted to his pledge brother.

Vahn stood up, "I never went to a single Rush event. I signed my name on a sheet at a Rush table, and that was it," Vahn said passionately. "If the brothers would have had the same attitude you do, I wouldn't be here. Maybe Aidan wouldn't have come out to the Omegas."

"I'm trying to make a point," Landon said getting heated.

"I am too," Vahn snapped with a lot of arm movement as he continued, "Some guys don't hear about us, until they come to the parties. I thought that was the whole reason we threw the damn things! Brody, are these guys Omega material?" Vahn asked.

"Definitely," Brody chuckled.

"I trust in my Rush Chairman, this is a moot point Landon, I'm sorry but you are wrong. I Call the Question," Vahn stated.

"Objection!" several brothers cried out and the room turned into chaos.

The night devolved into bickering, everyone wanted to talk about every guy, it became exhausting. In the end they were giving out twenty bids, a lot of brothers were angry they weren't giving out more.

"Guys I know some of you may be upset tonight, that some of the men you Rushed didn't get bids," Magnus said uncharacteristically soft toned and compassionate. "Always remember, quality over quantity. If you care that deeply about the guys who didn't get a bid, encourage them to come out next semester."

"Alright, let's go dorm stormin'!" Gabriel shouted out slamming both of his hands on his desk leaping up to his feet.

"You know we can't call it that," Jace admonished his Hegemon with half lidded eyes.

The men followed suit of their leader, jumping to their feet, thankful the meeting was finally over. Everyone barreled out of the meeting room shouting victoriously, the excitement of handing out the bids taking over. The brothers raced out to their vehicles, flying to campus, to let twenty lucky men know they'd been chosen for membership in the Omegas.

# Chapter 4 Rho Class

Wednesday night the brothers and candidates gathered at the amphitheater near the belltower. The candidates were lined up as such Vinny, Steve, Elmer, Flynn, Brett, Frank, Randy, Nigel, Colton, Zane, Cameron, Aidan, Homer, Tucker, and Jeramiah at the rear. This was Rho Class. Virgil looked down at the fifteen candidates, feeling overwhelmed. If every one of these guys made it in, they'd almost be doubling their Chapter size.

The group briskly power walked across campus to the edge of the forest that hung just on the outskirts. Once they were safely out of sight from prying eyes, blindfolds were placed on Rho class. The candidates were apprehensive, it was enough to make even the most fearless man uneasy. Vahn led the group forward, Vinny hanging onto his back for guidance and the group made their way to the secret Nephilim temple in a clearing in the woods. The stone temple was built hundreds of years earlier, resting atop an intersection of several ley lines. The temple had four stone archways, that led down to a center platform, with plenty of stone benches for seating. A powerful spell was laid over the structure, making it invisible to those without celestial blood in their veins. The spell also acted like a giant dome covering, no rain, snow, or any other foreign element ever fell inside the roofless structure. The temple was lit by three large copper colored basins that were filled with fire.

The candidates waited in the forest, with the Pylortes Zender, who loved intimidating new candidates. When you first met him, Zender came off as stern, cold, and demanding, with an authoritative presence. Only as a brother did you see that it was all an act, he was sensitive. He hid his true persona behind a sarcastic attitude, perhaps to keep himself from being vulnerable. He hadn't learned that in order to truly find compassion and acceptance from others, one had to open one's self up, exposing one's vulnerabilities and insecurities.

"Virgil, come here, I need to talk with you for a second," Vahn called out to Virgil. Vahn had quickly put on the traditional silver robes that the Omegas used for rituals.

"What's up Big?" Virgil asked him.

"I'm going around telling each brother, who their Little is going to be," Vahn told Virgil. "I've thought about it, and I want you to be Vinny's Big. You'd be a great mentor to him. I have a strong feeling he'll be one of the top pledges, and I only want to bring quality guys into our family tree. Being a Big requires a brother to be caring and nurturing, there isn't anyone in the Chapter better suited for a job like that then you," Vahn said proudly, a small smile peaking at the corners of his mouth. Virgil was quiet, he wasn't sure what to say. "Do you not want to be Vinny's Big?" Vahn asked his eyebrows knitting together, not sure how to take Virgil's lack of response.

"I do," Virgil nodded. "I'm just in shock. I'm a little scared to be honest Vahn."

"Why?" Vahn asked getting serious.

"What if I'm not a good Big?" Virgil asked, his fears of failure reflected in his eyes.

"You'll be great Virgil," Vahn said smiling, understanding where Virgil was coming from. "And a hell of a lot better Big than I was," Vahn chuckled.

"Not possible," Virgil said staring into Vahn's eyes. "I got the best Big."

"Thank you, my friend," Vahn said a film of moisture covering his eyes. "You humble me; I didn't do half as good a job as you deserved. But being a Big isn't about being perfect, it's about caring for your Lil, letting them know you're there to support them, no matter what. I know you'll be great, you're great at whatever you set your mind to," Vahn nodded. "You're going to be Vinny's Big. I won't take no for an answer."

"I'll do my best, to make you proud Vahn," Virgil said seriously.

"I'm always proud of you buddy," Vahn patted Virgil on the shoulder and moved onto the next brother.

"I better get Aidan!" Gabriel demanded stopping Vahn in his tracks. "Or I don't want to be a Big," Gabriel told Vahn with a sharp edge to his voice.

"Of course you'll be Aidan's Big," Vahn nodded, "I hadn't considered anything else."

Once Vahn had gone to all the Bigs he announced to the group, "That's everyone! Alright boys, we have fifteen guys that we are about to bring into our brotherhood. I know some of you are disappointed you didn't get to be Bigs. I'm sorry!" Vahn told them with attitude. "Everyone can't be a Big, and I picked the ones I thought were the best fit! I can't please everyone." Vahn took off his robe, and handed it to Gabriel, then left to bring in the candidates.

Magnus, Gabriel, Tarek, and Landon were getting everything set up on the center platform. A dagger was present on the table, with an open tome of spells, along with the chalice of their Chapter. The chalice filled when it was time for new members to go through the Oath of the Pledge, awakening their latent Judge blood, bringing their Nephilim powers online. Virgil noticed his Omicron brothers, Birdy, Louie, Nolan, and Troy were downcast and sullen. He walked over to the four of them, who'd gathered around to stand together, talking quietly.

"What's going on?" Virgil asked his pledge brothers with concern.

"We're just sad yo," Louie explained, clearly upset. "Omicron class got royally screwed just now!" Louie snapped angrily his voice rising.

"Keep it down," Birdy told him motioning with his hand.

"Why is that?" Virgil asked then he realized the problem. "None of you are Bigs," Virgil nodded feeling immediately guilty.

"Nope," Louie said angrily. "And after all the damn work I did Rushing these guys," Louie shook his head, his nostrils flaring.

"I was really hoping to be Cameron's Big," Birdy said sadly.

Troy was quiet, like usual, but he wasn't his usual self. Under his calm exterior, was a boiling rage, Virgil could see it in his eyes, he'd been hurt. Troy was one of the most devoted brothers they had, he came to everything, him and Agustin from Pi class were best friends, and inseparable. Virgil was glad Troy was standing with Omicron.

"Group hug guys," Virgil said.

"No," Nolan instantly replied.

"Oh what the hell," Louie said coming in for a bear hug, guy couldn't resist giving hugs. Birdy sighed and the rest joined suit. They hugged for a few seconds that broke apart.

"I'm sorry that I got a Lil guys," Virgil told them. "I don't understand why we didn't get Lils, all of Nu class got Lils?!" Virgil asked surprised. Almost all the Bigs chosen already had Lils, each brother could have a maximum of only three, but some never got to be Bigs.

"My Big got a second Lil, before I got my first," Birdy pointed out not happy.

"Yup, Abe got a Lil over me," Louie added in bitterly.

"He is a Jeweled Officer," Nolan pointed out.

Virgil hoped the reason he got a Lil wasn't because his Big was the Hegemon. He had been excited to do things with his best friends, and their Lils as a group. "There's always next semester," Virgil said trying to cheer them up.

"Vahn did say that Omicron will be first up for Lils next time," Nolan added. "As long as we have the grades, which that shouldn't be a problem."

Vahn was coming across the clearing with Zender, leading Rho pledge class.

"Let's go!" Louie yelled out happily.

"I'm in," Birdy laughed.

"You coming?" They asked Virgil together. It was tradition that brothers fly over the candidates as they approached the temple, to psyche them out a little before things got started. Birdy and Louie had Angel wings because Virgil had used his power on them. They'd been imprisoned in Hel, and the only escape route was flying out. Virgil looked to Nolan and Troy, he hadn't used his powers on them, and felt a little guilty. Perhaps he should offer to use his power giving everyone in the Chapter wings. Birdy, Louie, Magnus, Brody, Landon, Jagger, Spencer, and Virgil ran out of the temple, breaking out their wings they took flight. Rho class immediately reacted everyone shouting out different things, some were shocked, some scared, some excited, candidate Jeramiah, at the very back of the group, fainted on the spot.

"Oh for goodness sakes! Get your ass up!" candidate Steve barked.

"Don't talk to him like that," Colton admonished Steve going over to Jeramiah with Vinny, Flynn, and Aidan to make sure he was okay.

"What happened?" Jeramiah asked coming to quickly.

"You ate shit man!" Candidate Homer called out making the group laugh.

Jeramiah took notice of the brothers who had landed and were heading back into the temple. "What the hell is going on?" he asked his eyes bulging out of his skull his face beat red. "Why do those guys have wings?" he asked on edge.

"Let's get you up," Colton told him helping him to his feet.

"Rho class!" Vahn yelled. "Back in formation! We'll explain things soon."

"What's going on here?" Jeramiah laughed nervously. "Anyone want to explain?"

Zender narrowed his eyes and stomped to the back of the line where candidate Jeramiah stood. "You're already on my shit list!" Zender barked stepping into Jeramiah's personal space, "What's your name!"

"Jeramiah," he said nervously.

"Now you see, you've already messed," Zender cruelly smiled at Jeramiah. "You always begin and end your responses with sir!" Zender yelled.

"Sir, Jeramiah, sir!" Jeramiah said nervously.

"You've got one strike!" Zender reprimanded him. "Heads down no talking! Get your shit together!" Zender radiated authority and Jeramiah looked like he might faint again.

"Zender," Vahn said his name with a warning tone. "You can ask questions at the end." Zender backed off, but his message had gotten across, no other candidates dared speak out of turn. Virgil was in the temple watching, he shared a look with Birdy and stifled a laugh. It was all for show, but the unknown was always so much more frightening than the known.

Zender sealed the temple off with a barrier spell, making it impossible for even Omegas outside of the temple to see inside. The ceremony was the same as always, the brothers explained the history of the Paladins, reading from ritual books, and the Oath of the Paladin commenced. When it was time for the Bigs to take their oaths, Virgil felt shaky. He walked up to the center platform with the other Bigs and placed his hand on Vinny's shoulder. When asked who would be his Big, "I will," Virgil replied.

When it ended the fifteen pledges turned around and met their Big Brothers.

"Virgil!" Vinny smiled, "I thought that was your voice," he laughed.

"I'm excited to be your Big," Virgil admitted nervously. "We're going to have a lot of fun," Virgil said excitedly talking fast.

"I was hoping I'd get either you or Louie," Vinny said shyly with a smile.

"Vinny look!" Virgil exclaimed. Vinny's Devil Arms flashed into existence on his right hand, a ruby red symbol in the shape of an axe.

Virgil smiled brightly, "A fire axe," Virgil guessed.

"Wow!" Vinny exclaimed, staring down at the Devil Arms symbol, turning over his hand seeing the same symbol on both sides. "Hey!" Vinny exclaimed looking at Virgil's hands. "You have something on both hands!" He noticed.

"I've had them the whole-time bud," Virgil acknowledged extending them out for Vinny to see properly.

"WOW!" Vinny said sounding impressed, "Yours look cool."

"Thanks," Virgil laughed. "Each of us have a unique Devil Arms symbol, aligned to one of the six elements. They are a reflection of our souls, our personalities, and inner most selves. I'll work with you, and help you to master your Devil Arms," Virgil explained. "I know with all the wings and tattoos you probably have a lot of questions still."

"You can say that again!" Jeramiah said laughing to himself.

"Things will make more sense after your first Education Sunday night," Virgil offered.

"Everyone!" Vahn called out, "Eyes up here!" The temple went quiet. "Candidates, Sunday night is your first Education, and when the process begins. Be at the Omega house by 10pm! We'll go over what's expected and any lingering questions Sunday. Now let's head out!"

That night they went out for a late dinner, with almost forty guys, Virgil was both impressed and overwhelmed by how large their group looked with the fifteen potential new brothers. Vinny was riding the same high all pledges experienced in the beginning. He couldn't stop looking at his Devil Arms and everyone else's. Virgil sat with Vinny, Louie, Nolan, Nev, and Birdy.

"Vinny, I want you to know that if you ever need anything, you can always come to these guys for help," Virgil offered his Lil. "Think of them as your extended 'Big' family," Virgil joked.

"Alright," Vinny nodded laughing nervously. "But I already feel close to you guys, being Dante's close friends," Vinny said.

"I'm so excited, this is my first-time having pledges," Nev laughed a tad manically.

"Oh no," Vinny replied with a nervous laugh his face getting red. The table broke out into laughter.

"Do you know any of your pledge brothers Vinny?" Birdy asked him,

"No," Vinny said.

"That's okay," Louie assured him. "I didn't know any of my pledge brothers before we started, and now they're my best friends!" Louie smiled throwing his arms around Birdy and Virgil.

"Lucky us," Virgil said sarcastically earning some laughs.

"Hey!" Louie said taking his arm off Virgil's shoulder. "I remember saving your bitch ass from an Arch Demon just a few weeks ago. You remember that mister Seraph," Louie snapped back with attitude.

"What's he talking about?" Vinny asked totally lost. "Arch Demon? Seraph?"

"Don't worry Vinny, there is a lot to catch up on, but it's too much for one night," Virgil told his Little Brother. "I was just kidding Louie," Virgil sighed. "You're one of the best friends anyone could ever ask for."

"That's what I thought," Louie beamed throwing his large arm back around Virgil bringing his head into a tight embrace.

"You're choking me Louie!" Virgil exclaimed his face buried in a choke hold.

"Are you a part of Omicron class too?" Vinny asked Nev.

"No they're all Omicron, I'm part of Pi class," Nev told Vinny.

"Oh, okay. You seem like a part of their group," Vinny pointed out.

"He's an adopted Omicron," Louie said proudly.

"Hey!" Rowan called out from across the room. He was seated with Gabriel, Aidan, Dante, Vahn, Magnus and Colton. "He's MY pledge brother!" Rowan laughed.

"Pi class!" Nev said making a Pi symbol with his hands.

"What what!" Rowan replied doing the same, as well as Agustin.

"There is rivalry among the pledge classes," Virgil explained, "But it is all in good fun. We're one big, blended, happy family."

Virgil's friends asked Vinny lots of questions about himself. Vinny seemed a little out of his element with so much attention being lavished upon him. Vinny was humble, and he seemed so genuine and extremely caring, really rare in people these days. Virgil felt lucky, Vahn was right, he was going to be one of the good ones. Vahn stopped by for a moment.

"Hey Lil!" Vahn greeted Virgil warmly. "And Gran Lil," Vahn added acknowledging Vinny.

"What?" Vinny asked not understanding.

"Virgil is my Little Brother, he's very special to me," Vahn told Vinny. "Which makes you my Gran Lil. I just know you're going to be a great addition to our family tree," Vahn told Vinny.

"I'm the Lil Brother of the Hegemon's Lil?" Vinny said taking it in. "Damn!" he laughed his voice getting more gravely than normal. "That's a pretty high bar!"

"Not at all," Vahn told Vinny. "Just be yourself. We don't ask for anything more than that. The three of us should have a Bigs and Littles day sometime soon," Vahn suggested. "The whole family hanging out."

"Yes!" Vinny and Virgil responded together and then they shared a laugh.

Vahn laughed as well rolling his eyes. "You two are precious! I'm proud of you Virgil," Vahn told him and went back to his table.

"Wow," Vinny said after he left.

"What?" Virgil asked.

"My Hegemon must think a lot of me to give me to his Lil," Vinny said seeming a little intimidated.

"Don't sweat it," Louie suggested trying to ease the pressure, "Virgil isn't THAT great!"

"Are you sleeping outside tonight Louie?" Virgil asked as he drove their group there.

"Love you," Louie replied with a big toothy grin.

"You aren't driving home after this are you Vinny?" Virgil asked.

"I don't really want to," Vinny admitted. "I have a 10am class tomorrow morning."

"You're staying at the Omega house," Virgil told his Lil with no room for arguing. "There are dozens of empty beds in the pledge dorms, you can make yourself at home. You can crash at the Omega house as much as you need to help make this process easier on you," Virgil encouraged him.

"Thanks Virgil," Vinny said with obvious relief. "The gas was killing me driving back and forth every day."

Birdy chuckled, "Well staying at the Omega house may not be so nice, once the brothers find out you're there they'll be hitting you up constantly!"

"I don't mind," Vinny shrugged, "The way I see it, it's the best way to get to know the brothers."

"You're going to do well with that attitude," Nolan nodded. "Get a planner and stay organized," he suggested, "One thing this fraternity is good at, is teaching new guys how to time manage properly. It is the only way to stay sane through all of this."

"Agreed," everyone at the table said in unison. Virgil could tell his pledge brothers were still sad they didn't get Lils, but seeing how they were with Vinny, Virgil didn't mind sharing.

After their late meal the large group hit the road, everyone going their separate ways. Vinny was the only candidate to come back to the Omega house. Virgil showed him to the pledge dormitory on the second floor, where Rho class would be staying during the pledging process on late nights. Vinny had first pick of the beds and chose a spot he liked. Vinny followed Virgil, Louie, Nolan, and Nev up to their rooms. Vinny sat in Virgil's computer chair Vahn had given him the night he'd first moved in. They sat up for a while, just the two of them, talking about everything and nothing. Vinny was so excited he kept saying he wanted to make Virgil proud. Virgil kept telling Vinny that he didn't need to try to prove himself. Vinny started falling asleep in the chair and Virgil insisted he get some sleep before class. Virgil lay in bed feeling exhilarated, being a Big, a mentor to another Brother in the fraternity, was exciting!

Monday afternoon, pledging had officially started, and there were now fourteen official candidates as one dropped out. Virgil finished classes for the day and walked to the food court. The back section was usually taken up by fellow Greeks, Virgil saw lots of Omegas along with some Alphas sisters and Tekes he recognized. Virgil went over to his brothers greeting them and sitting at a booth with Louie, Birdy, and Nev.

"What's up Virg?" Louie asked.

"Just got done with classes, my brain feels fried," Virgil complained. "I'm starting to hate my major."

"Try being a Math major," Nev quipped. "There are no girls in any of my Math classes!" he complained. "It sucks!"

"Virgil!" Blair called out walking over to their booth and sliding in next to him. "How is it going with your new candidates?" she asked.

"It's day one, and already them bitches be messing up!" Louie joked.

"We have eight new girls this semester," Blair told them. "I'm pissed off at my sisters though. They didn't give me a Lil!" Blair exclaimed.

"Me neither!" Louie said slamming his hand on the table. "Damn Vahn, gave all the Lils to the upper classmen."

"I'm sorry," Virgil said.

"Did you get a Lil?" she asked him.

"Yeah," Virgil said sheepishly.

"Figures," Blair smirked. "Must be nice having the Hegemon as your Big."

"The only one from Omicron who did!" Birdy said with some heat.

"I'm sorry guys, I didn't chose for it to happen like this," Virgil sighed. "I wanted all of us to be Bigs at the same time. I imagined us doing Big and Lil bonding time as a group."

"Who is your Lil?" Blair asked him.

"Vinny," Virgil told her.

"I love that kid!" Blair exclaimed. "You guys are a good match. He's so sweet and cute! And Helene seems to think so too," she added a devilish grin spreading across her face.

"Oh Helene has a crush on our lil Vinny?" Louie asked his voice getting high pitched. "Ohhh shieeet!"

"Don't tell either of them I said anything!" Blair cut him off sharply.

"I won't," Louie purred a twinkle in his eye.

"I mean it Louie," Blair snapped. "Helene finds out I blabbed she'll freak out on me, and then I'll have to kick your Asian ass!"

"How are your candidates?" Birdy asked. "Any hotties?" he wiggled his eyebrows.

"I guess," Blair shrugged her shoulders. "There is this one Hispanic girl that looks like she could be a model. She's really humble about her looks, but she's like really intense! Not a girl you wanna mess with. Hey that's her over there actually," Blair pointed out.

"Where?" Birdy asked getting excited.

"Cool it Birdbrain, she is WAY out of your league," Blair joked.

"Hey! I got some moves," Birdy bobbed his head back and forth. "Oh my God, is that her!?" Birdy said his eyes getting wide.

"Yup, that's Amariana," Blair nodded.

Virgil turned around to get a glimpse, he froze in place when his eyes fell on her. Never had Virgil been captivated so strongly by a woman's beauty. Amariana was seated five booths down, sitting alone, intensely reading a textbook. Amariana had a mild Hispanic complexion, with an obvious strong Caucasian ancestry as well. Her hair was wavy and black as night, and fell around her in thick, soft curly locks like silk. Her eyes were emeralds, and her face...Virgil was so enthralled by her face his mouth slowly dropped open. She had full lips and smooth, perfect skin. She tucked a strand of hair behind her ear, revealing cute small ears. Her shirt was modest revealing only the slightest teasing of cleavage.

Blair cleared her throat, Virgil blinked closing his mouth turning to look at the others. Everyone was staring at Virgil, Birdy was wiggling his eyebrows, Nev's face was getting red, Louie was grinning ear to ear, and Blair...if looks could kill, Virgil would have died young.

"Like what you seen?" Louie asked his grin not leaving his face.

"What do you mean?" Virgil asked defensively his eyebrows knitting together.

"A Bulldog drools less than you were just now!" Blair snapped crossing her arms over her chest.

"I was not!" Virgil protested.

"You should go talk with her," Louie suggested shooing Virgil away with his hand.

"What! No!" Virgil said feeling terrified. A girl like that? I wouldn't have a chance in Hel, he thought. "She's out of my league," Virgil said simply.

"So, you DO like her," Birdy nodded starting to smile as big as Louie. "First time I saw a girl get that kind of reaction from you. Virgil's got a crush!" Blair gave Birdy an icy glare, and his smile was whipped clean off his face.

"She's not THAT good looking!" Blair said in a huff.

Virgil turned to look at her again, he felt his face grow warm, just from the sight of her. Amariana looked up and their eyes locked, Virgil quickly turned away, she'd caught him staring! Virgil's face grew flaming red.

"Go talk to her man," Nev said.

"No, maybe another time," Virgil suggested.

"Hey Amariana come over here!" Louie shouted out.

"Louie!" Virgil snapped nearly attacking his best friend.

Louie was laughing so hard he couldn't contain himself. Amariana looked over at them with an arched eyebrow, then went back to reading.

"She already caught me staring, she's gonna think I'm a weirdo!" Virgil spoke softly but harshly, trying to keep his voice down. "Don't embarrass me Louie!"

"Ol' Louie knows a thing or two about the romance son," Louie said proudly placing his hands on his big belly. "Let me help you out. We've all been hoping you'd find a special someone who makes your pants grow tight."

"I'm heading back to the Omega house," Virgil declared.

"You get up and I'll start shouting her name out," Louie threatened.

"You wouldn't dare," Virgil forced through clenched teeth.

"Amar," Louie started, and Virgil forced his hand over Louie's mouth. Louie started laughing so hard his whole body was shaking.

"I'm out of here," Blair declared with an icy tone. She grabbed her back pack and stormed away from them.

"What's her problem?" Virgil asked taking his hand off Louie's big mouth.

"Isn't it obvious?" Louie asked. "She's jealous this sexy Latina girl is giving you action in the pants, and she doesn't." Birdy and Nev chuckled at Louie's comment.

"What?" Virgil cried. "But Blair and I are just friends, we had a talk about it at formal."

"Girls are complicated," Nev shrugged, "Maybe she told you what you wanted to hear."

"Go man," Birdy told Virgil. "Introduce yourself and ask to sit down."

"Do I have too?" Virgil asked, feeling more scared then when he had faced the Arch Demon a few weeks earlier.

"Yup," Louie said happily. "Or I will embarrass the shit out of you!" he declared proudly.

"I'm going," Virgil said getting up. His legs felt like rubber, his hands were sweaty, his pulse was racing. Virgil walked past the booths approaching Amariana, he came to a stop at her table. Amariana didn't look up, though he was sure she could tell he was there. Virgil felt his face grow a little red, she wasn't going to make this easy for him.

"Hi," Virgil said and wanted to kick himself. Hi? Hi! Creator why did he walk over here?

Amariana looked up, her face was blank, she didn't smile at him, her eyebrows rose up, as if to say, 'what do you want?'

When it was clear she didn't plan on responding back Virgil had no choice but to speak again. "I'm Virgil, a brother of the Omegas." Virgil told her.

"I know," Amariana responded.

"You do?" Virgil asked confused.

"Some of the sisters mentioned you, said you had two Devil Arms, one on each hand. They said you were a nice guy," Amariana said.

"Cool," Virgil nodded, looking down at her right hand, she had a blue Devil Arms symbol in the shape of a small blade. They stood there staring awkwardly at each other. "They are a great sorority, one of my best friends is a sister, Blair, I don't know if you met her yet."

"I did," Amariana nodded. "She seems…lively."

"Yeah," Virgil replied. Why am I so nervous?

"Can I sit down?" Virgil asked at the same time Amariana said, "Well I should get going to class."

"Oh," Virgil said feeling like an idiot.

Amariana gathered her things and stood up, she was just a few inches shorter than him, tall for a woman, around average male height. Standing so close to her, it sent shivers down his spine, her scent wafted to his nose, lavender, she was intoxicating.

"Bye Virgil, it was nice meeting you," She said politely and quickly walked away.

"Bye," Virgil said in a pathetic tone he didn't recognize as his own. As he watched her go his eyes drifted down, in the words of his fallen comrade Boyd, she had a booty you could bounce a quarter off of. Virgil in that moment, decided he was an ass man. Amariana stopped dead in her tracks, and her head snapped around. Her gaze was icy, Virgil stood there gawking like an idiot, she'd caught him staring at her rear end! She arched an eyebrow in a sassy way, and Virgil quickly turned around, wishing he could just die from embarrassment already. He walked back to his friends a defeated look on his face, he slumped down into the booth.

"Epic fail!" Louie declared laughing hard. "I can't believe you stared at her butt for so long! Don't you know how to sneak a peek for the spank bank, then hit the road like you stole somethin'?" he jested.

"Dude, you choked hardcore," Nev laughed. "Your usually so smooth, what happened?"

"I don't know," Virgil shrugged, "She makes me feel so…nervous."

"You're crushing, hard!" Birdy laughed.

"Alright, let's get out of here," Louie suggested to Virgil. "I've got plans to hang out with two of the new pledges, Homer and Tucker. You're welcome to join!"

"Sounds fun," Virgil replied with a smile, and left with Louie.

# <u>Chapter 5 Devil Arms Training</u>

Louie drove them, in his black SUV, off campus heading west, towards Kawkawlin. They came to an apartment complex, the same one Blair lived in. Louie parked his vehicle, and Virgil laughed at the irony, the candidates lived right across from Blair and Helene's house! Virgil and Louie walked up to their place and knocked on the door. A mixed Hispanic and Caucasian male answered the door. He had a medium complexion, with dark hair, and dark eyes, he had a dip in his mouth.

"What's up guys!" Tucker greeted them warmly with a slightly country twang, people spoke with a nasally Northerner accent in Michigan.

"Hey Tucker!" Louie said coming in for a bear hug. Louie was the same way with everyone, and Tucker laughed hard.

"Get outta here!" Tucker said breaking the hug after a few seconds.

"Sorry man, we hug in this family," Louie told him moving aside for Virgil.

"I'm Virgil," Virgil said extending his hand to Tucker.

"Tucker," he told Virgil using his Devil Arms hand to shake hands. Tucker had an earth colored halberd shaped Devil Arms.

"Well come on in guys, we're happy to have you over," Tucker welcome them. The apartment was in the same style as Blair's, but instead of it being decorated in a feminine and cozy way, this was a bachelor pad. No pictures or decorations hung on the walls, save for a few posters with crude college humor. The place was messy, not unusual for guys their age.

"Hey Louie!" Homer greeted them from the living room. Homer had your typical white boy look going on. He had blonde hair shaved close to his head, like Magnus and Nev, with a hooked nose, and bright blue eyes. Homer's Devil Arms was a ruby red lance.

"Homer!" Louie shouted out and Homer got up to shake his hand, but Louie grabbed him in a bear hug. Homer's face grew a little red, and he slapped Louie on the back a couple times signaling he'd had enough hugging. "What are you guys up to?" Louie asked.

"Just chillin' man," Homer said, also with a dip in his mouth and a spit bottle in hand. Virgil thought it was a disgusting and unhealthy habit. "We're both done with classes."

"Well shit let's do something!" Louie said. "Show me around your place."

They greeted Homer and Tucker's other two roommates and followed them downstairs. Tucker lived in the basement, though there wasn't a room for him. Half of the basement was sectioned off and Tucker's things and his bed were at the far end.

"Man this is your room?" Louie asked looking around. "How the hell do you jerk off down here without a door?" he laughed.

"Those bastards are always coming down the stairs without asking," Tucker shook his head.

"Well Tucker doesn't have a lot of money," Homer explained. "He has the basement and pays the cheapest rent. I'll show you my room," Homer said, and they followed him back to the first floor, then up another flight of stairs. On the second floor were three rooms, Homer's room was set up nicely. His bed was a futon set up as a couch, with two extra chairs facing a large TV hooked up with the latest Xbox.

"Aww you're an Xbox kind of guy," Virgil commented.

"Hell yeah!" Homer told him.

"I'm all about Playstation," Virgil commented.

"Well, there's the door!" Homer joked. "No, I'm just kidding man, Playstation's alright." The four guys sat down and closed the door.

"So how is pledging going?" Louie asked.

"Good so far," Tucker said, "Haven't really had to do anything yet," he admitted.

"Don't you worry, shit is coming down hill," Louie warned, a devilish grin on his face.

"How was your first Education?" Virgil asked.

"Sucked," Homer admitted. "We were there until 2am! We have some real winners in Rho class. Jeramiah kept getting so nervous, he would screw up, and Vahn made us rip out our pages and start all over!"

"Yup, sounds like the first Education!" Louie laughed. "At least you weren't Omicron class, we set the new record for most pages ripped out."

"Oh we beat it," Homer said confidently. "Vahn even said so."

"Damn," Louie laughed.

They turned on a shooter game and the four of them played locally against each other. Virgil and Louie quickly bonded with them. Homer and Tucker were extremely chill, and Virgil found he had a lot in common with them. Homer was the more outgoing of the two, the more chauvinistic, cocky, and talkative one. Tucker was on the quieter side, but the guy was funny as hell, and had a goofy way of looking at things, that made Virgil laugh at his comments. Virgil liked them already.

"Well shit son, if we're just hanging out and talking," Louie commented, "We should knock out our interviews."

It was Homer and Tucker's first interview, so they were a little unsure of themselves. Louie did a great job of setting the pace, letting them know the right questions to ask; funny ones and serious ones, ones about people's past, the present, and what they wanted out of their futures. Hours went by, and the four of them were laughing for much of the time. Tucker and Louie were humorous, and they played well off each other. Homer had a harder life than Virgil would have guessed, the guy carried himself so well. Homer's Aunt was like his parent, she lived on the other side of the state. Homer revealed a humble and vulnerable side to himself, and even got teary eyed at one point. Louie gave him a big ol' bear hug and Homer really cried. Virgil was moved by his story and felt a kinship with him. Homer, though a little cocky on the outside, had a heart of gold on the inside. Tucker was from the small town of Brown City, the birth of the mobile home, in the Thumb of Michigan. Tucker's mom was Mexican, and his dad was white. Tucker had an older brother and a younger sister. Tucker wasn't the sharpest tool in the shed, but there was more to measure a man by, than his grade point average. Tucker was a genuine goofy guy and Virgil immediately felt these two could grow to become some of his best friends.

Of course, Louie and Virgil shared about themselves as well. As the conversation went on Homer and Tucker asked more questions about the fraternity, the Paladins, and what it meant living as a Nephilim in a world filled with humans unaware of the conflict that was threatening to overtake the world.

"I don't want to toot my own horn now, but I am one of the badasses in this fraternity," Louie bragged. "I have Shiva's Bow, an ice bow Devil Arms. I've faced off against Arch Demons, Death Dealers, you could say I'm one of the brave ones."

Virgil's eyes grew wide and he struggled to contain himself, Tucker caught Virgil's reaction and the two of them burst out laughing.

"I don't think Virgil agrees," Tucker told them.

"You got something to say?" Louie asked incredulously.

"You have more redeeming qualities than most Louie, but bravery is not among them," Virgil admitted still laughing.

"Hey! I saved you from that Arch Demon!" Louie cried out.

"You going to use that line every day until we're old men?" Virgil asked. "What about the vampires we ran into in the tunnels last semester?"

"Vampires!" Homer exclaimed. "I want to hear this!"

"Hey, I held one of the flashlights!" Louie protested. "They were UV flashlights that burned vampires if they came into contact with the light," he explained to the pledges making it sound like he was so brave.

"Yeah, at the *very* back of the group," Virgil added rolling his eyes, "And we had to beg you to come, and practically drag you down there with us."

"I was scared alright!" Louie admitted and everyone started laughing including Louie.

"Tell us about your Devil Arms Virgil," Tucker asked. "Louie has two symbols and he has a bow. But yours are different colors," Tucker pointed out.

"Yeah, I haven't seen any of the other brothers with those colors," Homer added.

"That's cause Virgil's s-p-e-c-i-a-l," Louie mocked. "He's not normal, even by Nephilim standards."

"Come on," Virgil said not wanting to get into this.

"Tell 'em," Louie shrugged nudging Virgil. "They're awesome man, you might as well share."

"Well, I guess there is this prophecy, about the end of the world," Virgil rambled wanting the explanation to already be over. "The War of Ragnorak, it is called. An evil being, a very powerful godlike entity, that created the race of demons, slumbers in the demon world called the Ever After. When he awakens, he'll destroy our world, and everything in it. It was foretold that seven powerful Nephilim, called Seraphim Nephilim, or just Seraphs, would be born heralding the coming of Ragnorak," Virgil's hands were getting sweaty. Everyone's eyes were on him and he had a hard time meeting their gazes. "Apparently I am one of those Seven Seraphs," Virgil admitted looking down at his Devil Arms. "I'm the Sixth Seraph, the Redeemer. This white symbol, it's the Holy Blade, Ragnorak, the most powerful Devil Arms in existence."

"It's pretty damn awesome," Louie admitted. "I've seen Virgil kick some major ass with that thing."

"It was once wielded by my father, the Fallen Judge Raphael," Virgil said, his face becoming saddened by the memories of him.

"Your father's a Judge?" Homer asked in disbelief.

"What's that again?" Tucker asked.

"Same thing as an Angel, just different term," Louie explained.

"That seems a little unreal," Homer added.

"I wasn't raised by him, I was adopted as an infant and grew up with a normal family. The first time I met my father was in June," Virgil told them. "There was a big tournament at the Paladin Capital, in Alexandros. The Death Dealers attacked at the end, and a group of us Omegas were taken prisoner into the Ever After. My father, he visited me in the Death Dealer prison, Hel. He wants me to join him," Virgil said sadly.

The room was quiet. "Are you going to?" Tucker asked.

"NO!" Virgil yelled startling them. "Sorry," Virgil added. "It's a sore subject."

"Okay you're the son of some powerful dark Angel," Tucker nodded, "I get it I think."

"How'd you escape?" Homer asked.

"Artreyu, the First Seraph, he freed me, and I helped free the brothers," Virgil explained.

Homer and Tucker responded in awe and amazement. It was a much more complicated story, but Virgil didn't want to go into detail, and they were smart enough to understand. "What are your other Devil Arms?" Homer asked.

"Soul Reaver," Virgil answered, and the black symbol glowed with dark light.

"Wow!" Homer and Tucker exclaimed.

"It's a Chaos Devil Arms," Virgil said sadly. "A scythe covered in dark black flames that burns away the aura, the very essence that gives mortals life, of whomever it touches, even my friends."

Homer and Tucker's eyebrows went up, with weary looks on their faces.

"Virgil is one of the good guys though," Louie stated attempting to shift the tone, draping his arm around Virgil's shoulder. "This guy has saved our brothers' lives more times than anyone. If you're ever in trouble, you can always count on him, to do his all to protect you."

"Louie," Virgil wanted to shrug his friend's arm off but the look in his eyes stopped him. Louie's chocolate eyes held such trust, and faith. Louie believed in Virgil, more than he believed in himself, Virgil smiled tightly, tears coming to his eyes.

"Sometimes, I feel like Soul Reaver's influence is growing stronger, like it wants control," Virgil admitted. "But I don't want that, I don't want to be that person."

"And you won't," Louie firmly added, "Cause I know you brother. You're stronger than any darkness. That freaking scythe starts wantin' more control, you tell it to mind its own damn business!"

"I don't think you're bad Virgil," Homer said firmly. "I'm good at reading people and you seem like one of the nicest guys I've ever met."

"Same here," Tucker said raising his hand in the air.

"Thanks guys," Virgil said trying not to choke up. "I'm sorry for letting things get so serious."

"That's it, bring it in," Tucker said standing up.

"Fo sure!" Louie cried out, jumping up open arms, and the four men stood up and did a group hug.

"You guys are awesome!" Homer declared. "This was amazing! I can't wait to do more interviews and learn more about the brothers!"

"You two are probably my favorite brothers," Tucker told Louie and Virgil softly.

"Aww shut up," Louie laughed blushing slightly. "It's only your first day, your knucklehead. You don't know any other brothers!"

"Yeah but even when I do get to know the other brothers," Tucker said sincerely an earnest and raw look in his eyes, "I can already tell I'm going to be closest with you guys."

"Shucks son!" Louie babbled. "Now I'm going to start crying."

Virgil laughed and the four of them felt connected, bonded. The interview had come to a close, it was one of Virgil's favorites, he knew he'd always remember that day, getting to know Homer and Tucker for the first time. He prayed they made it through the process, he wanted them as brothers.

"I can't wait to start Devil Arms training!" Homer exclaimed. "I want to see what my weapon is going to look like!"

"Me too!" Tucker added.

"Tomorrow night, your first brotherhood," Louie explained. "You'll get to practice with your Bigs and Hegemon, it might take a few times, but soon enough you both will be able to summon them to your hands just by saying their names."

"When Tucker told me you were coming over, I thought you were coming to mess with us," Homer admitted with a nervous laugh to Louie.

"No way!" Louie said waving off Homer's comment. "Omicron isn't like that. We're not interested in making your lives hell, we know what pledging is like. We're more interested in being your friends. Some brothers do like to mess with pledges like Zender and Jace, now those guys you have to watch out for!" Louie warned them.

"Jace is my Big," Homer said with a big smile, "So I don't have to worry about that!" He stuck his tongue out, thrilled.

"Who is your Big Tucker?" Virgil asked.

"Buck," Tucker replied.

"That guy got a third Lil before I got my first!" Louie yelled getting angry. "I'm mad at your Big Virgil," Louie laughed.

"Vahn's your Big?" Homer asked surprised.

"Yup," Virgil said proudly. "My roommate freshmen year, his Big was Buck as well," Virgil told Tucker.

"Oh yeah?" Tucker replied. "Which brother is it?"

Louie and Virgil got quiet. "His name was Boyd, he died last year," Virgil said sadly.

"Oh," Tucker responded with surprise.

"That is the dark side to this brotherhood," Louie admitted. "We're freaking half human half angel warriors, and sometimes we lose good men out there."

It was dark outside, they'd been talking for over four hours, and everyone was starving. The four of them headed out to grab some dinner and enjoyed each other's company even more.

They'd grown close in a short period of time, and it felt like they'd already been friends for a while. After dinner Louie and Virgil headed back to the Omega house. Virgil had his busiest day of classes on Tuesday and was feeling tired. Vinny was at the Omega house, hanging out in the living room with a group of brothers including Spencer, Landon, Jagger, Lamar, Mu, Jace, and Abe.

"Hey Virgil!" Vinny called out from the living room as Virgil and Louie came into the foyer. Virgil and Louie walked into the large living room to the right of the entrance.

"What cha watching?" Louie asked the room looking to the TV and taking a seat next to Landon.

"What did you do today?" Virgil asked Vinny who was seated next to Spencer.

"Your Lil is a really great guy," Spencer said to Virgil. "He spent the day with most of us, hanging out, and going on a few random adventures."

"I got a couple interviews done," Vinny boasted proudly. "I'd like us to have our interview soon," he added with less confidence and more shyness.

"Ehh," Virgil thought about it. "We can do our interview in a week or so. Vahn didn't do our interview right away, he wanted me get to know the other brothers first."

"Okay," Vinny nodded looking dejected.

"I'm proud you got so much done today," Virgil said to Vinny wanting him to know that he cared. "Tomorrow is your first Brotherhood. And I'll be there to help train you with your Devil Arms," Virgil smiled.

"I'm looking forward to it," Vinny nodded with a big smile. "Vahn said you're one of the strongest Nephilim in the world!"

"Ha!" Lamar laughed from a couch across the room. Virgil gave him a cold stare.

"I don't claim to be the strongest, or the best, cause I'm not," Virgil firmly put it out there for everyone to hear. "I honestly don't care about that. I only want the strength to protect the people who matter to me."

"Vahn said you'd deny you were," Vinny smiled proudly.

"Yeah well tell your Gran Big to quit talking about me," Virgil laughed. "I'm tired, and I have a full day of classes tomorrow, so I'm going to bed. Goodnight everyone," Virgil said to the room. His brothers bid him farewell. That night before Virgil went to sleep he went to his dresser, taking out the magicite he kept hidden. It was an opal colored gemstone, about the size of his fist, a gift from John, an Omega from another Chapter he'd tried to save in Hel. Virgil took the magicite, Optimum, and sat in his bed, he could feel the energy inside it, his energy. Virgil closed his eyes concentrating, seeing his aura around him. Virgil siphoned some of his energy off into the magicite, it could hold the size of his aura, ten times over. He had started making this an evening ritual, as his aura recovered over time. He knew there would be a day he'd have need of this extra source of power. Once he'd drained about half of his aura into the stone, he felt tired, and put the magicite back. Exhausted he fell asleep within a minute of laying down.

Virgil's Tuesday was his busiest day, he had both his History and Bio Statistics class Tuesdays and Thursdays, and his Communications class from 7pm till 10pm. He shared the history class with Nev, and the Communication class with Louie, which helped make those two classes more enjoyable. History was pretty simple, the professor just talked, and talked, and talked. Never on topic with the course, always about himself, and how great of a person he was. They had papers over assigned books for the class, which they never talked about. Nev and Virgil wrote back and forth through the class, making fun of the professor, and making each other laugh. Bio Statistics was Virgil's second hardest class; the professor was extremely intelligent but sucked at teaching. Virgil found he had to teach himself the material, the grade was based solely on four tests, and a final exam. Virgil had his first one already, and it had been brutal, he'd scored an 84%, not bad but he needed to do better next time. His communications professor was by far his favorite of the semester. She was sweet, and funny, and great at engaging the class and making people interested. Virgil sat next to Louie, and even though it was a three-hour class, it always seemed to take the shortest amount of time.

After class Virgil and Louie hurried back to the Omega house, it was Rho class' first Brotherhood. The candidates were already gathered in the foyer of the house in their line, heads down, Zender patrolling them, making sure they stayed quiet. The brothers were out back horsing around and pumped up.

"Anyone care to place a wager?" Magnus asked walking by.

"I'll put five bucks on Vinny," Spencer called out getting out his wallet.

"Five bucks?" Magnus asked in disbelief. "Come on now, you can dig a little deeper than that, you got a ten or a twenty? You believe in Vinny, you might as well go all the way," Magnus egged him on.

"You guys are terrible!" Landon admonished chuckling. "Spencer don't let Magnus take your money!"

"I got, ten on Zane!" Lamar proclaimed happily. "My Lil is the shit! He's going to be the star of Rho class."

Magnus took out a small note pad, taking note of Spencer's and Lamar's bets.

"Magnus who did you put your money on?" Landon asked his pledge brother with skepticism.

Magnus shut his notepad, his eyes betrayed his scheming ways. "Not placing any bets? Then it's not your concern," Magnus said nonchalantly putting distance between himself and Landon.

"He's putting money on his new Lil," Nolan said to Louie, Birdy, Nev, and Virgil who were standing together. "Guarantee it."

"Colton right?" Nev asked.

"Yup," Nolan nodded. "Magnus told me he only gets the best Lils, I was the best pledge in Omicron, and Colton will be the best in Rho class."

"Hey!" Louie, Birdy, and Virgil snapped.

"I wasn't far behind you buster," Birdy said with some attitude.

Nolan shrugged, "It is what it is, but Colton is determined to be the top of the class, and he will probably be the best warrior as well, something I wasn't in Omicron," Nolan said looking to Virgil.

"Colton's had a Devil Arms symbol since his first day of college," Virgil said, "There's a strong possibility he'll be the strongest Nephilim, he's a Pureblood."

"I wouldn't rule out Aidan," Louie spoke up, "He's Vahn's blood brother. Besides he already managed to summon his Devil Arms at Omicron's Brotherhoods last year."

"He did, so he's technically out of the betting," Nolan stated, "Only candidates who haven't already managed to summon corporeal forms of their Devil Arms are in the bet."

"Aww," Louie moaned, "I was going to root for our old pledge brother. I'm really glad Aidan came back," Louie said proudly.

"Me too," Virgil nodded. "He's a nice guy, and he'll be a great addition to the Omegas."

"Brothers!" Vahn shouted. "We're going to bring the candidates back. Everyone stay quiet, and no talking out of turn. This is my show, and I won't have ANYONE ruining this for Rho class." Vahn headed back inside. He came back out with the fourteen candidates in tow, Zender bringing up the rear.

Vahn went through a few traditional first night exercises, which Rho class blundered through like normal pledge classes. Afterwards came time for Devil Arms practice.

"The symbols that appeared on each of your hands, are a representation of who you are. Learning to master them, is also about understanding one's self. The Devil Arms can be used to protect yourself in the form of your soul weapon. My Devil Arms is Fury Brand," Vahn told them and his shortsword blazed into existence landing firmly in his hand. Rho class were shocked and most reacted with awe. "You can also cast spells from the element you're aligned with, we'll be going over that in a few weeks. Tonight, we'll focus on trying to materialize your Devil Arms into a physical form. Don't get upset if you don't make it happen on the first try, it can take weeks or even months. It took my Lil a while to master his, and he's gone on to become the best in the Chapter," Vahn boasted to the group.

"Says you," Gabriel spoke up his arms crossed over his chest, an unhappy look on his face. Virgil would never make the claim to be greater than Gabriel, Gabriel was more than powerful enough to kick his butt any day.

"Virgil, care to demonstrate with me?" Vahn asked.

Everyone turned to look at Virgil. Virgil nodded and stepped forward squaring off against his Big. "Dull!" Virgil said and a blue outline covered his black scythe symbol.

"The Dull spell is an integral component in practicing with your Devil Arms. It prevents your blade from piercing the flesh of another, helpful if you need to improve your skill and not maim your brother in the process," Vahn said sarcastically. "Dull," he commanded and the same blue traced around his symbol, and a light blue barrier formed around his sword.

"Soul Reaver," Virgil spoke aloud and the scythe snaked into existence, black flames creeping up his arm when he held it. The barrier was around his scythe's blade, but the flames could still burn Vahn. Virgil made the first move, breaking into a sprint he screamed and leapt forward flinging his scythe at Vahn. It whirled through the air, making an eerie sound, as it thirsted to suck the life of all it touched.

"Flame Geyser!" Vahn shouted extending his hand towards the incoming blade. A column of flame burst from the ground, overtaking the scythe, it was forced back coming to Virgil's hand.

The candidates were all impressed and a few whistled, "That a boy Virgil!" Tucker called out.

"Hey!" Vahn snapped at Tucker. "I'm your Hegemon, just remember that," Vahn teased.

"My bad," Tucker called out blushing with a shit eating grin earning a few laughs.

Vahn broke into a run, and Virgil did the same, their blades clashed and they strained against the might of one another. It was a familiar dance; one they'd done dozens of times in the year they'd known each other. Vahn had been Virgil's primary Devil Arms teacher, as was the norm for all Bigs and Lils, as such they grew to know each other's moves and tells. Putting on an exciting and convincing show for the candidates was easy to do safely. They knew each other's movements, and they purposefully exaggerated their strikes so they could block each other easily. Virgil would sooner harm himself than his Big. They'd grown close as they bonded over the art of the Devil Arms. Their blows were becoming more heated, they were striking at each other harder, with more force, the battle of the blades coming to a conclusion. Vahn cut across Virgil's guard knocking his scythe out of his hands, Vahn placed his blade on Virgil's shoulder. Virgil rose his hands to signal defeat.

The brothers and candidates broke into applause.

"Bigs pair off with your Lils!" Vahn instructed.

Virgil and Vinny walked side by side gaining some distance from the others.

"That was incredible!" Vinny was practically jumping up and down, his eyes were big and filled with excitement.

"Thanks," Virgil said shyly, "It was just for show."

"I could tell," Vinny nodded, "Vahn would never try to hurt you, it's easy to see he thinks a lot of you."

"And I think a lot of you Vinny," Virgil said smiling at his Lil. "Everyone is already really impressed with how you've been doing these past two days. Keep up the good work."

"Thanks," Vinny nodded beaming.

"Alright let's get to work," Virgil instructed, "Close your eyes Vinny." Vinny did as his Big instructed. "Bringing out your Devil Arms, is about searching inside yourself. Your soul weapon is connected to your feelings, thoughts, and perceptions. Clear your mind of doubt and negativity. Feel the air around you, the earth beneath you. The symbol on your hand, it has an energy and life of its own, listen, let it in," Virgil spoke softly.

They stood there silently concentrating. "Nothing is happening," Vinny said peeking out through his eyelids. "Is it just supposed to, appear?" he asked laughing nervously.

"You have to speak its name," Virgil said. "When you discover its name, you'll be able to use it," he told him. "Concentrate in your mind, the symbol on your hand. Envision it, what kind of thoughts does it bring? How does it make you feel?"

"It's warm, there is heat," Vinny said, "Fire, and strength."

"You have a strong moral character; your strength comes from the iron will of your convictions." Virgil nodded. "And your Devil Arms is aligned with fire. What else?" he asked feeling Vinny was starting to get on the right track.

Aidan summoned his Devil Arms with ease, earning some cheers and praise from the brothers. Vinny got visibly worried, it broke his concentration.

"Don't worry about him, he already has been able to use his Devil Arms since I was a pledge," Virgil told Vinny.

"Steel Plasma!" Colton shouted out and a longsword materialized into his hand. The blade pulsed with purple energy running along its length. It was similar to Terra's Devil Arms, the Prytanis of the Alpha sisters, only Colton's looked even more powerful. Colton slashed his blade forward and purple energy swam from the blades surface, thundering ahead of him. Everyone jumped out of the way. Colton's face held surprise, and triumph. A large grin spread across his handsome mug, and everyone cheered him on. Magnus looked pleased as well, and patted Colton on the back, promising him to train him to his full potential. He'd also won the bet. Vinny looked at his pledge brother's majestic sword with envy.

"Vinny," Virgil said gaining his attention back. "You have a Devil Arms all your own, unique from all others in the world. When you are able to summon it, I know it will be a great and mighty weapon, that will serve you well," Virgil placed his arm on Vinny's shoulder trying to instill his belief into Vinny.

"Okay," Vinny said sounding like he didn't believe it.

After an hour longer of practice, only Aidan, Colton, Flynn, and Zane were able to materialize their Devil Arms. The other candidates wore expressions of defeat.

"To everyone who couldn't produce a corporeal form of their Devil Arms, please do NOT be discouraged. You aren't in trouble, and no one thinks less of you," Vahn said passionately to his candidates. "We'll have Devil Arms practice again Thursday night!" Vahn announced with optimism. "That's enough for one evening! Candidates head inside and get some rest!"

"We'll get it next time Vinny," Virgil encouraged Vinny and they walked inside with the rest of the fraternity.

# <u>Chapter 6 Little Brothers and Vampires</u>

Wednesday after class Virgil was exhausted and went home to find it was abuzz with candidates, brothers, Sweethearts, and Paladins from Alexandros. The candidates were very curious about the Nephilim who always wore their wings, asking them questions, earning friendly banter from the normally stoic soldiers. It was only the third day of the process but already Rho class had bonded with the group. Vinny, Flynn, Brett, Nigel, Colton, Zane, Cameron, Aidan, Homer, Tucker, and Jeramiah were the eleven candidates who stood out among the fourteen. They all cycled through the fraternity house, spending as much of their free time with the brothers at the Omega grounds, a house that felt like a home.

Virgil snuck to his room, doing his best to dodge the others, a nap whispering to him from his bed. Virgil got to his room to discover his Lil and Zane chilling, playing the newest Playstation.

"What's going on in here?" Virgil barked.

The candidates jumped to their feet, the Dreamstone chains candidates had to have on at all times, dangling around their necks. "Sir!" Zane responded.

"At ease," Virgil jested, "Please," Virgil laughed. "You know you don't have to call me that, I'm not one of the brothers you have to worry about."

"It is best to show respect to each new man we meet," Zane said sternly, speaking so serious his brow was furrowed, his pointed chin set in a scowl. "I think it's important to bring back some class and respect in this society, and it starts with each interaction, passing it on to those you meet, leading by example," Zane spoke passionately.

"You make a good point," Virgil nodded slowly really looking at Zane. He had a profound natural street smart, and charisma, even though he wasn't the best academic, he was by no means out of the race for the sharpest mind.

"Sorry we're in your room," Vinny said to Virgil, his cheeks growing red, stuttering slightly. "There are just so many people everywhere, we came up here to take a short break."

"Calm down Vinny," Virgil smirked with an exaggerated eye roll for his Lil. "You're always welcome here, mi casa es tu casa." Virgil turned to Zane. "Sorry man, I know we've met a bunch of times now, but I feel like we haven't had a chance to really talk."

"Well I'm here now, let's talk," Zane suggested with a serious face, he could have been a model with his pouty fierce good looks.

"I guess I have a couple hours to kill," Virgil agreed, wishing he could just take a nap.

"Cool let's go out to dinner I'm starving!" Vinny shouted with a big grin. His Lil was a foodie.

"There is food here," Virgil suggested. "With Nolan as House Manager, we don't go hungry."

"Vinny's right," Zane shrugged. "Just the three of us, getting out of here, going on an adventure, that's the kind of stuff memories are made of," he smiled mischievously.

Virgil laughed, "Alright! I'm in. Vinny what do you have in mind?"

"Let's go to G's!" Vinny said getting excited. "I know how much you love Italian food."

"It shows," Virgil said patting his nonexistent belly.

"Whatever," Zane retorted. "Let's hit the road already."

The three headed out of the Omega house, Virgil drove them in his Blazer across town, over the Liberty Bridge to the east side of Bay City. Zane talked most of the way, Virgil got the impression he was the kind of guy that could fit in anywhere, he was personable and likeable. Zane told Virgil about his family; raised by his single mom, with younger siblings, they were lower class poor, growing up in rural Mayville. Zane told them he was the unpopular kid until he did sports in high school, because kids made fun of him for his clothes. They couldn't afford nice clothes or toys, Zane explained, it was go without, or go hungry. Zane's only real hope for college was a sports scholarship, but an injury in his sophomore year cut his chances of any college ball. Zane had come to Bay Valley because it was one of the cheapest Universities in Michigan, and it was close to his home. Zane didn't have a vehicle of his own, he didn't even own much clothing. The more they talked the more Virgil's heart went out to this amazing kid, who just didn't seem to have many natural supports, or resources available to him, yet was clearly such a great person. Zane's overall message was one of positivity, he never seemed to give up hope. He had a heart of gold. Zane's goal was to a get a good job so he could take care of his mom and be a good role model for his younger siblings. Vinny was touched as well by Zane's story, and they both had a newfound respect for him.

G's Pizzeria was owned and run by Gabriel's family, a long line of Nephilim warriors from Italy. They had amazing food, with great hospitality, and friendly service. A renowned Omega warrior owned the one in Saginaw, and the Bay City branch was just a block away from the Saginaw River. Narrow alleyways and streets were abundant in the downtown district. This used to be where lumber was pumped out of the city, the largest exporter in the State during the 1900s. Fish were plentiful as well back then, before men polluted the waters and over farmed them. And during Prohibition, this had been a major hub for alcohol, tunnels ran under the city, and had been used for illegal trafficking underneath the businesses. It was now home to the local Vampire coven. Just two blocks over was Ms. Morgan's Boutique, she was a friendly witch who made a living helping others in the community.

Quickly, the three of them power walked to the entrance, the bitter cold of the September night biting at their faces. They walked in, to find the place was packed with people! Virgil walked to the left, and was greeted by a chorus of voices shouting, "SURPRISE! HAPPY BIRTHDAY!"

"What?" Virgil was stunned silent. He'd been so busy and stressed out over classes, he'd completely forgotten it was his birthday…

"You didn't think we'd forget your birthday!" Dante shouted coming up to Virgil embracing him fiercely and briefly.

"Take a seat birthday boy!" Blair yelled seated near Louie and Vahn.

Virgil sat with his friends and brothers. Over half of the Chapter had come out along with half of the candidates. Sweethearts Raven and Lilly were there, along with TK and Selene. Virgil ordered some food, that Vahn insisted on paying for, and walked around visiting with everyone present. Virgil was overwhelmed by the affection from his friends, he felt truly blessed. After an hour people slowly started trickling out. People paid their bills and headed back home, biding goodnight to the others, and saying goodbye to Virgil. Zane rode home with some of the other brothers, and then it was down to just Virgil's close group of friends.

"How was your Birthday bro?" Birdy asked Virgil.

"I was so busy I honestly forgot it was!" Virgil said what felt like for the hundredth time. "But this was a great way to end it," Virgil nodded.

"Well it's not over yet!" Dante smiled hitting the table. "Let's go back to Blair's for the main event!" Dante suggested.

"We have to pick up a bit first," Helene stammered quietly looking at Vinny and looking away.

"Oh merr!" Blair announced. "You never like to clean! I wonder why you want to now?" she asked mischievously. Uncharacteristic of Helene, she lashed out at Blair, lightly slugging her on the shoulder, her eyes flaming. "What the hell!" Blair laughed taken back by Helene's outburst.

"I'm game!" Homer said.

"Me too!" Tucker called out. "Can we get some directions?" he asked seriously, earning a few laughs from those who knew.

Vinny, who didn't know where Homer and Tucker lived, started volunteering directions, "Well you head down State Park Drive," but Blair interrupted him.

"Vinny, I got this," Blair announced firmly, "Find your way back to whatever hole you shitheads crawled out of, and then directly across from your front door stumble across to our front door, you'll find it," Blair smirked.

"Got it!" Tucker laughed getting red in the face.

"I like her!" Homer smiled. "We should have met our neighbors when we moved in over the summer!"

"Let's roll out!" Louie declared.

"Mind if I tag along with you?" Vinny asked Virgil.

"Not at all!" Virgil declared and they left the restaurant heading around the corner to the large parking lot, which had just a few cars left now.

"See ya soon," Birdy called out, Louie and Dante got into his car with him. Birdy barreled out of the parking lot after Blair and Helene before Virgil and Vinny had even made it to their vehicle. Virgil and Vinny walked over to his Blazer, a figure moved out of the shadows next to the decaying building.

Virgil's instincts immediately sent him on edge, Virgil barely had time to call out, "Vinny!" The figure bolted towards Vinny grabbing him forcefully, in the blink of an eye, it turned towards the alley, and shot off like a blur.

"NO!" Virgil shouted. "Light Surge!" Virgil commanded as the Master Level spell sucked its power from Virgil's aura. Beams of Creation energy rained down on the roofs, and into the alley ahead of Vinny and his captor, cutting them off. Virgil sprinted after them, down into the alley's depths, his adversary stopped in his tracks by the spell still volleying from the sky. Two figures dropped from the rooftops to land behind Virgil. "Ragnorak!" Virgil shouted. The Holy Blade thundered down from the heavens, slamming into his right hand, the energy transforming into a crystal sword. The spell stopped raining from the sky. Virgil was facing off against three male vampires in the dead of night. Virgil put his back to the wall to keep the three of them within his sights.

Vinny looked scared, his captor had an arm wrapped firmly around his neck, he was at the mercy of the parasite. "We've heard all about you Nephilim," the vampire taunted him. "We have a message from our Master. Stay out of our turf after sundown. We won't tolerate your kind running through our streets like you own them any longer!"

"You couldn't have just picked up the phone and told us nicely?" Virgil barked. "You dare to take a Paladin hostage, and make demands?" Virgil asked angrily.

"Don't raise your voice to me, Judgespawn brat!" The vampire yelled barring his fangs and gripping Vinny tightly. "I'm the one in command here, not you!"

"You harm or maim him in any way," Virgil said slowly and carefully, feeling his aura's energy ebb, and flow with power. "And I will hunt down, every last member of your bloodline, until I have sterilized the world of any trace, of anyone, ever associated with your Master's coven!" Virgil raged out, his veins popping out along his neck. Soul Reaver's dark power glowed to life. Virgil thought its name and the Scythe came to his left hand, both Devil Arms firmly within his grasp. "So yes, you are in command here," Virgil nodded his words turning dark, "But do remember the consequences for wielding such dangerous authority, over one so determined, and deadly."

"You're just a mortal," one of the other vampires said to Virgil.

"Mortals are more than they seem," Virgil said coldly.

"I've had enough of this!" The other vampire snapped. "Let's take his friend for a meal and dump the body after we're finished. That'll send the message!"

Virgil snarled, a demonic growl, his eyes flashing black with darkness.

"We were told to give our message, and so we have," the vampire holding Vinny said throwing his Little Brother to the ground. "Next time we won't be so forgiving," the vampire warned. "Let's go!" Virgil watched and in the span of a blink, with supernatural speed, the creatures melted with the shadows, disappearing into the night.

Virgil ran to Vinny, "I'm fine," Vinny told him before he could ask, getting up from the ground dusting off his clothes from the dirty ground.

"No bites, or bruises?" Virgil joked.

"I don't think so," Vinny shrugged, "But I haven't looked in a mirror, might have a bruise around my neck, people will think I'm getting hickeys or something."

He was fine. Virgil was relieved. "Let's get back to my Blazer and get out of here."

"Wow!" Vinny nodded taking in Virgil's appearance with both Devil Arms activated. "That's incredible! Your sword must be so powerful!" he acted like a kid at a video game store.

"Gawk later, let's move!" Virgil yelled and they ran back to the Blazer. Virgil dismissed his weapons, they shimmered and disappeared. He fired up the engine and they raced home.

"Is it just me, or was that bad back there?" Vinny asked. "That's not normal is it?"

"No, it's not," Virgil said serious. "Paladins are responsible for policing vampires, lycans, witches, and protecting them from demons. But if the vampires are looking to push us out…to what purpose?" Virgil asked aloud.

"Can we listen to some music?" Vinny asked turning on the radio. He looked shaken up.

"You okay?" Virgil asked him.

"Yeah," Vinny nodded. "I'm just embarrassed."

"Embarrassed?" Virgil asked shocked. "About what?" he laughed.

"That I couldn't use my Devil Arms to help fight with you," Vinny admitted looking down into his hands.

"Vinny, I don't care about that!" Virgil said getting fired up. "Mastering your Devil Arms it isn't something that can be rushed, so don't attack yourself on the inside," Virgil said with passion and Vinny looked up at him. "I know what if feels like, to watch as your pledge brothers practice with their own mystical weapons plucked from lore and miracles of legend. While you stare at your symbol, hoping, and praying, wondering why it won't help you. You start to feel like it doesn't have faith in you, because you start to lose faith in yourself too."

"You really felt like that?" Vinny asked him.

"I did," Virgil nodded looking to the road, they went over the bridge, and were safely headed to Blair's house. "But I had Vahn there, believing in me, until I was able to believe in myself. I believe in you Vinny," Virgil spoke with conviction. "And someday you'll wield a Devil Arms greater than you could have ever known."

"I'll keep trying," Vinny nodded. "Thanks Virgil."

When they got to Blair's, everyone was relaxing, having a good time, and Louie was already tipsy.

"What took you guys so long!?" Louie stumbled into Virgil spilling some of his drink.

"Vampires got Vinny," Virgil whispered to him.

"SHIT!" Louie screamed. "VAMPIRES GOT VINNY!" The party came to a dead silence, and everyone barreled to the entrance of the house shouting and asking questions, all at once. Vinny came through the door behind Virgil two seconds later closing the door.

"What's going on?!" Helene demanded. "Vinny's right there!" She yelled at Louie.

"A Vampire picked me up and ran with me down an alley!" Vinny shouted.

"What!" Homer shouted.

"Shit, I rode in the wrong car," Tucker sighed. "I wanna see that!"

Virgil got everyone calmed down, and they went to the living room where they both told the story of the vampire's message from their local coven's Master vampire.

"Magnus needs to know about this," Dante said with a serious tone. "We have Paladins from the Capital at the Omega house, and he can talk this over with them and get the word out."

Virgil got on the phone with Magnus, retelling the story once again. "This is bad," Magnus commented. "Vampires have no right to bar us from protecting citizens. They must be doing something they don't want us interfering with."

"Is this about Omicron killing two of them last winter?" Virgil asked.

"No," Magnus said quickly. "Or else this would have happened sooner. I'll get the word out to the brothers and other Paladins, and we'll discuss it more on Sunday. For now, we're going to do as they say, and take this threat seriously, until we have reason to do otherwise."

"Take care," Virgil told Magnus.

"Same to you," Magnus responded before ending the call.

Thursday night Homer, Tucker, Cameron, and Brett all managed to summon their Devil Arms for the first time, leaving Elmer, Frank, Randy, Nigel, Jeramiah, and Vinny who hadn't yet managed to do so. Vinny seemed to be taking it the most personally, he was getting so worked up, by the end of practice he stormed off to the Omega house by himself.

Vahn came up to Virgil, "I think it's time I had a talk with Vinny," Vahn told his Lil. "He needs to ease up a little."

"I agree," Virgil nodded. "He's beating himself up, I'm not sure what more I can say."

"Let me talk with him," Vahn said with optimism. "He's doing great in this process. He'll get there," Vahn told Virgil heading inside.

Virgil mingled with the brothers after Brotherhood, playing a quick game of Euchre with Nolan, Birdy, and Cameron. Afterwards Virgil went to his room, Vinny was waiting for him.

"Is everything okay?" Virgil asked Vinny.

"I just wanted to tell you something," Vinny shrugged shyly, and Virgil closed his door.

"Whats up Vinny?" Virgil asked him, standing with his feet apart and arms open.

"I feel like I'm letting you down," Vinny told Virgil.

"What do you mean?" Virgil asked getting upset. "Where is this coming from?"

"I feel like I don't meet your standards," Vinny admitted. "You're too good of a Big for me. You should have Colton, or Zane as your Lil."

"My standards?" Virgil asked a little insulted. "Have I ever said I think you're no good? Bigs and Lils aren't assigned on how good of a warrior a brother is; they are based on how people connect. I'm glad I got you Vinny, I like the other pledges, but they're not you."

"It's just, well you're really critical," Vinny admitted shyly. "Not necessarily of me, but of yourself, and people in general. You expect a lot from others, and sometimes I don't think you understand, not everyone's best is going to be at the same level," Vinny spoke with raw honesty and Virgil felt so dumbfounded, so blown away. Is this how I am coming across? Virgil didn't want to be like that.

"I am critical," Virgil nodded owning up to what Vinny had said. "It is one of my worst qualities. I don't claim to be perfect. I do expect a lot from the people I care about. When I see potential in others, I push them to reach it, the same as I push myself every day."

"You're the most self-critical person I've ever met," Vinny said honestly to Virgil.

Virgil nodded, he was hard on himself, he always had been. "I'm sorry if I've been hard on you Vinny," Virgil said softly. "I get what your trying to say. Not every brother is going to be a Gabriel, or a Colton."

"Exactly!" Vinny laughed. "We're all not going to be as powerful as Magnus!"

"I do know that!" Virgil announced with vigor. "I realize this Vinny, and don't expect any more than an individual's best. Is this about you not being able to use your Devil Arms yet?" Virgil asked.

"I don't know," Vinny said frustrated. "I just, don't want you to get your hopes up, thinking I'm going to be something I'm not," Vinny said looking down at the ground dejected.

"Vinny, you're my Lil, and I love ya," Virgil said seriously. "No matter if you're the strongest Nephilim, or the weakest, that's not how I judge a person's worth. But Vinny, I KNOW there is greatness within you. You may not see it yet, but I do. Don't count yourself out, you may just be a Magnus yourself someday," Virgil finished, and Vinny smiled warmly.

"Maybe we just need to get to know each other better," Vinny shrugged, the fight leaving him. "Then maybe there wouldn't be miscommunication, I'm still trying to understand how you think about things."

"What are you doing this weekend?" Virgil asked.

"Work on Friday, and Saturday morning, and that's it," Vinny said.

"Saturday night, we're hanging out, and doing our interview," Virgil told Vinny.

"Really?" Vinny asked getting excited. "I thought you were going to make me wait for a few weeks?" he chuckled.

"No reason to wait," Virgil shrugged. "It's been forever since I've seen my mom. I'm going home to Caseville Saturday night. You can ride along, and we'll talk on the way there, and we can get to know each other better."

"I'd love to meet your mom!" Vinny said smiling brightly. "This is going be great! Thanks Virgil!"

"Of course," Virgil replied.

Saturday, Virgil and Vinny hit the road together. It took just under an hour to reach his mother's home in Caseville. Virgil suggested that Vinny start first and tell him about his upbringing to pass the time. Vinny told Virgil he was named Vincent Junior, but everyone called him Vinny since his dad was Vincent. Vinny's dad died when he was young, and his mom remarried and had a daughter with his stepfather.

"We never knew how my dad died exactly," Vinny told Virgil. "My mom seemed to find the whole situation very skeptical. My dad was a Paladin, and my mom, she never knew."

"How do you know that?" Virgil asked Vinny.

"I had my interview with Magnus," Vinny told Virgil. "He was able to look my dad's name up in the Paladin registry. He had joined a Paladin fraternity in college and died in combat when I was just a child," Vinny smiled getting teary eyed. "It makes me proud knowing I am following in his footsteps."

"Vinny that's amazing," Virgil was overcome by his Lil's story.

Vinny's childhood friend, Tanner, was in most of his stories. The two of them seemed to have many misadventures as kids. Vinny told Virgil, Tanner was planning on coming to Bay Valley next year and wanted to join the Omegas like Vinny. Vinny was fiercely loyal, and a devoted friend. Virgil enjoyed listening to him talk about his life. They got to Virgil's mom's house, and Vinny was sad because Virgil hadn't had a chance to talk much yet. The modest two-story home was just outside of Caseville, it didn't have a beach access, but Lake Huron could be seen from the yard. Sue Pitcher was working on her flower beds surrounding the house when they pulled up.

"Boys!" Sue called out happily. Virgil walked up to his mother, embracing her affectionately. "There is my son!" Sue said proudly. "You are looking more handsome, every time I see you!" She claimed.

"Mom!" Virgil cried horrified. "My Little Brother from the fraternity is with me!" Virgil told her.

"Oh, I'm sure he knows what it's like to have a mom, don't cha?" Sue asked Vinny.

"Yes mam!" Vinny told Sue. "I'm my mom's only boy, and the oldest!"

"Aww," Sue cooed.

"Vinny, I'd like to introduce you to Sue Pitcher, the wonderful woman who raised me these past nineteen years!" Virgil said proudly.

They shook hands and exchanged small talk, "I have dinner and cake for us!" Sue told them, finishing up her yard work and heading inside. "I can't believe you're nineteen already Virgil!" Sue said to her son. "It feels like just yesterday your father and I picked you up from the hospital."

They set the table and washed their hands. "What was Virgil like as a child?" Vinny asked Sue.

"Oh lordie," Sue laughed. "Virgil was as stubborn as a weed. I remember when he was a small child, I tried to teach him to tie his shoes. He couldn't get it right the first time, so Virgil threw the shoe against the wall, and declared he'd never learn how to tie his shoes!" Sue said in a very animated and rehearsed fashion.

"Really?" Vinny asked loving every minute of it, Virgil's face grew red. "Virgil's so nice and collected though," Vinny said.

"Oh yes!" Sue laughed. "He can be really sweet. He also can be a real brat with a short temper. Virgil quit everything he used to try within the first few minutes; his ABC's, riding his bike. If he couldn't be perfect his first go, he didn't want to do it at all!" Sue told them.

"How did you ever get him do anything?" Vinny chuckled. Virgil was hating this.

"Virgil is so determined," Sue said smiling, a twinkle in her eye. "When he sets his mind out to accomplish something, and he really wants it, he'll never give up. Virgil beats himself up, he'd quit, walk away and sulk, eating himself up on the inside for quitting, for giving up, for being weak. His words not mine," Sue raised her hands. "To the point where he stood up and came back, with more determination in his eyes than I'd ever seen. The next time refusing to quit. He's the most resilient person I've ever met," Sue added a tear coming to her eye.

"Mom!" Virgil sighed. "Don't cry!"

"I'm sorry," Sue smiled. "I don't get to tell these stories often. It is nice you brought home a fraternity brother Virgil, it is nice meeting you Vinny," Sue nodded to him and he smiled awkwardly. "But when are you going to bring home a girl?" Sue asked impatiently.

"Mom!" Virgil cried.

"Well I'm not getting any younger!" Sue declared. "Are you dating?" She asked.

Virgil's face was flaming red. "I haven't really gone on any dates," Virgil admitted. "I've been too busy with the Omegas."

"Well you're still young," Sue nodded. "Give it a few more years, you'll find a good one someday. Just remember to bring her home to meet mom!"

"I like your mom," Vinny whispered to Virgil as they ate dinner.

Sue had set up a cot for Vinny in Virgil's room, and that night they lay awake until late in the morning, sharing and telling stories. Sunday, they said their goodbyes to Sue and drove back to campus. Vinny's doubts seemed to dissipate as well, he was glad to be Virgil's Lil, and they both agreed they wouldn't have wanted it any other way.

# Chapter 7 The Werewolves of Standish

After an intense week of Homecoming competitions, Saturday arrived, and the judges examined the Omegas' masterful piece of art that was a float. Vahn had masterminded its creation, it was Indiana Jones themed. A large boulder of paper Mache made to rumble down a ramp. There was a large pedestal with a chest full of jewels, and at the top stood a chalice, with a football glued on top, the whole thing was spray painted gold. The Omegas won the float competition, placing them first overall for the second year in a row. The student parking lot was full of Omegas celebrating. There were some Betas who came over to congratulate them, led by Damian, with a few of his brothers and their candidates. Louie helped to ease them into the Omegas fold, and then the group really became a party. Virgil saw Malachi and Jamal, two powerful Nephilim who led the Betas. Malachi was pale and tall with long blond hair. He wore a permanent scowl on his face. Jamal's very presence was intimidating, he was a towering wall of muscle and power. His head was shaved bald, and had deep ebony skin, with dark, intense eyes.

"Damian, I'm glad we keep running into each other," Virgil said clapping his old roommate on the shoulder.

"You again?" Damian joked curling his upper lip in disgust before he lost it and smiled for real. "I'm glad that we can have our guys together like this," he added looking out over the group of people. Damian was helping to heal the rift that had formed between their two groups.

"You guys aren't going to get in trouble for this, right?" Virgil asked looking towards Malachi in the distance across the parking lot. Damian gave him a look that let him know he'd overstepped the bounds of their friendship. "Sorry," Virgil backpedaled. "I'm just glad to see you, let's stick with that."

Damian surprised Virgil by saying, "Malachi is losing his hold over the Chapter," Damian boldly rasped, stopping to take a drink. "Soon a younger E-Board will take control, and we want more unity with the other Paladin Chapters," Damian stared Virgil down stepping in closer. "Things are coming, Virgil. Worse than you could ever imagine," Damian's voice fell to a whisper.

"What's Malachi planning?" Virgil whispered back.

"He's not planning, he's supporting," Damian warned.

"There you are Damian!" Trent said walking up to them.

Damian became quiet and Virgil quickly began a new conversation for show. "Have you met any of the new sorority chicks?" he smirked and wiggled his eyebrows.

"I've met a couple that caught my eye," Trent boasted walking up to them, earning a shared laugh by Damian and Virgil. Virgil did not press the issue, he kept Damian's omittance to himself, a secret between friends. That exchange could cost Damian membership in his brotherhood, or worse, betraying fraternal secrets was the ultimate offense. Virgil wouldn't undo Damian. Virgil knew in that moment he'd have to face Malachi one day. He was the root of the rot that was seeping into the Betas…

After a few more minutes of friendly banter Virgil walked away seeing Landon's father and mother had shown up with Landon and Helene's youngest brother, who was only ten years old. Virgil introduced himself to Landon's family, ecstatic to meet his friends' parents. Virgil spoke with them until Troy came along to do the same. Virgil saw a face he hadn't seen in months. "Doc!" Virgil called out catching his brother's attention.

"Cupcake!" Doc replied coming over and embracing him in a bro hug. "Well if it isn't good to see Sprinkle's Lil Cherry!" Doc teased. The girl standing next to him giggled.

"It's good to see you brother!" Virgil beamed.

"Your nickname is Cherry?" She asked all bright eyed with a sparkling smile.

"It was better than the alternative," Virgil muttered to himself.

"Virgil I'd like you to meet my sister, Gina. She's pledging the Alphas."

"I heard that," Virgil nodded shaking Gina's hand, "It's a pleasure to meet you!" he exclaimed.

"Doc's told me all about you boys!" Gina smiled. "I feel like you guys are already my brothers too!"

"We're all one big family," Virgil grinned then gave her a side hug. "It's awesome that you're joining the Alpha sisters, you'll be a Paladin just like Doc!"

"I'm coming back up here," Doc said with confidence. "I'm going to Macomb Community College right now and hope to transfer back next fall. I want a Lil," Doc said seriously to Virgil.

"I'd love it if you came back," Virgil said honestly, "I miss having you around."

"Aww thanks buddy, that means a lot to hear you say that," Doc was touched and spoke with sincerity, unusual for a guy who was always joking around. "Come here, you miss daddy don't cha? Give me a hug, bring it in."

"You're definitely NOT daddy, but you can have a hug Doc," Virgil rolled his eyes. "How is pledging going?" Virgil asked Gina.

"Really good!" Gina spoke with a high pitch and rapid speech. "The sisters are great, and my pledge sisters and I are bonding. But not everyone comes around to the candidate process. Only me and two other girls have come to the Devil Arms practice," Gina told Virgil.

"Do you know Amariana?" Virgil asked.

"You mean Amari?" Gina replied smiling brightly. "ALL the guys ask about her," she sighed.

"I'm sorry," Virgil said quickly, feeling that had been rude of him.

"No it's okay!" Gina laughed. "I don't mind. Amari is a nice girl, but kind of guarded. She comes around to some things but hasn't been to a Devil Arms practice. Some girls are scared of that part, and we don't have mandatory candidate events," Gina shrugged. "The girls don't have to participate in stuff aside from the Oath of the Paladin."

"Yo yo!" Louie announced his presence practically jumping onto Doc's back.

"You're gonna kill me!" Doc struggled his face bright red, and Louie jumped off.

"Hi Louie!" Gina called out.

"Doc's Lil sis!" Louie ran up to her and they hugged each other. Louie got talking with Gina, making her laugh to the point she couldn't stop.

"Yo Virgil!" Dante barked. "Come get in this picture! You too Louie!"

They exchanged quick goodbyes. Gina said excitedly, "I love you guys!"

"Hugs!" Louie said embracing Gina again. "You're already a little sister to me!"

That night the Alpha sisters volunteered to have a get together, in honor of the Omegas win. By 11pm over three hundred students were crammed into the Alpha's sorority house. Virgil was surrounded by all his friends; he couldn't ask for much more. Virgil was walking around visiting with acquaintances, sober and enjoying the clear perception of reality, catching up with people he didn't see every day.

Virgil saw her out of the corner of his eye, and he couldn't stop himself from staring. Nothing else in the room was more intriguing. She was intoxicating, and he had no control over how he perceived her. Amariana was standing across the room, holding a cup, but not drinking. She looked stunning yet did so without looking like she was trying. She had a fierceness to her, something Virgil had not fully registered the first time he'd met her. She certainly was not the kind of girl that was easy to approach, but Virgil found himself walking over to her regardless. He wanted the opportunity to make a better impression.

"Hey Amariana," Virgil said his voice shaking slightly. He came to stand next to her, not invading her space, and not standing in front of her either.

"Virgil," Amariana said aloof like, but still acknowledging his presence.

"How are you doing?" Virgil asked her.

"Parties aren't all they're hyped up to be," she shrugged. Her clothes were conservative, in comparison to the other girls present, and that made Virgil more interested. It wasn't for lack of having the goods, it was that she had a class about her, an attitude about privacy that resonated with him.

"You haven't had a good week?" Virgil asked. "Classes or friends? Or boyfriends?" He added bravely at the end, feeling his heart race a million miles an hour.

Amariana didn't make eye contact. "You know, this is pointless," she suggested. "You're the tenth guy to hit on me at this party. I'm not dating right now, just trying to get to know the sisters and get through classes."

Virgil was stunned silent; this had taken a turn for the absolute worst. "I wasn't coming over here to ask you out on a date," Virgil sighed. "I was trying to have a conversation. I'm close with the Alphas and like to be friendly with them. I'm sorry if I came across as pushy." Amariana looked Virgil in the eyes, almost like she didn't know how to respond. "If you want to stand here alone, I'll keep mingling," Virgil said politely walking away.

"Hey," Amariana called out and he turned to look at her. "You're a sweet guy, we can try to be friends but, you're too nice for me," she said plainly. "It would never work between us."

"Way to judge someone before you get to know them," Virgil belittled her. "Do you always do such fine vetting of people who try to be polite to you?" Virgil flexed his left fist, Soul Reaver's symbol blazing with black light. Amariana's eyebrows knitted together, and the look on her face was one of a Tigress backed into a corner, dangerous and unpredictable. "I'm not as nice of a guy as you think," Virgil said defiantly his anger bubbling, black fire dancing across his eyes. He stifled his power back down, and turned away, leaving the room.

Sunday's meeting held eighteen brothers. The mood was high, still riding out the success of Homecoming, and fourteen potential new brothers, things seemed to be going well for the Omegas. It was Landon's turn for his report as a Jeweled Officer.

Landon stood up and looked out at the room with a heavy heart. "I wanted to let everyone know that I am going to be stepping down from being the Grammateus of the Chapter," Landon spoke with a shaky tone. The room became tense, and then brothers began speaking out of turn to ask him what was wrong.

"Simmer down!" Magnus griped, slamming the gavel, bringing the room back to a silence. "Landon please continue," Magnus insisted, clearly surprised as everyone else.

"I'm just, really overwhelmed with my classes right now," Landon said sadly. "I don't have time for myself anymore, and Stephanie feels like I'm putting the fraternity before her. I can't let it ruin the best thing that's ever happened to me," Landon spoke honestly.

"Alright everyone," Magnus said to the Chapter with a nervous laugh. "Looks like a Jeweled Officer position just opened up. If you are interested, please speak with me after the meeting, and we'll see about electing someone at the next meeting."

Vahn was going over how the candidates did in their second week, and everyone agreed that they did a great job in helping Omega win the Homecoming trophy. "At this time, I'm going to open it up to the brothers," Vahn said. "Is there any candidate that you would like brought up for removal? With GOOD reason?" Vahn stressed.

"I'd like to bring Frank up for removal," Zender said standing up. "And Randy."

The room erupted into chaos, everyone speaking at once.

"Settle down!" Magnus yelled using the gavel to get the room under control. "We will do them one at a time," Magnus instructed. "Let's start with Frank."

"Well," Zender thought about, "He's a piece of shit, do I really need to explain more?"

"Yes!" Vahn, Jace, and Louie yelled.

"Alright!" Zender sighed. "When I had my interview with this guy, he just came across as smug as hell."

"Look who's talking," Louie whispered to Virgil. That made Nolan and others laugh.

Zender continued, "He already feels like he's in, and doesn't have any respect for the brothers, the hierarchy of this fraternity, or the Paladins. I don't like him, and I don't want him as my brother," Zender said fiercely. "I'm finished," he said sitting down.

"Anyone else?" Vahn asked.

Birdy raised his hand. "I had my interview with him, and I get what Zender's trying to say. Frank is just one of those guys that rubs people the wrong way," Birdy shrugged.

"Do you think he'd be a good fit for the Oemgas?" Vahn asked. "Do you think he'd represent us well?"

"No," Birdy shook his head. "He's like the worst parts of Dante, Rowan, and Magnus thrown into one."

"Hey!" Rowan and Magnus responded.

"Enough said," Vahn shrugged, "Let's put it to a vote." It was close, but the room was in favor of removing him from the process. "Alright, looks like Rho class is down to thirteen candidates," Vahn said frustrated. "I'll let Frank, and Rho class know tonight. Next up, we have Randy, Zender you brought him up, you get to speak first," Vahn was more guarded and defensive while speaking about him. Virgil could tell this was going to be a fight.

"I don't trust him," Zender said plainly. "He's shifty and tells you what he thinks you want to hear. I don't see this guy being a valuable Omega. He gets in, he'll just be another empty seat at meetings, I guarantee it." Zender sat down.

They ended up talking about Randy for forty-five minutes, by the time Vahn called the question, everyone had spoken at least once, and the room erupted into arguing, because more wanted to speak. They had enough votes by one to move onto the actual voting of Randy. They did secret ballot, because the subject was so touchy. Virgil wrote on his piece of paper, IN, and folded it and handed it on. Landon counted the votes, and the room grew tense.

"He's still in," Landon announced. Some were displeased with the outcome.

"I hope that whoever voted against Randy, makes sure they actually go out, and try to get to know the kid," Vahn spoke with anger in his voice. "He didn't deserve this, I didn't like what I heard tonight, how can so many of you be so critical? I know you guys, and I am telling you all right now, you're not THAT great. None of you are better than Randy," Vahn admonished them.

"I am," Zender said proudly.

"Piss off!" Vahn spat at Zender.

"Enough!" Magnus cut across. "Can we please move on?" he asked.

Magnus gave his report, "Things have been getting heated in the area surrounding Bay Valley, demon activity is spiking all around us, and it's clear they're being drawn to the Chalice," Magnus said coldly. The hair on Virgil's arm stood up. "Six more Paladins from the Capital will be coming sometime this week, to help bolster our defenses. They've proven a great help in protecting and patrolling the city and surrounding area. If you see them in the halls, please be polite and introduce yourself, they are doing everyone a great service by being here."

"Tell them to clean up after themselves," Nolan barked. "I'm tired of cleaning all day. I'm the Omegas house manager, not theirs."

"I can have a dialogue about that," Magnus nodded looking like it was the last thing he wanted to do.

"We got an urgent request from the Ulfric, the King of the werewolf pack in Standish," Magnus explained. "Each lycan breed, has their own laws, titles, and ways of governing their packs. Werewolves choose a pack leader, called the Ulfric, he is the Alpha wolf.

"Wolf pack?" Louie asked aghast.

"I was part of the squad that helped the werebears over Spring Break," Brody spoke up. "They were awesome! If this group is anything like them, we should help them."

"There is a wererat nest in Saginaw, besides them the werewolf pack in Standish are this area's only lycans," Magnus said.

"What do they need help with?" Tarek asked curious.

"They didn't give too much information, other than to say it was urgent," Magnus shrugged. "We need a group to go there this week and find out what we can do to assist them." Magnus looked out over the room, looking for volunteers.

"I'll go," Virgil said raising his hand. He'd only gone on one assignment since Operation Flint, a simple pack of solider demons in Auburn, he was ready for something more.

"I'll go too," Birdy immediately volunteered. They shared a look; Birdy was a great friend.

"You need some more backup?" Nev asked Virgil.

"Always," Virgil nodded.

"I'll tag along with you guys," Rowan volunteered. "I haven't hung out with Virgil, or Nev in a while."

"I'll go with them," Tarek sighed sounding like he really didn't want to. "It'll be good to have a Jeweled Officer present, it's not every day our Chapter has a formal meeting like this."

"I'm satisfied with that," Magnus nodded ending the discussion.

The third week of pledging for Rho class, things started to pick up, the candidates were a little on edge from having lost one of their group. They'd been told Randy had been brought up for removal as well. Come Monday a fire was lit underneath the candidates, they were constantly at the house, and with brothers on campus. There were a few candidates still falling behind. Elmer and Randy seemed to become *less* motivated after the events of Sunday. The rest of Rho class had redoubled their efforts, and everyone took notice. Tarek had contacted the pack's Alpha, or Ulfric. They were going to meet him Wednesday night, he sent everyone the details.

Tuesday night after Brotherhood, the candidates had Devil Arms practice. They had a few guys like Colton, Aidan, Zane, and Flynn who were naturals. Vinny, Elmer, and Jeramiah were the only three candidates who hadn't produced their Devil Arms yet. They practiced hard, Vinny was still giving it his all, and he had stopped pressuring himself so much. The bonding trip with Virgil had helped give Vinny confidence that he was free to be himself. After practice everyone hung out at the Omega house and Virgil ran into Colton in the kitchen.

"Hello Virgil," Colton said enthusiastically with his signature charm. "How are you doing tonight sir?" he asked.

"I'm doing fine, how's your week going?" Virgil responded politely.

"Very busy," Colton laughed nodding. They walked past each other; Colton turned to Virgil. "Do you have a minute by chance?" he asked sincerely. "I was wondering if we could meet up for our interview sometime soon?"

Colton was one of the most popular candidates, and he was the new guy Virgil knew the least. "Sure, I'd like that," Virgil nodded

"Good," Colton sighed. "My Big, Magnus, told me I couldn't have his interview, until I was done with yours," Colton laughed breaking into a big toothy smile.

"What?" Virgil asked not understanding. "Why would he say that?"

"Magnus told me he wants our interview to be done right. He told me to go interview Virgil, he'll teach you what a great interview is about," Colton said fondly his smile reaching his brown eyes. "I'd really like us to have a chance to get to know each other. I've heard only great things about you, sir," Colton's smile left, his expression coming down to a more somber face of respect.

"I'm just another brother," Virgil flushed feeling uncomfortable with the praise. "I'm touched Colton," Virgil confessed. "When are you free?"

"You available Thursday?" Colton said checking his phone and planner.

"I'm free after 5pm," Virgil offered.

"Perfect," Colton smiled, "We can meet here, I'll see you Thursday, thanks Virgil," Colton said shaking Virgil's hand before walking back to the others in the living room. Virgil felt like he'd misjudged Colton, and decided he'd give the guy a real shot.

Wednesday after classes Virgil had dinner with Vinny, and they caught up, Vinny vented his frustrations, and they shared some laughs. Once 8pm rolled around, Virgil met up with Birdy, Nev, Rowan, and Tarek in the foyer to head out on their assignment. Colton, Flynn, Aidan, and Vinny came out to see what was going on.

"Where are you guys heading off to?" Flynn asked adjusting his ball cap.

"Super-secret Paladin mission," Birdy boasted bobbing his head with a large grin.

"Can I come?" Colton smiled brightly.

"Can't take pledges on missions," Rowan sighed, "It's against the rules."

"Whatever!" Tarek burst out laughing. "Coming from a guy who did just that."

"Whatttt?" Colton frowned. "That's not fair!" He joked, "How'd that happen?"

"Enough!" Nev laughed. "Let's go!"

"I'll drive!" Birdy volunteered.

"No!" Virgil, Nev, and Tarek shouted.

Rowan laughed, "Are you a shitty driver Birdy?" he asked.

"No, I drive fine," Birdy looked down at his phone with a scowl.

"I'll drive," Tarek volunteered, and they followed him to his car.

The drive from Bay City to Standish was a half hour north. Standish was a small city, and the seat of Arenac County. On the northern outskirts of Standish, houses started thinning out, nature taking over the landscape. They followed the GPS to the address they'd been given. They arrived at a ranch style home, down a long driveway, with lots of trees, concealing the property in the back. There were several cars, a dozen trucks, and a few vans parked around the large secluded home. The five brothers got out of Tarek's car and walked up to the front door.

"Hello!" a booming voice roared out from the front door as it burst open.

"Xiphias?" Virgil asked, a smile coming over his face.

"Hello there Virgil!" Xiphias beamed, having to hunch his shoulders to peak out the front door.

"Xiphias, these are my brothers Birdy, Nev, Rowan, and Tarek," Virgil said introducing each one. "We came here to speak with the Alpha?" Virgil asked unsure of himself.

"The Ulfric," Xiphias nodded. "This is his home, I'm here in support of their pack, please come in, your support is most welcome here!" The Omegas followed him inside.

The house was full of lycans, ranging from teenagers, to men and women in their fifties and sixties. They kept together in groups, talking softly to each other, aware of the outsider's presence, and trying to keep the tension low. The living room had a set of doors leading out to a large deck, expanding the already large open area. There was seating for twenty, and room to stand for even more. There was a loft on the third floor overlooking the room below. The Ulfric stood proudly in the center of the room, a man in his late thirties. He wasn't altogether physically striking; his demeanor was that of someone in command.

"I know this Nephilim," Xiphias said to the Ulfric gesturing to Virgil, and the room grew silent, "He helped our den with a demon infestation back in March. His people are trustworthy." The house gathered around the Omegas.

"Welcome," the Ulfric spoke smiling, and donning a tone of a hospitable host, "My name is Keaton. I appreciate the prompt follow up to our request, the matter is rather time sensitive," Keaton put it delicately vague.

"We will consider lending assistance," Tarek replied equally formal. "Of course, we'll have to be debriefed on the nature of your request," Tarek said pointedly.

"Fair enough," Keaton nodded. "I received an invitation from Voltro, the Master Vampire of Bay County," Keaton said with strained effort to remain neutral. "He wants our pack to pledge allegiance to his coven, and for our Ulfric to become the Beast of Power for his protégé," Keaton finished, his pressured speech sent the tension in the room up several notches.

The brothers were silent, Virgil could tell this was bad, but he didn't speak vampire and lycan politics. Tarek tried to make sense of what had been said. "The vampires in Bay City want your pack to bow down to them?" Tarek rephrased.

"In simple terms," Keaton nodded. "It is more complicated however, becoming a Beast of Power to vampire, forms a permanent metaphysical link between the two. Changing the physiological aspects of the lycan, granting them immortality, the same as the vampire they are bonded with."

"It would effectively make Keaton, and all his pack, slaves to the vampires," Xiphias said sadly to Virgil and the others.

"That's awful!" Birdy cried out in revulsion.

"Yes," Keaton nodded. "We first received a formal request, when we turned it down, Maya, Voltro's protégé, sent out a command for all wolves to come to her side. Every werewolf within a fifty-mile radius felt the involuntary response to her call, her demand," Keaton's words stung, his eyes blazed with rage. It infuriated him that someone could have that kind of power over his people. "The youngest of our pack, were literally walking out from their homes, headed to the vampire's lair. If I had been any weaker of a Ulfric, I wouldn't have been able to shield my people from her power, and enslavement."

"How can a vampire have that kind of power?" Virgil asked horrified by Keaton's words.

"Vampires are varied in power, and gifts, the same as Nephilim, and lycans," Xiphias explained.

"Voltro has an affinity for rats, his power extends to wererats," Keaton explained. "He brought the nest of lycans in Saginaw to heel over fifty years ago, their leader struck an agreement with Keaton willingly. They answer to the vampires now," Keaton said cautiously, "Bolstering their ranks. They want to add us to their powerbase, without any conflict."

"What can we do to help?" Virgil asked.

"We don't have the manpower to resist them outright," Keaton admitted, the words stinging his tongue. "I can shield my people from Maya's commands, but soon they will physically come to take us. Half our pack are elders or cubs. A few fights with their coven and we'd be cut down to size, they'd enslave the survivors."

"They need the Paladins behind them," Xiphias put it simply. "With the support of the Nephilim behind their pack, the vampires would have to openly go against your order, a very dangerous line to cross."

Tarek looked Keaton head on, showing steely resolve, his normal antics replaced with somber seriousness. "This is…more involved than we had originally anticipated," Tarek said carefully. "I think we need to discuss this with our Chapter, before making a formal alliance," Tarek went quiet but kept Keaton's gaze.

"Wise words," Keaton nodded. "But know this. My people cannot hold out against Voltro's force, for long, without a formal response. If they don't hear from us by Sunday, they'll take it as a show of disrespect. Vampires are all about pleasantries, and Voltro is an old-world vampire."

"Why does this Master vampire, want your pack?" Nev asked curiously.

"Vampires are all about building their power bases, and continuing their bloodlines," Xiphias replied. "My guess is Voltro is grooming Maya to replace him and wants her to gain a powerful lycan ally," Xiphias shuddered. "It's called a Beast of Power, and they can also have Human Servants, one of each, increasing their money dramatically."

Virgil shuddered at the idea, having never realized that vampires could form one link with a lycan, and a human, permanently connecting them. Virgil's instincts were to just say yes, of course they'd help. But their Chapter was a collective of all the brother's opinions and desires, they'd have to bring it to a formal vote at Sunday's meeting.

# Chapter 8 Clubbin' with Lust Demons

Thursday, after a stressful day of A&P lecture and labs, Virgil drove back to the Omega house mauling over his grade. His second exam grade came back today and was a mid-range C. He was growing frustrated with the studying, there was simply too much material to memorize, he didn't feel like he had enough time to learn it all. He got home and went to the kitchen to grab a quick snack, finding some carrots and apples. Spencer, Jagger, Jace, and Nev were at the table, Virgil nodded to them, and sat down at the row of barstools. Colton came within a few minutes, stopping by the three older brothers first, then walking over to Virgil.

"Good to see you Virgil," Colton said all smiles, "I was looking for you. Ready to do our interview?" Colton asked.

"Hey Colton," Virgil replied. He sighed setting his apple down on the small plate he was using. "Honestly man, I'm just worn out," Virgil admitted. "You think we could reschedule?" Virgil asked hoping he'd say yes. There were a ton of brothers around, and everyone wanted to be friends with Colton.

"I already had two cancellations this week," Colton said his face dropping. "I was really looking forward to speaking with you." Colton's tone was manipulative, but subtle, he knew how to communicate. "But if you need to reschedule, we can make it work," Colton offered half-heartedly taking off his backpack and opening his planner. "What day are you available?" Colton asked Virgil with a serious stare.

"Uh," Virgil felt guilty. "Okay let's talk for a few minutes."

"Lies!" Nev burst out making everyone laugh. "Get that in writing!"

They went to Virgil's room and began their interview.

"I bet you wish initiation was tomorrow?" Virgil jested.

"Yes and no," Colton bobbed his head weighing the thought. "Pledging is a lot of fun, if you know how to approach it that way," Colton explained.

"What do you mean?" Virgil asked putting his empty plate away.

Colton leaned back gesturing with his hands he explained. "I look at it like, the guys are opening up their family, their lives to us, and it's an opportunity to get close to your future best friends. If I was initiated tomorrow, there would still be a third of the Chapter I hadn't even got to know, like you," Colton smiled brightly. "I don't want to miss out on those opportunities," Colton said passionately. "When I see it like that, it doesn't feel like work," Colton shrugged.

"I agree," Virgil nodded. "You have a good mindset."

Colton asked all the typical questions, that Virgil had come to know from a standard interview. Virgil introduced him to a few new questions as well. Colton was more reserved and humbler than he portrayed himself to be. Though Colton could be outgoing and social, he was quiet with deep thoughts stirring underneath. Colton felt that's how he should be perceived so he lived up to that image. Colton grew up in Frankenmuth, with loving parents, and a younger sister just as good and in love with sports as Colton. Colton had played football for Frankenmuth like many of his brothers but was not involved in any university athletics. Colton explained that his father was a recovering alcoholic and had been sober for twenty years. Colton was proud of his father, he affectionately referred to him as 'Wayne-o' even to his face. Colton's father sounded devoted, supportive, and loving. Virgil was guessing Wayne-o was the one who'd taught his boy to have class. Colton impressed Virgil, and he understood how he'd won over the rest of the group.

Colton was very curious about Virgil's stories with the Omegas, more specifically ones involving him using his Devil Arms. "Magnus told me, you guys battled a Wyvern Queen demon together," Colton shivered. "That sounds scary," Colton laughed causing Virgil to laugh as well.

"Oh, it was!" Virgil admitted. "Thank goodness we had Lambda class leading the way, or we might not have made it."

"Magnus said a Fallen saved you guys," Colton added in a lower tone.

Virgil's eyebrows raised, that was something that not every brother knew about. "At first I just thought it was a brother. No brother has ever wielded their blade like this immortal," Virgil stared off. "We really are no match for them."

"I'd like to train with you sometime," Colton asked Virgil. "Your sword against mine," Colton gestured to Virgil's white symbol. "If I best you, Magnus told me I'd have bragging rights in the Chapter," Colton laughed cockily.

"He did?" Virgil sighed, what was with the pledges wanting to beat him up? Virgil laughed to himself. "I don't really use Ragnorak for practice," Virgil said out loud. I couldn't even if I tried, he said to himself. He'd learn soon enough he hoped. "I could use my scythe to spar with you for a bit if you insist," Virgil smiled slightly.

"I do, and we shall!" Colton laughed excited getting up, ready to go. "Everyone is going to be jealous!" Colton said happily packing up his things. Virgil hoped he didn't start something. He didn't need every guy in Rho class looking to kick his butt.

They went outside to the far edge of the backyard, Colton took off his bag and did some stretching, he wore an air of confidence, with his usual cocky demeanor. He had no intention of losing to Virgil. Magnus and Colton were the perfect Big and Lil pair.

"I want you to know this is to help you grow, and train as a warrior," Virgil said to Colton, "An exercise to bolster your skills," he explained.

"Of course," Colton nodded, a greedy grin on his face. "But that doesn't mean we can't have some fun with it," his eyes sparkled. "Steel Plasma!" Colton commanded and his amethyst sword symbol glowed, purple energy flowing out into his hand, forming a long blade. Colton firmly gripped the sword, and purple energy pulsed along the blade's edge. Virgil's excitement piqued, he had one of the more powerful, and aesthetically pleasing Devil Arms he'd ever seen.

"Soul Reaver," Virgil spoke and his scythe, welcomingly, came to his left hand. "Dull," Virgil commanded coating his weapon in a protective barrier, Colton did the same.

The two began to circle each other, Colton was bouncing on his feet, getting his blood pumping, his hand steady, his brown eyes sharp as a razor's edge. Virgil made the first move, sprinting directly towards Colton. Colton had a choice, fight or flight, Colton ran forward and swung out his sword. The scythe's sickle blade became locked against the amethyst glowing longsword, flames crackled against the sparks of electricity, each holding back the other. Virgil broke free, stepping back gaining some distance. Colton charged at Virgil, stabbing at him fiercely. Soul Reaver spun round becoming a blur, Steel Plasma's strikes rebounding off. Colton roared, swinging his blade into the air, he swung it down, a wave of purple energy swam towards Virgil. It blasted Virgil off his feet, he went rolling on the ground, his skin still feeling the shocking sting of the blow.

Virgil struggled to his feet, Colton approaching fast. Colton was agile, aligned with wind and lightning, making him a naturally lithe warrior. Virgil stood tall, Soul Reaver hovering just within his reach, waiting for his command. Colton stopped just outside of reach. They stared each other down. Colton genuinely challenged Virgil, in that moment he felt Colton would go on to become a leader of their Chapter.

"You good to call it quits?" Virgil suggested.

"Sure," Colton shrugged. "We'll tell everyone I beat you, if you're giving up," Colton's words stung, as they were meant to.

"I never give up," Virgil thundered back the flames of Soul Reaver rising off the scythe.

"Good," Colton smiled. "I don't want to win like that." He raised Steel Plasma, and charged Virgil. They began to duel fiercely, sweat beginning to pour from their bodies, neither willing to concede. Minutes ticked by, they both grew weary with fatigue. After twenty minutes, they were both breathing heavy, silently they agreed to leave it at a tie. Best if they didn't acknowledge the resolution, it would only bring strife. Virgil retired to his room for a late nap following their interview, he didn't set an alarm and decided he'd be alright if he slept through the night, training with Colton had eaten the last of his energy. He awoke to a loud pounding at his door, still feeling exhausted, wanting only sleep.

"Go away!" Virgil called out from his bed. He had been sleeping for two hours at most and was in a grumpy mood. The knocking came again. "Knock it off!" Virgil yelled. Realizing they weren't going away, Virgil got up to answer the door.

Birdy was standing in the doorway with Brett and Cameron. "Bout time you opened the door!" Birdy said with attitude walking in and taking a seat. "Boys you've met Virgil before?" Birdy nodded.

"Nice to meet you again sir," Cameron said shaking Virgil's hand in a very polite manner. Cameron reminded Virgil of a younger Birdy, he was tall and lanky, with dark hair and eyes. Brett, Blair's stepbrother, was average height with blond hair, blue eyes. Brett was still rather shy and quiet, though he had a goofy fun side. Cameron was more outgoing and sociable.

"So?" Virgil gestured with his hands. "What brings you here?"

"We're going on a road trip!" Birdy shouted throwing his arms up in the air doing a little dance and laughing.

"Birdy," Virgil sighed.

Cameron and Brett joined in, "Yup!" they agreed.

"You have one hour to get dressed. A group of candidates, brothers, Alphas and Betas are going," Birdy explained.

"Where?" Virgil asked yawning still not awake.

"That three story club in Pontiac, they have eighteen and up tonight, figured it would be a good mixer of sorts," Birdy said proudly. "Louie and I helped throw it together with Blair and Damian."

"Nice! That does sound like fun," Virgil thought about it. "I've never been to a club before."

"I have, back in Macomb," Birdy said, "It wasn't very busy though, and you can't drink, so it was whatever," he shrugged. "Didn't meet any girls that night."

"How is the process going for you guys?" Virgil asked.

"Good so far," Cameron nodded. "I've met some really good brothers. Birdy's like my adopted Big," Cameron laughed.

"Aww," Birdy sighed.

"Don't say that," Louie said sassily walking in, "It will hurt your Big's feelings! It's only the third week, cut him some slack."

"Sunday is the start of the fourth week Louie," Brett added. "Don't be adding on any more weeks now mister!" Brett said in a high-pitched voice. Everyone in the room broke out laughing.

"You are one goofy mofo," Louie said making himself laugh.

"Everyone I've talked to says you give the best interviews," Cameron told Virgil. "I want us to have our interview."

"Whatever man, brothers like to run their mouths," Virgil laughed.

"No not the brothers, Rho class says it too," Cameron said to Virgil. "I want us to get to know each other, like everyone else."

Damn these pledges were good at making you feel guilty, tricking you into spending time with them! "Okay well maybe this next week then."

"Great!" Cameron nodded.

"Anyways…can I have some space to get ready everyone?" Virgil asked.

"Sure," Birdy laughed rolling his eyes and they cleared out.

An hour later Virgil was dressed and following the group out to the cars. Nev quickly knocked on Nolan's door to invite him out one last time. "You sure you don't want to come?" Nev asked Nolan when he answered.

"I'm sure, have to study, and I work a morning shift. Have fun guys!" Nolan said closing his door.

"We'll get him," Louie said shaking his fist, Nev nodded. Birdy was driving with Cameron, Brett, and Nigel, their roommate and another candidate in Rho class. Louie was driving Nev, Virgil, Tucker, and Homer. Rowan was driving Brody, Tarek, Colton, and Zane. They met up Dante, Vinny and his friend Tanner, in Clio on the way down, and they joined their adventure. Blair was driving with a group of sisters that included Selene and Amariana. Damian was driving along with one of their candidates. The seven cars took off heading for the freeway southbound to Clio, thirty miles south of Bay City. They quickly met Dante's car and made the last fifty minutes south to Pontiac.

The club was more than Virgil had been expecting, a massive three-story building with dazzling lights and hundreds of cars. Each floor was packed with people. It was hard to feel self-conscious inside when no one was paying any attention to you. They had a big enough group that they made a comfortable space for themselves on the first floor and began to have fun. Most of them couldn't drink. Selene, Tarek, Rowan, and a few Alpha sisters were the only ones old enough. With the beating of the music, the energy of the crowd, jumping and moving their feet, you didn't need it. Virgil danced with Blair, and even by himself, loving the feeling the music gave him, giving himself over to the beat and letting his body follow the rhythm.

Virgil went to grab a water, he was breathing heavily, and needed a short break. Amariana was sitting down where their group had claimed a spot, she was by herself, watching the people she had come with dancing and having fun. Her green eyes looked out at the crowd with envy, and a little sadness. Virgil walked over, a smile on his face, he refused to let her wipe it off this time.

"Amariana!" Virgil said more confidently than before. "You should come dance with everyone," he suggested dancing a little in front of her.

She gave him a condescending look as she watched him shake his hips, "I don't dance," she sighed.

"You don't have to, just stand there and nod your head," Virgil suggested.

"That would look stupid," Amariana retorted a look of disgust on her face.

"Then just dance for real," Virgil laughed.

"I'm just watching," Amariana bobbed her head and crossed her arms, her left leg coming over her right leg as she leaned back.

"If you go through life just watching, and not participating, that is not living. You have to be present, and do things that make you nervous," Virgil laughed. "Or the things that you've always thought about, but never had the courage to act on. I try to, that's why I walked up to you in the cafeteria last week. I saw you, and just felt like I had to know you," Virgil said his face getting red. "And I'm glad I did, because you have already taught me a lot."

"Like what?" Amariana asked him her stern stance breaking, her posture becoming more relaxed, her eyes softening.

"That not everyone is going to like you," Virgil said his words coming out bitter, he hadn't meant them to. He inhaled, his next words softer, "That sometimes no matter how hard you try, there are people you can't impact, or show them a different perspective. You're a nice girl Amariana, I think more people could see that, if you let them," Virgil smiled and turned around leaving her at the table.

He didn't know if she was going to say something else, he wasn't going to chase after her. Coming on too strong, was intimidating. Amariana knew Virgil wanted to be friends, she knew how to find him. Virgil went to the top floor, finding Colton, Homer and Tucker dancing with a group of chicks he'd never seen. Virgil went over and started dancing with them, a few girls coming to dance around him. After a couple of songs, Virgil walked back down to the second floor. Selene was at the bar with Brody, Virgil took a seat next to her.

"Honey what's wrong?" Selene asked swiveling her chair to face Virgil, placing her hand on his side.

"I'm fine," Virgil smiled rolling his eyes.

"Nope, I can see it in your eyes, you're feeling sad, who hurt you?" Selene said getting a little snappy. "Did one of these little trollops break your heart?" Selene looked around like she might be ready for a brawl.

"Trollops?" Virgil asked.

"Skanks, ho's," Brody added laughing.

"Stop!" Selene cried out laughing. "You know I hate those words."

"Is streetwalker better?" Brody asked seriously, breaking out into a big laugh.

"I thought this girl was cute, but it is not a big deal," Virgil told Selene. "There are plenty of girls out there."

"What kind of girl caught your attention? I'm really curious now," Selene asked seriously.

"Amariana," Virgil felt like an idiot saying her name.

"Oh," Selene drew out the word like it was six syllables, stirring her straw in her glass, she took a drink, and smirked giggling to herself.

"What?!" Virgil barked.

"That doesn't surprise me in the least," Selene smiled brightly. "In a lot of ways, she kind of reminds me of you."

"What?" Virgil asked surprised. "Like how?" Virgil demanded.

"Amariana is a powerful woman," Selene said puttting it plainly. "She's an intellectual, a planner. She's bold, independent, inquisitive. She's knows what she wants, and why she wants it. She's down-to-earth and can be very persuasive. These could be used to describe you too," Selene said to Virgil raising her eyebrows.

"Yup," Brody laughed, "You can't deny that its true!"

"I guess so," Virgil shrugged. "But she seems so stubborn," he huffed.

"I'm sure Amariana can at times seem too stubborn, and overly critical of others, but she has a more practical approach or mindset about life," Selene suggested to Virgil.

"You explained her so well, but they've only been candidates for three weeks," Virgil shook his head.

"I'm good at people," Selene smiled batting her eyelashes and then laughing hard. She knew she was sharp minded, cunning, charming, and she was for the most part, a humble compassionate woman.

"What should I do?" Virgil asked Selene.

"Don't do anything different," Selene stressed. "If Amariana's a smart girl, she'll realize it's a mistake to let a guy like you slip past her."

"Thanks for that," Virgil smiled.

Brody spoke up about his girlfriend, "Everyone says Selene's nice, but she's only really great to people she cares deeply about."

"Oh shut up!" Selene said throwing her napkin at him. "If I can help, by putting in a good word or two, I will," Selene arched an eyebrow and smiled.

"Don't be meddling," Brody said sternly to Selene.

"I won't say anything tonight, maybe next week, next chance I get. I'll be subtle," Selene's voice was confident, and conniving.

Virgil sighed, standing up, he walked through the crowd, migrating to the first floor, most of their friends were still in the same area. Virgil went over to Blair and started dancing with her and the others. Virgil looked over to where Amariana was sitting, he didn't want to give her too much attention, though he couldn't help look after what felt like forever. She was still seated, a guy was on either side of her, and another was standing right in front of her. They were dressed like hoodlums, and were talking loudly, whatever they were saying, Amariana didn't like it. At that moment Virgil struggled with what the right thing to do was. Amariana could probably handle herself, Creator knows she'd probably belittle him if he did try to speak in the name of her honor. She wasn't his to protect, he turned his attention away from her.

A group of girls were walking past Virgil, they stopped to check him out. Virgil was flattered and started showing off, earning laughs, and introductions. They started dancing around him, the ones who couldn't dance grinded on him, the few who could dance, showed off their skills. Virgil smiled; he'd never had five women just jump at him. He was starting to enjoy this bonding trip. Virgil felt a forceful tap on his shoulder. He turned around, Amariana was standing there. He raised his eyebrows, she grabbed his hand, and led him away from the girls. Amariana started dancing with Virgil, she was really putting her all into it, and Virgil was surprised to find she was rather good. The girls moved on, leaving the two of them on their own.

"You don't dance?" Virgil asked Amariana.

"I don't like to," Amariana said to him, not looking him in the eyes. She calmed her moves to be more conservative.

"You don't like being watched," Virgil guessed, he didn't either really. "What brought you out here?" Virgil asked.

Amariana turned to meet Virgil's gaze, "I didn't like those girls dancing on you," she admitted. Her pupils got really big, she hadn't meant to say that.

Virgil raised an eyebrow, a manly smirk on his face, "You didn't like seeing them dance on me?" Virgil asked with a straight face, using his big blue eyes, long curly lashes, and full lips to attempt his best at making her crack up.

Amariana's eyes grew wild like Virgil had told an offensive joke, then she smiled and started laughing. It was the first time he'd heard her laugh, he smiled, feeling like he'd scored some kind of victory. She'd let her guard down, just a little. She was softer on the inside, he'd sooner fight a Fallen than say that out loud though. They danced for a few songs, soon Virgil felt like he was being watched, he looked around to see most of their friends, watching with intense interest. Amariana immediately stepped back from Virgil, crossing her arms over her chest, she walked away. Closing down again, Virgil thought to himself.

"Aww!" Louie groaned disappointed. "I was enjoying the show!"

"You bastards ruined it!" Blair joked.

The moment was lost and after Amariana kept her distance. The night wore on, and everyone still had a ninety-minute drive back to Bay City. They started gathering their cars of people and heading out in groups. Virgil found Louie and Nev.

"Where are Homer and Tucker?" Virgil asked them.

"Haven't seen them in a half hour," Nev said throwing his hands up.

"Let's check the higher floors," Virgil suggested. The club was emptying out, with only half the amount of people present, compared to when they arrived. Birdy, Dante, Vinny, Cameron, and Tanner were at a table crowded together on the second floor.

"Have you guys seen Homer?" Virgil asked.

"Or Tucker?" Louie asked.

"They are upstairs with Brett and Nigel," Cameron offered. Virgil walked over to the stairs to the third floor, ready to leave already, when women's voices called out in distress, followed by what sounded like men being harmed. Virgil stopped in his tracks, listening intently.

"Ohhhh shieeeet," Louie sighed.

"Déjà vu Louie?" Virgil asked his pledge brother.

"Yeah," Louie laughed, "You need me to get the car running?"

Everyone burst out laughing diffusing some tension, no one laughed harder than Virgil, Birdy, and Dante as that had been the same line Louie had used the *last* time they'd heard similar cries.

"Let's go," Virgil said to others taking point.

"Not the candidates," Louie said firmly. "I'm not getting bitched out again, remember what happened with Rowan?"

"Who is going to take them downstairs?" Virgil asked impatiently.

"What's going on?" Tanner asked confused.

"We can explain another time," Vinny said to his best friend. "Let's get out of here."

"Birdy take them down, I'll watch Virgil's back," Dante suggested.

"Alright," Birdy nodded heading outside with the others, leaving Louie, Nev, and Dante. Virgil's friends faithfully followed behind him and they entered the third floor.

There were a pack of Desire, or Lust, demons with slender feminine like bodies, and horns coming out of the front of their skulls. They levitated off of the ground, with long arms and claws, blood red eyes, and a mouth full of long fangs. They were stronger than a sloth demon, but weaker than a pride demon. They were a force to be reckoned with. In the center of the demons, were over a dozen people, the demons were floating above the humans, herding them together, and sucking at their auras. Homer and Tucker had their Devil Arms drawn, Homer wielded a flame mace, and Tucker wielded an earth polearm.

"Guys! Get outta there!" Virgil commanded the candidates.

One of the Lust demons turned to Virgil's group, the demon's voice was the typical deep, and fearsome demonic tone, but retained a note of femininity. "Leave now Judge Spawn!"

"Try again sweetheart!" Dante barked back.

"There's a knock on the door, intruders are trying to kill the children!" The demon told the people in the center.

"We won't let them!" The people shouted running at Virgil and the others.

"What do we do?!" Louie shouted. "We can't kill them!"

"What the hell? We're trying to help!" Homer shouted, sweat forming on his forehead.

"Their minds are being manipulated by the Lust demons!" Nev guessed. "We need to break the demons' influence!" he shouted.

"Dull Spells!" Virgil suggested. "Louie your arrows could knock them out!"

"Right!" Louie yelled and placed the Dull spell over both Devil Arms symbols. He summoned Shiva's Bow, and pulled his left hand back along the string, an ice arrow formed from nothing. He released it at the closest approaching person, the man was hit hard in the chest and fell down, he'd have bruises at the worst.

"Push through to the demons!" Virgil called out summoning Soul Reaver to his left hand. "Dull!" he commanded the blue barrier covering the scythe, and the symbol. Virgil ran forward and threw his scythe at the approaching people, they went down like bowling pins, laying on the floor writhing in agony. The scythe didn't cut through them, but the brief contact with the scythe's flames, were enough to put the strongest man on the ground.

There were eight Lust demons and they surged forward to attack! They flitted on the air like kites, doing flips, weaving swiftly to kill Virgil and his brothers. Virgil took the Dull spell off of Soul Reaver and charged a Lust demon swinging his scythe out. The Lust demon nimbly dodged the blow and descended behind Virgil swiping at his exposed side. Virgil cried out in pain as the demon's claws raked across his flesh.

"Cone of Lightning!" Nev shouted and from the tip of his staff, large arms of electricity reached out, connecting with the Lust demon attacking Virgil, immobilizing it for a second while the spell took its toll. Another Lust Demon swooped down to dive kick Nev, he caught the blow with his staff, just barely. It savagely assaulted him, and Nev backed up dueling with the powerful demon.

Virgil used the opening to slash his scythe across the Lust demon, it howled in pain, moving back, its body hanging limply. Virgil ran after it, eager to remove one of their numbers. Virgil threw his scythe at the fleeing demon, it cut through the demon's midsection, the demon screamed, falling to the floor as ash. The scythe whirled further and began to spin back. A Lust demon grabbed Virgil from behind. Virgil struggled against its pull, another descended on Virgil, holding his other side and they began to suck at his aura, feeding on his energy. Virgil thrashed his body, bucking his limbs against their steel grip, they were infinitely stronger than any mortal. Another Lust demon floated over and began feeding on Virgil's aura. It was getting harder for him to fight, his limbs were feeling heavy. Virgil saw his brothers locked in viscous battles of their own. Homer and Tucker were barely surviving one demon between the two of them, and there was no sign of Brett or Nigel. Virgil started to feel numb, it was getting harder to think, harder to breath. What was going to happen to him? What did he need to do?

"Get off him, you filth!" She cried. Amariana held her arms to her side concentrating heavily. She moved her arms forward and a sheet of ice materialized, it surged forward, cutting through the demon that hovered in front of Virgil, sending it crashing to the floor. Amariana held her hands at her sides and large ice daggers materialized into her hands. She spun around throwing both at the demons holding Virgil. The daggers hit them both in the chest and they released Virgil. Amariana ran over to Virgil shielding him from the Lust demons.

The three Lust demons hovered in the air once more, snaking gently back to Amariana and Virgil. Amariana closed her eyes and inhaled deeply. She spun around slowly in place, her hands dancing, her arms twisting, water glided into existence, dancing up around her, growing larger. It reached above Amariana's hands and she flung out her one arm aimed at the demons. The water shot forward expanding into ice, freezing midair, the ice wave cut through the Lust demons, destroying them instantly.

Virgil was stunned, his eyebrows were raised high, and his mouth hung open slightly. He tried to stand, his legs unsteady. Virgil's brothers had finished off their demons and came over to Virgil and Amariana.

"Thanks for your help!" Louie said excitedly to Amariana, "We wouldn't have made it without ya!"

"Where are the other two candidates?" Virgil asked.

Brett and Nigel rose their heads from behind an overturned table. "We saw things get a little whack-o, and decided we'd be better off chilling over here," Brett explained.

"Thanks a lot," Homer retorted rolling his eyes. "WE helped fight!"

"Damn straight, you guys did great!" Louie yelled giving Homer and Tucker a high five.

"That was impressive Amariana," Virgil said with astonishment. "I've only ever seen a few Nephilim with the ability to bend their element like that," he felt like there was more to her than she was letting on.

"It was nothing alright!" Amariana protested, blushing and embarrassed.

"Alright," Virgil nodded. "Thank you Amariana." He said walking over to his friends to assess how everyone was doing.

"Your welcome," he thought he heard her mumble as he walked way.

# Chapter 9 A Rocky Tradition

The brothers were a buzz with everything that was going on in the Chapter; a handful of candidates had fought Lust demons, there was a sensitive request from the werewolves at play, and Tuesday was Tradition. Magnus had consulted with the Paladins present at Bay Valley on the nature of the local Ulfric's request. The candidates didn't know exactly what was going on, though they could feel the tension in the brothers. Virgil had spoken briefly with Magnus, who was so busy he had little time for chit chat these days. Virgil requested to be in the voting for Grammatues on Sunday. Magnus just smiled and nodded saying, "It's about time you asked me," Magnus joked passive aggressively.

Sunday night, as the meeting was being prepped to begin, Magnus took Virgil and Troy out in the hall, they were both running for Landon's position. "I wanted to let the two of you know beforehand," Magnus said to them quietly. "I'm appointing Virgil our Grammateus."

Virgil was shocked, as was Troy, who couldn't hide his disappointment. "But we both had speeches prepared," Virgil spoke up in Troy's defense. "He even made a powerpoint! We should put it to a vote."

"When there is an empty Jeweled Officer position, the Prytanis fills it, he does not need the consent of the Chapter," Magnus pointed out coldly. "There is a lot to get done at this meeting, I don't want to slow it down. Troy, you're a great brother, and you'll have your time to be a Jeweled Officer," Magnus told his friend, placing his arm on his shoulder.

"Thanks Magnus," Troy nodded heading back inside.

"Thank you," Virgil said once it was just the two of them. "I feel bad though, for Troy."

"Don't feel bad," Magnus shook his head. "He'll be Grammateus someday. But it'll be good for you to get some experience for something bigger," Magnus explained.

"Like what?" Virgil asked.

"What do you want?" Magnus asked him. "Prytanis? Hypophetes?" Magnus guessed.

"Not Prytanis," Virgil shook his head.

"No?" Magnus asked.

"No," Virgil laughed, "It's a tough job, that I don't want. I want to be the fun brother, as the Prytanis you have to be the adult, in a room full of adolescent, sarcastic, boys!"

"It feels like that sometimes," Magnus laughed nodding. "But it shouldn't have to be! If brothers would just keep it together, we'd get through meetings faster."

"Please, this room of clowns?" Virgil asked pointing his thumb towards the door.

"Let's get this started," Magnus chuckled.

Virgil sat close to the front of the room near Magnus, as he was now in charge of taking notes, and making a speaker's list, to call on brothers when there were motions on the floor. The usual eighteen of twenty-four active brothers were present, it turned out to be a chaotic first meeting as Grammateus. Randy was brought up for removal once more, sending the Chapter into an hour-long fight. Virgil could barely type fast enough to keep up with his motor mouth companions. Once it came to a vote, the ballots were passed up to Virgil, he felt privileged looking at each person's slip of paper. In the end, it was close, ten to eight, Randy stayed in Rho class by two votes. After the dust settled from announcing the results, the room was still filled with tension, and people were irritable.

"Anything else?" Magnus asked Vahn sarcastically. The Hegemon was a hard position, there was no pleasing everyone.

"Nope," Vahn sat down, then immediately stood back up, "Oh yeah, one last thing!" Everyone groaned in irritation. "Shut up!" Vahn barked. "Brotherhood on Tuesday is Tradition! We should have 100% attendance, any brother who doesn't show, I'll bring up on charges."

"Now that everyone's in such a great mood," Magnus said sarcastically standing up and taking the floor, "We have to discuss the issue with the local were pack." Magnus explained, "The Master Vampire of Bay City, is looking to bring the lycans in the area under his control, to use for his own protection, and increase his own powerbase."

"That's awful!" Louie barked out.

"The wolves want us to help defend them from the vampires," Magnus shrugged putting it simply.

"Ooooo!" Louie cried out his pupils engorging to the size of quarters, his grin falling into a frown, "That's worse!" A few brothers snickered at his remark, it was clear where *he* stood.

"Internationals isn't keen on the idea of us intervening in this particular situation," Magnus put it delicately. "The Paladins believe, if we insight the wrath of the local vamps, they could try to take us down, and with the Chalice of Immortals being safeguarded here, our Chapter has to avoid the limelight at all costs," Magnus explained.

"Yeah but we can't just leave those werewolves to be enslaved!" Vahn cried out.

"We'll put it to a vote," Magnus sighed.

"I don't think we should even vote on this," Jace spoke up. "I'm not sure why we are entertaining the idea, if Internationals don't want us doing this, then we shouldn't."

"There are thousands of Paladins in the Capital," Virgil said. "Why can't they just send a squad down to tell the Vampires to leave the pack alone?"

"We're supposed to keep the peace between the various supernatural species," Magnus asserted, "But there are thousands of vampire covens and lycan herds across the world. We can't possibly intervene in the affairs of all other beings. It is a thin, hard line we walk as the peacekeepers," Magnus said sadly.

"Just sitting by while innocent kids, teenagers, and women, get man handled by some slimy vampires," Virgil shuddered, "Doing nothing isn't a hard job, and it sure as hell doesn't sound like keeping the peace," Virgil boldly fired off.

"Watch it," Magnus furrowed his brow at Virgil.

"From the Pylortes prescriptive, as the risk management chair," Zender said to the room in his usual sarcastic, and arrogant 'I'm the smartest guy in the room' mindset. "I feel like this would be a bad move for us. We don't want to spread ourselves too thin, that's just my opinion."

"Let's vote already! I call the question," Lamar called out and no one objected. They all wrote down their responses, and handed them in. Virgil was surprised by how many No's there were, only six of the eighteen brothers voted to help the werewolves, Virgil was disappointed.

"Well?" Magnus asked.

"We're declining assistance," Virgil said weakly to the room.

"I'll contact their Ulfric after the meeting," Magnus nodded sadly, and they moved forward with finishing the meeting. When it was over, the brothers burst from the room, everyone needing space. Being a brother, meant sometimes getting angry with each other. Virgil felt in his gut that they needed to help those people, he was scared for them, what would it be like, having a vampire for a master? He had a hard time sleeping that night, dark dreams haunted his mind. He looked on the Ulfric Keaton's house being attacked by monstrous humanoid rats and vampires. Virgil watched, and did nothing but cry mutely, some were devoured, others were dragged away screaming.

Monday morning Vahn sent out a mass text announcing Elmer had dropped out, only twelve candidates left. Rho class took the loss hard, and Monday all of them were feeling a little down. Elmer hadn't been a candidate too many people were close with, but still, losing someone this late in the game hurt. By Tuesday just Vinny, and Jeramiah hadn't produced a Devil Arms. Tuesday afternoon Virgil hung out with Birdy and candidate Cameron. Cameron was freaking out about Brotherhood, all the guys talked about it being something…big! Rho class didn't want to lose any more of their pledge brothers. Birdy had become good friends with Cameron, and Virgil found he felt the same about their new potential brother. Funny how new friends could become so important, so quickly.

The brothers gathered for Brotherhood at the Omega house once the sun set. Once the candidates arrived, Zender encouraged them to reflect silently on the lessons learned with their time in the Omegas. Virgil was proud of Vinny, he was among the most well liked of Rho class! He was polite, and a little goofy, but good hearted, with strong morals. It felt like he was already an Omega to Virgil. Virgil stood in the back yard with the rest of the chapter. Dante arrived and Gabriel, Tarek, Brody, and Birdy went up to him to greet him. Dante then came over to Virgil.

"It's great to see you here! I'm glad you drove up!" Virgil told his friend shaking his hand. "Tradition wouldn't feel right without you here," Virgil said warmly.

"Thanks Virgil. You're always encouraging me to come around, and making me feel welcome when I do, I appreciate you," Dante said uncharacteristically soft for a moment. "You know I couldn't miss Tradition," Dante smiled, and he walked on snuggling into the crowd.

It was 10:20pm, Vahn impatiently began to count the brothers. "Only twenty-one!" Vahn snapped, he was counting Zender inside with the candidates. "Why are we missing three actives?" he asked.

"Buck and Benson asked for permission to be excused," Magnus told Vahn, "I told them they didn't have to worry about it."

"What about Thiago?" Vahn asked. "He's a Jeweled Officer, he should be here!" Vahn argued.

"He didn't ask to be excused," Magnus shrugged.

"Whatever," Vahn sighed, "Let's get started."

"I'd like to bring Randy up for removal!" Someone called out.

"No," Vahn said horrified.

"If one brother has doubt, we are supposed to bring it to a vote," Magnus sighed getting very angry.

"NO!" Vahn shouted. "We are not doing this again! I am not putting that kid through this!" Vahn yelled. "I told Randy he was brought up for removal, *again*, and it broke him. He worked his ASS off these past few days," Vahn seethed, he was shaking he was so angry. "Did anyone here come to the get together on Monday? Randy was there, perfect time to bond with him. He tried guys! This is bullshit!"

"Enough!" Magnus yelled. "We get how you feel. We need to create a speaker's list, and get this moving to a vote," Magnus instructed. "Who is next?" Magnus barked.

"Lamar," Virgil quickly read off the first name he'd written down, *everyone's* hands went up. This was a crappy start to brotherhood, Virgil sighed pouting as he looked at a list of fifteen names. He didn't put himself on there, he didn't need to bog down the engorged list. The argument raged on, and it made Virgil understand a little better how challenging it really is for people, to meet at a common ground.

Lamar made a big deal about Dante not being able to vote, which caused a few minutes' worth of banter, and tension. Dante still spoke on Randy's behalf though, in favor of keeping him. The votes came in, Virgil's hands were shaky, everyone was staring him down, he didn't want to be the one to announce it either way. Zender's vote was collected by Landon. Landon told everyone the pledges knew what they were discussing, and they were all hoping to keep Randy. Magnus came over to stand near Virgil, helping him count the votes. Magnus and Virgil stared at one another, the votes were in, the numbers tallied, twenty-one votes, there was no tie. Eleven brothers voted to remove Randy, ten brothers voted to keep him. Virgil refused to speak, Magnus didn't ask Virgil to do it, but his eyes said he didn't want to either.

"Eleven votes, Randy's out," Magnus announced to the brothers.

Everyone started shouting, Magnus struggled to get the group back to order. Gabriel's fist glowed with the light of his aligned element, he stomped his foot, and the ground beneath their feet rocked, everyone went silent, as they struggled to keep their balance.

"ENOUGH!" Gabriel barked. "The votes are in, Randy is done. Vahn go tell the candidates, and let's get Brotherhood started, it is almost 11pm," Gabriel added checking his phone, everyone got upset, a night that was supposed to be fun, and bond them closer together, was off to a rocky start.

"I'm leaving," Brody declared. "I don't want to stay if Randy can't."

"Don't you dare!" Vahn snapped. "There are eleven other guys that deserve to have a great Tradition, and they won't have a chance if everyone walks away angry. I'm pissed too!" Vahn yelled. "I want nothing more than to get away from the brothers! But we need to come together for Rho class, before we scare them away. We need them!" Vahn told everyone.

"We don't need them," Landon said sounding disgusted. "Stop giving the candidates all the power."

"Our Chapter needs these guys," Vahn reiterated. "We're falling apart. We need new guys to revitalize our group, or we won't make it much longer."

"Stop being so dramatic," Tarek sighed. "The show must go on! Let's hit the road already." Vahn gave Tarek a dark look and went inside to break the bad news.

"No kidding!" Gabriel laughed and he walked off with Tarek, the two friends venting their frustrations. It took twenty minutes, for Professor Ramuh to get there to help with the depledging process, which involved a bit of a mind erasing, or so Virgil had been told. Finally, Vahn brought Rho class out, and they walked into the woods. Rho class was slightly crest fallen. The remaining eleven guys had been through a lot, Virgil felt bad for Randy, and the men who had called him pledge brother.

Rho class was blindfolded and formed a line, Vahn leading the way. The brothers led

Rho class to the Paladin temple in the woods. The mood of everyone improved as they walked

together, through the dark forest, trying not to laugh as people stumbled along the fallen brush.

Virgil was proud of Vinny, he stood at the front of the pack, fearlessly leading his pledge

brothers forward. They arrived at the open field near the temple, they entered and the candidates

took off their blindfolds. Zender used the barrier spell on the entrance, sealing them from the

outside. An important step when creating portals and leaving them open.

Virgil watched Magnus generate the portal to the Ever After, the swirling light coming

into existence in the stone archway. Vahn gave a brief lecture that whatever happened tonight,

stayed between the brothers present, and none of the Paladins from the Capital were allowed to

find out. Several brothers went ahead to make sure it was safe. Jagger came back through within

a few minutes, to report it was safe to proceed with Brotherhood. The Bigs ushered their Lils

forward, Virgil and Vinny were first. Vinny was hesitant, all of Rho class looked a little skittish,

even Colton. Zane had a cocky smirk, but underneath he too was weary of the unknown.

"You'll be fine," Virgil assured Vinny. "I'll be by your side the whole time, watching out

for you."

"I know you will," Vinny nodded. "I'll follow you anywhere Big."

They stepped through the portal, their bodies sucked through space and time, in the same

second falling out onto hard rock. Mountain towered all around them, the cliff they were on was

rather large, with plenty of room for the brothers to stand. Magnus and Zender were almost

finished with a large perimeter spell, that would cloak their presence within it while they stayed.

The sky above them was a mess of thick, black storm clouds, a dying red sun struggled to drift lazily above the never-ending storm. The Ever After, once home to the race of sidhe Fairies, descended from the Eidolons, was now a wasteland. Its beauty, and life devoured, drained, and obliterated. A fading world, stained by darkness…

The rest of Rho class came through the portal, and quickly ran into the enclosed barrier. Vinny was stunned, as was everyone who looked upon this world. It was so foreign and alien from their own. Once Rho class was gathered, Vahn spoke up.

"This world is connected to our own," Vahn said passionately taking everyone's attention. "All the demons and Death Dealers that plague Earth invade us from here. I was held in a prison in this world, this summer," Vahn recalled with anger, and some of Rho class looked shocked. "I used to believe we were safe from this place; we are not. Look how easy it was for us to get here, it's just as easy for them to come to us," Vahn warned. "We bring you here, to strike home the severity, the reality, of this struggle. Being an Omega, means being a Paladin, and this," Vahn stretched his arms out, "is what the Paladins are fighting against. To make sure this, CRAP, doesn't end up taking over our world."

Everyone was quiet for a moment, reflecting on his words.

"Let's head back to our temple," Magnus encouraged. The people at the back headed out from the barrier, stepping into the portal two at a time.

"MWWWAHH!" A loud avian like cry echoed against the rock. Giant bird creatures dive bombed the brothers walking to the portal, managing to pick up Jeramiah, Aidan, Zane, and Colton. The barrier spell around the brothers was brought down, and pandemonium ensued.

People were screaming for everyone to get through the portal, everything was happening so quickly, Virgil grabbed hold of Vinny and started running. The sky was becoming choked with the giant avian demons, Virgil had seen one back at Pi's Tradition. Their bodies consisted of two parts, a lower spherical body with gray plumage and two wings on each side, and a mouth at the center of the body, that held a thick tongue and dagger like teeth. The top portion had a humanoid figure, waist up, completed with a torso, arms, and head anchored to the top of the grey bird like body. Two powerful legs sprouted from under the stout body. Additional wings sprouted from top humanoid portion's back. Each bird's bottom section looked similar, but the tops were unique, with distinctive male and female variations. The eyes of the demons burned with an intelligence some of the lesser demons did not possess.

The demons that scooped up the pledges, quickly took flight, heading high up into the mountain ranges. Magnus, Gabriel, and Tarek drew their Devil Arms seeking to keep the demons from snatching any more people as they sprinted for the exit. Gabriel burned a large amount of his aura, commanding the rock beneath them to protect them. Pillars of earth erupted around the brothers, protecting their sides as they raced to the portal. Tarek released a stream of water that swam through the air, stretching out, then freezing, spraying like missiles at the birds. They cawed out in pain, backing off momentarily.

"Don't slow down Vinny!" Virgil urged his Lil as he heard Vinny's breathing becoming ragged. Shadows cast down on Virgil, and the other brothers ahead of them.

"Here they come!" Magnus shouted. The demons let out a deep bird like cry, Zender and his Lil, Flynn, were just ahead of Virgil and Vinny. Flynn was plucked off the ground, mid stride, the female bird demon flying hard, ascending higher up the mountain.

"Virgil!" Vinny cried and he was ripped out of Virgil's grip. Virgil's head snapped to his right side, his eyes locked with Vinny's, his Lil's eyes were stretched out in horror. Helplessness washed over Virgil, Vinny was clutched between the talons of the demon, immobilized. The male bird demon, with an old face, and one eye, ascended into the sky.

"Soul Reaver!" Virgil cried, throwing the scythe hard the moment it came to his hand. The scythe sailed after the demon, closing in, another demon flew into its path, screeching as the blade sliced through it. The demon fell to the cliff, a pile of feathers, bones, and ash. Vinny quickly faded from view. "Vinny!" Virgil screamed.

"Get through the portal!" Vahn said close behind Virgil. "NOW!" Vahn demanded physically shoving him forward.

"I'm going after him!" Virgil shouted ready to summon his wings from his flesh and take flight.

"There are too many of these things!" Vahn urged. "We need to regroup!"

"UHHH!" Virgil screamed in frustration Soul Reaver returning to his hand. Virgil ran through the portal, close on Zender's heels. The trip back was jolting, Virgil had never done it with his Devil Arms active, it felt like he was getting static shocks in his hand. Virgil came out the other side, the temple was full of brothers who were on the verge of a nervous breakdown. Several pledges had just been snatched up in the Ever After, by a group of demons, that looked like they had massive numbers. Homer, Tucker, Cameron, Brett, and Nigel were safe. The other pledges…

"What the hell just happened?!" Vahn yelled once he came through with the last of the brothers. Magnus immediately closed the portal, as they didn't want anything trying to come through after them.

"They got six pledges," Louie said sadly.

"We have to go after them!" Virgil declared to the group. Everyone was quiet, the looks in their eyes…the Omegas were shaken.

"We could ask for help," Birdy suggested, "From the Paladins."

"Nice thinking Birdbrain," Dante retorted. "If they find out we took candidates to the Ever After, they could shut our Chapter down!"

"We need to get them back somehow!" Jace barked.

"I'M GOING!" Virgil declared walking back to the archway. "Magnus! Help me get there!" Virgil asked.

"You're not going alone!" Vahn snapped.

"I'm going," Gabriel said walking up to them, "My Lil is out there."

"He's my little brother too," Vahn said sadly to Gabriel. They were talking about Aidan; he'd been one of the six pledges taken. "I'm not losing him," Vahn's voice broke, his eyes misted.

"We're gonna get him back," Gabriel promised his best friend, clapping his hand firmly on Vahn's shoulder. They both looked like they might lose their composure.

"Let's go!" Zender yelled impatiently.

"You're going?" Jace asked, not happy.

"You got a problem with that?" Zender asked.

"You're the Pylortes!" Jace snapped. "You shouldn't be condoning this kind of behavior, let alone be a witness, or party to it! What if the people from Internationals just stop over? What would they think?"

"Everyone who doesn't go, must stay here, until we get back," Magnus commanded. "The spell protecting the inside of this temple won't break unless someone steps out. No Paladins from the Omega house are getting in here, unless you let them in," Magnus smirked.

"My Lil is out there!" Zender yelled showing true emotion, "I have wings, and I'm getting up that damn mountain, and bringing him back! Even if I have to climb over a pile of damn bird corpses, I'll find a way!" Zender forced out through clenched teeth. The men were quiet. No one questioned Zender again.

"My Lil is out there too man!" Jagger said to Zender, referring to Jeramiah. "And he can't even use his Devil Arms yet. I'll watch your back frater," Jagger said uncharacteristically tender to his brother.

"There is no way just a few of you can bring them back!" Louie cried. "You'll never make it out there!"

"We'd have a better chance with you Louie!" Birdy volunteered.

"Oh hell no!" Louie laughed like the idea was the most absurd thing anyone had ever said. "I ain't no Jeweled Officer, or a Big Brother, I'm going to keep these fires going, and wait for y'all to get home safely." Louie grinned with nervousness taking a permanent seat on the steps.

"Figures," Dante sighed.

"Real mature Louie," Vahn said coldly to Louie.

"I do shit for this fraternity all the time!" Louie yelled. "Don't guilt me into doing something I don't want to do!"

"ENOUGH!" Gabriel shouted and everyone went quiet. "Who IS volunteering to go?" Gabriel snapped. "We need to make this quick!"

The temple quickly divided in two, those that were going back into the Ever After, and those who would be left to sit in the temple, unable to leave, with nothing to do, but await the return of their companions. They agreed that if the brothers did not return by sunrise, that they would leave the temple. They didn't discuss what would be said to the Paladins from the Capital, they didn't want to plan for that. Vahn, Magnus, Jagger, Gabriel, Tarek, Zender, Lamar, Brody, Virgil, Birdy, Dante, and Rowan were going to rescue the captured Rho Class candidates. Twelve brothers, that was a dozen, strong warriors, that could all fly independently. Most likely they'd have to carry the candidates back.

"Just come back safely," Landon said with deep concern to the twelve brothers gathered to head back.

"Be safe Birdy!" Cameron called out, concerned.

"We can't lose anymore guys," Jace said seriously, "If you can't save the pledges, just get out of there. We can't lose a single one of you," Jace said looking at each one of them. "You are too important, to too many people, to die in that hell hole. Just get back safely," Jace solemnly whispered, his eyes misting up.

"Yeah, and bring the pledges back if you can," Louie nodded happily. "I mean, we still got five pledges left but, well," Louie laughed nervously and so did several others, "They aren't the sharpest tools in the shed."

"Oh shit!" Brett said to Nigel. "I think he's talking about us!" he laughed.

"He's talking about you!" Nigel laughed pointing to Brett and playfully shoving him.

Magnus finished writing the spell for the portal, and it opened up, the familiar whirl of spiraling energy. "It's time," Gabriel said. And the brothers came together in one large circle, they held hands and said a prayer, for the safe return of all Omegas, and asked for the guidance of the Creator. Some hugs were exchanged, but the men did not dawdle, almost ten minutes had already passed since they got back. How long before those things…ate them? Virgil shuddered, he needed to get doing something, or he was going to go insane.

"I'll go first," Virgil volunteered stepping up to the portal. The eleven brothers parted for him, the Chapter stood breathless, uncertain where the future of Upsilon Delta would stand once the light of day, lit the horizon.

Virgil swung Soul Reaver around, and concentrated on his wings, they worked their way from his flesh, bursting out with a ripple of magic. The eleven brothers did the same. "For Brotherhood, and Valor!" Virgil called out.

"Omegas!" The Brothers echoed out in response.

Virgil ran into the portal, Vahn, and Dante close behind him.

# Chapter 10 The Bird Demon City, Ginangup

Virgil surged out of the portal, back to the large rocky cliff on the mountainside, in the western reaches of the Ever After. It was eerily quiet, Virgil landed on the cliff, looking around. Vahn and Dante quickly came to his side, they wouldn't be ambushed this time. Soon the twelve brothers were through the portal, it closed behind them, the brothers back at the temple would create a new portal for them every hour, leaving it open for five minutes at a time. They didn't want to leave it open the whole time…

"More Judge Spawn," a deep masculine voice cawed at them. The group turned to see a bird demon descend, and land on a small ledge maybe thirty feet above them. Virgil instantly recognized the demon, its top portion had the body of an old man, with only one eye, he was the one who grabbed Vinny!

"Where did you take Vinny!" Virgil shouted at the demon, the black flames along his arm and scythe rising to reflect his boiling anger.

"The Judge Spawn were taken to the Queen Mothers' nest," the old bird spoke from its hooked beak it had instead of a mouth. It stared Virgil down with his one red eye, the two yellow ones above the large mouth in its middle narrowed to slits. Looking on the demon with two faces was unsettling, but Virgil knew only anger, he could freak out once he had Vinny back.

Another demon landed near the old one, this one was female, she was older as well, with long wispy white hair, clinging to her small head. "The Mothers will be pleased!" the female bird demon said.

"Take us to your Queen," Virgil commanded.

"Mothers have enough meats," another demon cawed landing near the other two, "We should take these for ourselves!"

"Agreed," another demon added fluttering to land with the other demons.

"I warn you," Virgil said coldly, "Challenging us will only bring about the destruction of your people. We'll cut down anyone who stops us from taking our brothers home!"

"Your brothers are likely being fed to the new hatchlings by now!" the old demon with one eye laughed, a screechy bird laugh. "There will be no taking them home!"

"I tire of these cretins," Dante snapped. "Let's go up to this nest and grab our pledges!"

The bird demons started squawking loudly. "Her Highnesses will stop you!" they cawed. "You are no match for the mothers!"

"I'll burn down this entire mountain if that's what it takes!" Virgil spat at the demon.

The bird demons took flight, a few more descending from higher in the mountains, there were six circling overhead. Virgil didn't have time for this, he leapt into the air, flying straight for the closest demon. His brothers sprang into action, and the air above the ledge became a battle zone. The demon saw his intent, and the creature went into a dive, plummeting at Virgil, its sharp talons on its two powerful legs outstretched to Virgil. Virgil cocked his arm back and threw his scythe as hard as he could at the approaching demon. The demon squawked in alarm the scythe heading straight for it, beating its wings, it changed its flight path, coming out of the dive. Soul Reaver was now on a trajectory that would completely miss the demon. Virgil concentrated on the scythe and commanded it to veer right, the scythe took a sharp turn quickly approaching its target. The bird demon squawked in a terrified tone, the scythe cut through its middle, the demon exploded into ash and bones.

"Virgil!" Rowan yelled out panicked. Rowan was fighting a large demon of his own, with the help of Lamar and Brody. Rowan was a man who looked out for everyone else, his eyes reflected fear for Virgil.

Virgil turned his head, a bird demon slammed into him like a wrecking ball. He felt the bones in his left arm snap, his left side felt crushed, and they fell from the air together. The demon's talons pierced his left arm and the side of his chest. The large mouth in the middle of the demon's body opened wide, to swallow him whole. The demon sitting atop the large round body wailed in pain, Vahn flew straight at the demon, slamming his sword against the demon, it lashed out with his clawed arm. Vahn screamed in pain, and stabbed Fury Brand forward, the blade pierced through the demon's chest. The large mouth of the bird fell into a frown. The demon exploded into ash, Virgil beat his wings, and pain thrived along every nerve ending. He struggled to regain his composure, coming to a sloppy landing on the large ledge. Virgil fell to his knees, leaning on his right side.

Vahn landed next to him. "You're bleeding pretty bad," Vahn pointed out the obvious.

"I'll be fine," Virgil said his arm hanging limply. It was hard for him to breath, he had a couple of broken ribs, maybe a dislocated shoulder, and some broken bones in his arm.

The other demon birds were vanquished, and the men landed coming together.

"Tarek, can you patch up Virgil?" Vahn asked.

"No!" Virgil waved off Tarek who had immediately come over to help. "Save your energy Tarek, I'm sure there are others who will need it more by the end of the night."

"You can't fight like this!" Vahn said getting angry.

"I won't," Virgil said to Vahn. "Ragnorak!" Virgil screamed raising his right hand to the air. A bolt of light came down connecting with his hand, Ragnorak extended out, and a cloak of gold light surrounded Virgil. He felt the healing effects of the sword take over instantly, his wounds slowly diminishing, his bones repairing. "I'll be good as new in a few minutes," Virgil put on a brave smile getting to his feet. Soul Reaver came whirling back to Virgil, he didn't think he could hold it with his arm as it was, and commanded it follow at his side.

"What now?" Dante asked the group.

"We fly," Gabriel commanded, and the twelve men took flight, ascending up the mountain range, the black storm clouds looming ominously above. Virgil flew in the middle between Vahn and Gabriel. His left arm was knitting itself back into one piece, he heard his bones snap back into place and moved the arm carefully. The twelve men shared looks of determination. A rumble of thunder gurgled in the clouds above, a flash of lightning lit up the dark clouds. The mountains were incredibly massive, making the Rockies of America look like mole hills. They kept flying higher, several minutes went by, and still no sign of the bird demon's lair. Virgil knew he'd recognize it when they found it, a group this large would have some kind of nest.

The wall of storm clouds loomed on the horizon.

"Keep it tight!" Magnus commanded. "V formation!" The brothers formed an arrow in the sky, their wing beats just missing the men next to them. Magnus raised Tempest Staff and whispered to the wind. A gale of air surged forward, pushing a small enough space ahead of Virgil and the others to fly a little easier, he held Ragnorak forward taking point, the sword lighting the way for the twelve men. They entered the sea of black clouds and the storm battered the men mercilessly. To fall outside of the cocoon of air Magnus was creating, would mean getting engulfed by the storm. They beat their wings hard, the brothers growing tired, it took all they had to keep their path true. Seconds dragged on into minutes. They had to fly through the storm. Their aching bodies were availed by the sight of storm clouds thinning ahead. The brothers were climbing above the storm, higher into the mountains. Screeching filled the air.

"They come!" Virgil announced.

Bird demons descended from above, diving with their talons outstretched for killing blows. The men couldn't engage the demons like they were, and hope to fight tacitly. Virgil concentrated on Ragnorak, gripping the sword tightly the blade pulsed in his hand. Virgil sliced the sword through the air, a wave of creation surging forth cutting a space open through the top of the storm, the Omegas surging out. At this height, above the storm, the sky was an empty canvas of nothingness. The dying sun provided no light for the land. The brothers broke formation, outnumbered four to one, the sky was crowded above the storm, erupting into savage warfare.

Gabriel's magic was limited so suspended in the air. He was being chased by a male that was much larger than the average of his kind. Gabriel struggled to gain enough lead, the demon surged forward, his claws striking out. Gabriel midflight halted, and spun around, flying opposite direction, straight back towards the demon. LionsHeart gleamed with yellow light, Gabriel sliced the demon's torso, removing him from the lower half of his body and wings.

Tarek was one with the sky, having been born with wings at a young age, he was one of the best flyers in the Omegas. Two demons dived towards him. Tarek's Stiria's Lance glowed with power, "Twin Flow!" Tarek shouted twirling his ice-covered polearm. Two jets of water flowed forward, weaving in and out around Tarek as he flew forward. The birds screeched angrily, the talons and claws stretching out to rip his flesh. Tarek cut the ice lance through the water, and it crystalized, the streams of water becoming ice, each shot at a demon like a missile. Tarek went for the demon on the right, it was wounded and distracted from the ice, he sliced through it with ease. The other demon recovered coming after him. Tarek swiped his lance at the demon's outstretched attacks, riposting a lethal stab, causing it to explode.

Lamar like Gabriel he was strongest on the ground. Lamar was on the verge of being swallowed by a hungry bird demon, he raised his arm with the mighty Cybil Cleaver in hand, a massive hammer. Lamar brought the hammer down on the demon's body, slamming its gaping maw of teeth closed. The demon whimpered like a wounded pet. Lamar sprung off the demon, right into the waiting outstretched mouth of another waiting bird demon. Lamar screamed swinging his hammer wildly, knocking the demon on the side of its jaw. They both spun through the air from the momentum of the attack. Lamar's misfortune continued as he dizzily flew towards a plump bodied demon, twice the size of a normal bird demon. This demon opened its greedy middle face with a devilish grin, Lamar certain to be swallowed whole this time. Lamar was the loudest brother, and his voice boomed like a ferocious grizzly bear, he barreled to the demon's mouth, cocking his hammer back with all his strength. The demon began to close his mouth on Lamar. Lamar swung his arm and shouted, "Gravel Shot!" A spray of rocks erupted from Lamar's Devil Arms, it burst through the back of the demon's mouth. Lamar's hammer ripped the demon in two, he flew out the other side. Lamar yelled triumphantly, "You bastards aren't eating ME today!"

Rowan wielded his fire katana like he had been doing it since birth. Rowan's chauvinistic nature got the best of him, and he strived to be the brother to kill the most demons. His competitive streak shining through as he fearlessly hacked his way through every demon he could reach. Dante and Birdy were the best of Omicron, they fought close together, effectively protecting each other, and taking down approaching threats more expeditiously. Magnus's staff helped him to ride the winds, like a surfer on waves. Of the twelve, Magnus had the easiest time handling the flying fiends, spells zipping from his hands, blasts of energy erupting from his staff.

Virgil wielded his Devil Arms in tandem, slicing through another bird demon. A harem of birds descended on him, four demons dive bombed him. Virgil went into a dive, the five of them plummeting towards the sea of dark clouds below. Virgil looked to the sky above, and the demons quickly approaching. He stretched his right hand out towards the fiends, "Light Surge!" Virgil commanded. His aura was drained for the Master Creation Spell. Beams of Creation energy rained down from above, they pelted the birds reaching for Virgil, exploding on impact. The demons fell into the sea of storm clouds, ash and feathers; Virgil beat his wings climbing back up into the fight.

We'll never make it in time like this! Virgil thought with feverish irritation. They were handling themselves well, but the sky was still full of demons, ten minutes from now, they'd still be battling to make it through. Virgil didn't know how much time Rho class had! Virgil needed to get there, even if it meant going by himself. Virgil concentrated on Ragnorak, closing his eyes and breathing deeply. "I'm going on ahead!" Virgil screamed out to Vahn who was the closest brother. "Catch up when you can!"

"What?!" Vahn asked unsure of Virgil's words.

"Take me to Vinny," Virgil whispered to Ragnorak. The blade glowed gold, Virgil held on tight, and the sword surged forward like a beam of light, Virgil rocketing behind, struggling fiercely to maintain his grip. The world flowed past Virgil so rapidly, he could barely make out his surroundings as he passed them. He felt Ragnorak slice through several demons as it shot through the sky, at the speed Virgil was traveling, a demon wouldn't even slow him down.

Virgil climbed up into the mountains, several peaks coming into view. Virgil's speed slowed slightly, and he finally began to fly vertically, instead of horizontally. He had come to precipice of the bird demon's lair! Virgil's eyes widened in surprise. It looked like the lost Incan cities atop the Andes Mountains, meets the ancient towering gardens of Babylon. A sprawling metropolis spread out before Virgil, the remnants of an ancient city, once built by the sidhe Fairies. Though the metropolis was now a decaying ruin, the architecture was still among the greatest splendor Virgil had ever seen. This place had clearly been important. Temples and fallen statues were scattered and decaying everywhere, reflecting a lost culture. Virgil could feel the power in the land below, wondering if that was why Fairies had built this grand city. Sadly, the avian demons ruled these lands now, large nests, were spread throughout the hollow buildings. Virgil flew through the city skies, there were no bird demons jumping into his path, most must have gone down to intercept the brothers.

As Virgil approached the center of the city, a large building stood at the center, likely the castle or home of the ruler of this once proud nation. The roof was eaten away, a large field had grown in the center, and a nest had been built at the heart, the size of a football field. Eggs the size of trucks were laid around the nest, over a dozen of them. Virgil came to a stop, it was jarring coming out of the high speed so suddenly and Virgil's altitude faltered, he quickly landed, folding in his black and white wings. He was wobbly on his feet, scanning his surroundings with intense focus. Brittle, dry foliage crunched under his feet, he walked past a large egg, it was off white, dark purple veins running through it. The eggs were pulsing, with a lot of movement, Virgil got an unsettling feeling in his stomach.

"Virgil!" Vinny jumped at him hugging him fiercely. "I knew you'd come for us!" Vinny said proudly grinning ear to ear.

Virgil swallowed hard; he was so glad Vinny was still…

"Vinny," Virgil said breaking from him. "I'm sorry I didn't protect you back there," guilt had been eating at him, he was glad to get it out. "That's twice now you've been snatched away from me, and each time I feel like my world is ending. I'm just…so thankful right now," Virgil laughed nervously with tears in his eyes. "All the brothers are so worried, I just had to get here as fast as I could!

"Aww," Vinny crooned in his gravelly voice, getting red. "That's the nicest thing anyone's ever said to me."

"Virgil!" Colton called out coming around the corner through remnants of an old room. "Thank God! Guys this way! Its Virgil! Flynn you owe me twenty bucks!"

"Like Big, like Lil," Virgil sighed and started laughing, relieved to see him safe.

Aidan, Flynn, Zane, and Jeramiah came over quickly and Virgil greeted each of them. They looked shaken, eyes hollowed with fear, a few were a little banged up, but they were alive.

A smile spread across his face and Virgil hurried over to his friends.

"Thank God!" Jeramiah cried out almost jumping into Virgil's arms. "I thought we were doomed! That big ugly demon with the two bodies said she was going to feed us to her chicks!"

"Calm down Louie 2.0!" Virgil told Jeramiah getting his arms free. "We are gonna get you guys outta here," Virgil spoke rapidly.

"We?" Aidan asked Virgil.

"Vahn and Gabriel came to bring you back," Virgil told Aidan, who smiled and nodded, hope restored to his demeanor. "All your Bigs are fighting their way through!" Virgil told the rest of them.

"How come you're the only one here?" Jeramiah snapped.

"Because he's one of the Seven Seraphs," Vinny said speaking up for his Big. "Ragnorak brought him here!" Vinny pointed out. The candidates all reacted, it was the first time they had seen Ragnorak, let alone both his Devil Arms, they could be…overwhelming.

"That's badass!" Flynn laughed.

"We've gotta duel again sometime!" Colton grinned at Virgil.

"We can spar all you want later," Virgil quipped. "First we need to get you guys out of this city!"

"How are we going to get out of this building?" Jeramiah pondered nervously, "You can't fly us all down the mountain!" His voice was taking on a note of hysteria.

"Calm yourself!" Colton told Jeramiah. "We're just thankful you came for us," he said humbly. "It means a lot, knowing you'd risk yourself for us."

"That's what being a brother is all about," Virgil shrugged. "Sometimes you have to put yourself on the line for the people you care about, with no reward other than safeguarding and protecting that person you love."

The eggs that were all around them began moving violently.

"Okay, lots of love in the Omegas, we get it," Jeramiah nodded. "Can we please just get out of here?" He asked stomping his foot.

Virgil looked up at the ceiling, they were over ten stories from the roof, it was so high up, the only way out was to fly. The bird demons had sealed off this massive building, so it was *only* available to those who could fly. A venerable fortress, a safehouse for a treasure most precious to the bird demons. The only way out was to fly each one, or…

"I could give you all wings," Virgil suggested. "Then I could fight, while you six flew. I could carry maybe one of you, but then I'd be near defenseless."

"How are you going to give us wings?" Flynn laughed.

"Like Vinny said, I'm a Seraph, the Sixth Seraph," Virgil explained.

"Which means?" Jeramiah snapped.

"It means he's the Redeemer," Colton added. "A powerful Nephilim able to restore Fallen Judges. His power apparently works on Nephilim as well," Colton said. "Louie told me, Virgil used the same power on him, over the summer, when brothers were trapped in Hel. Louie, Birdy, and Dante wouldn't have escaped without the wings Virgil gave them."

"You can really do that?" Zane asked skeptically. He was having a hard time imagining wings coming out of his back, Virgil did too at first.

"Yes, let's give it a go," Virgil suggested.

The eggs started cracking, limbs bursting from the shell.

"Virgil," Flynn spoke up with a hesitant voice. "Whatever you're going to do, better make it quick!"

Virgil started to concentrate, and the egg nearest him burst open. Virgil stumbled back, as a large eggshell was thrown against him. The demons emerged and began to swarm them. They'd ran out of time!

"Vinny and Jeramiah, in the center!" Virgil commanded. "Everyone else create a circle around them."

"Oh God!" Jeramiah cried out. "We're all going to die! I'm going to get eaten!" He sobbed.

"Pull your shit together Jeramiah!" Virgil barked. "Don't you think the rest of us are scared?" Virgil yelled honestly. "Sometimes in life you must stand up to what you're afraid of, in order to keep on living! Don't sit back and let your fear control how you choose to live your life!"

"Rho Class!" Colton called out. His pledge brothers shouted in unison, he was their leader, and everyone materialized their Devil Arms. Aidan had a fire sword, longer and thicker than Vahn's. Colton wielded his lightning saber. Flynn wielded a short earthen polearm with a small axe at the end, very similar to his Big Zender's. Zane's Devil Arms was a wind lance, he was incredibly agile with his weapon, and had even strained Gabriel's capacity to remain victorious in practice. They gripped their Devil Arms and the newly born bird demons lumbered towards them, the mouths in the middle of their bodies opened wide to swallow them whole.

"Whatever you do!" Aidan called out. "Don't get eaten!"

The first bird demon ran face first into Colton and Aidan. Both men ran towards the demon striking out with their blades. They managed to dodge the demon and slice its sides. The demon kept running, straight into Jeramiah. The two crashed to the ground. Jeramiah started getting up and the bird demon began crawling towards him, its eyes narrowing, its tongue panting as it looked at him.

"Somebody help me!" Jeramiah panicked screaming to the others. But everyone was busy with demons of their own. No one had the extra hand to spare, and Jeramiah and Vinny were in the center, the others were fiercely fighting to keep anymore from charging through. Jeramiah scrambled backwards sobbing, "Please don't eat me, please don't eat me!" He begged the demon. The demon inched forward, gaining ground. The newly hatched bird demon reached its tongue out, Jeramiah's arm settling on its wide surface. The tongue brought Jeramiah's whole arm closer in, its jaws coming down.

"NO! PLEASE NO PLEASE NO PLEASE NOOOOO!" Jeramiah wailed, the golden-yellow Devil Arms symbol disappearing, as its jaws lowered further. Seeing his own arm disappearing into the hungry maw of a creature from a psychopath's worst nightmare, sparked something in him that he'd never felt before. "Fiora's Fist!" Jeramiah screamed, and his Devil Arms blazed to life. Light flowed from the symbol, and metal enclosed Jeramiah's fist, spreading down the length of his arm, up to his shoulder. The demon bit down on Jeramiah's arm, its teeth chipping in the process. The bird opened its mouth and howled in pain. The ugly demon sitting on top became enraged and started squawking.

"YEAH!" Jeramiah yelled victoriously and wrenched his arm from the demon's mouth. Jeramiah then charged the demon, slamming his metal encased arm into its face. The demon went flying into the air, until it slammed into the ground, rolling through a nest, destroying it in a shower of broken branches and feathers.

"Way to go Jeramiah!" Colton commended his pledge brother. "Now help us out!"

They were holding their own, and Vinny wasn't getting attacked. Colton, and Zane impressed Virgil, each able to completely handle a full demon on their own and lend support to the men on either side. Virgil was doing his best to hack through as many as possible. A wave of energy was released from Ragnoark and it destroyed the demon coming at him. Virgil had taken down seven demons, and with the candidates, it appeared they'd finished off all the new hatchlings. The group was breathing hard, the guys shared looks like, did we do it?

"Rho class! Fall in!" Virgil called out in urgency.

Virgil stabbed his weapons into the ground and extended his right hand out, closing his eyes and breathing deeply. He needed to concentrate on the part of him that was Judge, his godhood. Virgil felt the power, like opening a door, it flowed out coursing into his body. Virgil's eyes went gold, he opened them, and light surged out from Ragnorak's symbol. Like ribbons, six bands of energy snaked out to the pledges. Jeramiah flinched and dodged it at first, the others accepted it, and the band of light touched their Devil Arms. Jeramiah was finally caught, and Virgil's mind was berated with visions and memories from the six men. Time stopped, and in the span of a second, Virgil experienced six lifetimes.

Virgil fell into the worlds that spread before him, and it felt like time stretched forward, Virgil felt like he was growing older, with each new life he experienced. Only at the very end, was there a feeling of control once more. Virgil had the conscious decision to send out the power to each of them, or deny certain ones. Based on the images of their lives, Virgil found the six men, to be virtuous, with flaws and mistakes, yet there was good in them, that resonated throughout their lifetime of memories. Virgil sent the power forth and the instant he made the decision, the connection broke, and less than five seconds had passed. Virgil swayed on his feet, falling to his knees. He'd never done so many at once, blood dripped onto the ground, he wiped at his face, his nose was bleeding, he felt so dizzy. The six Rho class brothers, sprouted wings, it was always a little painful, the first time was the worst. They all made sounds of discomfort, as their body grew new appendages, bursting through their shirts.

"Virgil you okay?" Vinny asked concerned kneeling next to him.

"I'm fine," Virgil nodded trying to stand, he still felt shaky.

"Wow!" Colton cried out and Virgil fell back onto his butt.

"Virgil!" The candidates called out running over.

"I'm good!" Virgil insisted, struggling to get back to his feet, feeling embarrassed. The six pledges together reached out and steadied him.

"Take it easy!" Vinny said getting angry. "You're still part human, right? Just breath for a minute would ya!" Virgil looked at Vinny, it sounded like something he'd say to Vahn. Virgil smiled and nodded, Lils being overprotective of their Bigs, was all a part of the fraternity.

A large shadow fell on the group, they looked up and a massive demon landed on the side of the roof, causing the whole building to shake under its weight. Dust and debris fell from above. It was a larger form of the many bird demons they'd slayed thus far. This one was female, her body was massive in size, as big or bigger than the Arch Demons Virgil had faced. Atop the normal midsection with a face, were two female bird women, twins, two separate demons, sharing one larger body. They were old, with stringy white hair that barely hung to their scalps, with hooked beaks for mouths, sagging breasts, and two long arms, their midsections disappeared into the head of the lower half.

Virgil's eyebrows went way up as the demon swooped down from above to land on the ground with them. The impact of her landing sent tremors through the floor causing all of them to sway. The women looked down at their eggs, pensive. All at once the two old hags began to wail. Virgil and Rho class backed up slowly, bunched tightly together. Jeramiah tripped falling face first into the ground, cracking open a skeleton, and drawing the attention of the large demon. She turned on them all three pairs of eyes narrowing as her feet slammed into the ground, she quickly strode over.

"YOUS!" The old woman with wrinkly skin, and a pair of very saggy breasts squawked with a demonic tone.

"YOUS DID THIS!" The other old woman with a bigger and very croaked beak accused.

"What do we do?" Colton asked Virgil, Steel Plasma steady in his hand.

"We can't challenge her together," Virgil declared, not willing to risk one of the candidates. "I'll create a diversion, while you fly home! Fly east, opposite of the setting red sun!" Virgil quickly said to the six candidates. "Look for your Bigs!"

"NO ONE LEAVES THIS PLACE!" The old woman with the saggy everything announced, her voice holding power.

"WE ARE THE QUEEN MOTHERS!" Her twin sister with a big nose screamed.

"WE RULE THE LOST CITY OF THE SEELIE FAIRIE COURT, GINANGUP! ALL WHO ENTER OUR DOMAIN, ARE SUBJECT TO OUR RULE!"

"We were just going," Virgil told the Queen Mothers.

"KILL THEM KEEVA!" The saggy sister said to the big nose sister.

"WE'LL TEAR THEM APART KAURA!" The big nose replied.

"FLY!" Virgil shouted fearful for his men.

Rho class leapt into the air for their first flight lesson, the Queen of the Bird Demons, looming over them. She was a Greater Demon, one small step below an Arch Demon. Rho class had no hope.

"AEROGA!" The Queen Mothers said the moment the group was off the ground. A funnel of wind swept down from above connecting with the large nest, creating a deadly vortex that took up a quarter of the space available. Everyone was suspended in midair, the power of their spell so incredible, no one could move their bodies. The wind whipped around, and their physical energy drained. The vortex ended and the seven of them dropped to the nest below. Virgil lay on his side, his black wing under his body, his white wing covering his arm, Ragnorak loosely in his grasp. Virgil coughed hard, the wind had been knocked out of him when he slammed into the ground. Rho class wasn't getting to their feet, but they were still making noise.

The demon's large middle mouth inhaled sharply, "HOWLING BLADES!" The demon shrieked, and everyone covered their ears, the pain it caused was hard to take. Semi-circle shaped green energy rings exploded from the demon's mouth, shooting like individual bombs at the ground where the Omegas had landed. Everyone yelled out in terror and pain as the spell bombarded the land around them, exploding on impact.

Virgil had enough, he raised his head up to stare at the Queen of the Birds, "Light Surge!" Virgil commanded his aura draining even lower. From the sky above rays of Creation energy bombarded down, like missile strikes. The Queen demon screamed as her body was assaulted, the strain of the attack caused her to fall to the ground. Virgil didn't have enough energy to use that spell again. He'd be cutting it close with one healing bout of Cura. Virgil made a promise to himself in that moment. He'd start carrying the Optimum with him, everywhere he went. That'd likely mean it wouldn't ever have extra juice, if it was getting used so frequently. That extra aura pool of energy could mean the difference between getting these guys home, or never seeing the woods of their University again.

Virgil got to his feet, the spell Regen from the sword was slowly healing his body, unlike his friends who weren't recovering from the injuries she'd created with her spells. Virgil moved his wings, they were in working order, he started to run and leapt into the air, streaming straight for the Queen. She stirred getting back to her feet with a startling agility. The demon was airborne before Virgil reached her.

"NOT SO FAST JUDGE SPAWN!" The Queen Mothers shouted.

Virgil swung Ragnorak at the Queen, his scythe spinning around him while he fought. The demon wailed as it was hacked by the sword. The sisters quickly slammed into him, sending

Virgil back in the air. They flew forward and the sisters in tandem began to lunge out and strike at him, Soul Reaver barely managing to keep Virgil's flesh from being flayed off his bone.

"WE'LL MAKE YOU WATCH AS WE DEVOUR YOUR FLESH, PIECE BY PIECE!" Sister saggy screamed at Virgil.

"AERO!" Sister beaky commanded. A sphere of green energy sailed into Virgil whipping around, cutting him up like a dozen knifes were inside the wind. Virgil faltered momentarily. Virgil felt the claw dig into his chest before he saw it, he screamed in agony, as she ripped her hand down his pectoral to his abdomen. Soul Reaver lashed out cutting her hand clean off, she howled, and her claw was ripped free falling to the nest. Virgil fell back to the ground, hitting it hard. His chest was slick with blood, she'd cut deep. Where are you Vahn? Virgil wondered, praying his brothers would show up any minute to save them. Virgil wanted his Big, he was scared, he couldn't do this alone. Vahn…please help me, he prayed tears coming to his eyes. His breathing was ragged, he didn't want to fight right now, he needed to rest before he bled to death.

The Queen slammed into the ground close to Virgil. Her powerful legs lunging her forward across the ground. "WE'RE NOT THROUGH WITH YOU YET!" The long beaked sister said cruelly.

"THE FIRST STRIP TASTED SO GOOD!" The other sister laughed happily, and they both began laughing, it sounded like the most annoying squawking Virgil could ever recall hearing.

The demon went to grab Virgil, and Vinny ran in the way. "NO!" Vinny commanded holding a large tree branch he swatted the demon sister with a large beak, who still had two arms away.

"WHAT IS THIS!" The demon shouted out in delight. "A SNACK PROTECTING THE MEAL?" It asked with a sinister grin on the middle face, its tongue then emerging with eagerness.

Up until that moment, Vinny had never used his Devil Arms. He'd never spoken the fear aloud, that he was afraid of hurting people he cared about if he summoned it in practice. Vinny was a man who deeply loved those he cared for, they meant more to him than showing off, or having power. Practice was different than this, right now Vinny wasn't afraid of his Devil Arms harming someone on accident. Vinny was afraid of not being able to protect his Big. "Get away from him you!" Vinny declared. "I won't let you take him! I am a Nephilim, like my father before me! I won't lose another person I care about to your kind!"

The demon lunged at Vinny.

Vinny screamed at the top of his lungs, "Blazing Cleaver!" His ruby red Devil Arms flamed to life, fire spreading out into his hand. A long handle, half the size of Birdy's lance came into Vinny's grasp. The fire spread out into a large axe. The blade was thick and as the blade extended out it began to curve back slightly into a fine point, almost like Virgil's scythe. The axe was in Vinny's hand, and it took him two hands to wield it properly. The axe was bigger than Dante's, one of the biggest Virgil had ever seen. The sharp edge of the blade had flames dancing along it, they didn't dissipate, even as Vinny moved the axe around in his hand.

Vinny caught the demon's claw against the axe and they recoiled. Vinny shuffled his feet, trying to get better footing.

"YOU'RE NO MATCH FOR A GREATER DEMON!" The Bird Queen screamed. One of the sisters hurled a spell at Vinny. Vinny beat his wings, barely managing to dodge the blast, still getting adjusted to his newly grown appendages. Virgil struggled to stand, the spell hit him instead, he was thrown several meters across the nest. They needed more brothers! Blood poured from him, Virgil's vision became blurred, he had survived worse he told himself. It was hard to breathe; his breaths came out ragged.

"VIRGIL!" Vinny cried out in fear. He turned to the demon, rage burning his insides. "LEAVE MY BIG ALONE!" Vinny demanded flying straight for the sisters on top. Vinny swung his axe cutting in a horizontal motion, from the edge of his axe an arc of flames erupted, much like Colton or Virgil. The flames slammed into both sisters, who screamed as their flesh burned, and their feathers melted. Steam rose up from their bodies, they were damaged but still alive, and very angry. Vinny swung his axe around, circling the sisters, this time he was going all in. He'd either end them, or himself, either way, he wouldn't stop till he'd protected his Big, and his pledge brothers from this creature.

Vinny flew straight for the sisters, fearless in the face of death. Vinny swung the axe forward as he came at them. Blazing Cleaver hacked at the big beaked sister, literally cutting her in two, severing from the lower larger body, she fell back, no longer connected to her body. She instantly began to die. The other sister howled in pain, and anguish, her sister was a piece of her own body. Vinny screamed as a warrior. He charged the remaining bird woman, she raked her claws along his flesh, when his first swing missed her by inches. Vinny struggled to get his footing in place, the heavy axe hard to whip around quickly. The demon snarled at Vinny turning into a savage animal, she slashed at Vinny, looking to tear him apart. Vinny was clawed as he swung the axe around, yelling at the top of his lungs. Vinny took her head from her shoulders, and both sisters were silenced. The body began to dissolve into the nest, a goo of bones, feathers, and black blood.

Vinny ran over to Virgil, placing his axe on the ground he checked his Big over anxiously. "Virgil! Hang in there!" He said frantically.

"I'm alright Vinny," Virgil said meekly to his Lil, his blood-soaked clothes a bad indication of his status. Ragnorak had been healing him the whole time, he was starting to feel like he wasn't going to pass out. "That was…incredible Vinny," Virgil told his Lil. "I've never been prouder," Virgil struggled to smile.

"Don't push yourself!" Vinny barked. The rest of Rho class were getting to their feet.

"Damn Vinny!" Flynn commented seeing the giant axe laid next to him. "Got a big enough axe there?"

"Looks like Vinny was just a late bloomer," Colton pointed out. "He took down that demon by himself. That makes him the best in Rho class."

"His axe is even cooler than Dante's!" Jeramiah boasted.

"It is not!" Dante complained. The brothers had arrived at the roof of the building, they quickly raced down.

"Sick looking axe!" Tarek commented coming over to Vinny. "Easily one of the more impressive I've ever seen!"

"It's bigger than Dante's!" Lamar laughed.

"I have one of the best axe's in the whole Paladin order!" Dante barked. "Lots of Paladins said so at the Tournament!"

Tarek went to the candidates and healed their wounds.

"Way to go Lil!" Jagger said proudly giving Jeramiah a high five with his metal gauntlet.

"Thanks Big!" Jeramiah said ecstatically. For the first time Jeramiah felt like he belonged in the group.

"Vinny," Gabriel asked him.

"Yes sir," Vinny said to Gabriel.

"Did you take out the Queen demon here, all by yourself?" Gabriel asked seriously.

"No sir," Vinny said humbly. "Virgil did most of the work, I just did the cleanup."

Vahn helped Virgil stand, Virgil was completely leaning on his Big for support. "Yeah…cause I did soooo much laying on the ground, bleeding out," Virgil said looking down at himself, his clothes were ruined.

Gabriel clapped Vinny on the shoulder, "That's some damn fine work there candidate," Gabriel said proudly his eyes misting. Then he turned his attention to Aiden and gave him a crushing bear hug.

"Gran Lil!" Vahn snapped jokingly. "I'm proud of you!" Vahn laughed. "As for you Lil!" Vahn barked, "Flying ahead like that, making me worry, damn near gave me a heart attack! And what do I find when I get here? Your chest all torn to shreds, and your Lil saving your ass!"

"Your point?" Virgil asked getting inpatient with his Big's condescending tone.

"You're grounded," Vahn sharply retorted so seriously several guys chuckled.

"Sure," Virgil shrugged not caring at this point.

"But seriously, have some faith in my boys," Vahn said proudly. "It's looking like Rho class can handle themselves. And don't fly on ahead you jerk, nearly gave me a panic attack! We stick together, whether you like it or not!"

"Maybe," Virgil smiled and nodded. "Alright Big."

"The others flew off when their Queen died, but we could still be attacked," Magnus told the group. "Let's get out of the Ever After before something *else* decides to show up and challenge us!"

Everyone took to the air, and Rho class got a second chance at a first flight. As they flew over the ancient city of Ginangup, everyone got to appreciate the beauty of the lost city below for the first time, now that they knew everyone was safe. They were still very cautious, but they pointed out the different things they saw, and reveled in the fleeting experience of seeing this decaying wonder. The Ever After was such a dangerous place, but it held many beautiful relics, that held unknown and forgotten chapters of the universe's past.

Once safely home, the brothers who were waiting couldn't have been more overjoyed, everyone made it out alive! Vinny got a lot of attention, as did Jeramiah, for their newly discovered Devil Arms. The eleven Rho class candidates reunited, and they came together in a big circle, all eleven started balling. They promised to always stick together. Tradition had changed Rho class, and the Chapter. From that day forward, everyone in Rho class spent as much time as they could at the Omega house. The group had been bonded, through the harrowing experience, and their friendships had never been more significant.

# Chapter 11 First Annual Alpha and Omega Thanksgiving Dinner

Following the events of Tradition, pledging was much slower paced. The brothers felt like Rho class had proven themselves going into the fifth week, and the eleven men had bonded as a group. The brothers had also come together, what had started out as a night of bickering, had turned into a night of terror. In the end, they had somehow triumphed, and it put things into perspective. They did disagree at times, on very important matters, in the end they were brothers, and that friendship and bond were the most important part of being an Omega.

At Sunday's meeting Tarek rose to speak about position, the Hypophetes. "So besides setting up a few cool brotherhoods for us, once pledging is over, I don't have much but to pass on my position when we have elections towards the end of the semester," Tarek said to the brothers. "We still have study hours three times a week in the Omega house library. We do still attend a Sunday worship service, once a month, if any brothers are interested in going, Jagger is in charge of it. Shifting gears, I did take it upon myself to talk with TK, and together the two of us set up a mixer for the Alphas and the Omegas. Sorry Louie V, I know you're the social chair, wasn't trying to step on your toes," Tarek smiled with a flushed face.

"Your good dawg," Louie shrugged. "What is it?"

"We're going to have our first annual Alpha sisters and Omega brothers, Thanksgiving Dinner!" Tarek announced happily.

"What?" Brody asked confused.

"I want us to start some traditions, and I thought a good one would be having a Thanksgiving dinner every year with the Nephilim ladies of the Alpha sorority sisters," Tarek explained.

"I like it!" Nolan announced getting a few laughs from the room.

"Way to go above and beyond your position," Magnus congratulated Tarek. "We all enjoy their company greatly, and creating traditions like these, will help ensure our two organizations have strong relations for years to come. Greek unity is important, and let's not forget to reach out to the other Greek organizations on campus," Magnus encouraged. "Thank you Tarek. Anything else?"

"I am passing around a sign-up sheet. You HAVE to bring something, in order to come!" Tarek barked. "They are going to be bringing a lot of food, and I will not have us looking like shmucks! The event will be Wednesday night, at 10pm, at their sorority house. Everyone is to dress up nice, and bring a tie. We'll all be putting our ties in a big pile, and the ladies will be picking out ones they like, to pick their 'dates' for the night."

"Ooo!" Louie cried out. "I got a real sexy tie that's guaranteed to score me a hot date!" he joked making a few people laugh.

The rest of the meeting went much more smoothly than the week before. Brotherhood this week was Etiquette Dinner, just the candidates and the Sweethearts, so everyone was off the hook for Tuesday night. Virgil signed up to bring a Taco Salad, his mother Sue had the best recipe that always got compliments wherever she brought it. The brothers were a buzz about Wednesday night, Virgil was just as excited! This mixer sounded fun, and different from the stuff they usually did. Sunday night Virgil hung out with Birdy, Louie, Tarek, and Brody. They went over to Blair and Helene's to hang out and play video games after the meeting.

Monday morning came early, and Virgil dredged through the day. Virgil's classes weren't going so hot. He was getting an A in Communications, and a B in history. Virgil was averaging a D in his Bio Stats class. The grade was all tests, and he'd failed the last one miserably. Virgil was getting a C in A&P, which was the class that received all his study time! Monday after Virgil finished with classes, he walked over to the administration building. He'd been mulling it over all day, and finally reached a decision. Today was the last day you could drop a class, and Virgil had calculated out his grade, and figured there was no chance he could get the B he needed in A&P. He was going to have to retake it anyways, he decided if he dropped it, he could concentrate on his three remaining classes. Virgil felt guilty like a failure, he'd been studying hard, but in truth, hadn't put in enough time. If he was going to have a chance at passing in the future, he'd have to limit his social life.

Virgil went to the food court, and sat at a table with Birdy, Brett, Louie, Nev, and Vinny.

"Virgil why do you look so down?" Birdy asked him.

"I just dropped Anatomy and Physiology," Virgil said sadly. "I'm going to have to retake it."

"Happens," Louie shrugged. "It's just a class, you'll take it again, and do better!"

"I'm just not used to doing bad at school," Virgil sighed.

"It's a hard class," Nev encouraged him. "You know I'm smart," Virgil just smirked, one of the smartest in the fraternity he thought, "and even I would struggle with that class."

"Hey what are you doing after this?" Birdy asked.

"Nothing, free for the rest of the day, what's up?" Virgil wondered.

"Brett and I are running to the store to get the stuff we need for Wednesday, then we're going over to Blair's," Birdy told him.

"Sure," Virgil nodded. "I could use a distraction."

"Can I come too?" Vinny asked.

"Of course!" Virgil told his Lil. "Just be warned, riding in Birdy's car is likely to lower your life expectancy."

"Can't be any worse than last Brotherhood," Vinny joked.

Birdy huffed, "I haven't been in an accident yet! Let's hit the road!" Birdy yelled and the four friends headed out.

"He jinxed us, we're goners," Virgil said jokingly. Virgil had hung out with Brett on many occasions now, but Blair's younger stepbrother had a knack for being so goofy, he made everyone laugh. Virgil came to appreciate his own brand of humor. They finished shopping, and after a quick stop to drop stuff off at the Omega house, went to Blair's for another fun night. Blair was the kind of girl that everyone liked to be around, she was rowdy and the life of the party. Her place had become their de facto hang out spot most days. Vahn, Tarek, Brody, and Rowan came over soon after. Louie brought Aidan and Flynn, and Homer and Tucker walked over when they saw all the cars. They spent so much time together, every night seemed like a party, even when they weren't drinking.

"I am so pumped for our Thanksgiving dinner!" Blair told the boys as they played some cards.

"Thanks Blair! Me too! TK and I have worked hard on this!" Tarek said excitedly.

"It's like weeks away from Thanksgiving though," Helene pointed out.

"Gosh Helene, don't spoil our fun!" Tarek barked out sarcastically causing Helene to glow bright red, "Stop shitting all over our Traditions!" Tarek carried on in his usual loud obnoxious voice, that implied his friendly intent. Poor Helene thought Tarek was serious!

"Yeah! Cause one year is a tradition!" Blair made a solid point her usual laugh coming out as she rolled her eyes, she shared a look with Helene, who'd lost some redness. "Oh Omega boys," Blair sighed. "You tickle me."

Tuesday evening Virgil was in his room, he had stayed in and focused on getting some work done for his classes. He washed his face, and brushed his teeth, locking his door when he was ready for sleep. Virgil took out the Optimum magicite, the opal jewel feeling heavy in his hand, he'd been draining his energy into it most nights, it was starting to fill up. After Tradition Virgil was keeping it on his person more often. He realized that it was becoming necessary to always be prepared, and the magicite was an invaluable asset in emergency situations. Sitting in his bed he took a deep breath and sat back, closing his eyes. The jewel in his hand thrummed with energy. Virgil slowly coaxed his aura into the jewel, it was a slow process, anything more was too dangerous. A bright flash came from Virgil's open dresser, he put the Optimum down and ran over. The ornate mirror's surface, given to him by Alexa Diamond, was lighting up like a cell phone. There was a small diamond colored magicite, resting above the glass mirror, that powered the magic that worked this treasure.

Virgil picked up the mirror, placing a finger on the surface. The mirror flashed its surface and was replaced with Alexa who was staring up at him, her room in the background. "Alexa!" Virgil cried out in surprise with a smile. "This is so cool!" he beamed. They'd become friends by randomly running into each other in Alexandros over the summer. Alexa had created these mirrors herself. They were linked to each other, and provided a safe and direct line of communication, working just like a cell phone. They'd stayed in touch, and had spoken twice before through the mirror, catching up, talking about life, and video games.

"Hey Virgil! It's been too long!" Alexa cried out warmly. "I tried getting a hold of you last night, but you didn't answer," she said.

"I'm sorry about that," Virgil said sincerely. "I was at Blair's place until late. How are you doing?"

"Doing well!" Alexa nodded. "I turn seventeen on Saturday!" Alexa announced excitedly.

"Really?" Virgil responded in a high-pitched tone of surprise. He needed to go shopping. "What are your plans?"

"Mom and Grandpa have something planned I'm sure," Alexa laughed. "They refuse to speak when I bring it up, and Grandpa's been unusually tight lipped around me," she sighed. "How are you doing?" Alexa asked him.

"Things are going great, busy with classes and the fraternity, but always having fun!" Virgil smiled.

"You're so lucky!" Alexa sighed. "I hope Mom lets me go to America for college! Grandpa told me I can go to the Academy at Alexandros or stay home," she huffed.

"Like Hel you will!" Virgil said at the same time she snapped shaking her head, "Like Hel I will!"

They both burst out laughing.

"Do you have plans for the weekend?" Alexa asked him.

"No mam," Virgil told her happily sitting down.

"You should come spend the weekend in Alexandros!" Alexa cried. "You could stay in the guest quarters, or wherever Grandpa wants you. There are literally dozens of rooms that are available for when dignified diplomats stay at the castle," Alexa explained talking quickly. "It would be lots of fun, and would totally make my Birthday weekend awesome! I asked Mom if it was okay, and she seemed excited to have you over too! What do you say?" Alexa asked Virgil breathlessly.

Virgil beamed, he was slightly flushed, humbled by Alexa's sincerity. "Of course I'll come stay the weekend!" He replied confidently.

"Yes!" Alexa laughed. "I'll let Mom and Grandpa know," Alexa said happily. "I'm so excited! When can you come over?" she asked.

"Well," Virgil thought about it. "Friday afternoon? But wait, how am I getting there? Am I supposed to fly?" he asked with a nervous laugh.

"No!" Alexa cried out. "That would take you an hour or more! I'll have a portal arranged for you at the Upsilon Delta's temple. There will be Paladins from the Capital guarding it, waiting to escort you safely here," she explained.

"You've already planned it all through huh?" Virgil asked surprised, like she knew he'd already say yes.

"Well, Mom did, and Grandpa," Alexa laughed. "Part of the benefits of having the Oracle in your family. You start to know when people are coming over, before they actually do," she smirked.

"Oh," Virgil replied earning a chuckle from Alexa. They spoke for a few more minutes but Virgil was getting tired and had classes to attend once the day started.

"Goodnight Alexa, looking forward to seeing you," Virgil smiled after a yawn.

"Goodnight! See you this weekend!" Alexa waved goodbye.

Virgil placed the mirror and the Optimum safely in their spots, and then laid in bed falling asleep quickly, at peace with a smile on his face.

Wednesday night, Virgil hurried to finish getting ready, putting gel in his hair to look extra nice. The guys were all gathering downstairs, everyone finishing preparing the food they were taking over. The excitement and energy was reaching a fever pitch, everyone wanted to look their best to impress the ladies. Virgil was hoping someone he knew picked his tie, like Blair, or TK, maybe Helene, or even their Sweetheart Raven. He had a hard time talking with new people, and girls made him feel so nervous and awkward. Virgil went down to the kitchen to collect the Taco Salad he'd made. He just had to mix the dressing in once they got there.

"You ready to head over there?" Louie asked Virgil getting his pasta salad from the kitchen as well. Louie looked dressed to the 9's, easily out shining most if not all the brothers, the guy knew how to shop for clothes!

"Wow Louie, that suit looks great!" Virgil cried out.

"Thanks," Louie beamed, "I just bought it today. You look good, red shirt, black tie, always a good choice," Louie commented on his attire. "What tie are you bringing?" Louie asked. Virgil took out a solid turquoise tie from his pocket. "That's a nice one!" Louie whistled. "You're going to get a lot of attention with that tie on the table! Here's mine," Louie quickly brought a tie out of his pocket, it was orange, with white stripes. He stuffed it back in. "I wanted something a little brighter, that would stand out from the others," Louie said.

"You bitches ready to hit the road?" Dante asked walking into the kitchen with his hair gelled up, an orange dress shirt with a shiny striped black tie, and smug grin on his face.

"Well call me a pledge!" Louie cried out. "Our missing Omicron brother returns again!" Louie embraced Dante in a tight hug. "Good to see you brother."

"You as well Louie," Dante nodded. "I brought dip," Dante laughed, "And chips. I'm driving, you guys want a ride?" Dante asked.

"Yup," they both nodded.

"Where's Birdy?" Virgil asked them as they walked to the front of the house.

"He's driving Cameron, Brett, and Nigel cause none of them have a car," Dante said to Virgil leading the way.

They arrived at the girl's sorority house a few minutes later, they were just a few houses down the road. Their property was also gated, though they had a smaller front and back yard. They used the front entrance to decorate lavishly, with a fountain in the middle and non-native ornamental grasses and flowers, with large bushes and statues as focal pieces. Inside, the house was full of noisy and energetic chatter. You could tell from the collective of indistinguishable voices, that people were anxious, and having fun. Virgil walked into the main dining room to find most sticking to their normal social groups. Which meant Blair was in the center of a group of Omegas, Helene with her, making a bunch of boys laugh. Some of the sisters were a little jealous and looked at Blair with less than favorable glances. Maybe they didn't realize that Blair hung out with the guys three nights a week, minimum! Dante, Louie, and Virgil took their food to the kitchen.

Virgil had time to quickly say hello to Selene and Raven who were talking together with Lilly. Lilly wasn't in a sorority, but she was a Sweetheart of the Omegas, like Raven, making her an Omega. TK was busy running the party, but had time to give him a quick hug and a kiss on the cheek. A few minutes later Terra Peoples called the room to order, the girls listened to her, better than the brothers listened to Magnus! She looked stunning in a baby blue dress with her blond hair done up in a bun, with strands of hair falling around her face framing her deep blue eyes. She was the kind of woman you didn't cross.

"I'd like to welcome the brothers of Omega to our home," Terra said warmly. "We are so pleased to have you all here! I'd like to turn things over to our VP TK, who is responsible for putting this event on!" The sisters and the brothers all cheered for TK and she got slightly flushed stepping forward. The room turned their attention to her.

For all her social grace, charm, and intelligence, TK was a humble woman, and hated attention lavished upon her. Terra, her best friend, knew this and TK stared daggers at her sister. "Thanks Terra," TK joked, and the sisters shared a knowing laugh. TK wore something simple, but it did little to dull her natural beauty. "I'd like to thank Tarek Jeter who helped me get this together on such short notice!" TK spoke quickly and Tarek stepped forward to help her. "We wanted to start something, a tradition between our organizations. So that when we're all gone, the future members of our Chapters will hopefully share the same closeness, that we all have!"

"Now if all the guys could please place their ties in the other room, with the food, we'll have the ladies pick a brother to pair off with for the evening!" Tarek told them.

The brothers quickly placed their ties together, and they were brought out to the dining room table for the girls to look at. Immediately the girls started chattering over which ones they wanted, there were some exotic ties, some normal ones, some plain ones, and some that were rather striking. Terra told them to pick one out and the girls charged the ties, they didn't brawl over them, but just barely. Terra was perhaps the most aggressive, bee lining for a specific tie. She was a poor actress when she discovered the tie belonged to Jagger. Soft spoken, shy, Jagger blushed fiercely as she roped her arm through his, leading them to a spot she'd already claimed. TK saw a cherry red solid tie and picked it up, Tarek came over to her with a grin.

"I got yours!" TK laughed. "Cool!" She nodded and they sat down with Terra and Jagger.

"Whose tie did I pick?" Blair asked holding up a blue tie with a sleek silver pattern woven into it.

"Mine!" Vahn called out happily.

"YES!" Blair laughed and they gave each other a quick hug before picking their seats close to TK and Tarek.

Virgil looked around nervously, who had picked his tie?

He looked on to see Amariana with his turquoise tie in her hand looking around for the owner. He thought about running back to the Omega house before she saw him. He'd already shown it to Louie, and it'd be obvious with all the girls paired up but her, with Virgil mysteriously gone. Virgil sighed, and walked towards her. She sensed his movement and turned her attention, her face falling into her usual serious expression.

"Really?" Amariana asked already sounding annoyed.

"Yup," Virgil laughed nervously. I should have told Blair what my tie looked like, Virgil thought with regret looking over at Blair, Vahn, Tarek, and TK having fun sitting together.

"I could've done worse," Amariana said casually with a shrug, and walked to the table. She took a seat at the far end, away from the others.

Virgil walked after her taking the seat next to her. They sat there for several seconds, fidgeting and looking at each other, then around the room. What do I say? Virgil had no idea what to talk about with this woman. "So how was your day?" Virgil asked kicking himself after he'd done it.

"What?" Amariana asked raising her eyebrows at him, like he'd just slapped her mama.

"Uh," Virgil fumbled, "What did you do today?" he tried reframing the question.

"Class," Amarian shrugged. "And more class," she said with a small smile. "It's hard to understand how people can do it for so long,"

"What do you mean?" Virgil asked.

"This, school, college," Amariana gestured around. "It's...so stressful. Why do people put themselves through it?" she asked seriously.

Virgil was surprised by what she was saying, why had she come to this University? Was she regretting it? School wasn't for everyone, and juggling work, classes, and a life was extremely challenging. "People go to college so they can get good paying jobs to have a life for themselves," Virgil said in defense of every college student ever. "People do it because that's what we're told to do from the time we're kids. First, they tell us, you can be anything, do anything you want. That's the American dream. The older you get, the more you're told about the big picture. You can be anything you want, with the right education, or degree, or license," Virgil spoke seriously but passionately. "And what you end up learning the hard way, no one tells you the last part. The truth is, you can get ten degrees, with enough student loan payments, to make it so you can't afford to live, and you still won't necessarily get to be what you want."

"Why?" Amariana asked him. "Because the world is cruel and unfair?" she suggested bitterly.

"The truth is; the world has always been a cruel place. I don't know when Americans started believing they were safe, walking around with undeserved entitled pompous attitudes. Some civilizations have granted stability, and safety, though history shows it never truly lasts. This is a cruel world, it beats down those that try to raise order, out of the muck of chaotic mess that is humanity. Despite all that though, there are young people out there, just finding themselves. They have dreams of being more than what this world has to offer, of living in a world that is better than their mothers and fathers. That's why so many go to college," Virgil said finishing his rant. "It's the only way forward sometimes, even if the system is rigged, and the government is corrupt."

Quiet came between them again. Luckily Tarek announced people could start lining up for food and Virgil suggested they get in line. There was so much to choose from, Virgil had to use two plates. Virgil and Amariana sat back down, Brett, Zane, and Flynn were seated near them with three Alpha sisters Virgil didn't know. They started eating, it was so good, it helped with the little communication between them.

"Thanks for being my date tonight," Virgil joked to Amariana.

She raised an eyebrow way up, slowly turning to stare at him. "This is NOT a date," Amariana said firmly.

"I know," Virgil nodded smiling. "It is just a friendly mixer. But still, I'm glad you picked my tie," Virgil said half truthfully.

"You are?" Amariana asked. "Why?"

"Why what?" Virgil asked back.

"Why be glad?" Amariana asked him. "I'm not exactly nice to you."

"Not all the time no," Virgil shrugged. "But you have been nice to me, which means you can be, so…" Virgil smiled softly at Amariana.

"Why are you so nice?" Amariana asked Virgil.

"I'm not nice all the time," Virgil furrowed his brow, there were few absolutes when it came to people.

"Most of the time," Amariana pressured.

"Okay, most of the time," Virgil nodded.

"What do you get out of it?" she asked him seriously.

"I don't get anything really, I just…like being polite I guess," Virgil babbled getting a little flushed, feeling stupid explaining something so boring about himself. "I value people who are polite, civil, and courteous. I wish more people were like that, it'd be a better world. I could be just another jerk I guess, but why be that way? It does nothing for people, for this country. Sometimes it takes a little effort, but I like being nice to people," Virgil admitted. "I guess I do get something out of it. It makes me feel good about myself," he said honestly. "I feel good about who I am, when I treat people the way I want to be treated."

"You're weird," Amariana sighed.

"Why are you so cold, and abrasive?" Virgil asked regretting it once he said it.

Amariana turned to him like she might slap him. Instead she surprised him by saying, "You get kicked down enough, run into too many of the wrong kind of people…you start developing a thick skin, or you don't make it."

"I'm sorry," Virgil said to her, feeling the emotion in her words.

"For what?" Amariana asked him.

"It sounds like you haven't had the easiest run of things, and…I feel for you, I can't imagine what you've been through. I'm sorry," Virgil said simply shrugging.

Amariana rolled her eyes, "Don't apologize…it's not your fault," she said a little shyly.

"I know, I just have this bad habit of apologizing a lot, especially if I'm nervous," Virgil said and his eyes got a little wide at the end, why did I say that!?

"I make you nervous?" Amariana asked, a confident devilish grin spreading across her face, Virgil had never seen her smile like that before. "Is it because you think I'm hot?" She teased, flipping her hair and slowly blinking open lashes, turning the full weight of her emerald eyes, and pouty lips at him.

"What?!" Virgil asked getting instantly red. "I don't know," he replied meekly.

"You, don't know?" Amariana asked a little peeved, putting her hands on her hips and cocking her head to the side.

"I mean," Virgil changed gears instantly seeing the fire in her eyes. Women! They could be so temperamental! "Amariana!" Virgil laughed with nervousness. "Of course I think you're attractive! Any guy with eyes and a pulse should!"

"They should?" Amariana asked laughing her mouth hanging open slightly.

"No! I mean they could, or probably do," Virgil sighed and fought a grin from spreading across his face. "You're just loving this aren't you?" Virgil asked.

"Yup," Amariana said happily, "You're very easy to tease Virgil."

"Awesome," Virgil shook his head. "Great, I'm glad I can be entertainment for you tonight," Virgil chuckled and Amariana joined in.

Things became more relaxed between them. Amariana was warmer, still reserved, but Virgil felt a noticeable shift in her body language, and tone with him.

TK was walking around the room, people were mostly finished eating, and were mingling. TK came to the end of the table where Virgil and Amariana were a few chairs away from Brett, Zane and Flyyn.

"Virgil!" TK called out and he got up to give her a friendly hug. "I miss you buddy!" TK said warmly. They sat back down. "Hi Amariana," TK said mischievously. "How was your date this evening?" she asked curiously.

"This is NOT a date," Virgil said firmly. "Amariana made sure I understood that from the get go," Virgil laughed rolling his eyes to TK.

"I was hoping I was going to pick your tie," TK said to Virgil. "I always love talking with you, you're so upbeat and positive, you make me smile."

"Aww, TK, you're a Sweetheart," Virgil blushed and looked down.

"TK!" Terra called out to her. "Come get in the picture with us!" She asked. The Lambdas and their dates were getting into the picture. Tarek Jeter had gotten in the picture at the insistence of Vahn and Gabriel.

"I'll talk with you later," TK said to Virgil giving him a quick hug goodbye. "Bye Amariana," TK waved, "See you at Sisterhood," she said going over to her friends and Gabriel.

"She likes you," Amariana said to Virgil.

"We're good friends," Virgil nodded. "I've known her since last fall. We just get along really well."

"Do you like her?" Amariana asked cryptically.

"Wow, she's my brother's girlfriend! Has been since I met them!" Virgil said upset. "I've never liked TK like that, it's purely platonic!"

"I was just curious," Amariana said hastily, "I'm sorry, I shouldn't have asked that. TK just speaks so highly of you; I'm not used to people feeling like that for one other."

"You can be friends with people, and not want to sleep with them," Virgil pointed out.

"I agree," Amariana nodded. "I guess I'm a little envious of your friendships, people get powerful emotions towards you."

There was silence again between them.

"I'll take your plate," Virgil offered and walked away for a minute. Running into Dante and Birdy, he made quick conversation, with plans for an after party at Blair's, over half of the people were coming.

"Definitely," Virgil nodded. "Let me ask Amariana if she wants to come, and I'll be down to leave soon," Virgil told Dante.

"Take your time," Dante spoke quickly a devilish grin on his face, with raised eyebrows looking towards Amariana deliberately after he said it.

Virgil rolled his eyes and walked back, Amariana was standing by the table. "Hey Amariana, some of the sisters and my brothers are going over to Blair and Helene's, do you want to come?" he asked.

Amariana considered it, "I have class in the morning," she replied slowly. "And it's close to midnight. Maybe some other time?" she offered.

"Sure," Virgil nodded about to walk away.

"Hey Virgil, wait a second," Amariana stopped him.

"What?" Virgil stopping to look at her curious.

"Would you, maybe want to hang out sometime?" Amariana asked him quietly he almost didn't recognize her voice, was she, nervous!?

"Sure we can hang out!" Virgil laughed.

Amariana stared into his eyes, and his smile fell away. "Just us?" Amariana asked her face flushing slightly.

Virgil's face completely changed, is she, hitting on me?! Virgil's pulse began to beat faster.

"Like…a date?" Virgil was almost scared to ask.

"I mean if you wanted to, I don't know," Amariana shuffled nervously.

"I'd be game," Virgil nodded not wanting Amariana to back away. "Though I'm surprised in your sudden change of heart."

Amariana huffed, "I don't want you to think this is what a date with me would be like, doesn't a girl have the right to change her mind?" Amariana went to turn from him.

Virgil didn't give her the opportunity. "If you want to give me a chance, to take you out, so we can just talk, and get to know each other, that would be cool." He spoke trying his best to sound chill, his heart was starting to race in his chest.

"Just casual," Amariana suggested, "No strings or expectations."

"None," Virgil nodded. "Just hanging out, see how we click, and to see if we have chemistry."

Amariana stepped a little closer, she looked down and tossed her hair slightly, moving her bangs to the side out of her eyes as she looked up at him. "I think…we already have chemistry," Amariana said softly her words sending shocks of heat through his ears and down his limbs.

Virgil chuckled nervously, staring down into her emerald eyes, "When are you free?" he asked her. There was tension between them, she was looking at Virgil in a way he wasn't used to, women are sexualized more than men. He was flushed and flattered.

Amariana's eyes licked at his body. "This weekend?" Amariana offered.

Virgil was about to say yes but remembered Alexa, "I can't this weekend," Virgil said sadly and Amariana's face fell. "I'm going to Alexandros for the weekend," he explained which snapped her attention to him. "I'm not sure if you've heard of it from the Sisters yet, but my friend lives there, and it is her birthday this weekend. I haven't been there since the summer, and promised I'd visit."

"They've mentioned it," Amariana nodded. "Friend, huh?" She asked. "How good of a friend?" she wondered.

"She's turning seventeen," Virgil said flatly, she was no competition. "And her Grandfather is the Grand Prytanis of the Paladins, and King of Alexandros so…," Virgil laughed trailing off, it was obvious Alexa was not on Virgil's radar like that.

"Oh," Amariana replied smiling, she liked what she heard. "The Oracle's granddaughter."

"How about a night next week?" Virgil offered. "The candidates get inducted Friday night, so I'll be busy with their Initiation Party, but I'm free any other day," Virgil smiled.

"How about Monday night?" Amariana offered. "I don't have classes on Tuesday."

"Monday sounds great, I'll be free any time after 5," Virgil said.

"How about you pick me up at 6 o'clock and we go get dinner?" Amariana offered.

"Perfect," Virgil nodded, and they quickly exchanged phone numbers. "I'm looking forward to seeing you again," he said after and they shared an awkward first hug, goodbye. "Hope you have a good week, if I don't see you before Monday," he was nervous and yet so very happy.

"Thank you," Amariana smiled looking down, "For the record, I always thought you were good looking, I just didn't think it would work out between us."

"And now?" Virgil asked.

"I still don't," Amariana answered honestly looking up at him. "I'm willing to give it a try though." Virgil just grinned, he hadn't seen his night ending like this.

# Chapter 12 A Weekend in Alexandros

After catching up with his mom over the phone, Virgil left for a weekend trip to Alexandros. It was Friday afternoon, and the sun was shining brightly, but the weather was turning cold. In a month's time there would be probability of snow. The path through the woods was familiar to him now. There was a Paladin with a special garb just outside of the temple, Virgil recognized it as the uniforms the warriors who worked in the castle wore. They were similar to the secret service, the guards who worked just for the castle and the royal family.

When Virgil came up to the warrior guarding the entrance, he acknowledged Virgil calling out, "Good day Redeemer," with a thick English accent.

"Hello sir," Virgil replied in earnest. Then he recognized him, he was one of the guards who'd been standing outside the castle gates, the first time Virgil visited with Alexa. "I remember you, we've met before."

"That is correct sir," the Paladin nodded. "I'm Charles."

Virgil reached out and shook the warrior's hand, he had an Earth Devil Arms glyph. "It's nice to see you again Charles, I'm Virgil."

"I know," Charles replied shaking his hand. Charles tapped on the gateway; it was obscured with a veil of magic. Charles drew a glyph on the barrier, and it fell within seconds, a second guard at the doorway.

"You remember Philip?" Charles asked Virgil.

"Yes," Virgil nodded.

"Good to see you again 'ol chap!" Philip responded in earnest with a thick accent. Philip was louder than Charles, who was docile and easy going. It was just the three of them in the stone temple, it felt strange being in here without the Omegas. A portal was open, that must be why they had the place sealed off.

"Let's hurry through Master Virgil!" Charles urged. Virgil went first, stepping through the swirling black vortex. He landed on solid ground feeling queasy, he doubted he'd ever get used to it. There were several guards close by, watching over the active portal. The portal hung in a stone archway that sat in a small clearing surrounded by large hedges. The castle and small mountain peak towered overhead. He was in a large garden that stretched on for over a mile, complete with fountains, and hedge mazes. This must be the private grounds of the castle, Virgil thought, stepping out from the secluded transporter. The sight before him was resplendent, he was overcome by the gardens' splendor, stopping to gaze around, his eyes sparkling.

"Virgil!" Alexa shouted running up to him and embracing him tightly.

"It's so good to see you again!" Virgil told her picking her up, careful of her wings, and spinning her around. He set her down and they let go. Alexa was soon to be seventeen, she was tall for a woman, with gold blond hair, and dark blue sapphire eyes. She wore a baby blue dress with leggings. Alexa was intelligent, outspoken, and fiercely loyal. Charles and Philip came through the portal and it closed behind them.

"Princess!" The English guards yelled out coming up to them.

"Hey goofballs!" Alexa called back.

"Princess! Not in front of the guest!" Charles protested.

"Please! Virgil's like family," Alexa countered looping her arm through Virgil's. "Let's get you settled in, then we can figure out what we'll do!"

They walked through a small section of the gardens to the castle, Charles and Philip following at a distance. It towered over them, staring up at its peak was akin to leaning one's head back to stare up the length of a massive skyscraper. Alexa led the way inside to an elevator, powered by magicite. A few minutes later Alexa and Virgil where walking through the halls and had arrive at the royal family's quarters. Alexa brought Virgil to the same room he'd been in over the summer, when he'd been unconscious, after the battle with Tiamat. Alexa dismissed the guards and they were left alone.

"This is where you'll be staying!" Alexa announced. "You should know you're way around."

"I don't know," Virgil said hesitantly. "This is the royal wing, shouldn't I be in like, the regular guest quarters?"

"Why?" Alexa asked. "It's easier for the guards to protect us if we're close together, and then we have to do a lot of walking to see each other. Mom's the one who decided where you'd be staying, not me," Alexa shrugged.

Virgil nodded and put his bag down, he got out his present for her. "I want you to open your present early," Virgil smiled.

"Alright!" Alexa grinned taking the small gift bag from his hands. She took out an old Switch Nintendo system. Inside a little box were a dozen games for it, most were ones he'd already beat a couple times.

"Those systems are retired, so they are cheaper, and so are the games. I wanted to get you a variety, and figured we could battle each other in Pokemon," Virgil said quickly. "I hope you like it."

"I love it!" Alexa cried. "It is so hard to get this kind of stuff up here! You really pay insane amounts of money for anything from the surface, especially human technology. Thank you!" Alexa embraced Virgil.

Virgil and Alexa lay around on the furniture in the seating area of the room, talking and gaming. It felt like they hadn't skipped a beat, as if it had just been yesterday since they'd seen each other last. Virgil felt like he could be himself around Alexa, he wasn't trying to be macho or felt pressured to impress her, like he normally did at college.

Alexa was bubbly going through her new games, mostly RPGs which were what Virgil played. "This is really something," she exclaimed, "I won't be bored for months!"

"Lady Alexa!" Philip announced knocking on the door and walking in. He had a gift that was elaborately wrapped. "Look what I have!" He giddily laughed coming over to her. "An early birthday present!"

He placed the package in her lap, "From who?" Alexa asked surprised looking down at the package excitedly.

"Who do you think?" Philip barked sarcastically. "What hunk of muscle jock, with a fantastic booty wants to get his paws all over you?"

"Oh no," Alexa groaned looking at the present like it had turned into a stink bomb.

"I'm lost," Virgil said to them both.

"Master Whitefeather," Philip told Virgil.

"Axion?" Virgil asked Alexa. "He is still trying to court you?"

"His father is the Grand Crysophylos," Philip said off handedly. "He's been pursuing Lady Alexa since she started to…develop as a woman."

"Eh," Alexa uttered in revulsion. "Please don't say things like that."

"Open it," Virgil suggested.

"Nope," Alexa said walking the gift over to the trash can and throwing it away.

"Alexa!" Virgil and Philip cried out in surprise.

"I was sending the gifts back, but maybe he took that as I was playing hard to get," Alexa explained. "I want it to be clear, I'm not playing, EVER!" Alexa said fiercely.

"Can I at least open it?" Philip pouted.

"Nope," Alexa said kicking the can over.

Philip sighed and left the room.

"Why don't you like him?" Virgil asked.

"Aside from Axion being a vain, arrogant, and power-hungry asshole?" Alexa asked.

Virgil chuckled, "Obviously! Wow, you must *really* dislike him!"

"Well," Alexa huffed and fell into a chair, Virgil sat down close to her. "It's gotten to the point where, I have rejected him so many times, it kind of feels like harassment," Alexa said timidly.

"Has he ever threatened you? Or pressured you for…things?" Virgil asked his eyebrows knitting together in anger. He may have to go kick some ass before the day was over.

"NO!" Alexa protested. "Nothing like that. And to be honest, Axion's not my type," Alexa shrugged.

"We cleared that already," Virgil nodded the corners of his mouth peaking up.

Alexa became tense, Virgil could tell she was trying to tell him something important. "Well to be fair, even if he was the perfect guy, he still wouldn't be…my type," Alexa stared into Virgil's eyes. They were quiet.

"Oh," Virgil said his eyebrows raising, understanding. He needed to show Alexa that it didn't bother him, and why should it? It shouldn't be something that was even an issue. "Well I think, if a person is lucky enough to find love in this world full of hate, it shouldn't matter if they are a man or woman."

"Thanks," Alexa nodded looking relieved. "You're, the first person I ever told."

"I'm…honored," Virgil said speechless.

"Charles and Philip will probably freak out when I tell them," Alexa laughed.

"Why?" Virgil asked. "Wait! Are they like…together?" he wondered.

"Yes, they've been partners for ten years," Alexa said affectionately. "They've been my personal guards for a long time. Mom assigned them to be at a young age. She handpicked them to work for us. Some people in Alexandros, they, don't like gay people," Alexa hesitated, she was still finding comfortability with talking about this.

"America too," Virgil nodded. "People need to be more accepting, or at the very least tolerant. Hate does nothing but burn the world down," he said passionately.

"Let's go for a walk," Alexa suggested wanting to walk away from the room, and change the subject.

Virgil nodded, "I want to see more of the castle grounds," he admitted.

"You liked the gardens?" Alexa nodded. "We can take a break from gaming."

They walked back to the garden, Virgil caught Alexa up on his semester, censoring some details to protect the Omegas. Virgil mentioned Amariana, and Alexa became very interested.

"Ooooo, tell me more!" Alexa giggled all excited.

"It's one date!" Virgil laughed. "Not a big deal!"

"How many dates have you been on?" Alexa asked Virgil.

"With Amariana or all together?" Virgil asked.

"Both," Alexa answered.

Virgil pretended to count, "None I think," Virgil laughed getting red.

"A good-looking guy like you?" Alexa asked surprised. They took the elevator down to the garden entrance; the sun was still in the sky but beginning to set.

"I kind of dated this girl in high school, but it wasn't anything serious. And we never went on, like an official date," Virgil said feeling like an idiot.

"It's okay!" Alexa consoled him. "I'm not knocking you down. I've never been on a date either. Creator, Grandpa would probably have a stroke if a girl showed up to take me out."

"How doesn't he," Virgil was confused, Aseril was the Oracle, the Second Seraph, was given a powerful gift of divination.

"The power isn't all knowing, his reach has its limits," Alexa shrugged. "It's based on choices, and paths. I haven't met anyone special, so Grandpa probably hasn't seen anything. He'd likely come to have a little chat with me if he did see something on the horizon."

"I really like this girl," Virgil admitted to Alexa. "When I'm around her, I get so nervous, she challenges me, which I guess I kind of like. She makes me feel…alive, and on edge, with adrenaline rushing through my veins. She's a little feisty and unpredictable," Virgil said more to himself.

"Ahh, you like 'em fiery?" Alexa asked serious. They shared a look and burst out laughing.

"She sounds special," Alexa nodded. "The best way to know if you fit with someone is to spend time with them. If the first date goes well, maybe you two can hang out, and see how your personalities mesh," Alexa said.

"I can get along with most anyone," Virgil shrugged. "It's all about finding the inner strengths and assets in that individual."

"Shouldn't be hard for you to find assets, to like about Amariana right?" Alexa asked raising her eyebrows.

Virgil's jaw dropped. "Whatever!" He laughed getting red in the face. Alexa was as good at giving flack as the boys back at the fraternity house.

Alexa gave Virgil the full tour, the grounds were much larger than he had first thought. His favorite was a fountain with a series of steps, and stairs leading up to a small hedge maze. There were exotic fish he'd never heard of swimming in the ponds. The statues came from a time forgotten, filled with strange power. It felt like they were meant for something more than just decoration, their secrets were lost to Virgil, he was left to drink in unending, new discoveries. The gardens had a path that led up into the mountain, or rather behind it, to the Eidolon graveyard, the place that made Alexandros float. It was closed off from the public, a holy place to the Fairies, and the Nephilim. It was where Virgil, Artreyu, and an unknown Battle Maiden wielding Divine Light battled and defeated a powerful Fallen Eidolon, Tiamat.

They came upon a breath-taking pavilion, built out of marble and stone. It housed various statues, paintings, and monuments. The front was setup like a museum. Alexa led Virgil out behind the building, to the edge of the gardens, and the landmass. There was one last building, this one was set up for recreational purposes. Currently it was arranged into a dining hall. It was lit by magicite crystals, that glowed like torch fire. Sibylla and Aseril were in the room when they arrived with a group of people, dinner was being placed on the table by staff.

"Surprise!" Everyone shouted. Alexa was speechless, as was Virgil. A large cake was put out with the buffet of food. They started mingling with the crowd and Virgil felt awkward. Virgil didn't know any of these people, but everyone knew him. It was strange and off putting, introducing himself to someone new only for them to already know intimate details of who he was. Alexa was a gracious host and did her best to keep him at ease.

"The Redeemer!" A couple young girls came up to him. "We can tell from your Devil Arms! Is it true you killed that dragon that attacked the city this summer?"

"Uh, well not really," Virgil shrugged. "The First Seraph, Artreyu, he defeated her, I just helped." Virgil was so uncomfortable, another girl came up and all three started asking questions, one of which was, are you single!

"Virgil dear," Sybil said walking up to him, "We haven't had a chance to catch up. Might I steal him ladies?"

"Of course, Lady Diamond!" They replied in earnest.

Sybil rescued him at just the right moment, "Thanks for that," Virgil said walking with her over to the food table, making their plates. He was relieved to be near someone he knew. "Those girls were eyeing me up like I was a piece of meat!" Virgil exclaimed.

Sybil burst out laughing, her voice was soft and lyrical. "You're a Seraph, the people of this city know this, and that makes you akin to a celebrity," Sybil explained. "I'm glad you were able to make it this weekend," she smiled.

"I'm glad to be here," Virgil said honestly. They sat down together away from others and he felt comfortable to speak openly. Virgil told her about his fraternity, "I got a Lil Brother in the fraternity this semester, and I was appointed the Grammateus of my Chapter," he said proudly.

"A Jeweled Officer," Sybil nodded. "Congratulations."

"Thanks," Virgil nodded.

Virgil tried asking Sybil questions about herself, but she was good at driving the conversation. She would steer the topic back to Alexa or Virgil, he didn't mind though, she was one of the nicest people he'd ever met, it was easy to see how Alexa had turned out so good.

"What are your plans for after college?" Sybil asked.

"I haven't thought that far yet," Virgil laughed.

"No?" Sybil nodded. "That's okay it's a ways off," she suggested.

"No, it's really not," Virgil said seriously. "I'll probably move here, start playing a bigger role in helping against the Death Dealers, and the Fallen."

"You're only nineteen," Sybil said with a soft smile. "The end of the world isn't upon us yet. You still have time to enjoy your youth, while it is here."

"I have to help," Virgil said passionately. "I can't sit back, while the world falls apart."

"And you won't," Sybil nodded. "But the weight of the world is not yours to bear alone. You have friends, and allies who will be there when the time comes, never forget that Virgil." Sybil was kind and nurturing with her words. Virgil didn't feel the need to be defensive as if being admonished.

"Thank you Sybil," Virgil smiled.

Virgil finished eating and approached Aseril to have a conversation. The Grand Prytanis rebuffed Virgil just grunting at his questions and replying with a note of finality, "We will talk later." Virgil shrugged and moved on, they were allies, they didn't need to be best friends. After they had cake Virgil retired to his room for the evening. Alexa gave him a big hug before he walked back.

"Thank you for coming, you made my night," Alexa said as she held him.

"Thanks Alexa, Happy Birthday," Virgil smiled.

The next day Virgil had breakfast with Alexa, Sybil, and Aseril. Aseril drank his coffee and ate in silence, he seemed grumpier than usual. Sybil looked put together already, Virgil was starting to think she wasn't the kind of woman to be seen without looking breathtaking. The four of them headed into the city after breakfast, with a small escort of only four guards, including the royal families' personal favorites Charles and Philip. They did some looking around at various shops, the city was rather large, and they managed to spend most of the time in places Virgil hadn't seen last time he was here.

The day was filled with laughter, Virgil felt comfortable around the Diamonds, and they accepted him into their intimate fold without question. That evening after dinner, Virgil was watching a movie with Alexa in her room. She had her devices plugged into an outlet, that had a magicite attached to it, much like a battery. A knock came at the door and a guard entered reporting Lord Aseril would like to speak with him.

"If you take too long I'm going to pass out," Alexa smiled. "We can do breakfast and say goodbyes in the morning," she offered.

Virgil followed the Paladin down the hall. Two guards were posted outside Aseril's door, they knocked and Aseril called out, "Send him in."

Virgil entered Aseril's room and the door was closed behind him. The Grand Prytanis was dressed in casual satin pajama bottoms, with a fancy button up top. Aseril had been reading what looked like reports, he was seated in a chair, sipping on a glass of scotch.

"Take a seat Virgil," Aseril offered.

Virgil sat in the chair positioned next to him, facing the Grand Prytanis.

"We haven't had a chance to talk, Seraph to Seraph," Aseril said casually. Virgil wasn't sure where this was headed, he felt tense. "How is college going?" He asked unexpectedly.

"Fine sir," Virgil nodded.

"I am sorry about any inconvenience the extra security for the Chalice has brought to your Chapter," Aseril said with heart felt meaning. "It is an unfair burden, that no group of young men should have to bear."

"We won the Tournament," Virgil shrugged, "That's what happens. We're grateful for the extra protection, any inconvenience takes a back seat to that."

Aseril nodded taking a sip on his drink and setting it down. "We have made plans to smuggle the Chalice out of Bay Valley, and bring it back to Alexandros for safe keeping," Aseril said blatantly.

Virgil was shocked. "I thought, we were supposed to keep it until the next tournament?" Virgil asked. "Gabriel and Magnus asked you to keep it here, I remember they said you insisted we bring it to Bay Valley."

"Yes well at the time it was the best course of action," Aseril replied.

"It no longer is?" Virgil asked. "What is going on? Are my people in danger?" Virgil asked already knowing the answer.

"Your people have been in danger since the moment you touched the Chalice in June," Aseril said ominously. "We have reports that the Death Dealers are going to make a move on the Chalice. We have plans to move it the first of December," Aseril said slowly and deliberately.

"That's a month away," Virgil nodded, "When is the attack supposed to happen?" he asked concerned.

"We don't have an exact date," Aseril sounded tired. He usually seemed so put together, for the first time Virgil noticed that he was an aging man, and the burden of being the leader of the Paladins, and a Seraph must be a heavy weight. "But security will be strengthened for the remaining weeks the Chalice is on your campus grounds."

"Why do the Death Dealers want the Chalice of Immortals?" Virgil asked. "Is it because it is the key to the Oath of the Paladin?" He wondered. The ritual could help people with just a little Judge blood, Awaken to their latent powers, and bring out their Devil Arms.

"No," Aseril said simply taking a long drink. "The Judges could just grant us a new cup if our current one was destroyed to help us make more Nephilim warriors."

The silence between them became heavy. No? Virgil thought, then why did they want the Chalice so badly!?

"Do you know what the prophecy surrounding the War of Ragnorak entails?" Aseril asked Virgil.

"Sort of," Virgil thought hard. "Diablos is supposed to rise again, to attempt to destroy the world, right?"

"Yes," Aseril nodded. "The Creator ripped Diablos' essence into three pieces, and the husk of the Devil's body turned to stone. Once the binds imprisoning Diablos energy are destroyed, he will be free from his prison, and come to Earth to destroy humanity," Aseril spoke, with just the flames of a fire in the background.

"What does that have to do with the Chalice?" Virgil asked.

"The Chalice was originally safeguarded by the Judges. The Nephilim were being recruited by the Death Dealer Loiken, to his new order. The Judges came to the remaining Nephilim opposing the Death Dealers. As a show of their faith in the Nephilim, they brought the Chalice as a covenant of their alliance. To the public, the Chalice has always been as a symbol of the Paladins birth. In reality, our entire order was created for the sole purpose of safeguarding that golden cup," Aseril sighed. "Only a handful of people know what I'm about to tell you. You must keep this secret from everyone, Alexa, your brothers, *everyone.*"

"I promise I won't repeat this to anyone. Tell me Aseril, why is that cup so damned important?" Virgil asked on the edge of his seat.

"The Chalice of Immortals, holds a third of Diablos spirit, trapped within," Aseril said quietly. "If destroyed, only two pieces would remain in keeping him trapped in the Ever After," Aseril finished going quiet. Silence came between them, the roar of the fire suddenly getting louder as neither spoke.

Virgil was stunned. This was bigger than he had originally thought. This had nothing to do with the Death Dealers wanting to disrupt some Paladin ritual. The Death Dealers were trying to resurrect Diablos! A piece of his heart was sitting in the Omega house, begging every Fallen, demon, and evil Nephilim to storm its grounds, and be named the hero who helped liberate a third of their Master's binds. The Omegas were in mortal danger.

"My brothers, they are in peril," Virgil said out loud.

"They've been in danger for months," Aseril shook his head. "You just now realize how great that threat is."

"Why can't we move it now, tonight?" Virgil asked. "It would be safe in Alexandrus."

"If we were to move it tonight, Bay Valley would be attacked, and destroyed," Aseril said sadly. "Our forces would be decimated, and the Chalice obliterated, giving Diablos a portion of his power back. We need to wait," Aseril didn't leave room for arguing. "It's not safe anywhere," Aseril spat. "They have the Gatekeeper. The Fifth Seraph can create portals anywhere, bypassing barriers. With that warrior the Fallen can virtually send an army, anywhere, anytime."

Virgil had grown quiet, reflecting on the bombshell Aseril had dropped on him. Aseril was unusually kind towards him throughout all of it, it was a lot to take in. Virgil got up to leave, Aseril was leaning against the mantle staring into the flames.

Aseril said aloud, "You're not ready to face Sethos." Aseril's words were unexpected. Virgil stopped, turning to face the older warrior. "He's arguably tied for the most powerful of the Seraphs, with Artreyu," Aseril turned around looking Virgil in the eyes, he hadn't noticed before, they looked like sapphires. "Either way, be careful out there boy. Sometimes discretion, is the better part of valor. Walking away from a foe who is your greater today, can give you an opportunity to grow and take them out tomorrow."

Virgil left his room in a daze. Alexa was sleeping, so Virgil went to his guest room and laid in his bed. He had a hard time falling asleep. He wanted this semester to be over, so the Chalice could be taken from his fraternity house. As selfish as it was to want the Chalice in Alexandros, Virgil feared for his brothers, and Bay Valley, so strongly he felt sick to his stomach. If the Death Dealers came for it, they'd come in full force, with the strength to wipe out all who opposed them. December couldn't come fast enough.

# Chapter 13 Virgil's First Date

Sunday's meeting Virgil was unusually quiet, he had a lot on his mind and didn't feel like participating. Vahn was extremely stressed and relieved at the same time, the candidates were being Initiated on Friday, and his role as Hegemon would be completed. They were having a party Friday night, the last one of the semester. It was a list party, to keep the numbers down, every brother could only invite two people, every candidate could invite five. Virgil thought of inviting Amariana, if the date went well. Virgil had to give a Jeweled Officer report every meeting now, just like the older brothers he looked up to. It felt strange being one of them. Finally, it was Magnus' turn to speak, which meant the meeting was ending.

"Thank you to Tarek for the Mixer with the ladies this week. Taking it upon yourself to start new Traditions for this Chapter, that is leadership," Magnus said to the room, but he was facing and looking at Tarek.

"Aww thanks babe," Tarek grinned earning a few chuckles from the room.

Magnus rolled his eyes and moved on. "This is the final week of pledging, I know everyone feels like Rho class are already brothers, but they still have to go through the ritual on Friday. I'd like to say that the Chapter has really come together, I feel like we are more united now, than we have been in a while. That is in no small part thanks to Rho class either," Magnus pointed out. "These guys are going to be our brothers, so keep that in mind these last few days, and don't be rough on them. We have a Paladin assignment, involving some demon activity in Pinconning. I told Internationals that we were too busy to handle it this week. Next meeting when Rho class is here we'll discuss it, and have more volunteers to handle it. Besides that, we have something going on with the fraternity every night this week so let's adjourn this meeting!"

Virgil went back to his room after the meeting, he had some Bio Stats to study. He'd had an amazing time in Alexandros, he almost didn't want to leave Sunday afternoon when Alexa and Sybil walked Virgil back to the stone archway in the castle gardens. Alexa told Virgil he'd made her birthday, and Sybil urged him to visit again, affectionately she said, "We love having you around." Virgil had a chance to speak with Sybil that morning. He was still shaken by the information Aseril had shared. Sybil made tea for both of them, and sat down to talk with him. She didn't ask what was bothering him. She was never nosy. She was optimistic, and hopeful, and driven. She made Virgil feel better just by talking with her, and soon she had him laughing, and the dark knowledge that was plaguing his mind, fell away to his subconscious. Sybil was a great woman; he could see her being the next leader of the Paladins in her father's stead. Virgil hadn't seen Aseril since the night before, he didn't feel the need to say goodbye, they didn't have that kind of relationship. Virgil shared a heartfelt goodbye with Alexa and Sybil, and Virgil promised to come back over winter break from the university.

Trying to concentrate on learning the formulas, his mind wandered to his insipient date with Amariana. He was nervous, and not even sure why'd she'd agreed to go out with him. Amariana was so hard to read. She was so good to look at though. Virgil tried not to look too much, as to not make it obvious. Her beauty was almost intoxicating, Virgil wanted her like he'd never wanted anything. He needed to make sure he did everything to ensure tomorrow ran smoothly. Virgil brushed the Bio Stats book to the side and made a list of things to do tomorrow. Buy some flowers, iron his dress shirt, dress pants, and make reservations at Lucky's Steak House. Virgil was getting tired, he quickly set his alarm, and drained some of his energy into his Optimum. It would be full within the week. Virgil had a sickening feeling he'd need more than he could ever hope to store.

Monday afternoon Virgil had picked up some flowers and had them sitting in some water in his room. The candidates were stressing out, they only had three days till their Final Test, and four days till they were brothers. Virgil walked down to the second floor, to check out the pledge dorms. Aidan, Flynn, Homer, Tucker, Colton and Vinny were hanging out. They all jumped up when they saw Virgil walk in. Their Dreamstones were around their necks, Friday they'd get their fraternity rings and no longer have to carry the big magicite.

"Please, you don't have to stand when I walk in," Virgil sighed rolling his eyes.

"You're a Jeweled Officer," Colton pointed out. "Vahn told us to follow all the rules for the last few days of pledging, as to not piss off any brothers, and get ourselves brought up for removal."

"Well I'm one of the brothers you don't have to call sir, or stand up for," Virgil insisted.

"What are you up to?" Vinny asked Virgil.

"Killing some time, came down to see who was around," Virgil smiled.

"Take a seat," Homer offered.

"Has everyone had Virgil's interview yet?" Colton asked.

"Not yet," Aidan said.

"He's one of the best," Tucker boasted. Virgil just rolled his eyes.

"That's what I've heard," Flynn nodded adjusting his ball cap. "We never got to have our interview dude. We should try to do that sometime, I don't mind if it's after I'm a brother even," Flynn offered.

235

"I wouldn't make you do that," Virgil waved him off.

"No, I want to get to know you," Flynn insisted. "Everyone only ever says great things, and you did kind of saved my life at Tradition." Flynn smiled as did the other guys. Tradition had been a wild time, for the candidates who'd been taken and for those who had to wait behind. They had become closer as friends and bonded as Omegas.

"We can have an interview," Virgil nodded. "How about we do both of you together?" Virgil asked Aidan and Flynn. "Are you guys okay with that?" Virgil asked.

They looked at each other and laughed. "I'm closer with Flynn than anyone else," Aidan admitted. "We've done a few interviews together already so that will work."

"Awesome," Virgil nodded. "How are you doing Lil?" Virgil asked.

"Good," Vinny nodded. "Just studying the Omega guide, getting ready for Thursday night."

"Don't worry Vinny, Vahn won't let you down," Virgil told him. "He has prepared you all, I have faith in Rho class."

"I know," Vinny nodded. "I believe in my family." Vinny smiled meaning Vahn and Virgil, and Rho class, at the same time.

"What's up bitches!" Louie cried out walking into the room with Nev and Nolan. Nolan was carrying several bags from various clothing stores.

The candidates all jumped up once more, until Nolan signaled for them to sit.

"Wow Nolan, nice haircut," Virgil commented. Nolan always looked a little nerdy, he didn't spend money on grooming. This was the first time he'd seen his hair styled.

"What cha got there Nolan?" Colton asked.

"Clothes, hair product, cologne," Nolan said simply. "I'm going to take my stuff upstairs, see ya guys," Nolan waved goodbye to the pledges. Louie and Nev came and sat down.

"What's up with Nolan spending money on clothes?" Virgil asked Louie. "That guy pinches pennies tighter than Scrooge McDuck."

"He came to *us* for help," Louie said to Virgil, a smile spreading across his face.

Virgil raised an eyebrow and looked to Nev. Nev nodded and added, "Nolan said to us, I put aside money in my budget for the two of you. I want you to take me out, get me some good clothes, a haircut, the works. Whatever you think will get me a lady's attention," Nev said doing his best impression of Nolan.

"Wow," Virgil remarked. That was a big deal.

"Nev and I came together, and Nolan became our love child," Louie jested. "With our help we're going to help this boy get laid on Friday night!" Louie cheered laughing hard.

"I really hope so," Nev nodded, "Nolan wants to lose his V card, and he didn't stand a chance with his nerdy haircut, and thrift store clothes."

"I'm gonna help him get ready Friday night," Louie said, "And Nev's going to coach him on what to say."

"I knew we'd get him someday!" Nev laughed, and high fived Louie.

"We're meeting up for the group project on Thursday," Louie informed Virgil.

"We are?" Virgil groaned. They were working on a presentation with two other people.

"Hey! You're the one who wanted to be in charge," Louie added.

"Really?" Virgil asked not remembering that part.

"Oh yeah!" Louie laughed. "It wasn't me volunteering to be the leader!" Louie pointed out. "You said you'd rather be the group leader, so you knew it would be A worthy," Louie sighed.

"Oh yeah, that sounds like me," Virgil sighed.

"Yeah! You're such a snob when it comes to academics," Louie pointed out.

"I am not!" Virgil said, getting red in the face.

"Normally you're a very open and accepting guy," Louie shrugged. "But get you in a classroom," Louie shook his head. Then raised his hand moving to the edge of his seat. "Pick me, pick me professor! I know the answer!" Louie shouted out in mock imitation of Virgil, and started laughing uncontrollably.

"I don't do that!" Virgil protested.

"Nev! You have a class with him!" Louie shouted coughing hard. "Am I not telling the truth?" Louie asked.

All eyes turned to Nev, he got red in the face, "Damn it Louie!" Nev said nervous. "Why'd you have to drag me into it?" he asked.

"Well?" Louie asked.

"You do get pretty excited when you want the professor to call on you," Nev said carefully looking Virgil full on.

Virgil's mouth dropped open. "Which is like EVERY time the professor calls on the room for a response," Louie added.

"Whatever," Virgil sighed.

"I can see that," Vinny nodded.

"Vinny!" Virgil shouted and the room started laughing.

"We're just giving you shit," Louie said giving Virgil a playful shove. "You know we love your face!"

"Yeah yeah," Virgil rolled his eyes. Homer and Tucker got up to leave after a few more minutes, Virgil hadn't gotten a chance to spend much time with them lately. He felt bad, they had grown to be some of his favorites in the fraternity. "Hey!" Virgil said to them as they made their goodbyes. "I want to hang out, soon!"

"Me too!" Tucker nodded. "I miss you man."

"We'll have to set something up once pledging is over," Homer nodded.

"Let's help these guys study some," Louie suggested.

"Sure," Nev nodded. "I tutor brothers for free," he laughed. He was one of the brightest minds in the Chapter, along with Nolan, Magnus, Zender, and now Colton as well.

Virgil spent a little more time with his friends, before casually slipping out to get ready for his date. He quickly showered, and dressed, spending the most time getting his hair jusssst right. Virgil put his pea coat over his dress clothes a glowing smile on his face. Flowers in hand Virgil hurried to his vehicle. He didn't want anyone seeing him and asking him questions. Virgil came down the grand staircase to the first-floor foyer. Virgil smiled walking to the doors feeling confident he'd slipped out undetected.

A whistling sound called out and Virgil turned to see Gabriel grinning at him. "Look at you, all sharp, and dressed to the nines," Gabriel commented walking over to him from the living room. "Where are you going buddy?" Gabriel asked clapping him on the back and shaking his hand in a quick bro hug.

"On a date," Virgil admitted miserably, he got embarrassed so easily.

"Ohhh shit!" Virgil heard Louie call out from the living room causing a group of familiar laughs to echo out.

"Wrap it before you tap it!" Another brother called out. I need to get out of here, Virgil thought!

"With who?" Gabriel asked curious. "Blair?"

"One of the new girls, Amariana," Virgil said off handedly.

"Amariana?" Gabriel nodded with a grin. "Those flowers are for her?" he asked.

"Yup," Virgil nodded looking at the bouquet of roses.

"Be yourself and ask questions about her interests. If you're looking to see if you match with someone, chemistry and communication are essential," Gabriel was giving him advice and Virgil nodded.

"Thanks Gabriel," Virgil said, "I'll remember that."

"You're a great guy, just try not to talk her ear off," Gabriel smiled straightening Virgil's tie.

Virgil's eyebrows raised and he laughed. "Thanks!"

"I love ya kid," Gabriel patted his shoulder, "Have fun tonight!" Virgil nodded and quickly turned to head out the door before more brothers could come to speak with him.

"Good luck!" Gabriel called out as the door closed behind him.

Virgil drove over to campus housing, Amariana was living in the town homes, the upper classmen housing to the west of the education buildings, close to Greek Housing. Virgil parked his Blazer and walked around looking for her building. Virgil found her place and rang the doorbell. A woman he didn't know answered the door. She was Asian, short, with long dark hair. She smiled and welcomed Virgil into the kitchen. These dorms had four bedrooms upstairs, with the living space on the first floor. Amariana's roommate went upstairs. Virgil stood in the kitchen looking around, sweat beginning to bead on his forehead.

Amariana came down the staircase looking more impressive than he'd ever seen her. She was wearing a black skirt, with a matching top, and a small jacket over that. Her mild Latina complexion was accented perfectly with subtle makeup, shadowing around her emerald eyes made her gaze striking. Her dark natural curls were more tamed. Amariana came into the kitchen, owning the room, and Virgil could do little more than stand and stare.

"You brought me flowers?" Amariana asked surprised.

"Yes!" Virgil said blinking and handing them to her. "You look amazing Amariana," Virgil said stupidly.

"That's sweet," she said softly taking them from Virgil. "No one's ever gotten me flowers before." She got out something to put them in, and placed them on the kitchen table. "Thank you," Amariana said to Virgil.

Virgil nodded, "You're welcome. Are you ready to head out?" he asked her.

"Yes sir," Amariana nodded. Virgil was quick to open the door for her. It was a short walk back to his Blazer, the sun had set, and the November air was cold. "You look great by the way," Amariana said warmly to Virgil.

"Really?" Virgil asked an involuntary cocky grin spreading across his face.

"Oh whatever!" Amariana cried out. "You know you look good!" She sighed.

Virgil opened the door for her, "It is nice to hear you say so," Virgil admitted.

Virgil quickly got in and started the vehicle back up. It was already warm, so it kicked out heat, making it comfortable. The drive to Wilder Road was ten minutes. He knew his way around the small city and could drive without much thought.

"Where are we headed tonight?" Amariana asked.

"Lucky's, it's a steak house," Virgil said. "But they have sea food, burgers, sandwiches, and some Italian."

"Sounds good to me," Amariana replied.

"What kind of music do you like?" Virgil asked fiddling with the radio.

"Haven't listened to much music lately," Amariana said thinking about it. "I guess I like the older stuff, compared to what is being made today."

"I agree," Virgil nodded finding a song. "So where'd you grow up?" Virgil asked.

"I grew up in Chicago with my grandma. My mom died giving birth to me," Amariana answered with a detached expression. "I was raised by my grandmother, but when I was eleven, she passed away as well. Then I went into foster care. I ran away within in a few months, and I lived on my own for a while," Amariana finished open ended, and Virgil wasn't sure how to respond.

"That sounds tough," Virgil said sadly.

Amariana shrugged. "Most people experience suffering, and hardships. It's just a part of life."

"You made it through," Virgil pointed out. "Now you're at a University, getting an education, most people would call that a triumph of perseverance."

"I guess," the corners of her mouth rising. "What about you? Where'd you grow up?"

"In Caseville, Michigan. I was adopted when I was a baby, by a very loving couple," Virgil replied with enthusiasm. "I have the best mom in the world! She's supportive, understanding, and so open about stuff. I've always felt comfortable, and safe with her," Virgil laughed.

"What about your dad?" Amariana asked.

"He died of cancer a few years back," Virgil frowned. "He was a great dad. Mom's handled it pretty well. Sometimes I think I'm the only reason she held it together though. There are times I see her looking off, with a deep sadness, it hurts me to know I can't do anything to take that away," Virgil felt sad.

"You're sweet," Amariana smiled, it reached her eyes and they danced. "Sounds like you had a nice childhood."

"I did," Virgil smiled.

They asked each other some more random questions, arriving at the restaurant what felt like instantly. They went inside to sit down and continue their conversation. "Why'd you choose Bay Valley?" Amariana asked him.

"Well I always wanted to go to U of M," Virgil smiled. "I don't have rich parents though, and didn't feel like going into debt for eternity, so I looked at some other places. I was going to go to Grand Valley, though one-night, half way into my senior year, I suddenly realized how far that was from home. I started looking at places that were closer, and Bay Valley offered me a full ride scholarship for my academics, so it was a simple choice."

"You're here on a full ride?" Amariana asked impressed.

"Yeah well, we'll see how long that lasts," Virgil laughed. "You have to keep a 3.5 GPA, the standards are high." They got some waters and ordered, Amariana was getting shrimp scampi, and Virgil was getting chicken alfredo.

"So Amariana, tell me more about you," Virgil said looking across the table, batting his eyelashes, eyes resting on the splendor that was her face.

"Stop," Amariana rolled her eyes.

"What?" Virgil asked innocently.

"Don't look at me, like that," Amariana looked away shyly.

"Okay, I'm sorry," Virgil offered.

"Well what do you want to know?" She asked pulling her glass closer, twirling the straw around, the ice clinking against the cup.

"Why did you come to Bay Valley?" Virgil asked her. "Where were you before you came here?"

Amariana seemed like she was thinking, she took a drink of her water, looked up at him and swallowed. "I came here because it was cheaper than most places in the state. I wasn't anywhere special before here," she answered leaving no invitation for further prodding.

"What is your Devil Arms?" Virgil asked having been curious about it for a while.

Amariana rubbed her hand nervously, "Does it matter?" she asked.

Virgil was surprised, most people were usually eager to speak of their Devil Arms, boasting with pride. "No I guess not," Virgil smiled. "I'd like you even if you didn't have one," he said meaning it.

"What made you join the Alphas?" Virgil asked. "Was it your Devil Arms?" Her Devil Arms was blue, the symbol was in the shape of a sword. "You're a Pureborn right? You got your Devil Arms without the Oath of the Paladin," Virgil knew he was right.

"Yes," Amariana nodded. "I never knew I was Nephilim. Even after what happened when I was eleven, I didn't know what I was, just that I was a freak. My Devil Arms appeared when I was a few years later. I joined the Alphas by accident really, though it's nice to be around other Nephilim women," Amariana seemed to genuinely feel that way as she smiled brightly when talking about the sisters.

"What happened? How did you find out so young?" Virgil asked wanting to know what this story was, she mentioned it twice now.

Amariana's face fell, "I'd rather not say," she said apprehensively. "I've actually never told anyone about it, I'm surprised I even mentioned it to you."

"Well this is our first date," Virgil nodded, "We should keep the tone light. If you ever want to talk though, I'll always be here to listen to you," Virgil beamed brightly.

"Thanks," Amariana smiled softly tucking hair behind her ear. Virgil bit his lip, he'd seen her do that same thing a few times before, it drove him crazy, he wanted to run his hands through her thick curly locks.

Their food was delicious, Amariana complimented it, and Virgil knew he'd made the right choice on location. Though Amariana was usually guarded, and tense, tonight Virgil was getting to see more. She seemed to be trying. Virgil didn't feel any of the cold resistance she'd given off. Amariana had this, very assured way of handling herself, like she knew she was a badass, and didn't need cues of validation from others. Virgil wished he had that kind of confidence. Virgil was always drawn to women with strong personalities. Perhaps because he'd been taught women are equals or greater than men, never less than.

"What would you like to do after this?" Amariana asked.

"I figured we could go for an evening stroll on the Riverwalk," Virgil suggested after he'd finished chewing. "Down by the Saginaw River, they've put a lot of money into keeping that path up for the community. At night all the street lights are lit up, you can walk either side, and look across at the other path, it's really nice."

"Alright," Amariana nodded.

Virgil paid their bill, tipped the server, and they were off into the night. Virgil was feeling more relaxed than he'd felt at the beginning of the date. Amariana wasn't overly talkative, Virgil had a bad habit of talking too much, especially if he was nervous. She didn't seem to mind, she listened politely to him rambling as they drove across town.

"Sorry," Virgil apologized as they pulled up to the Riverwalk. "Gabriel told me not to talk your ear off, and I'm doing just that."

"It's dangling, but hanging on," Amariana joked making Virgil laugh nervously. "I'm enjoying your company," she said surprising him.

"Thanks," Virgil got embarrassed, "I'm glad. Your fun to be around," he blurted out.

"Really?" Amariana asked surprised. "You don't think I'm too quiet, or harsh?"

Virgil chose his words carefully. "I think it takes time to get to know someone, and it's not good to make assumptions of other people."

"Good answer," Amariana smirked and they got out.

It was cold, they agreed they'd only go for a short stroll. Amariana took Virgil's arm and they walked towards a small bridge down the way.

"I'm surprised you don't have a girlfriend," Amariana said to Virgil making him frown.

"Why?" Virgil laughed nervously. "I'm surprised *you* don't have a boyfriend!" Virgil said putting it back on her.

"Fair enough," Amariana conceded.

"My fraternity is having a party this weekend," Virgil said wanting to change the subject. "Would you like to come as my date?" Virgil offered.

"You mean like, together?" Amariana asked.

"Yeah, if you want too," Virgil shrugged. "If you'd rather just hang out as friends after tonight, we can leave it at that," Virgil said placing the decision on Amariana.

Amariana was quiet, they had reached the bridge, she stopped, turning to stare out over the water. "I'll go with you," Amariana turned to Virgil. "Let's just, take things slow, okay? I'm not really, experienced, with this whole dating thing," Amariana said nervously.

"Neither am I," Virgil laughed spreading his arms out. "We can take things slow! We're just getting to know each other. I want to spend more time with you," Virgil admitted feeling hot.

"Maybe," Amariana teased bobbing her head slightly, "If you're lucky."

Virgil raised his eyebrows and they both started laughing. Virgil drove them back to campus. He walked her to her dorm, wondering what would happen.

"Thanks for dinner, I had fun tonight," Amariana said turning to him at her door.

"Me too," Virgil smiled. "I'll pick you up on Friday?" he asked.

"Alright," Amariana nodded. They stood there, staring at each other, Virgil wondered if he should lean in and kiss her, he wanted to, more than anything. He'd been wanting to kiss her all night. She turned to the door before he could move, walking inside, he watched her go with regret. Their eyes locked, and Virgil's heart skipped a beat.

"Goodnight Virgil," Amariana said softly, her emerald eyes taking his breath away.

# Chapter 14 Rho Class Initiation

Virgil woke up with a grin on his face. Amariana was the first thought he had, he was still riding an emotional high from their date. She'd agreed to go with him to Rho's initiation party, like *together*. They were sure to draw a lot of attention. Virgil wondered if it was moving things too quickly being around his brothers, and her sisters like that. Amariana had stressed she wanted to take things slow, neither of them were into PDA, and they hadn't even kissed yet. Virgil thought about that for a moment, this woman has me grinning like an idiot and she didn't even kiss me? He shook his head, this is bad, he decided, getting dressed for the day. I've got it bad.

Tuesday night after Brotherhood, everyone stood around in the living room conversing with one another. The candidates were all anxious about Thursday night, their Final Test, and ready to be done with pledging. Virgil tried to walk around and chit chat with the pledges. Jeramiah had changed since Tradition, he'd gained confidence, and skill with his Devil Arms.

"I'd be down for a mission or two," Jeramiah bragged to Virgil and a few others. He was still an anxious guy, though that was beginning to dissipate since he'd gotten more comfortable with everyone. Virgil was glad to see he had gained some confidence.

Zane was still as slick, and cool, as he was the first day Virgil helped him move onto campus. Zane had women hanging around him everywhere he went on campus. He was more of the loner in Rho class, he wasn't particularly close with any one guy, but he could get along with just about everybody. Zane had clicked well with Virgil's close group. Virgil had a chance to talk with him briefly. "Thanks for all the support through this process," Zane said emotionally to Virgil, when it was just the two of them talking.

"I haven't been there more than any other brother," Virgil laughed. "We've only hung out a couple times."

"A couple times yeah," Zane nodded. "You're definitely one of my favorites bro."

"Why is that?" Virgil asked.

"Because you give a shit," Zane said looking Virgil in the eyes. "I can talk to you about my problems, and I can just see that you're listening, that you're hearing, that you *care!* Not many people seem to care enough anymore," Zane had a disappointed look as he said it.

"Hey," Virgil said placing his hand on his shoulder, "We're brothers. And all the brothers of Omega, we look out for each other."

"I'll always have your back Virgil," Zane said clasping Virgil on the shoulder his words thick with emotion. "I promise you that frater."

"Thank you, Zane," Virgil was touched he didn't know what to say back. "And I'll always have yours," Virgil promised. Louie arrived before anymore could be said.

"Let me scooch on in there," Louie said wiggling Virgil right out of his spot. "Don't hog all the pledges now," Louie said to Virgil shooing him off. "I want a chance to talk with Zane."

"We can talk Louie," Zane chuckled smiling brightly. Louie was one of the brothers Zane liked the most.

Virgil mingled with Tucker for a minute, he kind of felt like an adopted Lil to Virgil. Tucker's Big, Buck, didn't come around much anymore, he was close to graduating and looking at grad schools out of state. Tucker wasn't the kind of guy to need a Big to guide him, he was that guy in the crowd everyone laughed with, because he was such a goofball. He didn't have a problem finding people. "Dude I am so not ready for Thursday!" Tucker laughed.

"You haven't been studying?" Virgil asked concerned.

"Haven't had the time, been swamped with studying for tests and papers," Tucker sighed. "I'm going to study tonight; Rho class is hanging out to study together."

"You've got to put education first," Virgil nodded. "That's smart Tucker. You'll be fine," Virgil assured him. "Believe in your Hegemon, believe in your pledge class."

"We can still be friends, if I don't get in…right?" Tucker asked sincerely, he was nervous. Virgil thought he was joking and started to smile and laugh, he looked into his friend's brown eyes, and saw raw emotion reflected.

"Tucker," Virgil said his eyes getting a little wet as well, "We will be friends with or without Omega!" Virgil said fiercely. "If you fail the test, I'll still be over at your house twice a week for video games, cards, or to invite you over to Blair's."

"Good," Tucker looked relieved.

"We're friends," Virgil said placing his arm around Tucker in a side hug. "I don't abandon friends. Not the great one's anyway," he joked with a wink.

"You're probably the brother I'm closest with," Tucker admitted, "Louie and you," he nodded.

"Since our interview?" Virgil asked.

"Yup," Tucker nodded. "Everything changed for me that night. I started to care about the fraternity. I got serious about pledging, about Rho class, about the Paladin stuff. You guys are really something else," Tucker smiled.

"Whatever!" Virgil laughed. "Homer and you are going to be some of the greats!" Virgil stated. "Both of you have got talent, easily some of the best fighters in the Chapter."

"You think so?" Tucker got excited.

"Duh!" Virgil said obnoxiously earning an eye roll from Tucker.

"What are you doing after this?" Birdy came up to Virgil.

"I don't know," Virgil shrugged.

"We're going to Blair's to chill," Birdy said bobbing his head. "Ready to go?" he asked.

Virgil laughed, "Isn't that what we do every night?"

"Yeah so?" Birdy shrugged. "You don't have to come, I was just offering," he said.

"No!" Virgil cried out. "I wanna go!"

"That's what I thought," Birdy grabbed Virgil in a headlock and messed up his hair.

"Let me go Birdy! Birdy! Knock it off!" Virgil cried out. He was losing his temper, "ALEC!" Virgil shouted, and Birdy let go. No one called him by his real name.

"Alec?" Tucker laughed.

"Jeez, I was just messing around," Birdy said startled.

"I HATE having my hair touched," Virgil said irritated.

252

"I know," Birdy nodded laughing.

"Yeah yeah," Virgil huffed, and they walked together out to Birdy's car.

Birdy waited till they had gotten into the car, so he could speak his mind freely and not be overheard. He said kind of pouty, "Everyone likes you the best."

"What are you talking about?" Virgil sighed knowing exactly what he was talking about.

Birdy flew down the Omega's driveway heading to the apartment complex down the road from campus. "All the candidates, they've really taken a shine to you," Birdy nodded. "Most said you're their favorite brother during the Brotherhood tonight."

Virgil had been as surprised as Birdy. They'd been asked questions to answer to the brotherhood, and in turn they got to ask questions of the brothers, everyone had to tell the truth. When asked who their favorite was, and they had to explain their choices, three of the eleven candidates had said Virgil was their favorite. Louie had three candidates say he was their favorite as well. He had felt humbled by their words. He hadn't been looking for anything more from them than to spend time getting to know them, as friends. For them to have taken such a shine to him…

People look to others for direction in who they are. People act as a mirror reflecting for one to better see one's self, at least how others are perceiving them. What the pledges had showed Virgil of himself reflected back, it had made his heart race, and his eyes mist. He didn't feel like he deserved it. "That changes though, from being a pledge, to when you become abrother," Virgil pointed out trying to deflect the attention. "I don't think the same of the brothers now, as when I was a pledge."

"Yeah," Birdy nodded. "You still won 'em all over," he said with a jealous sting to his words.

"Okay," Virgil drew out the word. "What do you want me to say? I'm sorry?" he asked.

"No," Birdy shook his head. "I was just hurt a little, I guess. I was expecting a few more to say I was their favorite. Made me realize how much effort you put in with the pledges. I'm definitely going to do more with the next pledge class."

"I think you're a great brother Birdy," Virgil told him. "You're one of the best friends I've ever had."

"Aww," Birdy smiled. "I'm one of YOUR favorites, aren't I?" he asked.

"Yesss, Birdy," Virgil sighed rolling his eyes.

"I thought so," Birdy nodded his head confidently.

Wednesday afternoon Virgil ran into Aidan and Flynn at the Omega house and found room in the pledge dorms for an interview. Flynn had thinning blond hair, a slightly large nose, with a quiet demeanor. Flynn was a kind, selfless, and a giving individual. He owned a truck, and said he'd never drive anything else. He loved to hunt and fish. Flynn enjoyed country music and country living. Flynn loved sports, and women. Flynn didn't talk much at first. Aidan was close with Flynn, and their rapport helped to keep Flynn loosened up.

Aidan was like Vahn in some ways, physically you could tell they were family. Aidan's face was narrower, with a sharper nose. They even had similar Devil Arms. Aidan was into football, Vahn liked soccer. Vahn was better at English and the arts, Aidan like Science and Math. Virgil found Aidan to be more sensitive than Vahn. Aidan had this outward exterior of being a hard ass, but after talking with him Virgil realized it was a show. Aidan was a caring individual with a big heart. Aidan and Flynn were both great additions to the Chapter.

Wednesday night was the Final Supper, a dinner with the candidates and the Chapter. Raven and Lilly showed up instantly taking the spotlight. The brothers lavished attention and praise on them, so much so Raven got a little red in the face. After everyone got up to make sure they got their hug in, Raven had to wave the boys off to say something to the room.

"I feel bad I haven't been around as much," Raven admitted. "I took a Jeweled Officer position in the Alphas and haven't had as much time for the Omegas. You boys are my first family though, and every time I come around, you all remind me how loving it is here. The girls are great, but it's never the same kind of open and accepting feeling you get from being around the Omega boys," Raven told the brothers. Virgil was so moved by her words he had to fight his way through the crowd for his turn, finally giving her a tight hug.

"I miss you Raven," Virgil said warmly hugging her. "How have you been?"

"Good!" Raven replied cheerfully. "I'm still working at Scissor Wizards, cutting hair. Classes are going well," Raven nodded. "I'm on track to graduate in a year and a half with the rest of Lambda, five years isn't bad."

"Not at all," Virgil agreed.

"Hey!" Lilly barked playfully at Virgil with a stern expression. "Where's my hello hug!"

"Oh! So sorry!" Virgil said quickly giving her one.

"That's better!" Lilly laughed her stern expression softening.

"How have you been?" Virgil asked.

"Lovely," Lilly smiled with a bat of her eye lashes. "I'm getting into my teaching classes now, so it's actually fun. I feel like I'm getting something out of these classes, unlike the Gen Eds. Mu and I are doing as good as ever too. How are you honey?"

"Doing great!" Virgil nodded. "Classes are going good, Lil brother's about to be initiated, hopefully," Virgil added.

Lilly crossed her fingers, "Hopefully! I'm keeping my prayers up for them!"

"Aww," Colton and Aidan said from close by coming over to give her a hug.

"I made you boys snacks for tonight!" Lilly told Colton and Aidan. "I want to stay and study with you guys some. Figured I could learn a thing or two."

"You should!" Colton nodded. "We'd love the company Lilly!"

"Hey!" Mu barked walking in the room at that minute. "Don't get too friendly with my woman *pledge*!"

"Sorry," Colton responded, uncharacteristically red from embarrassment.

Mu burst out laughing, "I'm just kidding. I want Lilly to do more stuff with the guys. I'm not worried."

"Aww thanks babe," Lilly smiled rubbing Mu's arms. They were such a cute couple. Mu was a tall man, all legs, with dark hair and glasses. Lilly was short, coming up to Mu's chest, she had bright red hair, and a permanent friendly smile.

Virgil sat next to his Lil, Vinny. "What kind of food should I get you?"

"Whatever, I like it all," Vinny said in a huff his arms crossed not looking at Virgil.

"Is…something wrong?" Virgil asked confused.

"We haven't done much, these past few weeks," Vinny said to Virgil.

"WHAT?" Virgil exclaimed surprised this was where he was going.

"You're Rho class's favorite brother, and I feel like we haven't even got to spend much time together," Vinny said sadly.

"Vinny!" Virgil exclaimed. "You're one of my favorite people, you're my Lil! We've hung out, plenty of times. Yeah, in the beginning we were seeing each other every day, that's when you were still new! You were commuting and crashing here, and just still getting to know the brothers." At first Vinny had been shy, but once Vinny broke through his own block, he became a social butterfly, and everyone adored him. "Vinny, it didn't take you long to find confidence in yourself, you got popular with everyone quick. You didn't need to hang out with me every night because you had everyone else."

"Yeah but, I liked hanging out with you," Vinny told him honestly.

Aww, Virgil said to himself. "We'll hang out," Virgil promised smiling like an idiot. "Okay? I promise you Vinny, I'll prioritize spending some time with you above even Blair, Louie, and Birdy. And we can do whatever you like."

"Okay," Vinny nodded grinning back. "Sounds good."

"We good?" Virgil asked, his Lil eyebrows knitting together.

Vinny smiled, his voice as gravelly as ever as he drawled out, "Yeahhhh, we're good," Vinny nodded. "Now go fill up my plate before all the good chicken is taken!" Vinny insisted.

Vinny was a foodie, Virgil smirked and got in line to get his Lil some dinner.

Virgil brought the plate back to the table. "What no fruits, salads, or desserts?" Vinny asked.

"I didn't want the food to touch," Virgil said making the plate how he made his.

"It's all going to touch! Fill the next one up please!" Vinny demanded motioning for Virgil to go back.

Virgil's jaw dropped. He wants me to get him a second plate before I get myself one? Vahn immediately announced, "Bigs! Serve your Lils! This is *their* night!" Vahn was staring Virgil down as he spoke. Virgil rolled his eyes and did as he was told, getting Vinny an overflowing second plate that Virgil would have had to be tortured into eating.

After dinner Rho class went to the pledge dorms to study for the rest of the night, just Vahn, Lilly and Raven were allowed, though Louie managed to sneak in. He laid on a bottom bunk and put a blanket over himself with just his face sticking out. He studied with Rho class and none of them said a word. It took Vahn almost an hour to realize there was twelve pledges instead of eleven, probably because Louie kept shouting out answers, and Vahn recognized his voice. Louie was promptly kicked out much to Rho class' hysterical amusement.

"Sorry to see you go Louie," Colton said sadly.

Thursday night was the Final Test. Virgil had ordered Vinny a sweatshirt and long-sleeved shirt with Omega on them, bringing them to the test. Virgil gathered with the other brothers out in the woods. The small pond they had brothers jump into was cold, Zender and Vahn used a few fire spells to heat up the water. Funny how being on the other side seemed to make things go quicker. Virgil remembered waiting in a line with Omicron class, Jagger was their hardass Pylortes keeping them quiet. Looking back Virgil liked that Jagger was so strict with them. It made them take it more seriously. Virgil appreciated what Jagger was trying to do. To instill a sense of seriousness about these things, the traditions. Virgil didn't hang out with Jagger often, though he had an immense amount of respect for him.

Vinny was first up. Virgil wondered what he was thinking, looking out into the dark, being asked to jump into the murky water below. Vinny fearlessly leapt from the edge into the water below, Virgil felt so proud. Vinny had grown so much in such a short amount of time.

Vinny came out of the water, shivering and in tighty whities. Virgil came running out to him, to give him clothes to change into. "You come to us naked and cold," Virgil said to his Lil. "We clothe you, and bring you into our embrace, that you may grow warm, and strong."

Vinny started crying and hugged Virgil. "Alright, alright, Vinny get dressed," Jace grumbled, "Everyone else back into hiding! Ten more to go!" Jace was just as giddy.

That night after the Final Test Vinny didn't want to leave Virgil's side. He had a large grin on his face. "I've never felt prouder," Vinny said to Virgil as they walked back to the Omega house. Virgil sat in Louie's room that night, with Nev, Nolan, Vinny, Birdie, Cameron, and Brett. They talked about the pledging process and all the memories they'd made together. Tarek, Vahn, Gabriel, Brody, and Rowan came in after a while, and the group went downstairs to play some games together. The brothers couldn't have been happier.

Friday's Initiation the Upsilon Delta Chapter had eleven more brothers, bringing their Active roster to thirty-five! That would be the most they'd had since Virgil had been in. Dante and Doc came for the Initiation! They were both staying the night to bask in the candidate's glory at the Initiation Party. Professor Ramuh, and Gabriel's older brother Ezekiel came to the Initiation as well. It felt great having the older fraters there, it made it feel…special. It showed just how far back their fraternity stretched. The Sweethearts, Raven and Lilly, were anxious to come inside once the ceremony was over to welcome the new brothers. Lots of pictures were taken and gifts were exchanged between the Bigs and Lils.

Vinny handed him the paddle and Virgil was stunned. It was definitely in the top two of Rho class, Colton's paddle for Magnus was the only competition. Virgil could tell Vinny spent a lot of money on this. Virgil looked down at the paddle, he realized he'd always keep this. Virgil would always cherish it, and every time he looked at it, he'd think of Vinny, and how proud he was to be his friend. Virgil embraced Vinny. "I love you Lil Bro," Virgil said quietly.

"Thanks Virgil," Vinny said with heart.

After Initiation, Rho class headed out to dinner before the party. Virgil broke off from the group after dinner. He'd invited Blair and Amariana as his two guests for the party. Blair practically had a key to the house. Virgil wanted to escort Amariana personally. He drove the five minutes to campus and parked his Blazer. Strolling to Amariana's house with confidence in his step, a smile on his face, he was in a great mood.

Virgil knocked on the door and a blond answered the door.

"Hi!" She said with a big smile looking Virgil over with interest.

"Is Amariana home?" he asked her.

"I'll check," she asked leaving the door open slightly heading upstairs. She came back down, "She'll be right there," the blond nodded. "I didn't think she was here! Never makes a sound in her room, and I never see her leave once she goes in," the blond mused.

"Virgil," Amariana said coming down the stairs. Her hair was placed back with pins, she'd put some kind of product in, and her natural wavy hair was curlier than normal. She was in jeans and a lacy fancy top. She had a winter coat in her hands. He thought she looked stunning.

"Amariana," Virgil said breathlessly.

"Where are you two headed?" The blond roommate asked.

"My fraternity is having a party tonight," Virgil said.

"Oh, I want to go!" The blond sighed.

"It's a small, list only party, or else I'd invite you!" Virgil felt bad, he wasn't trying to be pretentious. "Next big party we have I'll tell Amariana to invite you!" Virgil tried to recover.

"Sounds good to me," the blond nodded, and they headed out.

"She likes you," Amariana said as they walked to his Blazer.

"Whatever!" Virgil rolled his eyes. "Every guy with good taste likes you."

Amariana gave Virgil a look and he regretted being sassy. "I'm glad you're coming over," Virgil said warmly. "I'm excited for you to meet some of my friends."

"We're just friends," Amariana said gently the corners of her mouth peaking up.

"I know," Virgil nodded acting like he didn't notice. "We're taking things slow, you're just my friend Amariana," he spoke aloud a large grin spreading across his face. He opened the passenger door for her.

"Why did you grin so big when you said that?" Amariana asked him her eyes narrowing.

"I don't know," Virgil laughed nervously. "I honestly can't help from smiling when I'm around you."

Amariana flushed and didn't say anything else. The drive was quick, just long enough to listen to a song on the radio, and exchange small talk about their weeks. Amariana was always so vague when talking about herself! Virgil did his best to be interested in her week, there were only so many questions he could ask. She would give short answers, and he'd ask a similar question, to get more info, just to get the same answer. Amariana was visibly more comfortable when the focus of conversation was on him. Virgil still had progress to make in getting her to open up, though he felt like they were making ground.

As they approached the Omega house, Amariana started squirming in her seat, visibly getting upset.

"What's wrong?" Virgil quickly asked.

"Are you sure…it's okay for me to be here?" Amariana asked him looking like she wanted to jump out the window.

"Of course, why wouldn't it be?" Virgil asked raising his eyebrow, she was acting strange.

"I don't know," Amariana wouldn't meet his gaze. They were approaching the gates to the Omega house.

"Amariana listen, you're my guest!" Virgil exclaimed. "I am a brother of the Omegas, and I like to think my word holds clout among my Chapter. I am saying you're welcome here. Anyone has a problem with that, they'll have a problem with me," Virgil smirked flexing his right hand so she'd she Ragnorak's symbol. She looked visibly relieved and they drove onto Omega grounds without a hitch.

"Easy Paladin," Amariana joked, and they both started laughing.

The Omega house was already full of guests by the time they arrived. Zender and Mu were working the door, making sure only the people on the list went inside the Omega mansion. The Paladins stationed there remained on the upper floors for the evening, staying out of sight, still guarding the Chalice. Less than a month till that cursed thing is finally gone Virgil thought. The house had over a hundred people present, small compared to their usual parties of over four hundred people. Most of the people present were friendly acquaintances Virgil knew well, though a decent amount of the guests were friends of Rho class.

Doc and his sister Gina were some of the first people Virgil ran into. "Hey cupcake!" Doc warmly welcomed Virgil.

"Hey Doc, Hi Gina," Virgil smiled.

"Amari!" Gina greeted her pledge sister and gave Amariana a hug. Amariana looked uncomfortable, though she didn't push Gina away, she didn't like being touched, or getting a lot of attention.

"Wow! Who is this?" Doc asked Virgil wiggling his eyebrows. "Dare I say…a special friend of yours?" Doc asked in a sultry voice elbowing Virgil with animated facial expressions.

Kill me now. "We're just friends," Virgil insisted.

"Hmmmhm," Doc drawled out.

A group of Alpha sisters came through at that moment, TK, Selene, Raven, and Terra. They quickly came over to Amariana and Gina. "Amari!" TK called out happily. "Didn't know you'd be here tonight! Who'd you come with?" Virgil furrowed his eyebrows; TK had some of the sharpest intuition of anyone that he'd ever met. She was playing dumb, unconvincingly.

"I came with Virgil," Amariana said plainly and confidently.

The group of girls all turned to stare at Virgil, he wanted to stand behind Doc to hide.

The girls broke out into rapid, low volume speech, they grabbed Amariana and dragged her away. They were all asking her questions at the same time, Virgil heard his name get dropped. Amariana turned her head to give Virgil an atypical, frightened look, he thought her eyes said she'd rather be with him, he smiled back at her and winked.

"You lucky bastard," Doc laughed placing his arm on Virgil leaning on him.

"Knock it off!" Virgil sighed shrugging his arm off. "We haven't even kissed yet man."

"Ohhh, she's one of those types," Doc nodded. "You're in it for the long haul?" he asked.

"I don't know, we're just getting to know each other," Virgil said defensively.

"Easy there princess, I'm sorry. You must really like this girl," Doc mused his voice losing its teasing edge. "Good for you."

"Thanks," Virgil nodded. "I should look for my Lil, I haven't seen him yet. I'll talk with you more later," Virgil said to Doc.

"I'm coming back up in a few weeks for Family Weekend," Doc said to Virgil. "I miss you buddy; we need to hang out."

"We will," Virgil nodded. "I miss ya too. Later Doc."

Virgil found Vinny, he was in the kitchen with Vahn, Gabriel, Tarek, and several random people Virgil didn't know. Vinny was just finishing doing a shot with the brothers.

"Another!" Vinny cheered sloppily.

"Hey bud, how you feeling?" Virgil asked worried.

"GREAT!" Vinny beamed stumbling a little then leaning against the counter. Oh great, he's already drunk, Virgil thought. He'd have to keep a close eye on him.

"I think you should pace yourself," Virgil suggested.

"I'm winning that banner!" Vinny asserted. "My Big won it, my Grand Big won it, it's mine!" Vinny declared angrily slamming his cup on the counter.

"Don't make that your goal," Virgil recommended to his friend. "It's not worth it."

"That was your goal!" Vinny insisted. Vahn gave Virgil a scathing look.

Virgil rolled his eyes regretting his words. "Yeah and I was a drunken fool, who blacked out," Virgil said thinking back. "I don't remember more than the first half hour of the party. It's just a banner bud," Virgil pointed out. After that night Virgil never over drank again, he didn't like blacking out, it wasn't fun.

"Yup, and its mine," Vinny said proudly.

"I'm winning that banner!" Jeramiah announced coming into the kitchen with his Big Jagger following close by. Jeramiah had gotten sloppy and was carrying a big mug, that he waved around, sloshing some alcohol onto the floor.

"Nope," Vinny shook his head confidently at his pledge brother.

"You don't even drink!" Virgil laughed at Vinny.

"Yeah I do! You gave me my first beer remember!" Vinny pointed out. Virgil frowned, please Creator let me not have corrupted one of your better creations.

"He's fine!" Gabriel waved off Virgil's concerns.

"I'm watching him Virgil," Vahn winked. "I'll help keep an eye on him for us," Vahn said warmly. Virgil sighed, he trusted Vahn unconditionally, so he nodded and dropped it.

Virgil kept moving on wanting to see the rest of Rho class. Homer was stumbling in the next room, bragging to a friend of his about the Omegas. Flynn was passed out in a chair, poor Tucker was passed out in the living room, and he'd pissed himself! Virgil felt so bad he asked a few brothers to help him get Tucker up to the pledge dorms. How had these guys gotten so trashed so quickly? Six weeks of no drinking could really lower one's tolerance.

Back on the first floor Virgil was mingling looking for Amariana when he saw Terra grab Jagger and take him to the bathroom. Several people had seen this, including TK. Virgil and TK shared a look and TK came to wait by the door. Soon there was a line, so TK knocked three times and was forced to opened it. Terra and Jagger were making out hardcore.

"Occupied!" Terra shouted slamming the door shut. TK just laughed and shook her head. "She finally went for it," TK muttered to herself. "She's had a thing for him since winter," TK explained to Virgil. "It just took a little alcohol for her to finally get the guts to make a move."

Virgil couldn't find Amariana so he started looking for Vinny. Flynn had pissed his pants, along with Cameron who was passed out next to him. Brett and Nigel were going strong and had started singing, horribly, swaying with their drinks in their hands.

"Rho class!" Louie said laughing pointing at Flynn and Cameron. "More like Piss class!" Louie joked laughing hard.

Virgil found Vinny on the second floor in the hallway. His arms were tangled in Helene's hair, they were in a tight embrace, sucking each other's faces off.

"Wow!" Virgil expressed surprise catching them. "Sorry! I was just looking to make sure you're safe!"

"I'm safe," Vinny grinned devilishly.

"Hi," Helene said meekly bright red in the face.

Virgil nodded feeling embarrassed and quickly walked away. Virgil saw Blair cozied up to Vahn in a private corner, the two looking way more intimate than friends. What was up with people tonight, he laughed to himself, the lovebug is biting everyone! Virgil went to the stairs, Amariana was walking down them, with a Paladin from Internationals following close by.

"Hey Virgil," Amariana said sweetly.

"Virgil," the Paladin said, "This woman was snooping around on the upper floors," the Paladin said harshly. "I escorted her down and told her not to go to the upper floors again."

"If you wanted a tour you should've asked!" Virgil laughed.

"Sorry," Amariana shrugged. "I was looking for you, and then I just sort of started walking around. This fraternity house is amazing!" She remarked. "I'll meet you downstairs," she said walking away.

The Paladin eyed her suspiciously as she left them. He waited till she was out of earshot and then said, "She was snooping Virgil."

"What does that mean?" Virgil asked the Paladin.

"I don't know. Keep an eye on her," the Paladin warned and walked back upstairs.

Virgil brushed the Paladin's concerns aside and went back to the party. Vinny was the last man standing, with some help from Virgil and Vahn, though they kept that to themselves. They'd secretly been only giving him pop, with no alcohol, since before midnight. Vahn said to Virgil, "We look after our own," with a wink. Amariana ended up having fun, she had opened up and was making people laugh. It was nice to see this side of her. Virgil took her back home when the party started winding down.

Virgil walked with her to her door. "Thank you for coming to the party," Virgil beamed. "I enjoyed seeing you again."

"Thank you, I had a good time," Amariana nodded. They stood at her door, and silence came between them, a chasm that started to grow with each passing second. What do I say?!

"Well, I'll see you again soon?" Virgil asked as he didn't know the answer.

"I'd like that," Amariana said not meeting his eyes, a hand in her hair.

They stood there a few more seconds, Virgil's heart was starting to hammer in his chest. "Goodnight Amari," Virgil said smiling brightly and they exchanged an awkward hug. Virgil went to turn away and Amariana grabbed his arm, she turned him back to her, and she was staring into his eyes intensely, her gemstone green eyes dancing with hidden thoughts.

"Why are you interested in me?" Amariana asked and Virgil smirked laughing a little. "What?" she asked her eyebrows furrowing and becoming defensive she crossed her arms backing up slightly. "Why did you laugh?" she asked in a huff.

"I don't know," Virgil laughed again. There was definitely a *wrong* answer to this question. He couldn't say he liked her because her eyes sparkled like gemstones, or because her hair smelled so good it made him want to tangle his hands in it, or that he liked her sexy bubble butt. Those were all lines that would move this to an immediate ending. He didn't want that.

"What?" she asked again irritated.

"I don't know!" Virgil answered honestly. "I can't explain why people develop attraction. I don't know why I like you. All I know is I do. When I look at you, you make me feel...special, and excited, nervous, and hopeful, and kind of scared. No one has ever made me feel this way Amari, and I," Virgil was interrupted. Amariana stepped forward and placed her lips on his. His eyes went big, hers were closed. Virgil closed his eyes, and they shared their first kiss. Virgil moved his mouth against hers passionately, not wanting it to end. She kissed him with a forcefulness that let him know, she felt the same desire he did. It felt incredible, everything Virgil had imagined. That's when Amariana stopped, and stepped back, staring into his eyes.

"Let's spend more time together," Amariana suggested. Virgil nodded his head vigorously like a bobble head idiot. "Goodnight handsome," Amariana smiled shyly. She walked inside closing the door slowly, staring into his eyes and smiling softly.

"Sweet dreams Amari," Virgil whispered before the door closed.

# Chapter 15 A Mission Gone Wrong

Sunday's meeting was Rho class' first as brothers, and it was a busy one. All eleven men showed up, there were thirty brothers present. The new brothers had recovered and were looking forward to a week of *not* being pledges. Virgil was looking forward to spending more time with Amariana. They were doing homework together tomorrow in the food court. Virgil saw all the brothers in the room, and wished he was sitting next to a friend, passing notes. Being the Grammateus, Virgil sat alone at the head of the room with Magnus, operating the overhead, and taking notes for the Chapter.

Vahn stood up for his Hegemon report, he had three trivia questions prepared, about the fraternity, and King size candy bars. "The Hegemon is the Chapter Educator," Vahn said, "That's so much more than overseeing the pledging process. The Hegemon is supposed to put on workshops to advance in the levels of the fraternal order and continue to educate the brothers. Next week I'll have more questions and more candy. I'm working on the workshops and will be asking different brothers to prepare different necessary presentations," Vahn spoke with a smile, he'd accomplished a lot, more than most Hegemons.

Tarek stood up next for the Hypopthetes report, "Now that Vahn's done with Rho class, I'm in charge of Brotherhood for the Chapter. This week we are going bowling, Thursday night, be there!" Tarek grinned. "Oh, and I am working on getting us some community service hours at a local AFC facility, maybe bingo, and some cards and music," Tarek sat down.

"Thank you, Tarek, colorful as always," Magnus nodded. "We appreciate all you do for us. Epiprytanis?" Magnus asked looking at Gabriel, the right hand of the Chapter.

Gabriel stood up, "We are having elections in a couple weeks. Think about what positions you want, Rho class, sorry but you're out this round."

"Dang it!" Colton cursed. "Just kidding I knew that already," he nodded.

"We encourage you to come vote," Gabriel stressed to the new brothers. "Also, Selene is putting on Family Weekend in a couple weeks. She is working hard to make it special so everyone, please, invite your folks to come visit the fraternity house. Siblings, and any close family are welcome within reason. Jagger!" Gabriel called out.

"What?" Jagger grinned sheepishly.

"You dirty bastard, don't invite your twenty cousins over!" Gabriel joked laughing hard. "We don't have the room!"

"My brother is an Omega at Northern," Jagger said proudly. "And both my parents are Nephilim. I'd just invite them," Jagger said simply.

"That sounds awesome!" Louie cried out. "I want to meet them. I'm bringing my folks out! Jo and Tu would love to meet all my brothers!"

"Are you finished?" Magnus asked Gabriel impatiently wanting the meeting to end.

"Yes sir," Gabriel nodded sitting down.

Magnus stood up, he was serious, holding a folder in his hands, his eyes said he was ready to work. "On the Paladin side of things, we have three requests this week," Magnus announced, "Including the one from last week that we didn't have time to handle, these HAVE to get completed!" The room groaned. This was supposed to be an easy week for everyone. They only had a few weeks left until the end of the semester. Everyone was worried about grades at this time of the year, it was make or break time.

"Internationals can't spare the manpower, and things are looking bleak on all fronts. We need to clear out some areas, and take some of the enemy's footholds back," Magnus said passionately. "I am expecting everyone to volunteer for at least *one* request!" Magnus demanded. "The Paladins from the Capital have taken care of a few missions for us lately. We need to fulfill our duties to the people of this area," Magnus was stern and commanding, leaving no room for arguing. "I have some dossiers drawn up on each request, and a sign-up sheet at the bottom. We'll pass it around, and at the end of the meeting the three groups will break up and determine when they can go." Magnus passed the three papers to his right, and each brother quickly flipped through, picking one and passing it on. "No more than three Rho class to an operation," he added quickly, "We can't have a pure Rho class squad tackling an assignment by themselves, we'd be short eleven brothers," Magnus smirked.

"Burn!" Louie laughed.

"We'd make it," Colton told his Big with confidence.

"Neither Lambda or Omicron were allowed to go by themselves," Magnus said to Colton. "Rho class is no different. We're better when we're blended," he smiled.

Virgil passed up the opportunity to sign first, he wanted to look at the final teams, and missions, then decide. As it got passed around the brothers completed the rest of their business. At the end every brother had an opportunity to speak to the room, Rho class took the time to reflect on their feelings. Bigs took the opportunity to give their Lil's official nicknames.

"Piss class," Louie laughed.

"Hey now!" Tucker said getting huffy sitting next to Louie.

"Five of you bastards pissed your pants!" Louie started laughing uncontrollably.

"Louie," Magnus sighed the meeting going off track for the seemingly hundredth time.

"Actually, it was six," Colton smiled sheepishly.

"What?" Several brothers asked at once.

"Yeah…my bad," Colton laughed, and the room erupted into laughter.

After everyone had a turn, the meeting was at a close. Virgil had to choose which group to join. One assignment was in Pinconning, another in West Branch, and one was in an abandoned town, more of an intersection really, near his hometown of Caseville. It was between Pigeon and Sebewaing, at a place called Kilmanagh. Virgil was concerned something sinister was going on so close to home, he read the description. A request came through to Internationals; police had been called numerous times to the location over the past few weeks. Residents close by swore that lights were on in the building at night, and figures could be seen inside. The authorities had discovered nothing, but a cop from Pigeon was an Epsilon class Paladin, meaning he was non-active in the order, and a registered Nephilim. He made the call, he confirmed demonic activity, hoping some Paladins could resolve it. Birdy, Louie, Nev, Zane, Homer, and Tucker were signed up to go and Virgil signed his name as well. Nev, Zane, and Tucker were from the Thumb like Virgil, that's probably why choose it.

After the meeting the groups got together to plan, as some of the operations had people, they had to make contact with. Virgil's group had to decide a night they could make the fifty-minute drive out to the country to search this deceased town.

"How about Tuesday night?" Louie offered.

"I have classes all day Tuesday," Birdy sighed.

"I have classes early on Wednesday morning," Tucker said.

"We have Brotherhood Thursday," Homer pointed out. "Bowling sounds fun. It'll be nice to hang out with the brothers, and *not* be a pledge," Homer remarked with smirk.

"Wednesday night?" Virgil offered. "That way if we can't find anything, and the cop gets another night where stuff is happening, we can go back for a second look."

"Wednesday night works," Louie nodded. "I'm not going to a haunted ghost town twice in one week though. We go once really quick, if we don't see nothing we're done," Louie insisted. "We don't go driving back late one night when the lights are on and the windows are banging," Louie whispered with a haunted expression, he was scaring himself!

"Awesome!" Zane laughed. "This is going to be great. We got a good group," Zane said to his Rho class brothers. Zane was closer with them than most of the others. Virgil was looking forward to going out with some of his best friends at his side.

"Wednesday night it is!" Nev announced. "We'll meet in the first-floor living room round 9pm unless any of you have class till 10."

"I have class till 10," Tucker sighed.

"We'll meet at 10:15," Nev amended. "That'll put us on the road round 10:25, and we'll get there after 11pm," Nev thought out loud.

When no one protested the plan, the meeting was adjourned for their group. "See you chums later," Louie yawned heading to his bedroom and the rest followed suit, the new guys heading back to their homes. The other groups were still talking, Virgil looked at his brothers making eye contact with Vinny. He was in a group with Vahn, Spencer, Zender, Brody, Rowan, Colton, and Flynn. He was confident his brothers could handle themselves. He skipped working with the Optimum magicite, it was full now, and ready to aid him.

Monday afternoon Virgil was with Amariana sitting in a booth at the food court. They sat by themselves at the very back, their brothers and sisters came and went around them. Amariana was relaxed and conversational, she did a good job focusing on her work, taking the occasional pause to talk with Virgil. Their friends came over to say hello, it was very casual, and Virgil liked the level of comfortability he'd gained with Amariana. She was warming up to him, showing a little more of her personality. Amariana was argumentative, bold, intelligent, outspoken, and determined. She had a softer side; Virgil was working on getting to see that more often. Virgil didn't count this as an official date, things between them weren't about official dates anymore. It was about seeing how they worked together, with others, and by themselves. It'd only been a week since they started dating, however to Virgil, it felt like it'd been several weeks. Funny how having a special someone to think about, could change the perspective of everything around you.

Virgil and Amariana planned to get together Saturday night. Amariana was going to make Virgil dinner at her place. Virgil was excited, a girl had never made dinner for him before, well his mom, but that didn't count! Virgil would have to cook for her next time. It was going to be their second official date. Virgil invited Amariana to the Bowling Brotherhood Thursday, as a few sisters from the Alphas had been asked. Virgil just wanted to spend as much time with her as possible, Saturday felt like so far away.

"We'll see each other before Saturday," Amariana rolled her eyes. "That's just our next official…date," she whispered quietly.

"Good, because Saturday is too long," Virgil said causing her to smile and blush.

"Yeah?" Amariana asked looking into his eyes leaning into the table, her face closer.

"Hmh," Virgil leaned in, they were practically touching now.

"How are things going over here?" Louie asked standing at their table.

"Great Louie," Virgil said through his teeth, Amariana leaning back. "What's up?"

"I figured I'd get some Amariana time in," Louie said wiggling in next to Virgil forcing him to scoot down the booth. "I'm Louie V," Louie waved grinning ear to ear.

"I know," Amariana laughed. Louie was hard to miss in a crowd. "It is nice to officially meet you. I'm Amariana, the sisters call me Amari," she said warmly to Louie.

"Amari, love it!" Louie declared.

Homer and Tucker came over, "What are you guys doin?" They asked standing at the table.

Virgil sighed. "Studying," he said annoyed and Amariana laughed. He wanted her all to himself, and she could tell that's how he felt.

"Would you boys like to sit down?" Amariana asked.

"Hell yeah!" Homer said sitting next to Amariana, Tucker sat next to him near the end of the booth. Tucker got out some cards and they started a game of Euchre. Amariana didn't know how to play so they switched to Spoons, Virgil wanted to play Pounce, except each person needed their own deck of cards. Amariana got very into the game, fiercely fighting the men for a spoon. At the end everyone would laugh and talk about their cards. Amariana had to go to class after playing for a while. She said goodbye to everyone, and Virgil walked with her.

"You have nice friends," Amariana smiled. "I reallllly like Louie," she laughed full heartedly. "You don't meet enough people like him."

"When have you ever met someone like him? He's a one of a kind," Virgil said with fondness.

"I'm looking forward to Saturday," Amariana casually said to Virgil. "I'll let you know about Thursday."

Amariana's class was in the next building over, they were there within a few minutes.

"Feel free to text me," Virgil said to Amariana.

"I do already," Amariana said confused shaking her head at him. "Ya goof," she sighed.

"I'll see you," Virgil smiled looking down into her eyes.

"Bye Virgil," Amariana said kindly and walked into class.

The next few days were productive, Virgil spent time on his studies, and he got to have lunch with Amariana on Tuesday. They'd bumped into each other on campus, and had time to spend, so they hung out together. Wednesday night Virgil ate dinner at the fraternity house with a group of brothers. Raven had stopped by to help with dinner, she drew in many more brothers than would have normally hung around, and they had to make more food. The days were getting shorter, it was November and getting cold, especially at night. Virgil milled around the front of the fraternity house, he had on a sweatshirt, shirt, and a coat he'd used his wings in before. He had the Optimum in his pocket, it was a tight fit, but his clothing hid the bulge. The group gathered together, there were seven of them.

"Louie let's just all pile into your SUV," Birdy insisted.

"That's illegal!" Louie cried out. Louie's SUV fit five guys comfortably.

Birdy shrugged, "Two of Rho class sit in the very back, it'll work. That way we can all be together."

"We need like, a fraternity van, or a bus!" Louie sighed.

"We could just take a portal there," Virgil suggested, "Ask someone to make a portal for us to get home once we're done."

"It's not that far of a drive," Birdy said defensively. "I thought the bonding time would be good for us. Magic and technology can take something out of social interactions. Let's do this road trip!" Birdy laughed excitedly. He made a good point, it was a good bonding experience, driving as a group to a destination. It was less than an hour anyway.

Louie whined for a few more minutes, then gave into the group consensus. Everyone gave him a few dollars for gas and they hit the road. Birdy rode shotgun, acting as the absent-minded navigator. Virgil sat on the left in the back seat, Homer was in the middle, and Nev on the other side, with Tucker and Zane in the very back. Louie had good music playing, his taste was wide ranged, and he had more knowledge than most. The guys sang along, or nodded to the beat, different conversations were going, snacks and drinks were available. Virgil knew what they were going to do was serious and having this chill environment before the stress of a mission was good for morale. It was Zane, Homer, and Tucker's first assignment. Nev had gone on a few, including the big one in Flint at the beginning of the semester. Even he seemed a little on edge. Virgil felt it too, they were walking into the unknown, it could be something simple…or it could be a complete shit storm.

"I'm thinking of running for Epiprytanis," Nev said to Virgil.

"Wow," Virgil had no words. "That's, huge! I think it's a great idea. You're one of the smartest guys in the Chapter. You'd make a great second in command," Virgil offered.

"He'll have to run against the older brothers," Louie pointed out. "And they'll say he's too inexperienced to have such an important Jeweled Officer position."

"I can do it," Nev said defensively. "I don't want to do a year as Grammateus to 'get ready' for the position I want. Leadership and positions don't work like that," Nev sighed.

"I would vote for you," Zane said from the back. "You're one of the smartest guys I've ever met," Zane laughed. "I wouldn't be passing Math without ya," he admitted.

"Thanks Zane," Nev said happily.

"I'd vote for you too," Louie said. "Just want to get us prepared for the others."

"Gabriel's running for Prytanis," Birdy said from the front and the SUV went silent.

"Who told you that?" Virgil asked Birdy.

Birdy turned in his seat to look at Virgil, "A little birdy told me," Birdy grinned.

"Cut the crap," Louie snapped. "Dish the dirt! This is big! Our Hegemon is running for Prytanis?" Louie asked.

"Gabriel told Dante, Dante told me," Birdy said to a demanding Louie.

"I forget that Gabriel used to be the Hegemon," Zane remarked, "It's weird thinking of anyone else but Vahn doing that job."

"He'd make a great Prytanis," Nev said to the SUV.

"He makes a great everything," Virgil joked and everyone laughed, because it was so true. It was quiet for a few moments, Virgil spoke again, "It is weird to think of someone besides Magnus as Prytanis. He was Prytanis when I was seventeen, I'm nineteen now!" Virgil said to everyone.

"Wow!" Homer laughed. "He did it twice?" he asked.

"You turned eighteen on our first night of pledging," Louie rolled his eyes at Virgil, "He was only Prytanis for three semesters."

"Three?" Tucker asked confused.

"Buck was the elected Prytanis," Virgil explained to Tucker, surprised he didn't know this about his Big. "Buck was Mu and Nu class' Hegemon as well. Buck stepped down from his position half way into the first semester, Vahn was Epiprytanis and became Prytanis. He stepped down before the start of Omicron's Freshmen year, and Magnus took over." Virgil remembered learning about this as a pledge, that felt like so long ago, like another lifetime.

"I want to be the Hypopthetes," Louie admitted.

"Good luck getting it," Nev laughed. "EVERYONE is running for that. Jagger, Rowan, Jace, and Lamar."

"I want to be the Hypopthetes as well," Virgil added.

"See?" Nev shook his head.

"You're running for Hypopthetes?" Louie asked looking at Virgil in his rearview mirror.

"Maybe not this election, maybe next year," Virgil said honestly. "I was only Grammatues for less than a semester. I would like to be elected to my own term, then step into one of the bigger roles," Virgil said.

"Good idea," Louie nodded.

"Have you thought of running for Prytanis?" Zane asked Virgil.

"No!" Virgil laughed. "Never, and especially not against Gabriel."

"I think you'd be a great Prytanis," Zane said softly.

"Me too," Homer agreed.

"I want to be a leader, not in that way though," Virgil tried to explain. "The president, he's the business side of the Chapter, the face of our group. All the responsibility, rests on his shoulders. I'd rather be one of the important generals, than the guy calling all the shots," Virgil shrugged. "I want to be the brother who is in charge of scholastic education, brotherhoods, and retreats. The brother people can lean on and talk to when they are hurting. The Hypopthetes is my dream job," Virgil said passionately.

"You already are those things," Tucker shrugged. "To me anyway. I don't think you need to be Hypopthetes, to be the kind of brother you want to be, to this Chapter."

"Thank you Tucker," Virgil was moved.

"The Hypopthetes is third in command," Homer said remembering. "You'd be a good third in command Virgil," Homer said kindly.

"Hey!" Louie barked from the front. "You want to walk there?" Louie threatened Homer. "Virgil already said he isn't running; I'm expecting you to vote for me!" Louie half joked.

They drove up M-25 for twenty-five minutes. The Thumb of Michigan was a flat area mostly utilized for farming. Houses were few and far between outside of the small villages, with just a few bigger towns in the Thumb. Large wind turbines were built throughout the Thumb, the red lights on them lit up at night. The fields they drove by were a sea of towering metal wind fans, built to store energy created by the planet. After passing through Sebewaing, the fun free conversation died down when they approached their destination.

Kilmanagh was nothing more than a three-way intersection. An old saloon, built in the late 1800s was the only real fixture, across from a small administration building that once served as a post office. There weren't many other buildings, this hadn't been a large village, now less than twenty people lived within the area. The saloon had been a bar, restaurant, and hotel, as was customary back in the days of expansion in the country before the industrial revolution, and the advancements in transportation. It was a condemned, decrepit building, Virgil wasn't sure if it was safe to go inside without demons. There was a dark unsettling feeling to the place, and Virgil's brothers sensed it as well. The front door showed evidence of being recently used.

"In and out, if we don't see anything we're leaving," Louie told the group.

"I'm not leaving till we figure out what's going on here," Zane asserted.

"Homer, sounds like you're going to be one pledge brother short before the nights over!" Louie joked to Homer walking next to him.

"You wouldn't leave us here?" Zane laughed hoping Louie couldn't be serious.

"If I come back out I'm leaving, you've got five seconds to join me," Louie said a little too seriously.

"Louie give me the keys," Birdy demanded.

"No!" Louie laughed.

"Yes!" Birdy insisted, "You just threatened to leave us if we didn't get back in the SUV five seconds after you. I've seen you run when you're scared, we don't stand a chance of making it back before you take off!" Birdy's voice was so sullen and serious Virgil started laughing.

"Fine," Louie sighed throwing his keys to Birdy.

"Birdy please do not get abducted or kidnapped, then we'll be screwed," Virgil said to his friend.

"Quiet!" Tucker yelled out.

They all went silent, as a group they approached the door. They had two flashlights; Virgil went in first. It was dark inside, the beam of artificial light illuminating a small point, casting shadows on the surroundings. Virgil sensed it, a presence, he took a deep breath and stepped inside. This had once been a proud structure, a testament to the American drive, and dreams of the past. His brothers accumulated behind him, forming a tight circle before moving forward, they were going to take this slow. Homer used the other flashlight, they walked into what would have been the main room. They hadn't spoken, it was so silent, they barely made a sound as they walked, their hearts racing. Virgil was starting to agree with Louie about leaving.

"SO, YOU'VE COME, JUST AS HE PREDICTED YOU WOULD," A deep demonic voice spoke to them from the dark, from everywhere, and yet nowhere specific.

"Who are you talking about?" Virgil asked the room.

"REDEEMER!" The demon cried out materializing before the brothers. It was a tall wraith, its form reflected a high-ranking demon, more intelligent, and powerful. A dark blade formed in its hand. The creature floated above the ground, it growled, and surged towards them.

"Ragnorak!" Virgil cried out light striking down from above, bathing the whole room in white energy, it slammed into his hand, stretching out into the Holy Blade. Virgil ran forward clashing his sword with the demon's. His brothers summoned their Devil Arms and they ran to Virgil's side. Zane circled around to the side of the demon, stabbing his wind spear into its side. Birdy did the same on the other side.

The Revenant demon howled and spun around, black energy sweeping out in a circle, knocking the men back. The demon rounded on Tucker striking out at him, Homer swung his mace, barely managing to catch the strike. The demon lashed out at Homer sending him sailing through the air landing hard on his back. The Revenant demon swung its blade at Tucker, and an ice arrow pierced its face. The demon groaned momentarily stunned.

"Virgil keep its attention," Louie shouted, "Everyone else give it all you got!" Louie instructed his friends.

Virgil ran forward striking at its exposed body with Ragnorak, inflicting massive damage. The demon rallied its focus, attacking Virgil fiercely. "Soul Reaver!" He called out his scythe blazing into existence. Virgil sent the sickle blade spinning at the demon, it parried the scythe, and Virgil stabbed Ragnorak at its exposed side. Screaming he ripped the Holy Blade through the being. The demon was so focused on Virgil it opened up its sides for the brothers to strike, they pounced on the creature, lashing out in fierce urgency. It started floating away from the group, it was weakening and needed to get a better position.

"Let's end this!" Virgil shouted running forward squeezing the handle of Ragnorak. The blade pulsed and he swung it forward, a wave of creation energy released from its surface barreling forward. It crashed into the Revenant demon who howled and slumped in the air. Zane ran forward screaming out with a warrior's spirit, he stabbed his spear through the demon's middle. At last it's strength gave out and it dissolved to the ground as ash.

"HELL YEAH!" Homer shouted jumping into the air. "Omegas saving the world!" Homer laughed out loud.

"Is that it?" Tucker asked holding onto his polearm with hesitation, he wasn't putting his weapon away so easily.

"Possibly," Birdy shrugged looking around. "It feels different in here now. You'd think that, if there was something else, it would have jumped in?" Birdy suggested.

"Should we finish searching the place?" Zane asked.

"I'm good, let's go!" Louie said urgently to the group. No one protested, and they hurried over to the exit of the building, a small sliver of light came through the opening, the night sky lit up, providing lighter than what was available in the old eerie building.

The sound of wings beating filled the air, a shadow passed over outside, something landed hard, they could feel it inside. Everyone came to a grinding halt, their Devil Arms firmly in their hands, you could hear a pin drop they grew so silent. The sound of footsteps started, growing louder, approaching them. The doors to the building were thrown wide open, bits of wood splintering and the brothers backed up. A being stood before them, tall and majestic, regal and handsome, with powerful black wings, and piercing glowing, golden eyes. Virgil had only met a Fallen Judge twice before. They were very different from a Death Dealer, there could be no mistaking the two. This Fallen *radiated* power, his aura so large and powerful it made the air thick and hard to breath in his presence. This was very dangerous…

Virgil placed himself between the brothers and the Fallen. No one spoke, the group looked to the Fallen for an indication of its intent, it hadn't lashed out, it wasn't friendly either. The Judge stepped forward, "You are the Redeemer?" The Fallen asked Virgil looking him over. "I hoped you'd come."

"You set this up?" Virgil asked him. "So, you could get a chance at Redemption?"

"Oh yes," The Fallen nodded. "I caught the scent of your power not far from here, I've been watching and observing, waiting for a chance to cross paths."

"I'll speak with you on one condition," Virgil said to the Fallen.

"That being?" the Judge asked impatiently.

"You let my brothers leave here unscathed, now," Virgil spoke with authority and power. On the inside he felt like he was shaking. "Once they are safely driving away, we can discuss what it is you seek," Virgil offered.

The Fallen laughed, the sound was so beautiful, Judge's had almost lyrical voices, it was off putting, such a peaceful sound, coming from such a malignant being. "Oh no," the Judge said coldly. "Your brothers are staying where they are. They are my guarantee that you'll do as I say," the Judge smiled.

Virgil stepped forward swinging Ragnorak, the sword glowing, the flames on Soul Reaver rising. "DON'T THREATEN ME!" Virgil screamed. "I'm NOT someone who can be bullied," he seethed through clenched teeth defiantly.

"I wasn't threatening, just making a statement," the Fallen put his hands up in a show of peace. "Give me Redemption, and I will return to Nirvana, never to bother you again," he waited for Virgil to respond.

Virgil nodded, he could at least try. Virgil concentrated on his power, gold bands of energy spiraling out from his hand, one rippled out to the Judge touching his hand. Virigl's mind was assaulted by the immortals memories. Mortals were far easier, Judges' lives were too long, their minds too complex to understand, Virgil's mind couldn't handle all of the information. It was hard to discern time, images and stories flew past, emotions colored things. This Judge was once named Zinnax, after his Fall he happily joined Diablos, taking his power and wings gladly. He'd served the God Generals faithfully, until he heard of Virgil's return. He was motivated purely by selfish gain, he hadn't learned the error of his ways, he had no remorse for the actions that had landed him in this predicament. The Judge was willing to torture and kill for this. The connection broke, the band of gold energy falling away. Virgil had made the choice not to spend power out to the Judge.

The Fallen furrowed his brow, "I don't feel any different. I expected something more," he asked surprised.

"I can't Redeem you," Virgil said sadly. "I've seen what's in your heart. I just, can't."

"Yes, you can, do it!" the Fallen demanded.

Virgil bit his lip, "No," he said not willing to discuss it further.

"The insolence of mortals!" The Judge spat a black blade materializing into his hand. "I'll have my Redemption!" The immortal leapt into the air and barreled at Virgil at blinding speeds.

Virgil's wings burst from his back, and he flew out to meet him, their blades clashed, Virgil's limbs were shaky, he'd grown exhausted after parrying just one blow! The Fallen's strength was beyond any warrior Virgil had faced, he fought with savage frenzy. Virgil feared his brothers would be torn to pieces, a Judge was far too powerful for any of them. The Fallen's sword broke past Virgil's guard, stabbing Virgil in the chest, he surged forward slamming his fist into Virgil's face. Virgil plummeted to the floor. His brothers raced to his side, ready to die defending him.

The sound of wings outside caught the group's attention, not more, Virgil begged, we can't handle another Fallen.

The Fallen turned to the door, and Artreyu stepped inside. The immortal was confused, Artreyu turned to Virgil smiling, "We really must stop meeting like this," he called out. "Perhaps next time you can invite me over for dinner like a normal friend?" Artreyu offered.

Artreyu was dressed like a royal, he had long snow-white hair, with olive skin, he was tall and lean. Artreyu's eyes had triple colored irises. The outer largest layer was a stormy grey that actually seemed to move around like thunder clouds. The inner layers of his iris were lilac, it looked like lightning strikes were happening from the outside of his eye into the black pupil. He squared off against the Judge. "I believe it is time for you to be on your way," Artreyu politely encouraged. "No need for things to go any further."

The Fallen looked at Virgil and growled. "I will have what I came for!" He yelled.

Artreyu flew forward on white wings with golden tips, he fought with the fluidity and skill of a sensei. Using his fists, he pummeled the Judge, who did his best to end the Avatar, the First Seraph. "Lunar Seal!" Artreyu commanded, rays of light zapping the immortal, sending the Judge to the ground. Artreyu's hands glowed with electricity, he concentrated his power, energy gathering. "Heaven's Wrath!" Artreyu shouted releasing his hands towards the Fallen, lightning raced forward, blasting through the Judge. The immortal recovered quickly; Virgil knew he needed to help Artreyu.

"Get out of here while you have the chance!" Virgil commanded.

"No!" Zane refused. "Not without you! I'll help you take him on!"

"Louie!" Virgil shouted. "Get everyone home! I'll fly back with Artreyu," Virgil offered.

"I'm on it!" Louie nodded grabbing the keys from Birdy and bolting for the door. The rest of the group followed, they cast back worried glances. Virgil heard Louie's vehicle drive off.

Virgil had been stabbed through his chest; the wound was healing from Ragnorak's power. Virgil surged forward, Ragnorak tightly in his hand. "AHHH!" Virgil screamed clashing blades with the Judge. Artreyu appeared instantly, moving so fast they hadn't seen him approach. Artreyu placed his hand on the Judge, a sphere of light exploding from the impact. Artreyu and Virgil began to fight in tandem. Fighting for every inch, Virgil didn't know how long he could last against such an unshakeable opponent. Artreyu managed to slip behind the Judge, and attempted to restrain him. Where Artreyu touched the Judge, light spread through his limbs. He tried to break free, but he was slowed immensely by Artreyu's power. Artreyu poured light into the Fallen, it was starting to glow out through the immortal's pores, destroying him slowly.

"Finish him!" Artreyu demanded.

Virgil yelled, Ragnoark screaming in turn. "Judgment Bolt!" The Soul Scream was unleashed, and a blast of power rocketed from the blade, it crashed into the Judge, who exploded in a shower of blue flames. Virgil was surprised and Artreyu saddened by the divine's death.

After, they were both breathing heavy. "Thank you for saving us," Virgil said with gratitude. "You always seem to arrive when I need you the most. How'd you know I was here?"

"I was in the area, and I sensed remnants of your magic, the same as the Fallen had. I respelled your mother's home, so you wouldn't be detected again. I went to check on you when I sensed you were in danger," Artreyu explained unconvincingly.

"Check on me?" Virgil asked. "You've never come for a visit."

"Glamour makes me practically invisible if I wish to be," Artreyu shrugged making it sound like he'd been to Bay Valley before.

"Dude, if you're coming by to make sure I'm alright, at least say hi," Virgil insisted.

"Perhaps I'll try that sometime," Artreyu smiled.

"Why do you care so much about me?" Virgil asked making them both feel awkward afterwards.

"It's not like that really," Artreyu shrugged looking embarrassed. "I mean, sure you're a nice guy, however I have saved you for more selfish gains," Artreyu admitted.

"Really?" Virgil asked raising his eyebrows surprised. "What did you get out of saving us tonight?" Virgil asked.

Artreyu replied, "The enemy has three Seraphs, we need you on our side."

Virgil nodded understanding, Artreyu was being honest, which is what he'd asked for. "Anything else going to jump out at us?" Virgil asked him.

"Not that I know," Artreyu shrugged. "But I'm not clairvoyant like the Oracle. I'll fly with you back to Bay Valley, if you're ready," Artreyu asked.

The flight home was relaxing. Artreyu was conversational, Virgil had never had a chance to just talk with him before. Artreyu was more proper and uptight than Virgil, he was more serious, more reserved, more intelligent. Virgil found he enjoyed speaking with the Avatar, he was far easier to get along with than Aseril. Though Artreyu was over a hundred years old, he physically looked like a teenager. Virgil felt comfortable talking to him like he was another college student, even though he was the son of Odin, King of the Judges, and the Queen of the Dark Fairies of the UnSeelie Court. Virgil got the sense Artreyu didn't get the opportunity to interact with other people like this often. They got back to the perimeter of the Omega house and they both wished they'd had more time.

"It'd be nice if we could do something sometime, when you're not saving my life," Virgil pointed out with a smirk. "Maybe game night at the fraternity house? My friends would love to have you around!"

Artreyu was taken back by this proposal, "Maybe," he offered with a small smile.

"Thanks again, for saving us, for saving me," Virgil said sincerely. "I hope to see you again soon friend. You're welcome here anytime Artreyu."

"I'm sure you'll be seeing a lot more of me in the future," Artreyu nodded. "Take care Redeemer," and he took flight leaving Virgil to ponder when they'd cross paths again.

# Chapter 16 Semi-Formal

Virgil's second date with Amariana went great, better than the first. Things were less tense, and it felt more natural being around her. At Sunday's meeting Virgil reported that their mission was a success, leaving out the part about the Fallen attacking the group. Virgil didn't want the brothers thinking it was dangerous to go on missions with him, his friends agreed to keep that part to themselves. After the meeting Virgil texted Damian and invited him over to Homer's to hang out. Virgil went with Louie to pick up Damian, and they stayed up late into the morning. Damian was starting to become friends with most of the brothers, and Virgil enjoyed how far things had come between them.

Monday afternoon Virgil was in the food court, sitting in a booth, studying with Amariana. When Virgil was sitting in Amariana's vicinity, it was impossible for him to focus on anything else. She was so beautiful to him, he didn't tell her how he perceived her, he worried she'd rebuff his compliments as cheap words to get something. Thoughts of kissing her lips came to his mind, and he smiled. Amariana raised an eyebrow still looking at her textbook, the corners of her mouth peeking up. Her eyes came to his, she knew what he was thinking about. Virgil's smiled broadened and his eyes sparkled, she rolled her eyes and looked back down.

"Virgil Pitcher, you are an incorrigible flirt!" Amariana sighed.

"I didn't say anything," Virgil said playing innocent.

"Over half of communication is body language, the actual words are only seven percent of the message," Amariana said playfully. "You didn't need to say anything, your body was doing the talking for you."

"Oh, my body talks to you?" Virgil asked batting his long curly eyelashes over his sapphire eyes. He leaned back putting his arms behind his head, doing his best to showcase the whole package.

"You're too much," Amariana laughed and looked down at her textbook.

Virgil went back to studying, for five minutes. Looking at Amariana was so much more appealing, more satisfying. He reached his foot underneath the table, gently caressing alongside Amariana's foot. She looked up at him trying hard to keep a straight face, "Are you always this flirty when you study?" Amariana asked.

"I don't usually flirt," Virgil shrugged.

"Oh, I guess I'm just lucky to get the pawing advances then," Amariana said sarcastically. "Slow your roll."

"Burn," Virgil hung his head, moving his foot back. "That one stung a little," Virgil pouted, but he did as she asked. Virgil never did well studying in a group. He was always someone who needed quiet, being alone was best, less distractions. Virgil's leg started to get massaged, the foot gently moved up his leg seductively. Virgil looked up surprised at Amariana. She was slightly flushed; her eyes were fiery.

"I do declare!" Virgil did his best to imitate a scandalized southern belle. "Is that you Amari playing footsy?" Virgil placing his hand over his mouth his eyebrows shooting up.

"Yup," Amariana admitted confidently.

"Salacious!" Virgil joked laughing. "The tortoise calling the snail slow."

"I'm sorry," Amariana said whispering in a sultry voice, "Am I not doing it right?" she asked playfully.

"You're doing great," Virgil whispered back.

"Are you two having footsy sex over here?" Louie asked out of nowhere.

Virgil and Amariana literally yelped and jumped. Louie started laughing his ass off.

"I caught you sneaky horn dogs!" Louie laughed. "Jeez," Louie shook his head. "Get a room!" He made himself laugh hysterically, Amariana got red, and Virgil got irritated.

"Go sit down," Virgil barked.

"Meow!" Louie cawed, "Someone didn't want sexy time interrupted."

"Louie!" Virgil snapped.

Louie walked over to the group of brothers he was sitting with several tables away. "I think they're having footsy sex over there!" Louie proclaimed to the group causing even non-Greeks nearby, to join in on the laughter.

"Well, that moments ruined," Virgil said sourly.

"Yup," Amariana nodded going back to studying for real.

Virgil walked Amariana to class, before they got there, she pulled him aside.

"Anyways, this is really last minute," Amariana said rushed. "I'm getting initiated this weekend, and it's our sorority's Semi-Formal. Would you like to go with me?" Amariana looked up at him, a hint of nerves could be seen beneath her guarded exterior.

"I'd love too!" Virgil was touched, and glad that she had asked him. "What color dress are you wearing?" Virgil asked.

Amariana looked uncomfortable. "I don't have any dresses," she said shyly. "Some of the sisters are taking me out after class," a look of pure dread overcame her face.

"You'll be fine!" Virgil encouraged her. "Dress shopping isn't torture," he said having never done it, and never wanting to experience the torture.

"Hmh," Amariana huffed like she didn't believe him.

"I'm looking forward to dancing with you," Virgil's eyes lit up as he said it, a grin peaking at the corners of his mouth.

"That sounds, nice," Amariana nodded. "I never got to go to a dance."

"Really?" Virgil was surprised. "Didn't you go to high school."

Amariana looked uncomfortable, "Sort of," she shrugged. "I'm going to be late for class," she tucked her hair behind her ear and looked down shyly.

"I'll text you," Virgil said already missing her. "Have a nice day Amariana."

"You too," Amariana called out as she walked away. She looked back at him, and there something was in her eyes, he wasn't used to, she stopped walking. They stood there, staring at each other. Amariana walked back, gripped his shirt, and pulled his mouth down to hers. She kissed him fiercely, unlike the previous times, she was more passionate and less restrained.

"Wow," Virgil breathed heavily when there were done, she was standing so close, her head just at his chin, she was breathing heavily as well.

"I'm looking forward to Saturday," she whispered against his chest.

"Now I don't want you to go," Virgil said wrapping his arms gently around her, then squeezing her in for an intimate hug.

Amariana started laughing and hugged him back, it felt so good, to be held, to feel…cared about. "I really need to go," Amariana said, drawing back slowly.

"Right," Virgil looked down at her, taking a deep breath, this was, so new, so exciting, he didn't feel he could get enough. "Miss you," Virgil said in a boyish, vulnerable voice, he hated himself for saying it, what the hell! Virgil yelled at himself, miss you? What an idiot!

Amariana's face softened, "Aww, I'll miss you too," she smiled genuinely her emerald eyes dancing, rewarding him with a quick peck on the lips.

She turned and walked away quickly, not looking back this time. Virgil was left watching her go, feeling better than he could ever remember being. Virgil quickly found out that over half of his Chapter was going to the Semi-Formal, it was going to be one big party. Virgil didn't have any Paladin assignments, so he focused his free time on trying to get his studies caught up. His brothers were constantly looking for him, inviting him to play some ball, or hockey, video games, or cards. You were never lonely when you were with the fraternity, it was one of his favorite parts about being a brother.

Saturday night Virgil and Amariana walked into the rented hall, down the road from campus, stunning in appearance. They turned heads, their arrival heralded excitement from their friends. They matched perfectly with her conservative, yet stylish white dress with a lacy black bosom. Virgil was wearing a black shirt, black pants, solid white tie, white suspenders, and white sock garters. There were a few guys from other fraternities on campus, a few Betas Virgil recognized. Sweetheart Raven was running the show, she'd brought her boyfriend. Gabriel was naturally TK's date; they were easily the most attractive couple there. Jagger was present with Terra, they hadn't left each other's sides since Rho class got initiated. They weren't official yet, but talk was, it would happen any day now. Tarek was there with a voluptuous and loud Alpha sister. Brody and Selene were sitting with Gabriel and TK. Vinny was Helene's date, Virgil saw them going steady soon. Zender, Lamar, Louie, Birdy, Dante, Rowan, Nev, Colton, Aidan, Tucker, Homer, Cameron, and Brett were the lucky brothers who'd been asked to attend as escorts for one of the sisters. Virgil saw Vahn as well, half surprised as Blair walked up with him. Were they into each other now?

They took a seat with Tucker, Homer, and Brett their dates were sisters Amariana was closer with and asked her to sit with them. Virgil took off his coat, Amariana started talking with her friends so he started walking around to see his friends. Virgil went over to Blair and Helene's table. Blair was sitting with Vahn, and they smiled at Virgil as he approached.

"How's it going Lil?" Vahn called out.

"Hey guys!" Virgil walked up and gave them both a quick hug. "I didn't realize you guys were coming together!" Virgil said speaking his surprise.

"We just came as friends," Blair rolled her eyes.

"I've been friends with Blair for a while," Vahn nodded. "You're not her only friend," Vahn teased.

"I know," Virgil huffed. "Anyways, this is going to be fun!" Virgil brushed it off, he was excited to be at such a fun party with so many good friends.

"We'll have to do some dancing!" Blair declared to Virgil.

"You know it!" Virgil laughed looking over to Vinny and Helene. "Hey guys!" Virgil beamed. "Well aren't you two adorable?" Virgil asked. They'd matched their outfits, and were sitting very close, it was clear they were smitten with each other.

"Thanks," Helene laughed getting red in the face.

"How are things going with Amari?" Vinny asked.

"Pretty good," Virgil nodded getting a little shy. "We've been on a few dates now."

"Bow chicka bowa!" Tarek called out walking over to them. "Sounds like things are heating up between Amari and Virgil!"

"Whatever," Virgil laughed getting red.

"Not so fun being on the spot," Helene quipped at Virgil.

Virgil looked over surprised at Helene's sassy attitude. Blair started laughing, "She's been mouthier since she started dating Vinny," Blair explained to Virgil.

"No I haven't!" Helene protested.

Virgil went back to his seat for the opening announcements. They had chicken salads, and a huge fruit bar. Drinks were being served, but only to those over twenty-one. Virgil couldn't keep his eyes off Amariana, she looked classy with her hair done up, a long curl hung off near her ear, he wanted to tuck it behind, and kiss her neck. Virgil did his best to be present with everyone else, it was challenging though. Once dinner was done, the dance music was turned on and people got up from their seats and started mingling with the other tables.

"Want to dance?" Amariana asked him.

"Sure," Virgil smiled following her lead. Virgil had danced with Amariana before, at the club in Pontiac. Back then they were little more than acquaintances. Amariana had been closed off, abrasive, and distant. Since then, she'd begun to show another side to him, he found himself longing to spend more and more time with her. Amariana was brave, she started dancing like she didn't care who was watching, and Virgil felt like he had to keep up.

"You've come a long way since that night at the club," Virgil said to her over the loud music.

"Well, it's easy to be confident with you around," Amariana replied back, she stared into his eyes, her face breaking into a smile, making him blush.

"I'm glad you invited me," Virgil said not knowing how to respond to her compliment.

"I wouldn't have wanted to come without you," Amariana laughed.

"Really?" Virgil asked surprised by her answer.

"This isn't really my thing," Amariana shrugged. "I'm not used to dressing up."

"You look…," Virgil stumbled for words, he just stared, and she rolled her eyes.

"Settle down," Amariana replied petting his shoulder and he burst out laughing.

The song ended and TK walked past, noticing them she came up and gave Virgil a big hug. "Are you two having fun?" TK asked hopefully.

"Of course!" Amariana nodded.

"What are you guys drinking?" TK asked them.

"Water," Virgil laughed.

"Oh yeah, neither of you are twenty-one," TK mused, "Come with me," TK announced grabbing Virgil's arm.

"Where are we headed?" Virgil asked.

"A little road trip to the parking lot," TK said happily. There was a small group gathered around one of the vehicles. Blair was at the center, passing out drinks to a group of their friends Dante, Birdy, Tucker, Cameron, and Homer were there.

"We came to do some shots!" TK announced.

"Right on!" Blair shouted.

"Hey Virgil!" Dante called out, coming over to give him a hug. "Haven't had a chance to talk with you yet, how have things been going?" he asked.

"Awesome," Virgil smiled feeling great. "Doing good in classes, and working," Virgil shrugged.

"Same here," Dante nodded. "I'm registered for classes next semester where I'm going, but I'm hoping to be back at Bay Valley in the fall."

"That would be awesome!" Homer called out excitedly after taking a strong shot. "We need you around more man! You're like, the craziest brother!" Homer laughed.

"Aww shucks," Dante laughed. "You're making me blush!"

"Yeah, I'm closer with you than most of the older brothers," Cameron told Dante. "Omicron is all of my favorites!" Cameron said to the guys.

"Amari girl!" Blair threw her arm around Amariana dragging her in. "We are doing shots together," Blair declared lining up a row of shots. "Virgil, get your scrawny ass in here!"

"Get me one too girl!" TK laughed.

"Shut up bitch, who invited you!" Blair joked spilling some liquor as she turned to taunt TK.

"Get your trashy ass back to pouring shots!" TK retorted making everyone laugh.

"Virgil is happier than I've ever seen him," Blair attempted at whispering to Amariana. "Take care of my boy. He's a sweetheart," Blair's tone was protective.

"Virgil really is," TK agreed. "He's the nicest Omega boy," she said to Amariana. "You're a lucky girl."

Amariana's cheeks flushed, "Thanks," she smiled. She didn't deny that they were an item, Virgil's eyebrows raised slightly. Just a few weeks ago, she would have insisted that they weren't dating, to a comment like that.

Drinks were passed around, then everyone clashed their drinks together before indulging. The group did another, then wandered back into the dance feeling looser and more relaxed. They all hit the dance floor, their energy contagious, causing everyone else to flock to the growing group. Virgil and Amariana became more focused on each other, over their friends. She was getting more handsy as they danced, and he wanted nothing more than to be alone with her, so he could kiss her. A slow song came on, and they got close, moving slowly to the music.

Amariana sighed, her head on Virgil's chest. "What?" Virgil asked.

Amariana picked up her head and looked around, "This night," Amariana remarked with a forlorn look in her eyes, "I never expected to experience anything like this," she said, almost sadly.

"What do you mean?" Virgil asked. "You didn't think we'd have fun?" Virgil's face grew clouded.

"No, I knew I'd have fun with you, and your friends," Amariana smiled weakly. "I never thought I'd get to experience things like this, in my life."

Virgil stared at her, really seeing her. Amariana was so guarded usually, what kind of past had she experienced to make her this way? Virgil folded her into his arms, "I don't know what happened to you before Bay Valley," Virgil said softly to her. "If I could, I'd take the pain away that I see inside you," Virgil said to her. "I want you to know that you can trust me, I'm here for you Amariana. Now that you're here, you don't have to go at it alone anymore. We stick together, all of us," Virgil's words were impassioned.

"Thanks Virgil," Amariana hugged him closer, they finished the song and went to take a break, sitting down at their table, sipping on their waters.

"You guys ready to head back out to the parking lot?" Birdy asked coming over to them.

"Round two?" Virgil asked with a smile.

"Round three son!" Birdy laughed.

There were more people gathered around Blair's vehicle than there were in the hall! They were singing and dancing loudly, drinks being passed around freely. Virgil shook his head, a grin spreading across his face.

"The party always seems to gravitate towards wherever Blair goes," Amariana spoke aloud Virgil's thoughts making him laugh, they walked over to the growing group.

"Blair has a certain charisma that draws people in," Virgil laughed not knowing how else to describe his friend. "She's got so much life in her, and she's not afraid to be loud, and live in the moment," Virgil smiled, there was a reason she had become his best friend. She was a lot of fun to be around.

"Amariana you bitch," Blair called out. "Your shot has been sitting there for ages, what took you so long?" Blair asked as they approached.

"This is a great Semi," Dante said to Tarek whose date was tipsy and trying hard to take him home.

"It's one of the better ones," Tarek nodded. "Sucks though all you guys aren't old enough to drink. It's cold as balls out here!" Tarek cried shivering.

"They should just let us drink inside," Dante sighed. "We don't put our guys through this."

"Because the Alphas have higher standards to adhere to!" Terra snapped interrupting everyone. They turned to stare at the President, who wore an irritated expression.

"Hey sexy!" Blair giggled nervously. Everyone went silent, it felt like they'd been caught, even the people like Tarek and TK, who were old enough to drink got quiet.

"Over half of the party is missing from in there!" Terra assertively spoke with a heated tone. "If you're underage, you shouldn't be drinking! Now everyone come back in, because the party sucks without you guys," Terra pouted.

"We'll come back inside," TK said in support of her friend. TK, and Helene along with a small group walked back in with Terra. The rest started packing up, finishing their drinks.

"I'm not going back in until I'm ready," Dante declared lighting up in retaliation.

After 11pm things hit their peak, they handed out awards to sisters, and the dance would be over by midnight. Virgil was feeling good, it seemed Amariana was as well.

Virgil found Vinny sitting with Helene and a few other couples. "Yo Vinny!" Virgil called out.

"What's up Big?" Vinny replied with a smile.

"Have you been drinking?" Virgil asked.

"Nope," Vinny said sadly, "Had to stay sober to drive Helene home."

"Aww," Helene replied, her face was flushed, she was exhausted from dancing, and talking a million miles an hour. "You're so sweet taking care of me," Helene smiled. "I'm a lucky girl," she spoke with sincerity.

"I'm a lucky guy," Vinny replied back staring deeply into her eyes.

"Hey!" Virgil called out getting their attention back. "Can I get a ride home?" Virgil asked. "Amariana and I, we've had a few," Virgil admitted. "I shouldn't drive my Blazer back to campus."

"Of course," Vinny was happy to help. "I'm giving a ride to Brett as well."

Virgil went back to Amariana, "You ready to go?" Virgil asked. "I got us a ride home," he announced proudly.

"We don't need a ride," Amariana laughed. "I can take us anywhere you want to go."

"I'm too tipsy to drive," Virgil admitted. "You can't drive us back."

"Oh, yeah," Amariana got quiet, then she recovered her expression and smiled. "Sounds good, I'm ready to go home."

The ride back in Vinny's car was fun, Brett was a riot, and Helene couldn't stop laughing. Amariana was so relaxed laughing, and joking with the others, especially Vinny, she seemed to like him. Vinny dropped them off close to Amariana's dorm.

"Goodnight guys!" Vinny called out.

"Be safe!" Brett called from the back seat.

"Shut up!" Vinny yelled at his pledge brother.

"Bye Helene!" Amariana called to her sorority sister. "Thanks Vinny, you're a real gentleman," she kissed him on the cheek, causing them to go flaming red.

"Just taking care of my Big," Vinny laughed.

Virgil and Amariana walked back to her dorm talking about the night, making it to her room, they were still laughing about the funny things that had happened.

"I'm gonna change in the bathroom," Amariana said grabbing a tank top and some shorts.

Virgil had brought some shorts and a shirt, he quickly changed out of his dress clothes, Amariana coming back shortly. She hung up her dress in the closet. Virgil was laying on the bed, looking for something to watch. Amariana slowly settled beside him. He couldn't help but turn his attention to her. She'd pulled her hair out of its pinned-up style, it now cascaded down around her.

"You are so beautiful," Virgil said breathlessly.

"Okay," Amariana sighed moving to get up, "I know where this is headed," and she wasn't having any of it.

"No!" Virgil laughed. "Just, relax," Virgil said looking into her eyes losing the playful smile. "You're so tense all of a sudden, let's just chill," Virgil suggested.

They started watching something and Amariana lay on Virgil's chest, snuggling against him. Virgil wasn't sure who made the first move, one minute they were slowly massaging one another, the next Amariana's lips were on Virgil's and they were kissing passionately. They'd both been wanting to all evening; they'd just been too reserved to start making out in front of the others. Virgil's hands moved to cup Amariana's bottom, she didn't tell him to stop, and a devilish grin crept up Virgil's lips. She felt better than he'd imagined, his pulse was racing, she pulled his shirt off, running her hands over his chest. Virgil pulled at Amariana's shirt, and she took it off, revealing a black lacy bra underneath.

Virgil's hands moved, cupping her breasts, Amariana stared down at Virgil, he looked up at her, a thousand words passed between them. She leaned down to kiss him, his hands stayed where they were. Things were becoming so heated, passion was overtaking them, they'd been fighting this for so long, in this moment they were acting on instinct and need, rather than conscious thought. Virgil's hands moved to the back of her bra, and Amariana became tense. Amariana withdrew from him, and Virgil's hands fell away.

"I'm not, ready yet," Amariana said meekly tension filling the air.

"Amariana, we don't have to do anything more," Virgil stressed. "I'm fine with just watching TV till we fall asleep. I'm sorry if I took things too far."

"You didn't," Amariana shook her head, "I think it was a little of both of us," she smirked looking down at his exposed chest. She giggled, "Wow, I got a little carried away."

"I kind of liked it," Virgil wiggled his eyebrows.

"I can tell," Amariana teased looking down, then looking back at his eyes with a smirk.

Virgil's face flamed and he rolled away to hide himself. Amariana grabbed him and rolled him back. "Don't be embarrassed," Amariana smiled.

They put their shirts back on and the heat between them cooled down. Both their pulses slowed, and the moment passed.

"Why do you call me Amariana?" she asked him after several minutes of silence. They were both starting to drift off.

"Hmm?" Virgil asked opening his eyes and looking over.

"People around here call me Amari, but not you. You still always refer to me as Amariana," she pointed out. "Why is that?"

"I don't know," Virgil shrugged not realizing he'd done that. "I guess I didn't know if I was allowed to call you that."

"You are," Amariana sighed rolling her eyes. "Are you always so proper?"

"Nope," Virgil asserted grabbing her and rolling on top of her pinning her down. "Amari," Virgil whispered breathlessly. "What are you doing to me?" he asked.

"I could ask the same," she looked up at him with a curious expression.

"Amari, I'll call you that from now on," Virgil smiled liking the way it sounded. "And I'll only call you Amariana if I'm angry or disappointed. Calling you Amari will be my way of telling you I care about you."

"I had a wonderful time with you tonight," Amari smiled.

"Me too," Virgil leaned down to kiss her gently. She held him close, the taste of her intoxicating. Virgil moved back to his spot before he lost control of himself. "I should get going," Virgil suggested, he was getting tired and wouldn't be able to keep his eyes open much longer. He got up from the bed.

"Virgil," Amari called out. He turned to see Amari with an expression he wasn't used to. She looked…vulnerable, a word that he'd never associated with such a strong woman.

"What is it?" Virgil asked coming back to the bed staring into her eyes with concern.

"Don't go," Amari pleaded her voice so low he barely heard it. "I, don't want to be alone anymore," she whispered sadly.

"You're not," Virgil told her with absolute certainty. "I'm here now," he said seriously.

"Stay the night here," Amari suggested. "We're just sleeping," she made it clear.

"That sounds nice," Virgil smiled climbing back into bed. They held onto each other and slowly drifted into sleep.

"Goodnight Virgil," Amari whispered holding onto him tightly.

"Goodnight Amari," Virgil murmured passing out, feeling complete.

# Chapter 17 Vampires Abduct Werepups

Things with Amari had changed since they'd spent the night sleeping next to each other. They'd bonded, he felt closer to her, and felt that closeness reciprocated by her actions and words. They weren't boyfriend and girlfriend, but they were more than friends now. Tuesday night for Brotherhood, they played board games and video games at the house, it was relaxed and easy going. Virgil needed the time with the brothers, and most of the Chapter showed up. Virgil had called his mom after the meeting inviting her to Family Weekend.

Sue had been overjoyed, "You've never invited me over to the fraternity house before!" Sue exclaimed. "I'm so excited to meet all these brothers, I've been hearing so much about!"

"You'll get to meet 'em all!" Virgil responded happily glad she was coming.

After 11:30pm, things were winding down, guys had class in the morning, and were heading home or to bed. Virgil got a call from Amari, he walked away from the others for some privacy.

"What are you up to?" Virgil asked after they had said hello.

"I just got out of Sisterhood," Amari said to Virgil, "I'm headed home. Would you like to come over?" she asked.

"It's almost midnight," Virgil said checking the time.

"So?" Amari countered. "Are you really going to bed right now? Or are you going to be up hanging out with your buddies?"

There was silence between them, "I'll be over shortly," Virgil said to Amari, "What would you like to do?" Virgil asked her as neutrally as possible.

"I thought we could watch a movie till we fall asleep," Amari suggested. "Then maybe go out to breakfast in the morning," she sounded excited.

"Sounds great!" Virgil said happily. "I'm going to let you go, so I can get ready, I'll text you when I'm on my way."

"See you soon," Amari said hanging up.

Virgil grinned, they'd never gone out to breakfast after sleeping next to each other, it sounded, sweet. "Aww someone's going to get their stick wet!" Louie cried out.

"Louie!" Virgil huffed. "You need to stop eavesdropping on me," Virgil sighed.

"Is she your girlfriend yet?" Louie asked eyes sparkling desperate to know.

"No," Virgil said honestly.

"Do you want her to be?" Louie asked a grin creeping up his face.

"Yeah," Virgil smiled, "I guess I do."

"Then go get her son!" Louie declared. "And tell me all about it when you get home!"

"Whatever!" Virgil exclaimed. "A gentleman doesn't kiss and tell," he affirmed.

Virgil quickly went to his to room to pack a bag for tomorrow, no one was using their bathroom, so he took a quick shower. Virgil was on the road within fifteen minutes of getting off the phone. The drive was so short he was there before the song he liked finished on the radio. He knocked on the door and walked in, closing and locking the door behind him. Virgil walked up the stairs and went to the door on the first left. Amari's door was open, she was in pajama bottoms and a tank top. He walked inside and gave her a hug, then she locked the door. They sat on her bed, flipping through Netflix.

Amari snuggled into Virgil, her hair smelled floral, she draped her arm across him, her head on his chest. His heart hammered loudly, she made him feel so special, so important, so alive, in ways he'd never felt before. They were talking about their days till they settled on something they both hadn't seen. Virgil never expected things to get where they were, he felt comfortable, maybe that was a bad thing.

"What are you thinking about?" Amari asked him her hand reaching out to caress his face.

"I was thinking that, I can't believe how lucky I am to be here, with you," Virgil said looking down into her eyes. "I thought, I am comfortable with you, in a way that makes me feel good about myself. I was considering if that was a bad thing, to feel comfortable so early," Virgil shrugged.

"You're so soft on the inside," Amari commented looking into Virgil's eyes. "Most have a little, some have a lot, but few have what you do," she said sweetly.

He leaned down and kissed her gently. Amari moved herself, so she could better reach him, she ran her hands through his hair, they fell back onto her bed together. They kissed and cuddled, soon the movie was to a point they didn't know what was going on. They turned it off and laid down, Virgil holding Amari close as they drifted off together.

In the morning Virgil awoke next to Amari, a little too happy. He quickly got up to brush his teeth, coming back into her room feeling less embarrassed. Amari woke yawning, "Morning," she sighed going to the bathroom. Virgil quickly changed while she was gone, putting his jeans on. She came back in before he put his shirt on. She pretended not to notice, so he took his time, he caught her starring at him shirtless, so he leaned back on her bed.

"Don't," Amari laughed.

"I have no idea what you're talking about," Virgil lied.

"If we start, we won't get out of here, and I'm starving," Amari admitted.

"Me too," Virgil agreed getting up and putting his shirt on, loving that her eyes watched him. "Let's go across the bridge, there are a lot of breakfast and lunch only places," he offered.

"I'd like that," Amari nodded taking her clothes to the bathroom to change.

Virgil drove them downtown. They parked and walked around, there were over a dozen restaurants within the few blocks of businesses. Virgil and Amari held hands, and walked around passing a few places, eventually settling on the Red Lion Diner. Virgil liked seeing Amari so real, she normally looked like a supermodel. Without her usual makeup, she seemed more approachable, though no less captivating. Virgil discovered she had a secret love for French toast, Virgil liked eggs over easy, with wheat toast and some tea.

After breakfast they were full and walked slowly away from the diner. It was a great day out, they both had smiles on their faces. Virgil wished they could spend the whole day together. Virgil saw Ms. Morgan's shop in the distance, it was open, though barely. Virgil wanted to take Amari there, the witch who ran the shop was wise, giving, and kind. Amari frowned when they approached the entrance.

"What are we doing here?" Amari asked strangely guarded.

"We did a mission for the woman who owns this place back in February, helped her take care of a demon in the basement. She runs a really cool shop, I figured we could look around," Virgil smiled.

They walked inside, Ms. Morgan was working on displays, rather than behind the counter. She turned when they entered and smiled brightly on seeing Virgil.

"Well hello Mr. Pitcher!" Ms. Morgan said kindly. "Good to see you again! What brings you by?" she asked.

"We came to look around, this is my friend Amariana," Virgil said introducing her.

Ms. Morgan stared at Amari intently, looking at her Devil Arms hand with curious interest, arching an eyebrow at Amari shaking her head. Amari tensed up and became uncomfortable clenching her aqua colored Devil Arms hand into a fist "We should go," Amari said to Virgil.

"Why? Amari don't be rude," Virgil asked knowing Ms. Morgan could hear them and feeling humiliated in the process.

"You didn't tell me she was a witch," Amari said defensively.

"Are you prejudice against witches?" Virgil asked surprised, "Ms. Morgan is trustworthy," Virgil insisted. Amari nodded weakly.

"Is there anything I can help you look for?" Ms. Morgan asked politely walking to her counter, she was still being hospitable, but was far more guarded than when she first greeted him. Something had happened between the two women, Virgil wished he spoke female, the secrets of the universe would be unlocked to him, and he'd be the most powerful man in existence.

"Do you have something that could help someone, relax? Like clear your mind if you're feeling stressed out, and help you concentrate? Finals are coming up," Virgil explained.

"I have some herbs you can burn, that make the atmosphere more relaxed, and clear negative energies. I make a potion that acts as an energy drink, though far more efficient, helps your mind focus, is non-habit forming, and has no negative side effects," Ms. Morgan offered.

"Okay, that stuff sounds good," Virgil nodded.

Ms. Morgan got to work getting Virgil what he requested, she wasn't very talkative, though Amari wasn't exactly making it easy. Amari hadn't said a word, and it made things awkward. Ms. Morgan rang Virgil up, and he paid for the products.

"I am glad you stopped by Virgil," Ms. Morgan said seriously as she gave him the bag, not letting go when he went to take it from her. "Have you spoken to the wolves lately?" Ms. Morgan asked Virgil her eyes staring deeply into his. His eyes reflected concern, hers were dripping with fear.

"No," Virgil shook his head feeling worried, "Last I heard they asked my Chapter for protection from the Master Vampire of the local coven, and after a vote, the Chapter turned down the request. Did something happen?" Virgil asked taking the bag and setting it down on the counter, she had his attention.

"The wolves made it clear they wouldn't submit to the vampires. Nothing happened at first, but," Ms. Morgan's eyes misted over, she looked scared.

"You can trust me," Virgil said seriously reaching across. She was powerful, he could feel her aura when they touched, it was stronger than he'd anticipated. "What's going on?" he asked.

"Two children have gone missing," Ms. Morgan whispered. "The Ulfric's children, an eleven-year-old boy, and a nine-year-old girl."

"The vampires stole Keaton's children?" Virgil asked his face falling.

"They haven't formally owned up to it yet, though I expect they'll be making demands of the wolves soon," Ms. Morgan sighed. "It doesn't look good for them," she said sadly.

"Do you have a number I could call, to reach them?" Virgil asked.

"Of course," Ms. Morgan got her business card, and wrote down Keaton's number on the back. "I wish I could do more," Ms. Morgan said sounding defeated. "There isn't a strong witch population in this area of the state. The vampires tolerate our presence here, though I fear they would force us out if they felt threatened," Ms. Morgan admitted.

"Thank you for telling me," Virgil replied solemnly. He walked towards the exit with Amari, his bag in hand.

"Virgil!" Ms. Morgan called out her eyes full of emotion. "Be careful," is all she said.

Once they were a short distance away Amari asked, "Are you going to help them?"

"The wolves," Virgil thought about it. "My brothers voted against it," he admitted.

"Then why did you ask for that number?" Amari asked concerned.

"Because, these are kids, innocent children, taken from their homes, their families," Virgil shuddered. Kids had a soft spot in his heart, only a feral monster would even register kids as a viable target. The idea of someone harming children, it boiled Virgil's blood. "He was willing to destroy, to kill, if that's what it took to protect these werepups.

"You have a soft spot for kids?" Amari asked nodding, seeming to understand a little. "I get that, but why risk yourself to help the wolves, when your own brothers don't want you to?"

They got to his Blazer and started driving back to campus. "Sometimes you have to do what you feel is right inside, even if it's different than what everyone around you is doing," Virgil explained how he felt. "I'm not the type to follow the crowd, especially if it means turning my back on the defenseless," Virgil looked over at Amari, her arms were crossed, her lips had grown skinny, like she was getting angry. "I take it you don't want me to help?" Virgil asked getting a little mad himself.

"I didn't say that," Amari huffed looking out the window.

"It seems that way," Virgil laughed irritated. "And what was that between Ms. Morgan and you? She's normally so personable, I've never seen her like that," Virgil mused.

"I just don't want you in danger like that," Amari sighed shutting down.

"Look, I don't know what I'm going to do," Virgil said to Amari not wanting to fight, things had been so perfect till they went to Ms. Morgan's. "All I know is, if there are children being harmed, or worse, and I knew about it and did nothing…something like that would eat me alive over time," Virgil gripped the steering wheel tightly. He didn't know where to start, and he knew something was about to go down soon. The radio was on low volume, the tension was still present, and they rode without talking much.

When they were pulling into campus Amari said to Virgil, "I don't get why you want to help everyone."

Virgil parked his Blazer and shut it off. "Amari, you don't need a reason to help people," his words full of passion. "Besides I don't want to help everyone, just the people who really need it. I wasn't given Ragnorak, so I could watch in safety while people around me suffer."

"You're different," Amari said simply in response. "Not bad different."

"Okay," Virgil said furrowing his eyebrows.

"I think you're sweet, incredibly naïve and idealistic," Amari sighed.

"I'm sorry," Virgil said not knowing what to say, "I'm not sure what happened between us, are we good?" he asked.

"Yes," Amari smiled leaning forward. Virgil leaned in, his lips meeting hers, she kissed him lightly and pulled back. She opened her door and got out. "I'll call you later," she smiled.

"I'm looking forward to this weekend," Virgil smiled. "I told my mom about you and she flipped out!" Virgil laughed. "She'll be excited to meet you," Virgil said laughing.

"Ohhh boy," Amari laughed. "I hope she likes me, I've never met a mom before," Amari admitted.

"She'll love you!" Virgil said warmly. "Goodbye Amari," Virgil smiled.

"Later Paladin," Amari smiled learning forward for another quick kiss. Amari turned to leave and looked back at Virgil, "Whatever you choose to do, be safe," she said before shutting the door.

Virgil drove back to his fraternity house, his thoughts were racing, he needed to think this over with a trusted friend. Virgil pulled out his cell phone.

"What's up?" Dante asked him through the phone.

"Hey Dante, hope I'm not bothering you," Virgil said apprehensively.

"Nope, just sitting down for some lunch, on break between classes. What's up buddy?" Dante asked him.

"Got a little hypothetical for ya," Virgil said nervously, "What I'm about to say stays between us, alright?"

"Dude, I won't say a word," Dante laughed. "What's the situation?" he asked, his tone implying he knew this was more than a hypothetical.

"Let's say I just found out that two werewolf pups were abducted by the vampires, to ransom the local werewolves' enslavement. Our Chapter voted to stay out of it, so I'm not supposed to do anything!" Virgil sighed frustrated.

"I'd say, in this theoretical situation," Dante said sounding wise beyond his years. "That you need to follow your gut. If inside you know you need to help those kids, then you don't need the Chapter behind you. You're a Jeweled Officer of the Chapter Virgil, you're a leader! Sometimes being a leader, means leading by example. Breaking a few rules don't mean shit if your protecting the sanctity of life. And even if you weren't, since when do we sit around waiting for permission to help people?" Dante asked making them both chuckle.

"What should I do then?" Virgil asked nervous.

"If I were you," Dante sighed. "I'd call together a few brothers you really trust, no older guys like Lambda, they'd shut it down in a heartbeat. The classes below us aren't likely to betray Omicron, we're the future leaders, and we'll be calling the shots someday. They'll respect you enough to keep quiet. Present your case, get a feel for the room, if you got enough guys, hit the road, and don't look back," Dante finished and there was silence.

"Thanks for letting me run that by you, that hypothetical situation," Virgil grinned. "I really needed a strong and steady voice for advice, I knew I could count on you to speak your mind Dante," Virgil said to his brother. "You mean a lot to me."

"Don't sweat it," Dante said with conviction. "I will always make time to help you if you're in need."

"I miss you frater," Virgil admitted making them both laugh.

"Ahh shut up!" Dante laughed. "I come around all the time, don't try to make me feel guilty!"

"I wasn't," Virgil insisted. "Thank you, Dante, for being there, I need you in this Chapter. You're an Omicron, we're not complete without you."

Dante was quiet, he wasn't the emotional kind of guy, and Virgil could tell that touched him. "You know, out of all the brothers, you encourage me to come back the most," Dante said his voice holding emotion. Virgil's face got serious. "Most people say they care, but don't show it. When you care about someone, you love so fiercely," Dante spoke from his heart. "Thank you for being there."

"We're pledge brothers!" Virgil exclaimed. "We're friends till death Dante."

"What time should I come to the Omega house for this meeting that's not happening?" Dante asked with his usual sarcastic charm.

"Maybe we can put you on speaker phone, no reason for you to make the drive unless we're springing into action," Virgil bit his lip, what he was about to do, could get him in big trouble. At the least he could get removed from his position as Grammateus, at the most…blacklisted from the scroll. Your name was literally stricken from the scroll, like you'd never signed it, like your number didn't exist. They'd never done it, in their Chapter's history.

"Are you second guessing yourself?" Dante asked.

Virgil furrowed his eyebrows, how in the hell? "How did you know?" Virgil asked making Dante laughed. "I'm worried, what if the brothers bring me up on charges?"

"Since when has that stopped you?" Dante asked. "Virgil, you doubt yourself far too often. You're too self-critical. Follow your heart, brother. You already know what you want to do, what the right thing is. You only called me, because you were looking for someone to believe in you," Dante said passionately.

"Maybe," Virgil nodded feeling Dante's words hit home. "I'm sorry I bothered you with this, I shouldn't be dragging you into this mess."

"Shut it! If you're going to fight the vampires, to get these kids back, you'll need some friends guarding your back. Truthfully, I'd kick your ass if you went without me! With just Birdy and Louie watching out for ya…" Dante and Virgil both laughed. "Louie would have run back to the car and Birdy's eyes would be glued to his phone, he'd be mid text, while you had three blood suckers draining you dry," Dante continued making them both laugh. "You need someone who's not afraid to charge in, Devil Arms first, and fight fiercely to the end."

"Let's make it out alive on this one," Virgil recommended to his friend.

"Get the meeting in place," Dante insisted. "Invite Blair, we'll need her. Give me a call back when its starting. I've got to get going now, but I'll talk with you soon," Dante said quickly checking the time.

"Thanks for the help," Virgil said goodbye to his friend.

"Always my friend," Dante affirmed before hanging up.

An hour later Virgil was in his room with a small group of people. Birdy, Louie, Nev, Rowan, Colton, Zane, Vinny, Homer, and Tucker were present along with Blair. Dante was on speaker, over Virgil's phone. Virgil went to his door and cast a barrier spell on it, making it impossible for people outside to eavesdrop.

"What did you bring us all here for?" Rowan asked restless as usual. The guy had more energy than a five-year-old. The room was packed, and people were getting antsy.

"Simmer down!" Dante barked from the phone. "Virgil's called all you bitches together for something important! Now shut up and listen!" Dante's tone was gruff. "Virgil, you have the floor," Dante ended sweetly as if talking to his first born.

"Thanks," Virgil said to Dante on the phone. Virgil took a deep breath and quickly explained the situation. The room was quiet, listening intently. Once Virgil had finished, he asked everyone for their input on what they should do.

"I don't think it's smart to do this behind the Chapter's back," Nev said apprehensively.

"Golden boy following the rules," Dante barked out from the phone.

"Shut it Dante," Nev retorted back. "Things like this can divide a Chapter, make people turn on each other, break trust."

"We're not stealing cookies from a girl scout troop for fuck's sake," Dante huffed from the phone, "We're rescuing two kids!" Dante yelled.

"Dante, you're not helping," Virgil said to his phone across the room.

"I agree with Nev, we shouldn't do this without Gabriel's approval," Rowan said speaking up. "I won't say anything I've heard in here, I swear on my bond," Rowan said seriously. "But this is dangerous Virgil. I went with you in the tunnels this winter, I've seen vampires up close. We weren't a match for them, they ripped through us easily, and that was only two! We barely made it out alive," Rowan laughed nervously.

"That's right!" Louie nodded remembering. "I passed out from saving your injured ass," Louie grinned shaking his head at Virgil. He'd poured spell after spell into Virgil and Blair till he'd used his aura to the point of physical unconsciousness. It was a noble and brave act of selflessness.

"I'm not denying this is dangerous!" Virgil shouted to the room. "I'm not saying it isn't wrong to go behind the Brotherhood's back. I didn't call you guys here, for you to tell me why we shouldn't do this. I brought you here to tell you a group of people asked us for help. Now those people, who we turned away, are about to be enslaved, ENSLAVED!" Virgil yelled. "In America!" Virgil shook his head. "The supposed Land of the Free," Virgil looked around. "The vampires kidnapped two children from the werewolves. They don't have anyone helping them," Virgil said sadly. "We're it," Virgil spread his arms out. "If you don't want to help, that's your choice. All I ask is, if you don't want to help, please, don't get in my way," Virgil said to the men looking each of them in the eyes. "I'll find out if one of you talks, and I swear I'll never forgive whoever that brother is."

"I'll go," Blair confidently said to the group. "Someone on this operation has got to have some balls. Pretty clear it's got to be me in this room of pansies!" Blair joked.

"Whatever!" Dante called from the phone. "You've only got the biggest balls, because I'm not there!"

"You wish!" Blair said playfully to Dante, earning another retort from him.

"I'll go," Colton said firmly, surprising Virgil. Colton seemed like a play by the rules type of person. Colton was easily one of the strongest new brothers, the smartest, the most…everything of Rho class. They needed him, perhaps he saw that. Virgil stared into Colton's soft brown eyes, "Thank you, frater," Virgil said with heart.

"I'm not doing this for you," Colton said very seriously. "I'm doing it for the children."

"Hell, sign me up," Tucker said spitting out some dip into a bottle. "Can't be any worse than the Fallen Judge we ran into."

"What!" Rowan shouted looking at Tucker. "What Fallen Judge?"

"Never you mind about that," Louie waved off Rowan. "One more headache we don't need," he sighed. Louie didn't look at Virgil, he was thankful his friend was protecting him.

"I'm out," Nev said crossing his arms. "I'm not condoning this kind of dissent. We make decisions like this AS A CHAPTER! Not one brother taking our men to the fight the battles he sees as worthy!" Virgil nodded not having a response, he was surprised. He'd expected Rowan and Colton to decline, not Nev, he considered him to be one of his closest brothers. Nev thought differently on this, on most things when it came to the fraternity. That wasn't wrong though, Virgil had to respect his friends' opinions. Virgil's thoughts weren't the only right path.

"I'll go," Zane offered. "Never seen a vampire or a werewolf before, sounds badass."

"I'm in," Birdy said raising his hand.

"Me too," Vinny said seriously. "I can't let just Dante go, you're going to need another Clio fuck!" Vinny declared proudly. There was a running joke going around about the brothers from Clio, Lambda's Hegemon, Dante, now Vinny…it got people laughing.

"I guess," Homer sighed. "I really don't want to, but I can't let Tucker go by himself."

"I can handle myself," Tucker said incredulously.

"If you die out there, I wouldn't be able to sleep at night man," Homer said to his roommate and best friend. "I have to watch your back, we're pledge brothers!"

"Thanks," Tucker smiled. "I've got yours too," he said to Homer.

"Aww, now they're gonna kiss!" Louie cried out.

"Shut up Louie!" Tucker cried out draping his arm playfully over Homer. "You're ruining a private moment!"

"Louie?" Dante asked from the phone.

The room turned its attention to Louie.

"I'm thinking!" Louie cried out.

"Hmm," Dante came back with in a fiery tone, "Thinking of ways to get out of this!"

"Going back into those tunnels, sounds like suicide," Louie defended himself. "I wasn't much help with my bow either."

"We sure could use the healing," Dante said from the phone, "You know how clumsy Birdy is, do you want to be short one absentminded loveable goofball?" Dante asked.

"Stop making me into this walking time bomb of death!" Birdy yelled at his old roommate. "I'm one of the best warriors in the Chapter."

"Eh," Dante said like he was shrugging, "I calls 'em like I sees 'em."

"Why do I got to save everyone?" Louie sighed over dramatically. "Fine! Whiny ass bitches can't do shit without Louie V," he mumbled to himself.

They'd reached an agreement and the room dispersed. Rowan stayed back till it was just Virgil and him.

Virgil raised his eyebrows, Rowan was hesitant, "I'm worried about you guys."

"We can handle ourselves," Virgil insisted.

"I understand," Rowan nodded looking at the ground. "I really don't want to go behind my Big's back with this, it doesn't feel right," Rowan admitted ashamedly to Virgil.

"Then don't, I won't hold it against you Rowan," Virgil gave a small smile. Rowan was honestly, one of the greatest brothers in the Chapter. He openly cared for everyone and was the first to volunteer to help any brother that asked for it, regardless of how close he was with them. Virgil had the utmost respect for Rowan.

"I don't like this, it's too dangerous. I can't let a group of youngin's like you go out there. You need more people with experience keeping the group safe," Rowan smiled.

"Hey, I'm Omicron, what class are you again?" Virgil asked Rowan with a tone of arrogance and superiority.

"Pi," he smiled nervously his face getting red, his blue eyes dancing, "So what if you're older in the fraternity! I'm four years older than you, and I was in the US military! You may be the Redeemer, but you're still just a teenager! You can't carry the world's problems alone! And you certainly can't protect everyone who was just in this room, so don't make them believe you can, because you just can't Virgil," Rowan said clearly upset.

Virgil went quiet, his fiery will to argue left him like a deflated balloon. Rowan spoke from his heart, he was worried for them, all of them. "I know I can't," Virgil admitted. "And I've never promised I could!"

"I know," Rowan nodded the fight leaving him.

"Why do you think I asked all of you for help?" Virgil looked into Rowan's eyes. "I'm not Superman, I can't do this alone," he admitted. "I can't protect us all…though I will try," he finished confidently.

Rowan nodded, "I'm going with you guys," he said sounding like he didn't want to, he went to the door, and looked back at Virgil. "I believe in you Virgil. Don't lead us astray," Rowan said fiercely, and he left the room.

# Chapter 18 The Vampire's Lair

The next night they flew to the werewolf Ulfric, Keaton's home. They coordinated the flight from the Tobico Marsh, so they wouldn't be seen taking off into the sky. It was a thirty-five-minute drive and took them less than fifteen minutes to fly. There were eleven of them, ten brothers and Blair, who had come to help the wolves. Virgil had called Keaton immediately following his meeting. Keaton had been surprised by Virgil's offer to intercede in their affairs, regardless he welcomed their invitation desperately. Keaton hadn't slept since his children had disappeared. Keaton informed Virgil the vampires were coming Thursday, the very next night. Keaton believed it was to take the pack back to the vampire's domain, with threat of torture or death to his children if they refused. Virgil offered to have his group be present during the negotiations. He wanted to hear about the missing children and show the vampires the wolves were packing more muscle than they realized. Virgil and his friends awkwardly mingled with Keaton's group outside the home, their pack had over forty people present. They were guarded, and visibly shaken. Virgil sensed that they were thankful for their presence.

A thundering came from the nearby trees, the Omegas reacted instantly most summoning their Devil Arms to their hands. Two large bears, twice the size of a normal bear, came bounding out from the trees, they were both pure black, one was much larger in size. These weren't vampires. Virgil had an idea though he'd never seen him shifted into his bear form. The two bears slowed their gait, coming to stand on their hind legs as their approached the wolves. Their bodies transformed, hair disappearing, the painful sound of bones reshaping, a slick clear fluid leaked from their bodies onto the ground. Seconds later they were naked men, the wolves provided them with clothing. The largest was Xiphias, he was hard to miss towering over everyone present.

"Short stuff!" Xiphias called out to Dante walking over to him. Dante didn't appreciate the nickname. "And Virgil of course. Thank you for changing your minds," he said warmly.

"Well we didn't really," Virgil said honestly. "We came against our group's wishes." This caused a stir among the wolves, lycans had superhuman senses, they could hear from great distances.

"We heard what happened," Dante said to everyone present. "And we aren't willing to let you go through this alone!" He said passionately earning a few shouts from the men.

"This is my son, Bolverk," Xiphias said introducing the other werebear. "He's only twenty now, someday he will take over as the head of our den. I wanted him to meet Keaton and his family. Our two clans have been allies for generations!" Xiphias boasted.

Bolverk was the opposite of his father. He was every bit as physically intimidating, yet introverted, and quiet. Xiphias was perhaps even more outgoing than Rowan, and louder than Lamar, if that combination was possible. The group exchanged small talk, though the tension hung in the air, coloring the conversation. Colton and Zane were popular with the group, especially the women. Louie got jealous of all the attention and did his best to win over the crowd, working his Louie magic, earning a few chuckles despite the pervasive sadness.

"Who is that woman?" Virgil asked Xiphias. She looked like a hot mess, that hadn't been cleaned up in a while.

"She's the pack's Lupa," Xiphias explained. "Keaton's mate, and wife. She's the pack's queen, though there is a second in command, most Lupa's rule second only to the Ulfric. Her children are the ones that were taken," Xiphias added sadly.

They came quickly, and silently, over fifty of them. One moment Virgil and the others were talking quietly, looking around nervously, the next vampires were across the way, a wall of immortal flesh. A female stepped forward, she was of Asian descent, with breathtaking looks. Dark hair that cascaded to her waist, prefect facial structure, supple lips, and a toned figure. She strode through her group, clearly the leader, towards Keaton. His wolves protectively encircled him. The vampire reached her hand towards the wolves, her almond shaped, dark eyes dancing with a strange light. The wolves seemed to cower, then seemingly involuntarily were forced away from Keaton, eight men and women, sliding across the ground like marionettes.

"What are you doing to them?" Virgil asked sensing her power at work.

"I've an affinity for wolves," she said simply. "My Master has an affinity for rats, vampires have unique gifts same as Nephilim. Some vampires can control animals, those that can, are able to bond a lycan of that animal to themselves, forever increasing their power, tenfold." She turned to Keaton looking him over like he was a piece of meat. She raised her arm to him, her eyes alight with vampiric metaphysical powers. She was trying to make Keaton obey her, he visibly shook, his eyes cutting into hers, he grinded his teeth and pushed his hands forward, the vampire faltered slightly. She couldn't sway the Ulfric of the pack, he was too strong! His ability to rebuff her compulsion seemed to excite her. "I want you Keaton. You're a strong Alpha, with you bonded to me as my Beast of Power, we'll become unstoppable!"

"I have my own pack, my own family!" Keaton yelled. "I don't want to become a part of yours Maya!"

"Oh darling, who ever asked what you wanted?" Maya laughed wickedly. "If you want to see those brats of yours alive, you'll do as your told!" Maya said like a vixen with a pouty smirk, narrowing her eyes and flicking her hair.

"Like hell he will!" Dante huffed flexing his arms his Devil Arms symbol of an axe glowing. Vinny's symbol began to glow a fiery red, his friends were poised to fight if need be!

"What's this?" Maya asked disdainfully sneering at the Nephilim. "You invited some hired help to fight us off?" Maya laughed, and the vampires began to laugh. The vampires all produced their fangs, and went from standing menacingly as a group, to looking savagely feral and hungry. Virgil was shaking a little at the sight of all them, they moved faster than people could see, this was going to be a blood bath! "Where are the other children?" Maya asked looking amongst the wolves, not seeing anyone underage.

"They are somewhere far from here," the Lupa of the pack smiled proudly. "Even if you manage to enslave us, you'll never get your hands on the others."

"Dear, sweet, deluded mutt," Maya purred. "We'll torture every one of you, till there is nothing left, if we must. We will take what we want. You are a pet from hence here forth, learn your place, dog!" Maya demanded.

The Lupa growled like a wolf her hands extending into a demi human wolf arm. She was ready to shift, ready to fight!

"If you fight us here, you'll never see your children again!" Maya laughed. "We'll take turns, bleeding them dry. It's a shame lycans can't be turned, child vampires are so deadly. I guess we'll just have to use their bodies up, till they have nothing left to give," Maya smirked.

The Lupa screamed, going into a full sprint, she shifted midstride, coming out as a pony sized grey wolf, Keaton hot on her heels. The rest of the pack followed suit, Xiphias pounded his legs against the ground sprinting towards the vampires, he transformed into a bear twice the size of the Lupa! Virgil screamed the names of his Devil Arms and spread his wings flying as fast as he could. The wolves and vampires collided, and began to tear each other apart! Both lycans and vampires could survive mutilation, and even lethal amputation, depending on how quickly their healing kicked in. Virgil's friends stuck together, keeping their small numbers grouped as one powerful unit.

Virgil reached for the Optimum in his pocket, this was the moment he'd been saving this energy towards. "Firaga!" Virgil spoke the Master spell, an explosion of fire erupted in the front lines of the vampires, encasing a quarter of their people in the flames. Vampires ran around, ablaze, howling in true terror, rolling on the ground to put out the flames. Vampires were extremely flammable. Blair, Rowan, Vinny, and Homer followed suit swiftly throwing out a few fire spells that kept the advancing bloodsuckers at bay. It quickly turned the tide in their favor. Maya's gaze turned towards Virgil, she started sprinting for him. "Eruption!" Virgil commanded again columns of fire bursting from the earth lifting vampires off the ground, and out of existence.

Maya launched herself off the ground with a powerful kick and went sailing through the air. Maya came at Virgil so fast he didn't have time to swing either weapon, she kicked him hard in the chest, sending him crashing into the ground. Maya landed near him, circling him like a powerful feline, ready to pounce on its wounded prey. Ragnorak fought to heal Virgil's wounds. He had blood coming out of his mouth, internal bleeding; she'd hit him hard, his breathing was ragged, he didn't have the strength to get up yet. Maya seemed to glide across the ground, her incredible speed making her a blur to him. A large black form barreled out to snatch her from the air, Maya screamed, and was tossed against the ground with tremendous force, snapping one of her arms. Xiphias growled menacingly edging close to Virgil, protecting him. She struck at Xiphias with such savagery, Virgil started screaming. She was ripping chunks of his flesh away, he fought fiercely, his strength greatly surpassed hers. Maya had superhuman speed, she used this to dodge Xiphias, and lash out with her own superhuman strength to deal devastating damage. He was stronger, but she was faster. Xiphias breathed heavily, his blood coating the ground, he swayed on his feet, he wouldn't last against her.

"NO!" Virgil screamed standing up, he swung Ragnorak, a wave of golden energy spreading towards Maya. She sprinted back and dove into the ground, narrowly missing its embrace. "Cura!" Virgil commanded three clouds of white energy flying out from his hand, two sought injured werewolves nearby, whose lives hung in the balance. The other went to Xiphias. The spell immediately went to work, his flesh rapidly repairing. The bear turned to look at Virgil, its dark eyes reflected gratitude. Virgil smiled and placed a hand on the bear, the bear's mouth opened with what Virgil took to be a smile. Two vampires descended on them, and Virgil went back to back with the large bear, working as a team they fought the vampires.

Zane and Birdy fought side by side, their Devil Arms complimenting one another. Zane's agility was second to none in their Chapter. He could go hand to hand with his wind spear against the younger, weaker vampires. Colton's lightning sword glowed with purple energy. He released waves of electricity at the vampires approaching the Paladins, keeping their group from being swarmed. Rowan's flame katana cut through vampire flesh with ease. Blair had fought these creatures before, she kept Flametongue extended out into a fiery whip, lashing it all around, keeping wandering hungry hands and mouths at bay. Vinny's large fire axe wasn't useful in fighting the vampires one on one, however he could unleash a wave of flames from the blade, which gave him a safe way to be extremely effective in fighting them off. Homer expended perhaps the last of his available aura to fire off a beam of energy, frying a vampire that had a wolf in a death grip.

"There are too many of them!" Colton yelled. "What's the game plan here!" he shouted out to the group.

"I'm not the ideas guy!" Tucker chuckled, excusing himself from that responsibility.

"Take her down," Virgil commanded to his group. "Maya's the general, topple her, and they will retreat!"

Maya started laughing, she was battling two wolves and Bolverk, Xiphias' son. She beat the three of them back, they fell on the ground wounded and unable to stand. She slithered like a serpent towards the Nephilim once more. "I wasn't told you'd be here," she growled at Virgil. "You ruined my victory!"

Virgil rushed forward his wings propelling him with dusts of magic trailing behind him, racing towards Maya, vampires came at Virgil, seeking to protect their leader. Virgil spun in midair sending Soul Reaver out like a boomerang, the scythe cut through one, the creature disintegrating into ash, the second managed to dodge the flaming sickle blade. The Lupa was suddenly at Virgil's side racing towards Maya, Virgil looked into her eyes. They'd take Maya down together. Virgil dived close to the ground barely above the grass, his eyes narrowing, the two warriors yelled and attacked. Virgil hacked at a vampire that ran to Maya's side, the Lupa tore at Maya's flesh with her mighty jaws. The vampire smacked the wolf's jaw back, the Lupa whining in pain. The Lupa ran at her again growling, ready to tear her limb from limb, she struck

333

out, closing her jaws on Maya's side, she ripped back and forth, sending Maya to the ground, the wolf spit out the chunk of flesh. The Lupa went in for the kill, Maya raised her hand to the Queen wolf her power flowing out. The wolf slowed down as she approached the vampire, her limbs visibly shaking the closer she got. Maya laughed, her power over lycans with the wolf strain was almost insurmountable, only a strong Ulfric of a pack had the power to resist the compulsion and protect the pack from that said power.

Maya approached the Lupa, an evil glint in her eye, a grin spreading across her face. The Lupa tried to run, but she could barely move under the vampire's control. Maya ran forward, wrapping her arms around the wolf, she picked it up in a tight embrace, squeezing hard, the Lupa yelped her spine cracking. The wolf sagged in her arms, her fur quickly receding, lycans transformed back to their human state when they died. The dead bodies of many wolves, returned to human form, littered the ground. Wolves began to howl, their Queen had been slain. Keaton became a savage beast, racing towards Maya. Virgil rushed Maya to prevent her from harming Keaton. He swung both Devil Arms at her, she dodged his blows, swiping at him in turn. The Veil spell that surrounded him, a boon from holding Ragnorak, helped to divert Maya's attacks from landing. One hit from her was enough to break bones and send him to the ground. Virgil was barely able to keep pace with Maya, she snarled at him, desperate to finish him. Virgil's limbs grew weary, he was coated in sweat, he wanted this to be over, he couldn't take anymore death.

"My Master has ruled over this area for more than a century! He grows weary of the small city life, and is ready to move on to bigger, better places. He made me into a vampire, most powerful vampires do but a few times. I was to take over his empire here, I inherited the lycan nest of wererats in Saginaw, and before he left, our plan was to consolidate my power with this lycan pack," Maya's eyes narrowed, her brow furrowing, her dark eyes alight with bloodlust. "I lost dozens of soldiers tonight because of you!" Maya screamed. "I'll taste your blood as I drain the life from your eyes!" Maya cruelly spat, meaning every word. She lashed out with a renewed vigor, Virgil could do little more than protect himself. She crouched down and swept her leg out, taking Virgil by surprise he fell back. She pounced on him within the second. She snapped his left arm, screaming in pain from touching his flaming flesh. Her tactic worked, with his arm as it was he couldn't fight with Soul Reaver, and she effectively kept his scythe away from her. Maya snarled and sank her fangs into his neck.

Virgil struggled against her, she had him pinned down, and trying to break free, was like lifting a school bus that had landed on his chest. Virgil's thinking rapidly became sluggish, she was going to drink him dry! Keaton's panting approached, his focus like that of an Olympian, his jaws closed around Maya's head, and he twisted with everything he had. Maya screamed, reaching back with her claws, she dug into his flesh, the wolf banged her head around, struggling to finish her. Virgil got to his feet, screamed in a loud rage, and ran forward swinging Ragnorak, cleaving her in two. Maya fell from the wolf's mouth, decapitated.

Keaton began to shift back. "We must set her ablaze!" he ordered. "The stronger ones, and even the weaker ones, can come back from death. They must be permanently erased from this world!"

Virgil's left arm was slowly healing. He reached it toward Maya, his symbol coming to life, black fire spreading, it leapt from his hand to Maya, quickly engulfing her body. The dozen or so vampires that were still alive, quickly retreated into the woods.

"Keaton, I'm so sorry, about your wife, about all of this," Virgil said to the werewolf King.

"We don't have time for sympathy," Keaton's words were steel, he was clearly shaken. "They still have my children. With Maya dead, Voltro will be enraged. She was almost a hundred years old, and already very powerful among her kind. She was his protégé, he'd made her into a vampire and raised her, the closest thing their kind can come to really having a child. Voltro's wrath will be insurmountable. We'll have to evacuate immediately, flee the state," Keaton said sadly.

"What about your children?" Virgil asked.

Keaton stared out, looking at his wife's dead body, at the dead bodies of his people. There was still over twenty of them left in good shape, and several more were alive, just injured. They shifted back to human form, their wounds not transferring through the shift. The transformation was physically exhausting, most had heavy lidded eyes, and were ready to pass out. Only Keaton shifted and still looked like he could keep going. He quickly put on pants, while the group was gathering the dead. Miraculously, none of Virgil's companions had been seriously injured, he was thankful for that.

"I don't know," he said sadly. "I will go to Voltro's domain, and make an exchange, my life for theirs. I did kill Maya, and he will want to speak with the one who took her life."

"He'll kill you and them!" Virgil shook his head. "I'll go with you," he offered. "Besides, I'm the one who dealt the finishing blow. Don't take the responsibility for it, please," Virgil insisted.

"No, there is a good chance whoever goes in won't come back out," Keaton argued, "It's still hours from sunrise, if you need to escape, you won't be able to get far."

"I won't be escaping," Virgil said darkly. "I'm coming out of there, with a kid in each arm," he asserted.

"Let me get my people in motion, then I will tell you where to meet me," Keaton said moving to speak to the grieving pack.

Virgil walked over to his friends, Colton read that something was going on.

"What are you doing with Keaton?" Colton asked.

"I'm going with him to the tunnels," Virgil said to the group.

"Are you crazy?" Louie laughed wildly. "This was a win here! Can't we go home?"

"A win?" Virgil asked angrily. "Keaton's wife was just killed in front of me! His children are still in those creature's clutches. What happens to them, after they hear about this?" Virgil asked fearfully. "I'm not asking you guys to come along; each of you helped these werewolves keep their freedom. We saved these people. I'm proud of everyone. You should all go back to Bay Valley, and don't tell a soul what you've seen here," Virgil commanded.

"I'm coming with you," Blair and Dante said at the same time. "You'll need us," Blair said looking at Dante and nodding.

"I'm going back to the Omega house," Rowan said quietly.

"Me too," Colton nodded.

"Do you mind if we go home?" Tucker asked Virgil. "Homer and I are going to sleep at the Omega house tonight."

"Please do," Virgil nodded.

"I'm gonna come," Zane said to Virgil.

"Maybe you should go back to the house," Virgil offered. "You're still so young. I saw how great you were tonight, you have more potential than I've ever seen in a fledgling Paladin. You could be one of the greats," Virgil said clapping his arm on Zane's shoulder. "We're going to need you for many years to come bud."

"Precisely why I need to be fighting at your side," Zane declared very serious not dissuaded, "I'm never going to get better unless I challenge myself. Besides, I don't like the idea of you going into a vampire lair. I'm coming with you Virgil, whether you like it or not!" Zane affirmed in his cocky attitude, like he knew better, was better. He had never used it with Virgil, but he'd seen him speak with the tone to most of the brothers.

"Wow," Louie laughed. "You're making me feel like a shitty friend right now," he sighed.

"You coming?" Birdy asked his best friend.

"Yesss," Louie sighed obviously not wanting to go.

"I'll lead the others back home," Rowan offered.

"Please do, fly safe," Virgil asked of his brothers.

"We just fought off an army of vampires," Colton laughed, "I think we can find our way back to Bay City."

"Point taken," Virgil nodded. "Vinny," Virgil said. "Would you be willing to go back to the house with them?" He didn't want to be worrying about his Lil in the tunnels, it was tight and disorienting down there.

"Why?" Vinny asked almost offended.

"Because I don't want to be worried about you the entire time," Virgil insisted.

"Zane's going," Vinny pointed out.

"I don't want Zane going either!" Virgil sighed. "I can't make you leave. I just want you to know that I'm scared. This is going to be even more dangerous than what we just faced," Virgil said seriously.

"Precisely why you need me along," Vinny offered. "I'm aligned with fire, my axe can burn those things better than anyone who doesn't have a fire Devil Arms," Vinny argued.

Keaton came back over, "Alright," Virgil nodded. Seven stayed back, the other four brothers took flight back to Bay Valley.

Keaton's people were quickly burying the bodies in the woods, then fleeing the state. Keaton was going to drive himself to an upscale condominium complex on the river, south from the restaurants in the downtown area. Apparently the vampires owned them, and the tunnels led to an underground facility beneath the apartment buildings. They wouldn't have to go stumbling through the tunnels after all. They were going in through the front door. Keaton was sure the vampires would happily bring them unscathed through their lair to meet with Voltro personally. Virgil and his friends agreed to fly and meet him there. Keaton got into his truck and took off. It would take him twice as long to get there.

Virgil and his friends took to the sky, they didn't fly as hard this time, the seven of them taking their time. They were shaken up, they'd already experienced so much this evening, Virgil prayed this was going to be simpler than it seemed. He didn't see the seven of them fighting through hundreds of vampires. Virgil hadn't Ascended yet tonight, if things turned desperate, that was his trump card. They came into Bay City, landing on a small battleship that was docked near Independence Bridge, permanently stationed there as a museum. They checked the time, they only had a few minutes, they didn't want to wait over by the vampire's lair, afraid they might be snatched up. Dante was a motor mouth, listening to him ramble nervously helped to occupy their time. Louie and Blair interrupted making Virgil smirk, helping to defuse the tension. They were going somewhere no sane person would walk into willing, they were all on edge. They checked the time a few minutes later, taking flight. They caught sight of Keaton's truck descending to the ground near the river.

Keaton was visibly shaking, steeling his nerves, and swallowing the inner turmoil threatening to unravel him, he led the group to the entrance. The stretch of buildings stood five stories tall. There were restaurants, hotels, condos, and other businesses nearby, including a medical emergency center, down the road from the city's hospital. There wasn't anyone stationed outside, but security was top notch, cameras were everywhere, and the doors looked like they'd survive a bomb blast. They approached the doors and they opened. There were armed guards just inside a reception area. A female vampire dressed up like a stewardess was behind the counter. She worked on her computer, like nothing was amiss when the armed soldiers searched them. Vampires didn't normally wield guns; these men were lycans, wererats most likely, the muscle of this vampire coven. The eight of them were escorted back to a group of elevators. The guards operated it and motioned the group inside. They did as they were told, the elevator descended what felt like twenty floors. It opened into an underground sanctuary; a large facility had been created down here. It was modern, yet cozy, Virgil nervously looked around, memorizing their way back to the elevators.

They arrived in an audience chamber, that was an enormous living room. Furniture was arranged in a rectangle, the floor descended several steps in the center of the room where the seating was available. Guards were posted at every door, a few vampires were seated on the plush, expensive, and decadent looking sofas. A young boy, and a younger girl were tied up, bound and gagged, they were seated on the floor, at the feet of a vampire. He sat at the head of the rectangle seating area, he had a plain face, with long straight black hair, and sharp hazel eyes. He smiled warmly welcoming the group.

"Welcome back Keaton!" Voltro said to the Wolf King. "I see you brought us some guests," he said looking to Virgil and the others. "Please have a seat."

"Thanks for the offer," Keaton nodded. "We won't be staying long. I came to take Kanin, and Kiala home," Keaton said firmly.

"Oh, but they have grown so fond of it here," Voltro smiled placing his hand lovingly on the boy's head. He began to tremble. Virgil noticed his neck was all bloody, it was marred with deep puncture marks. He'd been bitten many, many times for his natural lycan healing to have not been able to close the wounds, either that or he'd lost too much blood.

"I have to say I'm fond of your boy," Voltro purred, his hands trailing down to rub gently on the boy's chest. "He was a bit naïve at first. We saw to it to break him in for you," Voltro laughed, pulling the boy against him suggestively, and Kanin began to silently sob.

"YOU MONSTER!" Keaton growled jumping into action.

"Don't move!" Voltro yelled grabbing Kanin's hair and yanking back on his skull. The boy cried out his pain. "I'll rip his head right from his neck," Voltro said plainly. "Now, Sit, Down," he commanded.

Virgil and the others sat down. Keaton looked like he was about to explode. Virgil's pulse was racing. Blair's eyes reflected real fear, Virgil was wishing he hadn't offered to come here. His friends were no match for these people.

"I would offer you refreshments, however I was just told by the few of my servants who did return, that Maya was murdered," Voltro spoke tightly. He sounded like a politician, collected and poised. Virgil sensed a madman dancing behind his eyes. "Keaton, was it you who took her from me?" Voltro asked angrily.

Keaton went to speak, Virgil interrupted him standing up. "That Asian vampire?" Virgil asked. "I'm the one who killed her," Virgil said confidently.

"You?" Voltro asked sitting back, his stare hardening, the full weight of his gaze falling on Virgil. The hair around Voltro began to dance, Virgil felt queasy and wobbly.

"I sliced clean through her with my sword," Virgil moved his right hand, Ragnorak's symbol visible to them.

"A white and a black Devil Arms," Voltro nodded. "I've heard of you," he said coldly. "How kind of you to offer yourself so willingly." Voltro stood up stretching casually. He shot forward like a bullet punching Virgil, hitting him hard, sending him into the air. Voltro leapt into the air, and kicked Virgil hard, sending him into the pavement floor. Virgil heard his name being called out, and vampires moved across the room to restrain his friends. Virgil for the second time in one night felt like he was dying. He was suffocating, he'd suffered severe internal damage, he needed Ragnorak or...

"Cura!" Virgil shouted in his mind holding onto the magicite in his pocket. White light surrounded him, as two similar clouds of energy leapt over to mend the children. Virgil felt like he could breathe again, he coughed hard getting to his feet.

"The joys of being born a Nephilim," Voltro sneered. "Magic, AND magic weapons," Voltro flashed forward, one moment he was standing by the couches, the next beside Virgil. Voltro ripped the Optimum from Virgil's pocket, it was over halfway full. Voltro threw the stone across the room, he smiled at Virgil. "You won't be using that trick again," he said through clenched teeth. "I'm anxious to taste you. I want this to be slow, and miserable for you," Voltro ran his hand over the front of Virgil's jeans. Virgil's face flamed, he shoved against Voltro who only gripped him tighter.

"Let him go!" Blair shouted being held down by a vampire, all of his friends were being restrained. Keaton threw his head back, smashing the vampire's nose that held him, he bolted towards his children. Voltro threw Virgil to the floor, bruising his shoulder. Voltro tackled Keaton to the floor, flipping off him to grab Keaton's son. Voltro lifted the boy from the ground and held him tightly. Virgil and Keaton got up, Keaton squared off against the Master vampire, Voltro was hundreds of years old, and radiated power.

"Please, do what you want with me!" Keaton shouted. "Just let my children leave this place!" Keaton pleaded. "I'll do anything!" Keaton begged.

Voltro stared deep into Keaton's eyes, he coldly replied, "No." Voltro ripped his fangs into Kanin's neck, he bit down with his whole mouth. Voltro ripped Kanin's throat open, and Kiala screamed.

Keaton raced towards Voltro, vampires leapt out to grab either arm, a wererat coming up to hold his head and make him watch. Tears streamed down Virgil's face, he was screaming and crying. These were monsters, who had lost touch with their humanity long ago. Virgil was going to have to go through the same thing with every friend he'd brought with him. Watching Voltro ruthlessly end the boy's life snapped something inside Virgil. The dark part of himself, was something he fought every day to control and tame. His inner monster, he had no desire to hide it anymore. He hated Voltro, he wanted to see him suffer. He wanted revenge, revenge for the abuse and pain that had been inflicted on the innocent siblings. A growl rumbled in Virgil's chest, his eyes went completely black, dancing with dark flames. A quote came to his mind from the anime Attack on Titan, "Sometimes in order to defeat monsters, we have to abandon our humanity, in order to rise above them, we become monsters ourselves."

Vampires ran at superhuman speeds to grab Virgil, they reached him, forcing him to the ground. Virgil grinned, he felt like there was someone else in his mind, someone who was desperate to take control. Virgil let his hate and anger consume him, he relinquished his body to Soul Reaver, for the first time in the year since he'd first gained it. The black symbol on his left hand blazed with dark fire. The flames spread out, cascading across his entire body in two seconds. The vampires howled as the flames hungrily consumed thrm. Virgil stood at his full height, grinning wildly his body completely ablaze, his eyes pitch black and dancing with dark flame. He couldn't be touched like this! "Soul Reaver!" Virgil commanded, the dark scythe materialized into his hand, flames dancing on the blade's surface, ready to feed.

Virgil ran forward, and vampires gave chase. Virgil was faster in this state, he leapt up spinning Soul Reaver around at blinding speeds. The scythe sliced through two vampires, they fell to the floor as ash. Vampires and wererats swarmed Virgil, flooding into the room. Virgil began laughing, his voiced sounded like a demon's, deep and very dark. "Fools!" Virgil cried. "As if an army of you could ever hope to match me! DIE!" They came at him and Virgil danced. Flames leapt from his flesh; he commanded the flames to lash out. Wererats began firing their guns at him, they were unnerved by his visage. His scythe spun around, cutting down bullets, the fire burning anything it touched. Virgil used the fire as a weapon, crafting it with his thoughts, the black flames lashed out from his flesh, the room was quickly a sea of fire. Every vampire and lycan became engulfed in flames, Virgil blasted them with a feral and sadistic fever, dealing swift death to growing numbers. After dozens had burned, the rest were starting to back away in fear, they couldn't approach him let alone touch him. Virgil had burned through a large number, and it hadn't taken a drop of his energy. He could burn a thousand more.

"There is no escape for you! Burn, BURN!" Virgil laughed setting a line of fire near the doors, blocking the vampires inside the room, and discouraging more from entering. "This is what you get, for being what you are! Pay for your crimes!" Virgil threw fire at the vampires holding his friends, he accidentally burned Vinny and Blair slightly, but they were able to escape the clutches of their captors. Voltro went to grab the little girl, Virgil's eyes narrowed. He threw his hands out at the Master vampire, a beam of energy shot out, blasting the vampire backwards. Virgil approached the vampire, his body encased in flames, his eyes pitch black, he looked more like a monster than the evil vampire.

The vampire scrambled back, fear was in the old immortal's eyes. "What are you!?" he yelled "You're more demon than Judge!" The vampire declared.

"You'll never harm another child again!" Virgil declared through clenched teeth. "Feel the pain, you so eagerly inflict," Virgil grabbed Voltro and held him close. The vampire screamed into his ears, and the creature burned away, struggling against him. Virgil held on with delight, a gleeful grin on his face. He felt...numb, like his limbs had fallen asleep. He felt like he was watching himself, he wasn't the one moving his body anymore.

Voltro fell from Virgil's arms as ash. Virgil turned and walked back to the girl. "You're safe now," Virgil said to the child. She screamed and ran into her father's arms. Virgil was puzzled, he looked at his friends, they wore harrowed expressions. He moved towards them and they recoiled, their eyes showed fear, and concern.

"We need to escape!" Keaton yelled. He had his son in his arms, his daughter's hand tightly on his pants.

"Can you put that out already?" Dante suggested. "You'll burn the place down if you keep running around like the Human Torch," he smirked.

The room had fire everywhere, they needed to escape, Virgil let go of his scythe and willed it away. The scythe hovered in front of him, the black flames on his skin not receding. Virgil strained hard, go away! He thought fiercely straining against his Devil Arms, something had happened. Soul Reaver didn't want to return to the void, it enjoyed having control of his body, it enjoyed inflicting pain, it loved to hate.

"What's wrong?" Blair asked concerned.

"Tell that damn scythe you won't take no sass back, and it needs to get its ass on home, now!" Louie cried.

The flames on Soul Reaver grew in stature almost screaming, the scythe responding to Louie, its voice dark, deep, angry, and powerful. Louie looked like he'd crapped his pants backing a healthy distance away from Virgil.

"Enough!" Virgil commanded, and the black flames consuming the room dissipated, along with Soul Reaver in a cloud of dark flame.

"Follow me!" Keaton called, and the group ran from the room, out the door they'd come through, Virgil quickly pocketed his Optimum before following the group.

The group summoned their Devil Arms, vampires could attack them at any moment. They thankfully reached the elevator, everyone was silent on the ride up, not sure if the worst had passed. Nothing ambushed them in the lobby, and they ran out of the building safely.

"I'm taking my daughter to meet up with the rest of our people," Keaton said to the group beside his vehicle. "Thank you, for everything," his words were filled with unspoken gratitude.

"We're glad to have been there for you," Dante said sadly. The man had lost his wife and son and was thanking them, no one really felt worthy of praise.

Louie gave them both a big hug. Virgil was numb, Keaton came up to him, and he didn't know what to say. "You saved my little girl's life," Keaton had tears in his eyes. "Thank you," he said embracing Virgil.

Virgil felt like a failure and fought back tears. "I'm sorry I couldn't do more," was all he could say back as he hugged Keaton.

# Chapter 19 Loss and Love

Virgil was back in his room, his friends were going over to Blair's to decompress, since they weren't allowed to talk about what had just happened with anyone else. He told them he wanted to be alone. Virgil went to his bathroom and took a hot shower, wanting to wash away the blood, and bad memories of the night. He went to his room, laid on his bed, and called Amari. She didn't answer, he didn't leave a message, he just lay back staring up, feeling empty.

His phone buzzed, he picked up on the first ring, "Virgil?" Amari called out to him.

"Amari," Virgil sounded hoarse.

"Virgil, what's wrong?" Amari asked her voice showing real concern. "You don't sound like yourself," she commented.

"I need you," Virgil said almost sobbing, "Where are you?" he asked.

"I'm home, come over, are you hurt?" she asked concerned.

"I was bloody and bleeding out twice tonight," Virgil joked, "Not hurt physically at the moment."

"You helped them," Amari said quietly.

Virgil took a deep breath, "Yeah."

"IF you want to talk about it, I'm here for you," Amari said warmly. "Or we can just cuddle till you fall asleep."

"I'm on my way," Virgil said. He was at her dorm room within five minutes. Virgil lay down, Amari stroking his hair. He told her what mattered, she listened intently, not interrupting, gasping at the right parts. Virgil trusted her, she made him feel safer. Virgil felt so alone, she was helping to fight that.

"Seeing that little boy die before my eyes, I lost it. I couldn't control my anger, Soul Reaver...I gave it control. In return it gave me the power to end those monsters. When it was time to take control back, it wouldn't let me," Virgil said frightened. Amari was quiet. "I enjoyed killing those vampires and wererats. I became someone I didn't recognize though. I'm evil, inside. There is an untapped wellspring of darkness in my heart. The thing that frightens me the most is, part of me enjoyed being that way. I didn't feel the pain of the boy's death when Soul Reaver was in control." Virgil looked down, ashamed. "You deserve so much better than me," Virgil said miserably.

Amari grabbed him and turned his face towards hers, her eyes were fierce. "You may have darkness in your heart, so do all who walk this Earth. I'm no better," Amari looked sad. "I've seen evil, true evil Virgil. It has no empathy, no love, no remorse for inflicting pain, it thrives on misery, sadness, agony. Before I met you, I didn't know there were people who loved so fully, who gave of themselves so freely, with no thought to reward," Amari had tears in her eyes. "You are many things Virgil Pitcher, evil, is not one of them."

"I love you," Virgil said looking into her eyes.

Amari was caught off guard, she looked away, she didn't respond, and Virgil didn't ask her to. "The truth is Virgil, you're out of my league," Amari said not looking into his eyes.

Her words cut deep. "Why?" Virgil asked fearful. "Cause I'm the Redeemer?" Virgil reached out to Amari. "That doesn't matter to me, I'd still want you, even if you were human. I care about you Amari," Virgil meant every word.

"I care about you too, Virgil," Amari said looking into Virgil's eyes. "I'm just worried," she trailed off.

"Worried?" Virgil asked.

"That I'm going to end up hurting you," Amari said softly. "I already know I will."

"Where's the strong sassy woman who told me it'll never work between us? I saw a mother and a son die tonight," Virgil told Amari. "Nothing is promised Amari. Finding someone you care about in this world, its everything. We may hurt each other in the end," Virgil nodded. "Even if we don't stay together forever, I want that time with you. In this moment, right now, we care about each other, in the future even if this isn't what we want anymore, I'll be happy knowing that I had that at one time with you."

"That's...sweet," Amari admitted, she lay next to him and they stared up at her ceiling.

"I always believed, as a child," Amari told him staring up, a forlorn look in her eyes. "That what mattered most was what you knew. If you were good at something, you'd just do that in life. If you can draw, you're an artist, if you're athletic, then you play sports. It's such a hard world, it wasn't until I was thirteen that I realized, no one cares how brilliant or intuitive, or revolutionary you are. People just want to use you up, take from you what they want, only to leave you out on the curb once they've sucked you dry. What matters is the people you know," Amari said darkly. "Than what you know."

"That's...deep," Virgil bobbed his head slightly. What had happened to you at thirteen? Virgil stared at her wishing he could take away the hurt. Amari rolled over, placing her hand on Virgil's chest, snuggling against him. Virgil hoped his heartbeat didn't start bouncing her hand off his chest.

"When I was a little boy," Virgil recalled his face lighting up as he spoke, "I would get scared of the dark, alone in my room at night. I would go to my parents, down the hall, and my mom would put me back to bed. She always said that there was something special about me. I felt different from the other kids, even though I looked just like everyone else. Some nights, I'd hear a song being sung, outside my window. It brought comfort to me, when I felt alone," Virgil got misty eyed. "I would sometimes go to the window, and it would stop. I never knew where it came from. One time I saw something big fly away from my house, it was, startling," Virgil's eyebrows jumped. "But I began to yearn for those nights," Virgil's face softened. When he heard the song, it made him feel safe, and less alone then he could ever remember feeling. Like a piece of him was complete. "As I got older, I stopped being afraid at night, forgot how different I really was from the people around me, I didn't feel so alone, and I didn't have visits anymore."

"Virgil," Amari stared deep into his eyes, rubbing her hand across his chest. She lay her head down on his chest and sighed.

"What was growing up like, for you?" Virgil asked a small, warm, happy smile on his face looking down into Amari's eyes.

Amari's face darkened. "It was alright when I was younger, my grandmother raised me until the sixth grade. She was a kind, but quiet woman. She loved me and taught me to be strong. It got bad, after she died," Amari looked off not wanting to make eye contact.

"You want to tell me about it?" Virgil asked her running his hands along her face, cupping her chin gently.

"Another night," Amari nodded. "Not now. I'm feeling too good, to tell that story," she smirked. "I'm sorry, you just had a traumatic night, I shouldn't have said that."

"No, it's okay. I need this Amari, I'm having a really nice time with you," Virgil confessed moving his hand to move a piece of her hair. He'd been feeling so low, she'd helped him greatly, maybe he'd be able to get some sleep after all.

"Come here," Amari commanded reaching out to grab his shirt, she pulled his face into hers. They kissed and Virgil felt happy. There was a lot of bad things going on around him, for right now though, he was going to enjoy just being with Amari.

The next day Virgil went back to the Omega house, he had a lot on his mind, Family Weekend was starting today, his mother would be driving down to Bay Valley tomorrow for a visit. There were only a few weekends left in the semester, and elections for Jeweled Officers was approaching. Virgil was hoping his brothers didn't hear anything about the local vampires being decimated, or the local werewolves being attacked and fleeing town. He silently worried that the Chapter would find out, someone would talk, and he'd be kicked out of the Omegas. He felt like life was so fragile, having seen so much death so recently. Keaton had his loved ones torn from him forever, and was forced to live on. Virgil thought that was worse, he'd rather be dead then to have to live without his friends, his mom.

Virgil's thoughts turned to Amari, she made him happy, and it was hard not to smile and feel good with her on his mind. Things with her couldn't be more perfect. Amari was everything he wanted in a woman and more. Virgil wanted to ask her to be his girlfriend, he was just afraid to do it, and didn't know the 'right' way to ask her. They hadn't talked about a relationship yet; he'd been too scared of ending things before they happened. He couldn't help himself from wanting more. Virgil suddenly thought, maybe I'll ask Vahn for an idea. Virgil found his Big in his room, on the second to last floor, where the eldest brothers in the Chapter resided.

"Hey Vahn, can I bother you for a second?" Virgil asked knocking and walking in.

"Sure, what's up buddy?" Vahn asked sitting at his computer working on a paper. Virgil explained that he had strong feelings for Amari, and wanted to ask her to be his girlfriend, but in a way that would impress her. "That's a challenge," Vahn nodded biting at his nails, Virgil had noticed he did that when he was nervous or thinking hard. "DO you know if she'll say yes?" He asked emphasizing the 'do'.

"No," Virgil shook his head laughing.

"Then what you need is an exit strategy," Vahn mused. "Something sly, so that if she's not interested you can walk away, with an unbruised ego. Yet it also needs to be romantic," Vahn nodded.

"Okay," Virgil said rolling his eyes, he had no ideas, and that sounded impossible.

"Buy her some red roses," Vahn suggested. "With one white rose. Write on a small card with the flowers, 'When you're ready to be more than friends, return the white rose to me,'" Vahn said spaced out, thinking hard.

"That's incredible," Virgil blinked blown away by his Big's romantic creativity.

"I know, well don't just sit there, write it down before I forget!" Vahn laughed and Virgil sprang into action.

"How'd you come up with that?" Virgil asked his Big.

"I'm a genius," Vahn boasted. "No, I'm an English major, read crap every day. Now go get the flowers, write the message, and see if she responds. You might want to get an artificial white rose, in case she takes her time in making a decision," Vahn joked.

"That's a good idea too," Virgil nodded. "Okay I have a lot to do, I gotta go!" Virgil said hurriedly. "Thanks Vahn!" Virgil called out to his Big.

"Anytime!" Vahn called after Virgil, who raced to his Blazer, driving around for the nearest flower shop. He bought five red roses, and a fake white rose planted in the middle. Virgil wrote what Vahn had suggested, and went to Amari's with a large grin on his face. She was surprised when he showed up, even more surprised by the flowers.

"Virgil, what are these for?" Amari asked gently, he was glad she wasn't so defensive with him anymore.

"To show you I care," Virgil smiled. "Read the card after I leave, think it over, and get back with me some time," Virgil suggested putting his hands in his pockets.

Amari quipped a curious eyebrow at him but let the statement slide. "I'd ask you to stay but I have some things I have to do," Amari said disappointed.

"Family of all the brothers will be showing up tonight and tomorrow for Family Weekend," Virgil said knowing he'd be busy. "I won't have a lot of time. My mom is coming tomorrow remember? It'd be nice if the three of us could do something, maybe get lunch?" Virgil suggested. "I'd like for you ladies to meet."

"I'd like that as well," Amari nodded. "Maybe then I'd understand a little better how you got to be so sweet," she winked.

"Let me know what you think about that," Virgil motioned to the card in the small envelope. He hugged Amari and kissed her goodbye.

The families started pouring in. The siblings, who wanted to party with the brothers, were coming Friday. The parents were coming tomorrow for the day of activities, and for a dinner put on by the Omegas at their house. Doc showed up, his sister Gina, Amari's pledge sister, came with him. Dante came telling Virgil and Birdy his older half-brother and his father would be coming to the Omega house tomorrow. Birdy's parents were coming for the family dinner, and so were Louie's parents. Most of the brothers had at least one person coming on Saturday to Omega house for dinner. Spencer brought his younger brother, who was a quiet hippy skater guy. Brody's sister came that night; his parents were coming the next day. She had a fun outgoing personality like him. And quickly became a crowd favorite with her high energy. Lilly showed up with her younger sister. Raven brought her brother who was staying with her for the weekend.

Selene came over, she brought her younger brother, Cesare, who planned to go to Bay Valley when he was a freshman in two years. Cesare was different from Selene in every way, except they were both intelligent, polite, and incredibly attractive. He had icy blue eyes that you could fall into, where she had chocolate brown. Cesare was only sixteen and he had a Devil Arms. It was shaped like a sword, and aligned with water, while Selene had a fire lance. Cesare was quiet and shy, though he tried to be friendly. The brothers were all keeping their fingers crossed he'd join their fraternity. Virgil kept getting introduced to so many people he was having a hard time remembering names. Virgil didn't let the previous night get to him, he threw himself into having a good time with his best friends, and their families.

"I miss this," Dante said with a forlorn look in his eyes as he looked around. Virgil, Birdy, Louie, Doc, Tarek, Brody, his sister, Vinny, Tucker, Homer, Cameron, and Brett were sitting in a smoking circle. "I can't wait to be back at Bay Valley, I miss being around you guys every day."

"I know what you mean," Doc nodded. "Its hell being away from the boys."

"We miss you too!" Tarek said overly dramatic making a kissy face to Dante.

"Hey!" Doc laughed getting red in the face. "I was your pledge brother! Where are my kisses?" He asked jealously making everyone crack up.

"Oh no, you get more than kisses," Tarek wiggled his eyebrows leaning back, putting his hands behind his head. "Come here baby, give me some of that Nu class love, make daddy feel good," Tarek had everyone laughing and Doc rolled his eyes.

"Tarek Jeter you crack me up," Virgil said sitting next to him.

Tarek's gaze was sharp, he looked annoyed with Virgil. Virgil furrowed his eyebrows, he asked Tarek, "Did I say something wrong man?"

"No bro, it's cool, it's cool," Tarek said when it was obviously NOT the case. "It's just, we're friends right? So why do you gotta keep calling me Tarek Jeter all the time?" Tarek asked Virgil.

Virgil didn't understand what he was saying. "Everyone calls you that," Virgil said feeling lost. "There are several guys in the Chapter who everyone calls by their first and last name."

"It's just, how I feel is, if you're my friend, don't call me by my full name. Chicks do that all the time to me in the food court, and it drives me crazy! Hi Tarek Jeter," Tarek imitated in a high falsetto voice. "How are you doing Tarek Jeter! You're so dreamy Tarek Jeter! Let me just," Tarek was getting overly excited and Virgil grew red in the face.

"Okay! I get it!" Virgil interrupted him. "I didn't realize that bothered you. I'm sorry, I'll just call you Tarek from now on," Virgil smiled.

"Thanks," Tarek nodded ending his rant. "I appreciate it bro," Tarek smirked.

"You guys are too much," Brody's sister laughed. "I see why Brody never comes home, he's found a family away from home," she said fondly looking around.

"Yup!" Brody laughed hard. "I can't wait till you guys meet my parents!" Brody exclaimed. "They are a couple of old ass hippies!" Brody burst out laughing with his sister. "They are so chill, and down to earth, they'll fit right in. They'll definitely be down to party with us!"

"Oh yeah!" Brody's sister exclaimed.

"Hey Vinny," Tarek said mischievously. "Tell us how things are going with Landon's little sister," Tarek grinned.

"Great," Vinny grinned. "We've gone on a couple dates."

"Do tell," Tarek grinned leaning forward batting his eyelashes.

"Jagger and Terra have been inseparable since the Initiation Party," Brody pointed out starting a sidebar conversation.

"Good for him!" Brett and Cameron cheered.

Nev walked up to the group, "Hey guys!"

"Nev!" The group called out affectionately.

"Virgil," Nev nodded his head to the side. Virgil got up and followed him out of the room. When they were safely out of ear shot Nev said, "Amari's in your room, I passed her coming downstairs. She told me to pass along the message she was here."

"Oh," Virgil casually said surprised. Inside he started freaking out, he'd been having so much fun, he hadn't been concentrated on Amari. "Thanks man," Virgil clapped him on the arm.

"Something's going on between you two," Nev grinned. "Something new?"

"Yeahhhh," Virgil grinned getting red. "And?" Virgil asked.

"Nothing, I'm happy for you," Nev said cutting the teasing edge from his voice. "You've been more relaxed and happier since you've been talking to Amariana, smiling more," Nev grinned. "Couldn't be gladder for you," Nev said. "Though we haven't had you around as much lately," he added at the end.

"I'll come around more," Virgil laughed, "Thanks Ninny," Virgil smiled calling Nevin by his fraternity nickname.

"Aww, you never call me that," Nev replied heartfelt.

"Later," Virgil called heading for the foyer.

Amari was sitting on his bed, turned away from him when he entered. She rose to greet him, the white flower in her hand. Virgil couldn't help but take notice of it the moment he saw it. She walked up to him, looking down, "I was really flattered by your token of affection," Amari looked up into his eyes. "What would, more than friends, look like for us?" Amari's words were deep, her gaze cut deeper.

"That's for us to decide," Virgil smiled liking what he was hearing.

"I've never," Amari sighed, she was obviously uncomfortable. Strange that this strong, vibrant, and sassy woman seemed so affected by him lately. How she'd treated him had changed over time, she was still the same person around everyone else, she just, grew softer towards him. Virgil thought she was really kind and loving, she'd just been hurt enough, she felt she had to keep her walls up constantly. "I've never *had* a boyfriend before," Amari admitted glowing a little red. "So I'm really inexperienced in all this."

"I think we should keep things how they are now; nothing has to change if we're a couple," Virgil offered. "I'd like you to be my girlfriend because I care about you Amari. I want you, and no one else, and I want you, to want the same as well. Though that is, only if that's what you want," Virgil was uncertain of her response and started laughing feeling nervous. "If any of that made any sense."

Amari flicked her hair slightly, and she offered the white rose to Virgil, he took it. "I want you, Virgil. I don't want to share you with anyone else," Amari moved forward into his arms, and they embraced tightly.

"You want to get out of here?" Virgil asked.

"Sure," Amari nodded.

Virgil grabbed a large blanket from his closet and they left his room. They walked down to the first floor, passing a few people they knew along the way. Homer, Jace, Doc, Spencer, and Landon were near the front door.

"And where are you two hot and heavy love birds off to at this hour?" Doc asked them looking them both over.

"With a blanket?" Homer asked causing the men to laugh.

"We're going to look at the stars," Virgil said honestly.

"Hmh," Homer raised an eyebrow at his friend like he didn't believe him. "In this weather? Have fun bro!" Virgil pushed through wanting to get out of that gauntlet. "Bed him well!" Homer called out as Virgil and Amari made it through the door. Virgil was horrified, they'd just decided to become official boyfriend and girlfriend, he hoped Amari could handle the teasing. He looked down at her, she looked fierce, she walked forward with purpose, and confidence. He'd like to watch his brothers try to shake her down, Amari was the type to fight back, not cower away. She had steel confidence holding her head high, he smiled, he'd never seen her really fight before, but he was betting she kicked ass. His gaze caught her attention, earning a raised eyebrow.

"Grinning fool," Amari whispered under her breath causing Virgil to laugh.

He drove them to the Tobico Marsh. They parked his car, and walked along the path. It was rather cold, Virgil summoned a small blaze of fire, and had it float around them as they walked. At the tower Virgil dissipated the flame, they walked up to the top, and the view was breathtaking. They could see out to Lake Huron, the constant background to Bay Valley. Virgil went around the top of the building, creating a perimeter. He placed illusion symbols, with the sign for fire, so when the barrier came into place it stopped anyone from entering the tower and created a warm atmosphere. It was a spell he'd been taught a long time ago by Vahn.

Amari had spread out the blanket, and they lay back, staring up into the night sky. Stars lit the canvas of the cosmos. With such a clear night, the lights felt like they were alive, pulsing and shining with life. Virgil felt the massive universe beyond their planet was the greatest and most mysterious part of being mortal on Earth. Amari's hand found his and they cuddled closer to one another, with the spell in place they weren't cold. It felt good to be close. They talked about everything and nothing, neither had never had a connection with another being like this.

Amari sat up, wrapping her arms around her legs looking away from Virgil. She'd been growing tense the past several minutes. Virgil sat up and tried to make eye contact with her, she wouldn't. "Virgil," Amari said her voice thick with conflict. "I've been wanting to tell you something, something important for a while now. I've just been, scared," Amari seemed visibly shaken, she was holding herself tight, Virgil saw a tremor running through her limbs.

"Amari," Virgil said concerned reaching out to her. "There's nothing you could tell me that would change the way I feel about you," he said honestly. "I love you Amari, I hope that, you love me too?" Virgil asked hesitantly.

"Of course," Amari looked at Virgil. "That's not it," she looked down.

Virgil's phone rang, he ignored it, and it started ringing again. Virgil saw it was Louie, "Hang on," Virgil sighed taking the call. "This had better be good," Virgil answered gruffly.

"Where you at homie?" Louie called out insanely loud. "Things are getting crazy back at the house, and everyone's asking about ya! Get over here you slut!"

"I'll be back," Virgil sighed realizing it wasn't anything.

"Where are you?" Louie was being nosy, he heard someone whisper in the background.

"Goodbye Louie," Virgil muttered irritated ending the call. "I'm sorry, my friends can be a little overwhelming at times," Virgil turned his phone off. "What were you saying?" Virgil asked Amari.

"Well," Amari trailed off looking into Virgil's eyes. Her gaze was so solemn, his face fell, what was going on? Virgil was about to ask her, when she moved forward, and kissed him. She kissed him passionately, like it was the last time they were going to be together. Virgil was taken back; Amari was being more aggressive than normal. He gave himself into it, wrapping his hands in her hair, the smell of her skin, and the taste of her lips arousing him. Amari got on top of him, sitting on his lap, and the heat began to build between them. Virgil grabbed her butt with both of his hands sitting up.

They stared into each other's eyes, pausing for a moment, then fell into each other, with almost ravenous hunger. She started pulling his shirt off, and he helped her out of her blouse. She got up and her hands went to his pants, she'd never touched him there before, he inhaled a little surprised. Amari didn't stop, she bit her lip and yanked his pants down in one motion.

"Wait," Virgil hesitated. "I don't have protection or anything here." He'd never been naked in front of Amari, or any girl for that matter. He wanted to go further but being the Redeemer with a pregnant girlfriend in college…sounded stressful. Amari reached into her purse and pulled one out. Virgil's eyebrows lifted, and she blushed laughing nervously not able to meet his gaze.

"Someone's prepared," Virgil smiled sheepishly.

"I got some after Semi," Amari said meeting his gaze again. "I wanted to be ready if the moment ever happened between us."

"I'm a virgin," Virgil admitted blushing a brilliant shade of bright red.

"Oh the brothers have told me, many times," Amari laughed full heartedly.

Just like that, Virgil lost the action in the pants, his demeanor fell, and he sighed feeling frustrated with the brothers. "What did they say?!" Virgil asked trying not to sound worried.

"Nothing!" Amari sighed. "Virgil, it doesn't matter, alright? Your brothers love you, and yes, they do tell humiliating stories as often as possible when you're not looking," Amari tried hard not to laugh.

"I bet it was Louie!" Virgil sighed and then they both laughed. It diffused the tension.

Amari bit her lip. "It doesn't matter to me either way," Amari sauntered up to Virgil, her emerald eyes practically blazing with fire. Her lips moved to his neck, then his ear. She whispered to him, "I want you."

They kissed slowly, laying down, and gave into the desire that had been consuming them both. Amari was everything Virgil wanted, he was in love with her, and being with her physically only strengthened the growing connection. Virgil understood now what the brothers were always talking about, why men thought about sex so often. He'd never felt such physical pleasure. Once awakened his vigor and passion become unbridled. Virgil was glad they were alone and in the woods. It was intimate, private, and special, as it should be. After, their bodies lay next to each other on the blanket, staring into each other's eyes, the eternal night sky overhead. He wanted to live in this moment forever.

They couldn't stay at the top of the observation tower forever. They prolonged leaving, not wanting to lose the moment they had shared. Neither of them had ever connected with another person like that. They decided to go to bed early and went back to Amari's place. They fell asleep, wrapped up in one another's arms, smiles on both of their faces.

# Chapter 20 Family Weekend

"I'm so glad we can finally meet!" Sue gushed to Amari. Virgil, Amari, and his mother were sitting in the cafeteria on campus, they'd been together long enough for the initial introductions to be out of the way. "How'd you two meet again?" Sue asked as they ate.

Amari started laughing to herself and stopped when they looked at her puzzled. "She's in a sorority that's close with the Omegas," Virgil explained to Sue.

"What's your family like?" Sue asked excitedly. "Are you from around here?"

"Mom," Virgil sighed embarrassed.

"What!?" Sue hit her hand on the table. "I have a right to get to know my son's girlfriend!" Sue protested.

Amari smirked, "It's alright Sue, I don't mind. I grew up in Illinois. My mom died giving birth to me, my family never knew who the father was."

"Sounds like Virgil," Sue remarked.

Amari nodded, "My grandmother raised me till she passed away."

"I'm sorry to hear that honey," Sue patted Amari's hand. "She must have been a great woman, to raise such a respectful granddaughter."

That made Amari smile, "I came to Bay Valley because I liked the dorms, and it has cheaper tuition than most places."

"How'd you join that sorority?" Sue asked. "I was honestly worried when Virgil said he was joining the fraternity. It's confusing, I feel like he's speaking another language sometimes," Sue laughed.

"It's about comradery, community service, and being a part of something that's important," Amari explained to Sue. "When you're looking for friends like yourself, sometimes you find them in unexpected places," Amari looked over at Virgil and smiled.

Sue looked at them both and smiled as well. "What's your major dear?" Sue asked interested in Amari.

"I'm a Communications major," Amari replied eating her chicken and rice. "I'm still trying to figure things out though, might switch."

"I'm thinking of switching too," Virgil added chewing his food.

"You are!" Sue exclaimed with surprise. "Since when? You don't want to be a doctor anymore?" Sue asked with concern.

"Mom, it's not a big deal. I just…don't think that's the right path for me anymore," Virgil shrugged.

"Did something happen?" Sue asked.

"No," Virgil lied. A lot had happened, Virgil wasn't human, he was Nephilim. His father was a General leading the dark forces of the Ever After, and Virgil was the Redeemer, shepherd of Fallen Judges. He wished he could tell her all these things, bring her into the fold. He felt inside that was dangerous though, the more she knew, the more dangerous she became to herself. If the Death Dealers wanted to get to him, all they had to do was take his mother. He'd be completely helpless. He shook such thoughts from his mind, enjoying his time with his mother and Amari.

Amari and Sue got a long great. Amari was more talkative than Virgil had ever seen her, she asked lots of questions about Virgil. Sue was only too happy to tell all the embarrassing stories Virgil wished could just go away.

"Anyways this smell was coming from somewhere in the house, and I was in a cleaning frenzy, tearing the whole place apart," Sue told Amari.

"Please stop," Virgil was mortified, Amari was having a great time.

"No! Keep going," Amari laughed.

"Finally, I narrowed it down to Virgil's room. On the floor was the little train set. The one part had a compartment that opened up, I threw it open and screamed!" Sue shouted.

"What was inside?" Amari asked leaning in.

"Virgil's messy diaper!" Sue said excitedly causing them both to burst out laughing. "He was only ten months old when he was potty trained, he hated diapers, and demanded to go on the toilet. He started walking that day. He started talking early too, sixteen months," Sue smiled.

"He was a smart baby," Amari smiled.

"Oh yes," Sue nodded. "I woke up one night to Virgil bouncing around in his crib. I demanded that he lay down and go back to sleep. He turned around and gave me this pouty expression and said, 'I did!' after he started jumping around and laughing again. I was so shocked I had to ask him what he had said," Sue laughed.

"His first words were a sentence?" Amari laughed.

"Not even two and already a sassy mouth on him," Sue gave Virgil a look.

"I'm sassy?" Virgil asked his mom.

"You think you know everything, and that you're always right," Sue told Virgil.

"Sorry I asked," Virgil rolled his eyes.

"See?" Sue asked Amari pointing to her son and they started laughing again.

"It's about time to be hitting that old, dusty trail," Virgil stretched out as he stood up.

"Oh, sit down, we're having fun," Sue demanded, and Virgil frowned, sitting down.

Amari gave Virgil this look like, someone's a mama's boy. Virgil was just glad they were hitting it off, so he suffered the stories.

Once they finished eating they went for a short walk. The campus was full of families with students. There were different activities across campus, planned throughout the day for a variety of age groups. Kids were playing on bounce equipment in the courtyard, preteens and older were doing tye dye, there was a mini casino, all in good fun of course, set up for the adults, a lot of parents had migrated over there.

"This is really impressive," Sue gestured around them, "I'm glad your University does events like this," Sue beamed.

"Selene put this on," Virgil smiled. "She's the student body President, Amari's sorority sister, in a community service fraternity, in like four other organizations, oh yeah and she's Brody's girlfriend, he's a brother," Virgil explained to his mother. "She's pretty much going to cure cancer someday," Virgil joked making them both chuckle. Virgil didn't know how else to explain her. "When Selene gets an idea in her head, she doesn't stop till she's done the very best she's capable of," Virgil spoke of her with respect and reverence. He wished in some ways he could be as ambitious and giving as she was, how she had the time to have her hands in so much was beyond him.

They paused, Amari was going to walk back to her dorm, and Virgil and Sue were going to the Omega house. "Bye Amari," Virgil smiled.

"Bye Virgil," Amari smiled back.

"We'll have to do this again soon!" Sue exclaimed saying goodbye to Amari. "Maybe next time Amari, Virgil and you can come to my place!"

"I'd like that, get to see where Virgil grew up," Amari smiled looking at Virgil. "You raised a very fine young man, Ms. Pitcher," Amari complimented her.

"I can't take all the credit love," Sue laughed. "His father helped too, and Virgil is just a great guy to begin with, just has to watch that temper of his," Sue admonished him.

"I hardly ever blow up," Virgil sighed feeling his temper bubbling in response, funny how moms could know their children so well. He walked with Amari a few paces away from his mother. They held hands and looked into each other's faces. "Thanks for being so great back there, moms can be…overwhelming," Virgil sighed. "I'm her only kid so, she kind of wants me to find someone already," Virgil said uncomfortably laughing.

"That was fun," Amari shook her head in protest. "I like her."

"When will I see you again?" Virgil asked wishing he could just bring her along, the event was strictly only family, there were already going to be a lot of people.

Amari looked down not meeting his gaze. "I have stuff going on at the Alpha's house with the sisters, but it'll be done by the evening. Maybe you could come spend the night Sunday?" Amari pondered.

"I'd like that," Virgil pulled her in close and embraced her tightly.

"I'll see you soon," Amari whispered to him staring into his eyes.

"Miss you," Virgil whispered back.

Amari reached in for a quick kiss, it got Virgil's heart racing, licking at a fiery desire. She pulled back, leaving him only wanting more. Amari waved goodbye to Sue before walking home.

"Ready to see the Omega house?" Virgil asked his mother hoping it wasn't obvious how madly he was in love with that woman.

"Lead the way!" Sue said excitedly.

Virgil drove his mother to the west side of campus where Greek housing was located. At the end of the long path, sat the majestic red brick wall surrounding, and protecting the Omega grounds. The gates were wide open; from the head of the driveway they could see the place was packed with vehicles.

"This is so exciting," Sue said to Virgil as they got out and walked to the front of the house. "I can't believe you live here, feels like we're walking into a millionaire's home," Sue laughed.

"It is overwhelming the first time you come here," Virgil remembered coming to this place his third week of college, with his roommate Boyd. He'd met Gabriel, and Magnus that night, little did he know how important they were, or how important they'd become to him.

Just inside the entrance, the house was alive with activity. It was loud, music wasn't even playing, there was laughter, and lots of conversation. Virgil heard his name being called out as they walked into the foyer. Doc waltzed over with Gina, and a woman who could've passed for Gina's older sister. Doc had a young mom, she had a gentle smile, but eyes that reflected the tenacity of a single mom who'd raised four kids.

"Hey there Cherry!" Doc smiled embracing Virgil. "Welcome home cupcake," Doc's overly lavish tone made Virgil chuckle. Sue was going to think his brothers were a bunch of nut jobs!

"Gina, always nice to see you," Virgil nodded. "This must be your mother?" Virgil asked.

"Garnet," She introduced herself shaking Virgil's hand.

"This is my mom, Sue," Virgil introduced them.

"What do you think of your son being in this whole, fraternity business?" Sue asked Garnet surprising Virgil. Sue was serious, she wanted another parent's perspective.

Garnet didn't pause she knew what she thought, "Well my Gareth has been home now for six months, he failed out of Bay Valley last year," she told Sue honestly.

"Mom!" Doc yelled.

"Oh, he doesn't even go here anymore?" Sue was surprised.

"I'm going to community college back in Macomb County," Doc told Sue, "I plan on transferring back."

"Gareth loves this fraternity," Garnet sighed, "They are a second family to him. Gina tells me the boys are nice to her as well, which is reassuring having them looking out for her. Gareth swears they are the best friends he's ever made. Do I worry however, if it's a bad influence? Of course," Garnet nodded. "This fraternity, it's good for them though," Garnet looked at Gareth. "It gave my son self-confidence, he's so much more driven, and sure of himself since joining the Omegas. I like seeing that in him," Garnet smiled.

Sue was pleased with her response; Virgil could tell their moms had hit it off. Virgil wanted to show Sue around the house, so they kept moving. They didn't make it far, just to the dinning room.

"Wondering when you were gonna show up!" Louie called out.

Birdy and his parents, Louie and his parents, Dante and his brother and father, Troy and his parents, along with Nolan and his parents, were all standing around. They were mingling and getting to know one another, Virgil smiled to himself having stumbled across his pledge brothers.

"Mom these are my Omicron pledge brothers!" Virgil exclaimed excitedly. "And their families."

Virgil noticed instantly that Louie's parents, along with Dante's dad and brother, had Devil Arms symbols as well. It was shocking to see some of the parents, in on the fold of what was going on. Virgil made eye contact with them, and they took notice of him as well, his Chaos and Creation Devil Arms starkly stood out on his hands. Louie was the closest, so they stood by them.

"Virgil, this is Jo my dad, and my stepmom, Tuh. You say it like the number two," Louie introduced his father and stepmother. Jo had a blue symbol shaped like a katana, aligned with water like Louie. His stepmother had an amethyst Devil Arms, like a fan. They were both Asian like Louie, though Louie's father had darker skin tone, with a smaller face. He was a quiet man, the exact opposite of his son. Louie's stepmother was a petite woman, with gorgeous skin. She was aging beyond gracefully, with a welcoming presence, air of grace, and a facilitating attitude.

"Virgil, so good to meet you," Tuh, Louie's stepmother, said smiling kindly. Louie's parents had the thick accent Louie had most of his first year at college. It came from speaking primarily Vietnamese, their English had a shortness to it, there were no plurals in their speech. Louie had mostly kicked that habit, though funny around his parents, his thick accent came back. "Louie tell us all about you. Brave man, and loyal friend. Louie thinks of you as family," Tuh said with a kindness. "We would love to have you over sometime," Tuh offered.

"I'd love that!" Virgil nodded.

"This is Sue," Virgil introduced his mom.

Jo and Tuh took notice she didn't have a Devil Arms, they didn't skip a beat however, they were some of the politest people Virgil had ever met. Sue asked them all sorts of questions about Louie and themselves. They lived in Sterling Heights, where Louie had grown up. Louie had eight brothers and sisters, between his father, mother, and stepmother.

"My son from a young age was a talented artist," Jo boasted.

"Didn't a guy offer you money for my paintings dad?" Louie asked.

"Oh yes," Tuh answered for Jo. "Louie is very special; his work was beyond his time. Jo refused to sell it; he got many offer." Tuh smiled gazing at her husband with respect. "It mean too much to Louie father, give him great pride." Jo nodded a little misty eyed. Louie smiled embarrassed, Virgil could see that making his father proud meant the world to Louie, he was a great son.

Birdy's father was your typical Republican, man's man. He was also named Alec, like his father before him, and his before him. He had a big bushy moustache, he was intimidating at first, but a good guy underneath. Birdy's mother was a bombshell house mom, who could easily have been nominated mother of the year. Birdy talked to his mom three times a day; they were close. Virgil always thought he was close with his mother, seeing how close Birdy was with her though, they were best friends, it made Virgil envious. Sue instantly clicked with Barb Birdman, Birdy's mother. Barb was charismatic, outgoing, social, and fun.

Dante's father was a quiet man until he opened up. Dante's brother was built huge, and over six feet tall. Dante was the little brother, and he liked to remind him of that. Troy's parents were quiet, wonderful people. It was easy to see how he'd turned out to be such a good person. Nolan's parents couldn't be prouder of the man their son had become. Nolan really was an all-star brother, straight A student, workalcholic, and doting son. What more could a parent ask for?

Virgil and Sue went onto the patio in the backyard. Fires were lit, and though it was late November, it felt warm. They had been lucky with the weather. Magnus, Gabriel, Vahn, Jagger, Landon, and Spencer along with their families were out back. It was funny how the pledge classes had gravitated towards each other. Helene was there with her parents; Landon's father had a Devil Arms similar to his son's. Most of the parents of Lambda class had Devil Arms.

"You must be Sue," Vahn came up to them introducing himself and shaking her hand. "I'm Vahn, Virgil's Big in the fraternity."

"Virgil's told me about you!" Sue nodded. "You look after him, and I appreciate that greatly, from a mother to a brother, thank you," Sue smiled.

"Oh, it's my pleasure, Virgil's a great brother, we wouldn't be the same Chapter without him," Vahn boasted.

"Please," Virgil rolled his eyes.

"Never mind my sassy son," Sue waved off Virgil. "Tell me more about this fraternity," she asked Vahn. "I've been wondering how do you guys recruit people?"

Vahn looked at Virgil, then at Sue's hands. He gave Virgil a look like, it's your call. "People who join Omega are, different," Virgil suggested to his mother. "Fraternities were first founded, hundreds of years ago, to recruit people like us."

"What? Smart people?" Sue asked not understanding.

"Kind of," Vahn laughed. "Our fraternity was founded on the idea that men should be judged for who they are as people, rather than by wealth, or ties they have to powerful people."

"It seems like there is more than that," Sue mused skeptically. She knew there was something more, Virgil didn't know what to say. Luckily Nolan walked out.

"Dinner is being set, you guys can make your plates, oldest scroll numbers first," Nolan announced.

Lots of the new brothers wanted Virgil to meet their parents. There were too many faces, and names to learn all at once. Zane's mother was the youngest mom present. She had a natural beauty, worn from working hard and raising five children. Zane was fiercely proud of his mother, she was a fun, and kind woman. Virgil hadn't met one person who he didn't like.

Virgil and Sue ran into Vinny which made Sue excited as he was one of the few brothers she knew. "The Little Brother!" Sue called out to Vinny wanting a big hug. "Good to see you!"

The Omegas sat down for an early dinner. Sue, Vinny, and Virgil sat next to Louie and his parents. Tarek was the Chaplain, or Hypophetes, so he gave the blessing before dinner. Tarek's mother was present, a beautiful fierce, sandy blond Nephilim. She didn't have her wings present like the last time Virgil had seen her, she lived in Alexandros. She gave Virgil an enthusiastic wave, she seemed to be having the time of her life, mingling with humans in disguise.

Virgil noticed Tuh setting a place of food next to where Louie sat. Virgil had to ask, "Louie, what is she doing?"

"It is Louie duty, to pass on the family," Tuh explained.

Louie elaborated. "I'm the eldest and only son from my dad, so the family name, and whole family line rests with me. My grandfather, watches over me, guiding me to keep the family line going. Tuh sets a place for him at the table, to welcome his spirit. He is my guardian," Louie shrugged. It was a different practice, something Virgil had never heard of, but they came from a different religious belief than his mother. Sue Pitcher was a Lutheran Christian. Virgil had always been more spiritual, than religious. If more people could just move past religion, and accept or at the very least, tolerate other's religious beliefs, humanity would be well on its way to the next chapter of their journey, and the next step of their evolution.

The family dinner couldn't have been more filling or filled with great conversation. Everyone was getting along, and those over twenty-one were indulging in some adult beverages. Birdy's father and Dante's dad loosened up and started getting a little louder, they were sitting close together and getting along. A lot of the parents were connecting with other parents. After Virgil ran into Brody and his parents, they were tied for Virgil's favorite, along with Louie's. Hippies through and through, they were young in spirit, open minded, and hard working.

Sue was talking with them about the fraternity. "Before this event I was worried about the fraternity's impact on Virgil. I think all fraternities need something like this to assure the parents their kids aren't getting involved in anything bad," Sue made Virgil smirk.

"We were worried too," Brody's father nodded. "Then we saw how it changed our son. He became more mature, confident, and driven."

"Brody and Selene are both very passionate about their organizations," Brody's mother said to Sue. "They work very hard, you've got to, in this day and age just to get by."

"Oh Selene," Sue nodded. "The one who put on the Family Weekend events, she's your girlfriend?" Sue asked Brody.

"Yup," Brody laughed getting red in the face. "I'm a lucky guy," he admitted.

"She's lucky too," Brody's mother insisted. Brody's sister was there from the night before. She'd bonded with the brothers and was floating through the group with ease.

There were hours of daylight left, and so much more fun to be had. Everyone was starting to let loose; Virgil couldn't have been happier. A Paladin from the Capital walked in, his attire was that of all official Paladins, out of place in normal American society. It caught Sue's attention right away and she gave Virgil a look. The man walked over to Magnus whispering to him. Magnus immediately went stiff, he gave Gabriel a look, and all of Lambda class got up and left the room. Everyone was spread out, so not everyone had noticed. Virgil didn't like the look on Magnus' face, something big had just happened.

"Oh crap," Louie sighed as Gabriel and Magnus came back ten minutes later.

"We're having an emergency meeting on the second floor, brothers only," Magnus announced. "Everyone please make yourselves comfortable." The families didn't pay it any mind, going back to conversing while the brothers headed to the meeting room. Once the door was closed Zender placed a barrier spell over the door, sealing off the room.

"Demons just struck Midland," Magnus said carefully. "They've overtaken Dow. This will likely be all over the news by the evening," Magnus spoke with deliberate calmness.

"How?" Jace asked. "Its broad daylight!"

"Obviously the Death Dealers are at work here," Magnus pointed out like it was the most obvious thing. "A powerful shroud has been cast, a black barrier like cloud has covered a portion of the city, allowing demons to materialize in the daylight."

"I guess from what the Lieutenant told us," Gabriel spoke up adding in, "It looks like giant storm clouds to the civilians in Midland. The clouds are so thick though, they are blocking out the sun, making it seem like night in one half of the city."

"Why hit Midland?" Spencer asked.

"The Paladins believe the Death Dealers are mounting their forces, preparing for an invasion of our University," Magnus said honestly causing a few reactions. "Reinforcements are already being mobilized. The Chalice will be moved out of here by the end of the night."

"A group of Paladins are going over to Midland, to stem their forces from gaining ground so close to campus," Gabriel told everyone. "We are going to keep most of our brothers here, to protect our home and our families. A few brothers are being asked to go to campus, just as a precaution. The Paladins requested a squad of brothers go with them to Midland."

"We should go," Dante said to Virgil and the rest of Omicron, who had sat next to each other.

"We need to get our families to safety," Virgil suggested. "I don't want my mom staying here."

"I don't want my parents staying here either," Louie added.

"We'll be evacuating the parents who don't live near Midland," Magnus announced. "Otherwise they are welcome to stay in the safety of the Omega house.

"Fine we send our parents' home, then go to Midland," Dante said to their group.

"Maybe I should protect the house," Louie suggested.

"Louie why don't you just come with us?" Birdy asked. "We could use your help on this one."

"Damn! Y'all act like you can't do shit without me! How many times do I got to keep saving you guys!" Louie yelled at them.

"You say that like you do it all the time!" Dante grouched back. "I don't recall you pitching in a whole lot lately."

"I do a lot for this fraternity!" Louie defended himself.

"No one is saying you don't!" Dante fired back. "But it would be nice if you could come along and watch your best friends' backs! Feels like we beg ya to come along every time! Or kiss your ass and constantly thank you." Dante began acting a fool. "Please protect us Louie V!" He mockingly pleaded. "We shouldn't have to ask!"

"Knock it off," Birdy sighed.

"Fine!" Louie caved in. "I'll come along! But if I die out there, I am coming back to haunt you for the rest of your life Dante!" Louie challenged.

"I'll make sure there is always a spare bedroom, for your ghost, wherever I live," Dante said happily.

Virgil, Birdy, Dante, Louie, Rowan, and Nev volunteered to go with the Paladins heading to Midland. They weren't taking anyone without wings, so a lot of the brothers couldn't go. They needed the rest of the Omegas to stay anyways to defend the house and campus. They were released, and everyone headed downstairs to have uncomfortable conversations with their parents. Gabriel volunteered to make the announcement, calling everyone together in the living room.

"Something has unexpectedly come up," Gabriel said carefully to all the brothers and their parents and siblings. "The campus has been warned of a possible attack. Midland has just been hit, and everyone is being advised to evacuate the area if possible, staying away from the

Mildand and Bay City area," the room was breaking out into frenzied conversation and Gabriel's voice was being lost. He raised his voice speaking above everyone. "If you so desire, you are welcome to stay here, and ride this situation out!" Gabriel shouted.

Sue was at Virgil's side, she turned to him confused. "What is going on Virgil?" Sue asked concerned. "What kind of attack? Is it Terrorists?"

"I want you to go back to Caseville," Virgil spoke deliberately, wanting his voice to come out even and controlled.

"Why?" Sue asked fear on her face. "Maybe you should come with me," she added. "If it's not safe for me here, I don't want you staying either!"

"I have to stay, make sure nothing happens to this place," Virgil smiled, "And maybe help out if someone's in danger."

"Help out!" Sue shouted. "What are you going to do?" she asked incredulously. "No, you're coming home with me Virgil Pitcher, and that's the last I'll hear of this!" Sue declared like the conversation was over. She grabbed his hand and started walking for the exit.

"Mom!" Virgil shouted startling her. She turned to her son, she looked so confused, and Virgil felt so guilty seeing the puzzlement in her eyes. "I can't go with you," Virgil said feeling like he was ripping her heart out.

"If you aren't going home, then I won't be going either," Sue said stubbornly. Virgil looked around; his brothers were having the same awkward conversations. Most parents were listening and heading out. Louie's parents embraced him fiercely, before heading for the foyer. Lamar's grandmother was refusing to go, along with Jeramiah's parents. Only a handful of parents were being stubborn and wanting to stay at the Omega house with the brothers. Virgil didn't know how he was going to sneak off to Midland with his mother there. She would freak out if he told her where he was headed.

Professor Ramuh, Professor Ifrit, and Gabriel's brother Ezekiel came into the room. The Chapter Advisors were a welcoming presence, the brothers were all visibly relieved. Professor Ramuh came over to Virgil and his mother, sensing the tension. "You're staying here?" Professor Ramuh asked Sue.

"I'm not leaving my son alone, somewhere dangerous," Sue said defiantly.

"Perhaps you would be more comfortable back home?" Professor Ramuh offered. "We'll keep an eye on your son, and you can keep in contact with him by phone."

"Who are you?" Sue asked with attitude.

"I am one of the Chapter Advisors who help watch over the brothers and provide them with guidance. I'm Professor Ramuh," Professor Ramuh said introducing himself.

"I'll go home, if Virgil comes with me," Sue crossed her arms over her chest.

"If you wish to stay, you have my promise that we'll do everything we can to keep this house safe," Professor Ramuh nodded, patting Virgil's back, before walking away.

"Virgil," Dante called out to Virgil. "We'll be outside waiting." A group of over thirty Paladins had headed out the back. Virgil's brothers went too, waiting for him to finish.

Virgil took his mother's hands in his own and looked deep into her brown eyes. "Mom, I have to go," Virgil said sincerely.

"Go where?" Sue asked angrily.

"I'll be back soon, don't worry," Virgil smiled.

Sue's eyes started to water, and Virgil's expression fell. Sue was really scared, and Virgil felt like crap for putting her through this. He'd been looking forward to this day, his mother meeting his fraternity, and all the other parents. Why did this have to happen now?!

"Mom," Virgil said taking her into his arms hugging her tightly.

"I'm so worried about you," Sue whispered. "I don't want anything bad happening to you. You're my whole world Virgil," Sue's voice was tight. "I can't lose you too. I'm not strong enough to survive that."

"You'll never lose me, mom," Virgil promised moving back to look into his mother's eyes. "If I tell you something, do you promise to keep it a secret?" Virgil asked her.

"What?" Sue asked.

"I'm Nephilim mom," Virgil said feeling like a giant weight had fallen off his shoulders. "Part human, part Angel."

"Virgil this isn't the time," Sue replied sounding annoyed.

Virgil's words were filled with passion as he spoke, "You wanted to know what was going on, why it feels like there is more than I am telling you, this is the truth! Ragnorak!" Virgil raised his hand to the ceiling. A bolt of lightning crashed into his hand, extending out into his sword. Sue cried out in surprise jumping back. Virgil burst his wings from his back, extending them out for Sue to see. Sue stared hard at her son, trying to make sense of what she was seeing.

"Can you seem them?" Virgil asked her moving his wings.

"See what?" She asked.

"My wings," Virgil moved them slightly floating off the ground, causing her hair to move from the wind.

Sue wore a concerned expression. "What just happened?" Sue asked. "What did you do?" Sue wasn't staring at the wings; she was looking at his sword, and his feet floating off the ground. She couldn't see the wings, what did she see when she looked at him?

"I'm Nephilim," Virgil said to his mother landing. "Every Nephilim is born with a Devil Arms, a celestial weapon. I was given Ragnorak once wielded by my father."

"Your father?" Sue looked confused. "What do you mean?"

"I met him, over the summer," Virgil said feeling guilty for having lied to her for so long. "Remember when I disappeared for over a week this summer? I was taken prisoner," Virgil admitted. "My father is a Fallen Angel, who has pledged allegiance to the Devil."

"NO!" Sue shouted.

"Yes," Virgil nodded.

"Has the fraternity put this nonsense in your head!" Sue looked like she was about to blow up. "Are you on drugs?" she asked ready to start shouting.

"No," Virgil sighed frustrated. "Mom, everything I just said was the truth."

"Your son isn't lying," Vahn said coming over to stand by Virgil. Virgil was grateful for his presence, everyone else had left the room. "Virgil is the son of a powerful Judge, probably the strongest warrior I've ever known. He's a leader among the Nephilim. He's saved my life, and the lives of countless others time and again. You raised a kind, and loyal son Ms. Pitcher, you should be proud," Vahn spoke with passion and pride. It brought tears to Virgil's eyes.

"Not you too," Sue sighed.

"Your son was brave for telling you the truth," Vahn said to Sue. "Most humans without Judge blood can't see past their own auras and are blind to magic and Devil Arms. My mother didn't believe me when I told her, to this day she doesn't believe me." Virgil was shocked, Vahn had never told Virgil that. "It took a lot of courage for your son to tell you the truth. Now think hard about this, are you going to reject what he has said, or are you going to trust in your son?" Vahn made Sue really think, she looked shaken. Sue shook her head staring at Virgil.

"This is…a lot," Sue looked down thinking to herself, "There was always something special about you," Sue said softly. "I never understood it. Your father thought you had a guardian Angel coming to the house every night for years."

Virgil was quiet, it had been a while since they talked about the visits at night. "I have to go," Virgil said to Sue. "There are people in danger, and I have the power to help them."

"You do this kind of thing a lot," Sue looked up at Virgil. "Don't you?" She asked not liking the thought of it.

"Yes," Virgil answered truthfully.

"I, I don't want to wait for you at home," Sue said looking down at her hands. "I need to be here," Sue got tears in her eyes. "Promise me, you'll be careful. Promise me, you'll come back to me," Sue stared Virgil down. Virgil commanded Ragnorak to leave.

"I promise mom, I'll always find my way home, and home is where my mom is," Virgil had tears in his eyes. They embraced fiercely.

"I'll watch over her while you're gone," Vahn said to Virgil, more serious than he'd ever seen him. "I'll keep her safe, no matter what happens."

"Thank you Vahn. Mom, hear that? You got the Chapter's Hegemon protecting you," Virgil smiled weakly to his mother. "He's one of the best fighters, he trained me," Virgil smiled.

"Oh," Sue chuckled nervously.

Virgil ran to his room. He threw open his dresser and carefully placed the Optimum in his pocket. It was halfway full, and he felt reassured having the extra energy available. Sue was sitting down, looking a little shocked and overwhelmed.

Sue stood up and gave him one final hug. "When you get back, I want to talk more," her voice lacking the anger it held moments ago. "I want you, to feel comfortable telling me about this stuff. I'm sorry you felt you had to keep it from me for so long."

"I didn't," Virgil answered wanting her to know. "I never told you because I wanted to keep you safe. I trust you more than anyone, I need you to know that." Sue was moved by his words and he could do no more than smile, she smiled too, knowing her son loved her unconditionally. Virgil wanted to talk more but he didn't have time. "I love you mom."

"I love you too! Be safe!" Sue called out to him as he left the room, both their hearts weighing heavy.

# Chapter 21 Betas Betrayal

Virgil's brothers were waiting for him on the back patio, the Paladins had already gone on ahead. Virgil had a dejected look on his face, Louie asked him, "Everything alright?"

"I'm fine," Virgil nodded. "Let's not keep the others waiting."

Virgil, Birdy, Dante, Louie, Nev, and Rowan followed the well-worn path to the Nephilim temple in the woods. A group of Paladins from Alexandros were already inside, discussing tactics and battle strategy. The brothers approached the temple, when Virgil heard his name being shouted out.

"Virgil!" Blair cried out. She was flying over the trees, landing hard, with a panicked crazed look in her eyes. "I went to the Omega house, but they said you'd left already!" Blair was winded, and her words were coming out breathlessly.

"What's going on?" Virgil asked knitting his eyebrows together.

Blair was coughing, she struggled to compose herself. "It's Amari!" Blair managed to get out. Virgil's ears started ringing, everything around him became muted, his whole body became very hot.

Virgil's friends let out expressions of surprise and concern. Virgil was still trying to process this, "What happened to Amari?" Virgil asked Blair tension filling his body.

"The Betas, they took her!" Blair shouted. "A group of them stormed our sorority house, and just, everything happened so fast," Blair was upset and shaken.

"Did they hurt her?" Virgil asked concerned and feeling like his world was crashing down. What nefarious schemes were the Betas planning?

"They knocked her out when she put up a struggle," Blair said weakly. "Jamal and Malachi along with a handful of older brothers barged in and went right for her. Terra stopped me from kicking their asses, she was worried some of us would end up getting killed if we fought back," Blair shook her head feeling guilty.

"Why would the Betas take Amari?" Dante asked not understanding this.

"I thought you guys were friends with that Beta, Damian," Rowan asked them.

"I am," Virgil nodded. "He wouldn't do this. I know its Malachi, it's always been him," Virgil said to the others. "Damian warned me at the beginning of the semester that Malachi and some of the older Betas were helping with something, something big," Virgil remembered. He shook his head. "This couldn't be worse timing."

"We're leaving!" A Paladin shouted from inside the temple.

"Give us a second!" Virgil shouted back. "What do they want with her?" Virgil asked Blair not understanding this. Why did the Betas take his girlfriend?! Virgil felt like shouting until he went hoarse with rage.

"I don't know," Blair frowned, "I'm so sorry Virgil," Blair looked down.

"Where did they take her?" Virgil asked stepping closer to Blair. "I have to go after them."

"We're supposed to be going to Midland!" Rowan laughed nervously. "The Paladins need our help!"

"I have to go after Amari," Virgil cut across, leaving no room for arguing. "All of you can go with them to Midland, I'll confront the rogue Betas on my own," Virgil said.

"Like hell you will!" Dante stomped his foot. "I've been wanting revenge on those bastards since they took Louie last year," he grumbled. "I'm not about to let you just fly off into some trap! It's about time those Betas owned up to their treacherous ways," Dante gritted his teeth. "Let's kick their asses, and make them regret ever fucking with the Omegas!"

"Hell yeah!" Birdy shouted

"Shieeeeet man, we're all gonna die!" Louie groaned nervously.

"I'll go explain the situation," Rowan sighed walking over to the temple to engage with the Paladins. They didn't talk long, the Paladins were displeased but unconcerned, these were soldiers. A Paladin quickly made a portal and the group headed through. The temple emptying of over forty Nephilim warriors within a minute. "They said that Internationals will complete a full investigation once this is over. This is the second time in less than a year that this Chapter of the Betas are being linked to Death Dealers," Rowan shook his head. "They should have been shut down the first time."

"Blair, do you know where they took her?" Virgil asked his friend again.

Blair nodded, "As they were leaving Malachi said to tell the Redeemer, if he wants his…girlfriend," she laughed nervously as it was obviously not the term he'd used. "To come collect her at the abandoned factory on the Saginaw River, south end of Bay City," Blair remembered.

"It's a trap!" Louie shouted his tone filled with dread.

"Duh," Birdy retorted.

"It'll take just a few minutes to fly over there," Rowan nodded. "Let's go."

"Better than going to Midland anyway," Nev shrugged. "I was feeling kind of nervous being surrounded by those Paladins from Alexandros."

"I'm coming with you," Blair asserted.

"I'm sorry to have to ask you to help," Virgil felt so lost he wasn't thinking straight.

"You didn't, I volunteered," Blair huffed. "Besides, you'll need my help."

"We always do," Dante smirked.

"Let's go!" Virgil commanded and the seven of them extended their wings from their backs, jumping into the air taking flight. The University sat at the mouth of the Saginaw River and Lake Huron. They followed the river, keeping their altitude high, as to not attract attention. It was evening, with dusk not far off, people often mistook Nephilim for birds, or planes. Virgil didn't care about people seeing them, his mind was racing with horrible thoughts. If the Betas did anything to Amari, he'd tear every one of them apart with Soul Reaver! Virgil felt bad for not going with the Paladins, they were likely outnumbered, and were heading into a war zone completely blind. Virgil prayed that all the Nephilim aligned with the Paladins would be kept safe, as they fought to protect the lives of the innocent people caught in the middle of all this.

The group flew fast, passing the four main draw bridges of Bay City. The old building that was their destination, came into view. The city was working on knocking down most of the abandoned factories and buildings along the river, in an effort to gentry the city. This was one of the buildings that hadn't been replaced with condos or restaurants yet. The property it was on, was massive, and empty. The seven of them landed near the building, it was unsettlingly quiet. Virgil led his friends inside, there was broken glass, and garbage everywhere. The condemned building was very open, the sounds of their footsteps echoing throughout the decaying husk. As they walked slowly, deeper inside, visibility became low. Everyone was tense, they stayed tightly grouped together.

Lights came on just ahead, Malachi and Jamal were standing before them, with six other brothers, all had white wings upon their backs. A portal hung in the air behind the Betas. There weren't as many as Virgil had thought there would be, he smiled not seeing Damian. Not all of the Betas were loyal to Malachi. Malachi's men looked tough though, they had one more person than Virgil's group, and all the Betas were older. Amari was nowhere to be seen.

"Where is Amari?" Virgil demanded.

"You actually thought she'd be here?" Malachi chuckled. "Even you aren't that gullible."

Malachi had an amethyst polearm Devil Arms, Jamal had an earth Devil Arms, shaped like a giant axe. They were powerful Nephilim, he'd never battled either warrior, and was hoping to keep it that way.

"Tell me where she is, and I'll be gone from this place," Virgil offered wanting to end this meeting.

"In that case we'll not say a word," Jamal laughed his voice deep and booming. "You just stay there and die with dignity."

"In your wet dreams asshole!" Dante growled, his Devil Arms glowing with light. "Omegas go down gouging out eyeballs and ripping out tongues!" Dante's eyes were fierce.

"Brave words from such a puny man," Jamal jested and his brothers broke into laughter.

"Why did you take Amariana?" Virgil asked Malachi.

"I do everything my cousin Sethos asks of me," Malachi said affectionately.

"The Harbringer is your cousin?" Virgil asked Malachi surprised.

"My parents raised him, we were like brothers," Malachi explained. "My mother was his mother's older sister. His mom died giving birth to him. On his sixteenth birthday he Awakened, and his father came to make him an offer. Sethos went into the Ever After with Lucifer, and I didn't hear from him again until the summer before I started college. My cousin Sethos came to me, asking me to join the Paladins through a collegiate fraternity, and serve as his spy on the inside," Malachi smiled proudly. "There are hundreds of spies within the Paladins! I proved my worth when I discovered you on your first night of college. Sethos was seeking the right kind of Nephilim's blood to break the seal on that Arch Demon."

"You've been working for the Death Dealers," Virgil looked at each of the eight Betas. "And recruiting other men to turn against the Paladins."

"We had more, until you turned Damian against us," Malachi sneered.

"Where is he?" Virgil asked.

"With the rest of the Betas, at our fraternity house," Malachi shrugged. "We don't plan on sticking around Bay Valley any longer. We'll be joining the Death Dealers in the Ever After, now that our cover is blown."

"You plan to finish us off, and collect your reward from Sethos?" Dante asked angrily.

"Our job was to lure the Redeemer here. By now Bay Valley is all but defenseless, Sethos should be leading the Death Dealers there as we speak," Malachi grinned.

"The attack on Midland was just a diversion!" Nev shouted. "The Death Dealers plan to hit campus!"

"We need to go back!" Blair urged the group.

"Not so fast!" Jamal barked.

Virgil clenched his fists, he was tired of this exchange, he stared Malachi down. "Where is Amariana?" Virgil demanded to know.

"With Sethos I imagine," Malachi shrugged. "You'll have to take it up with him, if you want your whore back."

Virgil growled Soul Reaver materializing in his left hand, its flames standing high off the scythe.

"Virgil we need to get out of here!" Louie urged. "We don't got time to be wasting on these clowns, campus could be under attack!"

"I know!" Virgil shouted. His mother was there; he knew all too well how little time they had. The Betas weren't just going to let them go though, if they tried to fly out of here, they'd just chase them down, and try to blast them out of the sky.

"We have to deal with these skuz buckets first!" Blair summoned Flametongue, her fiery shortsword. She came to stand next to Virgil. They didn't make more loyal best friends than her.

Malachi began to laugh, "You don't actually think we've been waiting here to duke it out with you losers?" he asked. "We took the liberty of arranging a playmate for you to keep you company. Once it has finished you off, it'll make its way into Bay City, another mess to distract the Paladins," Malachi grinned.

"What are you talking about?" Rowan asked.

The portal began to ripple, then it expanded, rapidly growing, something was coming through… Suddenly a large demon burst through the portal, it stood almost as high as the ceiling, with dozens of slimy tentacles, protruding from a twisted revolting body that had hundreds of human faces moving along its torso. It was the Arch Demon, Vagningula! Virgil had battled against the mighty foe, and only due to Louie's bravery had he survived the encounter.

"Hmm, we meet again Redeemer," the Arch Demon purred as its tentacles tasted the air in the direction of Virgil. Its demonic voice sent shivers down Virgil's spine. The demon had said it like Virgil was a delicious plate of chicken alfredo.

"Dispose of them, then destroy the city!" Malachi commanded the Arch Demon.

The Arch Demon's attention turned towards the Betas, they were standing directly in front of it, between the Omegas and the Arch Demon. "I will do as I wish mortal," the Arch Demon sneered at Malachi. "I do not take orders from Nephilim!" The demon bellowed.

The Betas looked tense, and Malachi's confidence faltered, his face losing its permanent confident scowl. They grouped close to their leader, eyeing up the Arch Demon nervously, they were inching away slowly. Jamal looked to Malachi for direction. "I am the cousin of Sethos! He told me you'd be coming to deal with the Redeemer!" Malachi said trying to have confidence in his voice.

"Yes," the Arch Demon confirmed. "I was asked by Lucifer to assault the city, and draw more Paladins away from Bay Valley. Though, he did not tell me I couldn't feast on every juicy Nephilim I found," the Arch Demon chuckled.

The Betas realized their danger too late, they leapt into the air, looking to escape the macabre horror that was Vagningula. The Arch Demon's tentacles descended on the Betas like lightning. Every one of them became wrapped up in one of its arms. The Arch Demon did not waste time, and opened its massive beak, underneath it's disgusting mantle like head, similar to an octopus. The Arch Demon quickly swallowed the Betas whole, Jamal and Malachi screamed with such fear and agony, Virgil's stomach twisted and he looked away. Louie lost his dinner.

When Virgil looked back, he saw eight new heads materialize on the body of the Arch Demon. Malachi and Jamal's faces stared out in horror, like they'd been pushed against the creature's skin, from inside it's body. Their mouths hung open, and moved like they were screaming in horror, yet they made no sound. Malachi deserved to be punished for his actions, though Virgil felt this was a fate no man should have to suffer through.

"Can we please get out of here?" Louie asked the group tightly.

"And leave this…monster to ravage the city?!" Rowan asked incredulously.

"Are we even a match for something like this?" Nev asked fear thick in his voice.

"We need to get to Bay Valley!" Louie urged them.

The Arch Demon turned its attention on their group and lumbered forward.

"To Arms!" Virgil commanded and his friends summoned their Devil Arms. They had no choice but to fight for their lives. The demon's tentacles squirmed forward, the demon lurching towards them awkwardly, seeking more meals. Virgil knew from his past experience there were just too many tentacles to contend with. His only hope was to immobilize the creature. Virgil gripped the Optimum in his pocket, reaching out with his aura, feeling the power within him.

"Eruption!" Virgil commanded his hand extended towards the Arch Demon. Columns of flame erupted from the ground, Vagningula howled in pain scrambling to keep its body off the powerful columns that were spewing flame from the ground. The spell began to die and Virgil shouted, "Searing Beam!" A ray of fire and raw energy burst from his hand blasting into the Arch Demon. Louie quickly began firing arrows into the Arch Demon that towered over them.

Nev's staff, Loki's Rod, was blue, and at the top the wood twisted up into a cone. Inside the sphere cone of his staff it looked like a lightning storm had been captured within. "Storm Ray!" Nev shouted, a white bolt of light crashing down from above, striking into the demon, moving around once in a circle before dissipating. Tentacles and black blood fell to the ground, the demon stumbled back.

"Explosion!" Blair commanded and a dozen fireballs shot from her palm racing out to the Arch Demon, exploding like bombs as they hit their target.

Nev wielded a staff and therefore could cast more spells before his aura was too weakened. "Thundara!" Nev commanded a clap of thunder rumbled the air slamming into Vagningula.

His friends had caught onto his plan, using spells Virgil was hoping to keep it from overpowering them. "Smite!" Virgil commanded and the area around the Arch Demon was rocked with an explosion of powerful Creation energy. It fell backwards crashing hard into the ground momentarily stunned. Everyone leapt into the air their wings soaring higher.

"Light Surge!" Virgil shouted draining another spell from his Optimum. Beams of Creation energy rained down upon the revolting horror.

They dived bombed the demon as a group to hack it to pieces! Nev continued to blast it with spells from above with Louie, who used his arrows to keep the tentacles from taking hold of them. Virgil spun through the air, his scythe and sword whirling in a circle around him, slicing off disgusting appendages, that fell to the ground with loud crashes. Rowan's katana, Crimson Edge, never stopped moving, his body was slick with sweat as he worked faster than any other to carve up the demon menace. Virgil saw several faces on its body give silent death screams, then they withered and sagged, like the energy had been drained from them. Vagningula instantly became revitalized, its arms growing back, and its body rapidly healing from the damage they'd caused. The Arch Demon forced itself back up, shaking off the comparatively small flying Nephilim. Virgil and the others were sent reeling into the air, quickly recovering and flying with urgency, the tentacles close behind, eager to ensnare them.

The tide of the battle had turned, Vagningula pounced on them with renewed vigor. Suddenly they had gone from being on a full out offensive, to barely managing to stay inches ahead of pursuing tentacles. The slimy powerful arms came at them with a savagery!

"Virgil do something!" Louie demanded. "Use your Soul Scream or Ascend, go super saiyan on this bitch ass! Anything!"

Virgil wished it were that simple, "You use YOUR Soul Scream Louie!" Virgil fired back. "It seemed to work really well last time!"

"I don't know how!" Louie cried out as he was chased by a tentacle.

"Great!" Dante quipped in. "Our futures are in Louie's hands? Pack it up people!"

"Dante, I remember you using your Devil Arms' Soul Scream on Rassler," Louie shot back. "Make Gaia's Wrath get fired up!" Dante grumbled under his breath, apparently it wasn't so easy for anyone to use their soul weapon's Soul Scream.

Their squabbling came to a screeching halt as the intensity of the fight skyrocketed, it became a fight for their lives! Rowan barely managed to avoid getting squashed, as he quickly cut down a tentacle that had grabbed hold of Virgil. Virgil had only been held for seconds and quickly recovered, nodding to Rowan, surging forward on his wings. Blair sliced the tip off one, only to have another come up from under her, slamming into her body. Like a spider wrapping up an insect, it swiftly entangled her in its arm. The tentacle squeezed her body, her wings snapped, crushing under the pressure.

Dante came sailing through the air, dodging a tentacle that dived for him, his eyes narrowed on his friend Blair. He swung out Gaia's Wrath, his axe slicing through the arm that was holding Blair, and dived hard gaining immense speed, racing towards the ground. Blair and the tentacle fell to the floor. Another tentacle hot on his heels, Dante pulled up just before he hit the ground, the tentacle crashing into the floor.

Virgil gripped the Optimum, "Cura!" Healing energy flowing out to seek the injured. One went straight towards Blair, her wings began knitting themselves back together, silent tears came down her face, the spell worked quickly, and her pain was alleviated. Tentacles began to descend on her before she had a chance to stand, Louie fearlessly landed by her side. He pulled back a glimmering arrow of light. Releasing the arrow, it sunk into the closest tentacle, which quickly turned to ash, half of the appendage falling to the ground. Louie didn't stop, halting them in their tracks while Blair got to her feet.

"You didn't have to do that!" Blair shouted spreading her wings and leaping into the air, Louie beside her.

"Listen warrior princess," Louie shouted out. "You may be more badass than the rest of us, but I just saved your skinny booty back there!"

"Thanks Louie," Blair smirked knowing he was right.

"I'll be damned if I lose my Blair to this monster!" Louie looked back with a fierceness, firing off an ice arrow at a tentacle that descended down on them.

"Louie," Blair smiled touched. "You're braver than those boys give you credit for!"

"That's what I'm saying!" Louie grinned.

A tentacle slammed down between them, they quickly swerved out of its reach, narrowly missing its suckers. Nev was blasting the demon relentlessly with spells, but his aura was shrinking, and now he didn't have the energy to keep up the assault. Nev switched to sending out wisps of energy from his staff. They were enough to stun and harm a tentacle, but not enough to kill one. Vagningula sensed Nev was growing tired and the demons' focus became him. Six tentacles descended on Nev, and he was helpless to stop them.

"Bolt!" Nev shouted expending precious energy. A small ray of energy zapped down striking one tentacle and frying the whole thing in its tracks. Five tentacles descended on Nev.

"NEV!" Rowan screamed racing through the air to help his pledge brother. Two tentacles intercepted him, closing off his way forward. Rowan flew towards them not willing to back down, swinging his fire katana forward he fought through. Dante and Birdy flew towards Nev in desperation. Nev was snatched out of the air, and the arm began to coil greedily. Dante and Birdy had to contend with an army of tentacles to get anywhere near Nev!

"Hold on!" Dante shouted fighting relentlessly to get through.

This creature was too much for them, Virgil knew. They needed the whole Chapter present to deal with a demon of this caliber, and even then, what hope did they have? It used the many faces on its body like mini Optimum, keeping them there until it needed a boost of energy, then it drained them dry, repairing its body. They could bring the Arch Demon to the brink of death a dozen times over, and it'd just devour more trapped souls, regaining its strength. It needed to be destroyed quickly.

The Arch Demon moved Nev towards its beak, Dante and Birdy didn't have a moment left to spare. They dove together, their axe and lance cutting a path forward. Dante reached him first and brought his axe down in a mighty swing, freeing Nev from his prison. Before Dante could get out, a tentacle snatched him up, immobilizing him within a second. The demon brought Dante towards its eagerly open beak instead, he was already there. Everything happened so quickly, Virgil didn't even have time to react. Dante was going to be swallowed whole!

"DANTE!" Everyone screamed.

NO!" Birdy cried out tears in his eyes. Dante was Birdy's best friend, they had a love hate relationship, but they meant the world to each other. Birdy streamed across the air on his wings towards the Arch Demon's beak. An army of tentacles raised up in the air, ready to strike down Birdy, the Arch Demon was determined to take this meal.

Birdy's Devil Arms began to glow, the amethyst lance symbol radiating light. Birdy's lance exuded purple energy. Birdy streamed towards the creature's mouth with no fear, only determination to save his friend's life. "Ixion's Glaive!" Birdy screamed the name of his Devil Arms, and the polearm let out a howl. A bolt of amethyst electricity showered down from the heavens, colliding with Birdy's lance, the whole thing glowing. "BOLT TEMPEST!" Birdy screamed and threw his lance directly towards the Arch Demon's open beak. The lance sailed inside, moments before Dante. The lance collided with its flesh and a sphere of energy radiated out like a mushroom cloud. The Arch Demon tried to scream as it was filled from the inside with energy and electricity. Vagningula exploded in a shower of black blood, and slimy flesh.

Dante erupted from the demon in a shower of gooey mush, landing on the ground. He stood up with disgust quickly shaking off the demon gore.

"Dante!" Birdy yelled barreling into him from the air, flying so hard, he almost knocked him back over. "I thought you were a goner!"

"I'm alright!" Dante complained being smothered by his much taller friend. "Get off!"

"That was impressive Birdy," Rowan whistled as the rest of the group came to land near him. "I didn't expect you'd be the one to take down the Arch Demon."

"Neither did I!" Birdy laughed.

"I'm just glad we're all alive," Blair sighed catching her breath.

Virgil was relieved they were safe as well, but they did not have time to revel in their triumph over the Arch Demon! "Let's get back to Bay Valley!" Virgil urged the group. He was worried, about his mom, about Amari, about campus. Virgil just prayed the Death Dealers hadn't leveled the University to the ground.

"Right behind ya," Blair answered for everyone.

# Chapter 22 Battle at Bay Valley

Virgil and his companions flew hard, racing through the sky to get back to Campus. Sue and Amari were heavy on Virgil's mind. Virgil was worried what Sethos would do to Amari, and he needed to get back to the Omega house before anything happened to his mom. They arrived at the main entrance to the campus, the large sign that held the university's name had been blown to smithereens. They slowed down as they flew towards the first group of buildings and parking lots. Everyone came to a halt midflight, they went to the ground, landing and staring in horror around them, their university was in ruins. Fires were raging everywhere, with no one around to put them out, except the lifeless bodies of men, women, and children littered across the grounds. There were police cars and ambulances. All the rescue workers had been cut down. Everyone was dumb struck by the sheer brutality of the violence that had taken place. No one had been spared. Virgil saw among the dead two Death Dealers, their black armor indicative as foreign. They'd struck campus! Virgil was overwhelmed, there were so many bodies, who could murder defenseless people. They were dealing with monsters who were willing to cut down kids, tears came to his eyes, Virgil couldn't stop them from flowing down his face. Virgil had to be willing to do the same to every Death Dealer he found!

"This is BAD!" Louie cried out hysteria taking over his voice. "What are we supposed to do? What can we do? We should go back to the Omega house and check on the parents that haven't evacuated," Louie suggested.

"There might be parents here!" Dante shouted. "OR CHILDREN!" he screamed looking at the body of a little girl not far from them. "Fucking Family Weekend, a hell of a time to make a grab for the Chalice," Dante mumbled filled with frustration. Dante slammed his fist into a car, his knuckles bloodied.

"Settle down!" Nev and Blair yelled.

"We need you in top shape," Rowan told Dante.

"Oh, I'm better than top shape," Dante laughed coldly. "Every damn Death Dealer that I see is going to be cut down. They wanna kill kids? I'll tear them to PIECES!" He screamed tears in his eyes.

"We're all shaken up," Blair said calmly. She gently placed a hand on Dante's shoulder. "They tricked us into leaving campus, but we're back now," Blair said confidently. "I say we do what we can to secure this place."

"Think we got the people for that?" Nev asked. "There are seven of us," he pointed out.

"We just took down an Arch Demon," Rowan laughed. "A couple of Death Dealers too much for you?" he smiled.

"I'm worn out," Nev admitted. "I don't think I can handle many Death Dealers," he looked off, fear in his eyes.

"Sit back and watch what we can do," Dante said defiantly fire burning in his eyes. He wanted to punish the people responsible for this. "Right Virgil?" he asked.

Virgil met Dante's steel gaze and nodded confidently, "Let's go," he told them spreading his wings launching himself into the air. His friends followed closely behind him, and they flew over the first group of buildings with ease. Blair saw it first, he heard her gasp in panic, ahead of them TK and Selene danced through the sky, battling six Death Dealers by themselves.

"RAGNORAK!" Virgil shouted and a bolt of white lightning met his hand, his golden blade growing into existence from the energy. Virgil beat his wings with a powerful stroke, and he propelled himself through the air like a rocket. TK and Selene fought for their lives! They were holding their own despite being outnumbered. Selene attacked with a viciousness that was out of place for someone so kind, and TK was the most graceful warrior he'd ever seen. His heart raced with fear, not them, please Creator don't take them from us, Virgil begged. Ragnorak pulsed with energy, Virgil swung the blade in an arc, a massive field of energy blasted from the sword over the battling warriors. The Death Dealers dove down, and again Virgil released a wave of energy at them, driving the warriors further down, they landed on the ground. One of the Death Dealers had been hit by the wave of Creation energy, he fell to the ground with a hard crunch, and did not rise. Virgil and his friends landed opposite the Death Dealers, TK and Selene safely beside them.

"TK!" Blair yelled out running over to her sisters fiercely grabbing TK. "Selene! What the hell are you two doing out here!" she demanded.

"No time to talk," Selene told Blair spinning her flame lance, she stared down the five remaining Death Dealers. "You'll pay for what you've done here!" Selene said aiming her weapon at them.

"Tough words, now that you have a Seraph backing you up," one of the Death Dealers told her.

"I need no man to fight for me!" Selene screamed and charged into battle like an Amazonian warrior woman. TK and Blair were close at here heels, Selene launched herself into the air using her lance, and struck the ground ahead of the the approaching Death Dealers, erupting it into a sea of fire.

"Howling Flames!" Selene cried and the fire intensified, the flames almost reaching out like fingers for the Death Dealers. One unlucky soul got touched by the flame, and it coiled around him like a python, he wailed in agony as the flames cooked him. Virgil had never seen a spell so vicious, and so terrifying.

"You bitch!" A Death Dealer screamed swinging his sword to cut Selene down. Blair's shortsword broke apart into a fiery metal whip, latching onto the man's sword, and knocking him off balance. Blair cracked her fiery whip, and TK did battle with another Death Dealer. Virgil and his friends jumped into the fray! Virgil fought at Selene's side, she was a woman on a mission, dodging and weaving like a deadly ballerina with a flaming lance. The remaining Death Dealers were overwhelmed and overpowered. The last one was knocked to the ground, Virgil and his friends surrounded him.

"Where are your leaders?" Virgil asked him. "Where have they taken Amariana!?" Virgil demanded to know.

"They have Amari?!" Selene asked fearful, she'd been too busy with running Family Weekend, she must not have been at the sorority house when the Betas struck.

The Death Dealer began to laugh hysterically. "You're doomed," he managed to say. "Sethos will accomplish our goal, no matter what you try to do, no one can stop him," he laughed.

"Where did Sethos take Amari?" Virgil asked him getting angry. The Death Dealer just laughed.

"We won't get anything out of him," Dante said, "Its best to finish him," he added bringing down Gaia's Wrath on the Death Dealer. No one said anything, thankful to Dante for doing what had to be done.

"Now you want to tell us why you two are fighting off Death Dealers, all by yourselves!" Blair yelled. "Safety in numbers, isn't that the general thinking?" she asked angry.

"I didn't have a choice," TK said defensively the stress of everything weighing down upon her, "I couldn't keep Selene inside, she charged out here to shepherd families to safety, immediately organizing a lockdown announcement through campus."

"I couldn't sit inside knowing one family might be out here, trying to get to safety, while an army of Devil Dealers falls from the sky," Selene said clearly shaken up. "This Family Weekend was MY event," Selene said sadly. "I'm the reason all these…these," Selene got tears in her eyes.

"No, you're not," Virgil told her. "Believe me, when I say YOU are not the one to blame for this," he said sadly knowing he was. "Come on, we need to get you ladies inside, and kept somewhere safe," he told them.

"I don't think so," Selene said flatly, dismissing Virgil entirely. She turned from him and began to walk to a nearby building.

"Selene wait!" Virgil said walking after her. "What would Brody think of you out here by yourself? What would he do if he found out I let you go off on your own, without one of us protecting you," he told her concerned.

Selene turned to Virgil, the full power of her conviction and determination in her gaze, Virgil almost buckled meeting her eyes they were so fierce. "I do not," Selene's fiery words came out clipped and short, "Need a man to protect me."

"I'm sorry Selene," Virgil apologized realizing he had offended her.

"I've taken care of myself since the day I turned eighteen Virgil," Selene said not with attitude, but from the heart, "I don't need you, or Brody, or anyone else to take care of me. I will do what I want in this world, and when I see things or people that need my help, I will never stop giving all that I am to do what I can," Selene said with passion. "And I'm certainly not going to sit around waiting for a *man's* approval, to do what's right!"

"Alright," Virgil nodded rethinking his words. Selene didn't need his protection; she was one of the greatest warriors he'd ever known. "If not a man to protect you, how about a friend to stand at your side," he asked softly wanting to keep Selene safe so bad it hurt. He stared into her eyes, feeling overwhelmed with emotion.

There was silence between them. Selene smiled tears in her eyes, "I could use one of those," she smiled and they hugged.

"I'm glad you're safe," Virgil told her softly in her ear, he had been so scared seeing TK and her battling in the sky, his adrenaline had kicked into overdrive.

"Thanks," Selene said with a lighthearted laugh that lacked soul in the midst of her inner turmoil. "I'm glad you guys are alright as well, but I knew you would be," she said stepping back.

"Why is that?" Virgil asked her.

TK walked up and rubbed Virgil's arm, "Because we knew you were with them, and we knew as long as Blair, and your brothers were with you, you'd keep them safe," she smiled at Virgil.

"We keep each other safe," Virgil smiled hugging TK quickly. Virgil's friends nodded in agreement. Virgil would be dead a hundred times over if it wasn't for his friends fighting beside him, protecting him.

Selene went up to a building and a group of people came out of hiding and began to follow her. "This is why we were fighting that group of Death Dealers," Selene explained. "They were about to harm these people!"

"We'll get you folks to a safer location," TK assured them.

"Where is that?" Nev asked.

"The administration building, it's at the heart of campus, but its where the most Paladins are at as well," TK informed them, and they started making progress in that direction. There were fourteen in the group of civilians, they looked like parents, and a few younger siblings, maybe three students. Virgil was surprised they didn't ask questions about their wings or weapons, what did they see when they looked at them? Perhaps since they were NOT trying to kill them, maybe they just were keeping quiet. It was hard to tell how much normal humans could see, their own mundane auras blinded them to the real world, perhaps they didn't see the wings or weapons at all.

Virgil rambled quickly, "Do you have names of people who are safe? Have you seen Vinny, is he okay? Have you seen Rho class?"

"Yes, Vinny is there, and a few of Rho class as well, lots of sisters and brothers, and a few Paladins from the Capital," TK assured him. "We started getting as many people off the open grounds as possible," TK explained, "Damian showed up with a few other Betas and warned us of the attack. Death Dealers showed up within a minute afterwards," she said sadly a haunted expression on her face.

"Damian!" Virgil shouted. "Where is he?" Virgil asked concerned.

"We can't be sure who is still there because it has been a solid twenty minutes since we left there," TK added. "But Damian was helping rescue people off campus grounds like us, so he could be anywhere."

Damian was brave to turn his back on his fraternity, in pursuit of doing what was right, helping to protect innocent lives. Virgil needed to find him, as well as his brothers, he was frightened wondering who among his people were fighting for their lives at this very moment? Virgil knew Vahn was at the Omega house, with his mother, making sure she was kept safe, but he worried for the many brothers not at the Omega house, a portion of the Chapter had volunteered to be on campus in case they were attacked. They ran across the ground, fallen students and foes abundant, but they didn't have time to stop and absorb what they witnessed.

Finally, they passed by the Arts building, coming to the open courtyard in front of the administration building, the campus bell tower was in there as well. The group had stumbled across a battlefield! The Death Dealers had their people hopelessly outnumbered, at thirty-five strong. They were making a push to enter the administration building, where all the students and families they could find were being protected, and another group of warriors were throwing spells at the bell tower trying to tear it down. A few Paladins from the Capital were in the fray, grouped near the bell tower they were fiercely protecting it. Virgil's brothers, consisting of mostly Rho class, savagely fought for their lives against the mighty legion of ebony armor-clad adversaries. Virgil saw Vinny, Colton, Aidan, and Flynn fighting as a unit, keeping near the entrance of the building, defending it with the utmost priority. Virgil went still mid stride, paralyzed by fear, his Little Brother parried a deadly sword strike that almost cleaved his arm off. Vinny shoved the Death Dealer back and dealt a devastating riposte directly into the Death Dealer's gut, between his armor plates. A Death Dealer charged Vinny, while his large axe was still stuck in the warrior's fallen comrade.

"VINNY!" Virgil screamed launching himself into the air. Virgil streamed through the sky, dive bombing the warrior sprinting at his Lil. Virgil almost speared him through with Ragnorak, but the warrior turned his sword to deflect the blow, and was forced back by Virgil's momentum. Virgil landed and summoning Soul Reaver he spun around slashing at the warrior. Soul Reaver sliced through his armor cutting into his chest. The Death Dealer grunted, feeling his aura being drained.

"Virgil!" Vinny yelled out happily from behind.

Virgil ran towards the warrior, using Soul Reaver to keep him off guard, he stabbed Ragnorak forward, finishing their duel. Virgil turned back and quickly got to Vinny's side, they were far from safe. Virgil's group had joined the fray but there were still thirty some Death Dealers, and these were seasoned warriors, with the skill and power to prove it.

"What the hell are you fools doing out here?" Virgil asked them with anger. "Why aren't you inside with the others?"

"Then who'd be left to stop the Death Dealers from coming in?" Colton asked with attitude, fending off a Death Dealer with a spear. "Troy, and Jeramiah are inside!" Colton yelled to Virgil. "We can't leave the people inside defenseless!" Another Death Dealer came at Colton, two on one. Colton's purple sword pulsed with power, he swung it forward and an arc of electricity leapt forward colliding with the oncoming assailants. They were flung from the force of the power, slamming into the ground like ragdolls. They didn't rise back up.

"We had to come out here, they were going to destroy the bell tower!" Aidan yelled fighting off another armored warrior. The bell tower was constructed using powerful magicite, it held the barrier in place on campus that protected it from demons, while it was in place no demon could set foot on campus grounds.

"If they destroy that, campus will be flooded with demons!" Virgil yelled.

"Exactly," Flynn said charging a Death Dealer coming at Aidan's flank.

"Stay close Vinny," Virgil turned to his Lil, relieved beyond measure that he was unharmed.

"I can handle myself," Vinny's determined voice came out angry swinging his mighty fire axe in a show of power to his Big, "I'm sticking with Rho class, we're not letting anything through!" he yelled with conviction.

"RHO CLASS!" Virgil heard a chorus of cheers from the battlefield causing him to smirk.

"Virgil help Doc!" Colton shouted nodding forward. Virgil looked towards the center of the courtyard, a group of people were trapped in the middle, in the center were over a dozen unarmed students, parents, and children. Doc and his sister were fighting to defend them, along with Lamar, Abe, Brett, Cameron, Nigel, Mu, and even brave, sweet Lilly was fighting! Dante,

Selene, and Blair were embroiled with the enemy, desperately trying to make progress towards them. TK, Louie, Birdy, and Nev joined the fight to protect the bell tower. I f it fell there would be no protecting Bay Valley, it would be engulfed in an army of soulless soldiers, ready to drain the grounds dry.

Virgil held onto his Devil Arms, feeling their power flow through him. He opened his wings and propelled himself forward towards the intense battle unfolding. Virgil charged the group of Death Dealers, they nimbly dodged out of the way right before he rammed into them. Virgil spun around, the flames from Soul Reaver extending out burning one warrior. Virgil threw himself at the enemy using Soul Reaver to protect himself and terrorize his opponents. With every burn from its flames, and every cut from its blade, it sucked aura's dry. Virgil swung Ragnorak with impudence cutting down every metal clad Nephilim he could reach. Virgil had to reach his brothers; they were close to being overwhelmed!

"Doc!" Doc's little sister screamed out in terror, a Death Dealer slashed her across the chest with his lance. She fell back to dodge his attack, narrowly missing a deathblow, she suffered a severe laceration to her chest, blood flowing onto the grass.

"Gina!" Doc screamed, racing to his sister's side her life in mortal danger.

"Gareth!" Gina cried out to her brother as the Death Dealer was poised to finish her off.

There was nothing Virgil could do, there was a phalanx of soldiers between him and the others! "Fira!" Virgil shouted draining another spell from the Opitmum, and a column of fire burst up from the ground, between him and the others. Virgil knocked three down, but Death Dealers were everywhere! More moved forward to replace the gap. He wasn't any closer to getting through! Virgil launched himself in the air, and four Death Dealers rose into the sky to meet him. Virgil tried to barrel through, but they were acting defensively, not taking any risks. Their only goal was to keep Virgil separated from the small group at the center of their troops. Virgil flew hard flying straight and fighting with everything he had.

Doc threw himself into the Death Dealer before he could harm his sister, swinging his hand axe with fury. The Death Dealer's lance had far better reach, he blocked Doc's small axe with ease. The Death Dealer slammed Doc hard in the stomach with the shaft of his Devil Arms, Doc doubled over stunned. The Death Dealer spun the lance around, stabbing Doc through the chest, Gina started screaming. Virgil felt like his world came closing in on him, blood coated the Devil Arms that had gone through Doc and come out the other side. The Death Dealer ripped his lance out of Doc's chest, Doc fell to his knees, his face in shock, and he slowly fell face first into the grass.

"DOC!" Virgil screamed out along with many others. Virgil heard brothers and friends wailing around him, his ears started ringing, he couldn't handle this, he couldn't lose Doc! Doc was the first brother he'd ever interviewed; he'd been one of the first brothers Virgil had felt close with. Virgil's body overflowed with power, he Ascended, his 'godhood' taking over, his eyes radiated gold light, and his aura expanded out. "NO!" Virgil roared raising Ragnorak above his head, the Holy Blade screamed with Virgil's fury! The blade filled with golden light and Virgil swung his sword at the Death Dealers, a wave of golden energy swam from its surface, barreling through his enemies. Virgil turned towards more of the Death Dealers and swung Ragnorak at them, another wave of light blasting across the ground from his sword, a shockwave of fire and energy bursting forward. Virgil slaughtered them with ferocity, Ragnorak's power destroying everything in its path. Ragnorak overflowed with power, and as more Death Dealers charged him, he released another wave of energy that devoured them all.

Smoke rose up from the battlefield around Virgil, Ragnorak's power had created deep rivets within the grassy courtyard, like ugly jagged scars. Virgil breathed heavy, most of the Death Dealers on the battlefield lay defeated, but the Death Dealer who had impaled Doc on his spear rounded on Gina. She was so overcome with emotion she didn't have it in her to fight back, she knelt by Doc's side holding onto him tears flowing from her face.

"Gina!" Virgil called out. He couldn't let Doc's sister be taken from this world, he owed it to Doc, as his brother, to protect her! "Howling Blade!" Virgil called out and Ragnorak began to howl for all to hear. "Judgment Bolt!" Virgil called out and a beam of energy like a bolt of lightning exploded from Ragnorak, colliding with the Death Dealer about to impale Gina, hurling him across the courtyard. The Death Dealer's body rolled across the ground, his limbs twisting at impossible angles, and the sound of his spine snapping rent the air as his body bent too far for his back to support. The Death Dealer lay lifeless and Virgil landed, sprinting to Doc's side. The few Death Dealers left, took flight fleeing, the one's that still fought were defeated by Virgil's friends. Virgil felt his Ascended state begin to dissipate, his eyes returning to normal. Virgil dropped to ground next to Doc, both his Devil Arms disappearing back into the symbols on his hands. The grass and dirt around his brother was flooded with blood. Virgil helped Gina roll him over, Doc's expression was lifeless staring blankly ahead.

"Gareth," Gina sobbed.

Virgil held his right hand over the hole in Doc's chest. "Cura!" Virgil commanded eating what precious little energy was left in the Optimum. A white light flowed from his Devil Arms symbol going into Doc and Gina. Virgil watched as his spell slowly reknit the wound together. But the magic faded after several seconds, and Doc's wound still hadn't been fully closed.

"You have to save him Virgil!" Gina yelled at him her face fierce. "Please!" she begged.

"I'm trying," Virgil said his words coming out as a sob, tears beginning to blur his vision. "Cura!" Virgil commanded once more and another burst of the healing magic flowed into Doc, draining the Optimum of its last reserves. Virgil didn't care what the cost was, he'd use Cura until he passed out if that is what it took to bring Doc back. Doc's wound finally began to close, weeks of healing completed in a minute's time, the injury was still far from completely recovered, however.

"Do it again!" Gina demanded.

"Alright," Virgil nodded he'd have to use his aura for spells now.

"Virgil, stop," Lamar said sadly walking over to Virgil's side with Abe. The battle was over, and everyone gathered around Doc, including the Paladins from the Capital. "He's gone, there is nothing you can do brother," Lamar said softly to Virgil.

"I have to try!" Virgil yelled at Lamar filled with anger and sadness.

"You're only making yourself weaker," Selene tried to reason with Virgil, "Your spells can only heal the body's physical damage, they can't bring the dead back to life."

Virgil stared down at Doc, frater Gareth, not knowing what to say, not knowing what to do.

"Let's get him inside," Mu suggested. "There could be another assault at any minute."

"I'll help you," Dante offered his Big.

"He was my pledge brother, I'll help too," Abe offered as well.

Doc's brothers carefully picked him up and carried him to the building they were using as shelter. Virgil was in shock, he stood and watched his brothers carrying Doc, dragging his feet following them. Everyone went inside, the group of students that Doc and the other brothers had rescued found places to sit and huddle together. The brothers that had stayed inside, Troy, and Jeramiah came forward, when they saw Doc's lifeless body being laid down, they lost it. There wasn't a dry eye among Virgil's friends.

"Virgil," Vinny said softly to him. Virgil turned to see his Lil Brother standing next to him, he looked so lost, so vulnerable, exactly as Virgil felt. Virgil embraced his Lil and began sobbing uncontrollably. Blair, TK, Selene, Lilly, Mu, Louie, Birdy, and Dante came around Virgil and they formed a group hug. Then all the brothers present joined in.

"I failed him," Virgil whispered to Vinny. "I wasn't strong enough to save him."

"You can't save everyone Virgil," Vinny told him.

"This is my fault!" Virgil screamed. "All of this is!"

"Knock it off!" Gina yelled at Virgil breaking the group hug and bringing everyone's attention to Doc's younger sister. "You think my brother would want to hear you, tear yourself apart?" she asked him her lips trembling. "Gareth, he loved being an Omega. He fought today, protecting innocent people, who didn't have a Devil Arms to defend themselves. My brother died fighting for what he believed in! You fought with everything you had, and you couldn't have given anymore," she told him. "If it wasn't for you, I'd probably be dead as well," she said sadly. "You saved me, and I know he'd be grateful to you for that. If he was here right now, he'd probably say, 'Go out there and kick some ass cupcake!'"

Virgil laughed, "You're right," Virgil nodded. "He'd also call me something embarrassing, like Cherry or Virg the Virgin. I'm so sorry," Virgil told her too ashamed to meet her gaze. Gina smiled a tear sliding down her face.

"Thank you, Virgil," Gina said, her voice filled with pain. She walked over and wrapped her arms around him.

Virgil hugged her back, and the group came together in another group hug, everyone embracing Gina and Virgil. After they broke apart, the group milled around, no one knew what to do, no one was really talking. After several minutes, Selene started hanging around the doors to the outside, staring out with a forlorn look on her face.

Virgil walked over to her. "What are you doing?" he asked her.

"I should go back out there," Selene said leaning against the door. "I have a feeling, inside, there are more people out there who need my help," she told Virgil.

"It's dangerous Selene," Virgil said fearful, "You should stay in here."

"I can't stay in here, knowing people out there might be dying," Selene turned to Virgil. "I'm going," she said with determination.

Virgil stared into her eyes knowing he couldn't persuade her, Selene's will, was stronger than steel. "Then I'll tag along," he smiled weakly.

"You guys are leaving?" Colton asked approaching them. His handsome features were marred in a disapproving scowl, he didn't look very happy with either one of them.

"Selene's heading out, whether we like it or not," Virgil sighed.

"Let's go," Dante said walking up next to them with Birdy and Blair.

"Campus is dangerous!" Louie shouted freaking out. "It's suicide to head back out there! We already lost Doc!" Louie pointed out. "Can't we just all stay in here and wait for this to be over?" he asked them.

"If we sit around waiting for the Death Dealers to leave, who knows how many more people will be lost to their bloodlust!" Selene yelled. "If there is a chance, I can save one more life, I'm taking it!" she shouted fiercely towards Louie.

Louie looked down ashamed. "You don't have to go Louie," Selene said softly to him. "We do need people here to defend this place, and you're one of the few brothers who can use Restoration spells."

"You guys don't mind if I stay behind?" Louie asked looking into his friends' eyes, he looked conflicted.

"Not at all big guy," Dante smiled patting his friend on the shoulder. "It'll put my mind at ease knowing our big lovable panda, is protecting the bell tower."

"We're coming too," Lamar said coming over with Abe.

"We need a good amount to stay behind," Selene stressed. "We HAVE to hold this place, I'll probably be coming in hot, with a group of civilians before long."

"I'll hold this place," Colton told them confidently, his amethyst Devil Arms coming to life. Colton was one of the strongest brothers in Omega, he was still young, but he had potential to be one of the greats, like Magnus, like Gabriel. "Go if you need to but, be careful." Colton's eyes reflected his thoughts, he was good natured, and genuinely cared for people.

"I'll stay behind as well," Nev added, "I'll add a layer of barrier spells around this building, get this place more secured."

"Sounds perfect, I'll help ya," Colton nodded. They'd bonded since Colton had gotten in, and had become each other's best friends in the fraternity, something neither had in their own pledge class. They both loved Magnus and emulated his personality, they say the best form of flattery is imitation.

"We'll stay," Lilly said placing her hand on Mu's shoulder, who nodded in agreement. "If more come back, we'll defend these people," she told them.

"We'll stay as well," a Paladin from the Capital said speaking up for himself and three of his brothers in arms. "Defending the bell tower and keeping the spell in place will protect campus from a wave of demons invading."

"Virgil," TK called out, walking up to him and embracing him tightly. "Stay close to my girls," TK said quietly in Virgil's ear. "I don't trust them with just anyone, you know?" Her words were tight, she was scared, his strong brave friend whom he'd always looked up to was shaken.

"I will," Virgil nodded. "You're not coming with us?" Virgil asked surprised, TK was one of the best warriors.

"I'm staying close to Gina," TK said quietly, "She's in a fragile state right now, and she needs someone she knows looking out for her."

"You're amazing," Virgil chuckled to his friend. TK was majoring in social work; you don't get more selfless than that.

"Come back safely," TK's words unusually commanding, "And if you see Gabriel…" TK didn't say anything else, Virgil could sense the anxiety and fear within her.

"Isn't Gabriel at the Omega house?" Virgil asked her.

"That's what is worrying me," TK said with a shaky breath, "He hasn't been answering his phone, he's strong, you know that, one of the best, but," TK pulled away and stared into Virgil's eyes. "You've always looked out for us, God knows you've saved his life enough times already, but if you see him…make sure he comes back to me," she pleaded blinking once, a layer of moisture filling her eyes.

"I promise you TK, I'll always look out for Gabriel, and you," Virgil told her with a small smile.

TK nodded, "I know," her words came out cracked, emotion taking over she turned away, and walked away to sit down with Gina.

Selene nodded to those following her, she was the de facto leader, and no one would dare argue otherwise. They headed out the door. Virgil, Blair, Dante, Birdy, Lamar, and Abe were hot on her heels. The Paladins from the Capital went outside and headed back over to the bell tower. Colton and Nev slipped out behind them and started tracing spells around the building to shield it from Death Dealer spells, and blocking them from just walking in.

"Where are we headed?" Birdy asked Selene.

"The western edge of campus," Selene told them. "We haven't checked over there yet, and that's where Student Life and the cafeteria are located."

They spread their wings and took flight, higher up in the air they could see further. Smoke billowed into the air, their university, which had become like a second home to Virgil, was decimated. Selene led the pack, Virgil keeping close. It didn't take long for them to run across people in need. They heard shouting, flashes of magic exploded close by, Selene dived to the ground, and everyone followed closely.

The building with the cafeteria and Student Life was in shambles. There were a group of Death Dealers embroiled in battle with a group of Alpha Sisters over thirty strong led by Terra, Raven, and Helene. They were defending a group of over fifty children, parents, and students from being slaughtered.

Terra turned her attention to them shouting, "It's about time! We needed some reinforcements ten minutes ago!"

"Zip your lips precious!" Blair shouted back barreling into combat sword first.

"Virgil!" Terra yelled he landed near her. "Jagger, and the other boys at the Omega house, I'm worried about them!" Terra said fearfully.

"What's wrong?" Virgil asked.

"You need to get to the Omega house," Terra said to Virgil. "We can handle things here," she said to him.

Virgil looked to his friends, they all gave him this look that said, go, for all of us. Amariana wasn't here, and he needed to check on his mother and the Omegas, he was starting to get a bad feeling...

"May the Light guide you," Selene told Virgil.

"You need some backup?" Dante asked.

Virgil couldn't afford to take away anyone, "I'll be fine," Virgil said to his friends. "Get these people to safety, they need your help more than me!"

His friends couldn't argue, there wasn't an opportunity, they had to jump into the fight helping the Alpha sisters. Virgil trusted his friends could handle the Death Dealers and escort the people back to the safe house they'd created out of the administration building. He looked at his friends for only a second, a part of him wanted to stay and protect them. Another part of him knew that this is what he needed to do. Virgil took to the sky alone, his heart pounding, what lay before him? Doc had just died, and yet none of them had a chance to process that, they didn't have time. How many more brothers, and friends would be lost at the end of this? The sun was beginning to set, darkness started to leak across the sky like paint spilt on a canvas. All Virgil could do was to keep going, there were still too many faces he'd yet to see again, too many fates unknown. He started to fear for the Omega house, it held the Chalice, which held a third of Diablos' soul. Their house was the primary target, he wished his mother would have left when she had the chance. He silently prayed she had driven home after he'd gone to the Betas ambush. And Amari…Virgil was desperate to get her back. He'd do whatever it took to secure her freedom.

# Chapter 23 The Fifth Seraph

Virgil sped across the sky on Angel wings, dusts of magic trailing behind him in the twilight of dusk. On the outskirts of campus, towards Greek housing, was the beach located at the mouth of Lake Huron, along with pavilions next to a large playground set. Virgil hadn't flown long before he saw something that made his heart fall. Damian, Homer, Tucker, and Damian's fraternity brother, Trent were battling three Death Dealers, and by the looks of it, they weren't doing well. Virgil descended to the ground, their opponents were elite Death Dealers, and Virgil leapt into the fray! Virgil joined Tucker in dueling a Nephilim with a large axe Devil Arms.

"About time someone shows up to help us," Tucker grunted catching the warrior's axe on his polearm, his arms straining to keep the blow from sinking into his shoulder.

Virgil summoned Soul Reaver and swung it at the warrior, he leapt back narrowly missing the scythe's reach. "What the hell are you fools doing this far out?" Virgil yelled angry.

"We've already saved a couple dozen people, not like we've been busy or anything," Homer retorted with attitude. "But yeah, nice to see you too," he said looking towards Virgil a nervous smile spreading across his face, with relief, and hope in his eyes. Virgil hated how people got that look when they saw him.

"We were headed to the Omega house," Damian said doing battle with the strongest of the three Nephilim. "To help protect the Chalice."

"Have the Death Dealer's taken the Omega house?!" Virgil asked fearfully.

"We're not sure!" Homer shouted narrowly missing having his arm cut off. "Blazing Flame!" Homer commanded and a burst of flames engulfed the Death Dealer.

"Searing Beam!" The Death Dealer fighting Tucker and Virgil commanded, from his Devil Arms symbol a ray of fire and energy erupted slamming into both of them, picking them off their feet with the momentum of the spell. Tucker and Virgil hit the ground hard, Tucker yelled in pain, they'd been burned from the spell, Virgil's flesh felt like it was still on fire. The Optimum was empty, Virgil had no choice but to use his aura now.

Virgil shouted. "Cura!" The Basic Creation Restoration spell leapt from Virgil's right hand to cover Tucker, Trent, and himself. The pain from the burns began to dissipate immediately, as his skin was promptly repaired.

"Thanks!" Tucker said getting to his feet with a spring in his step. "I feel like I didn't just get hit in the chest, with a large fire beam, that tried to cook my insides."

"Stay focused!" Virgil told his friend, "Let's remove this trash from our campus!"

Tucker spun his long polearm around and nodded, Virgil ran towards the Death Dealer, who raised his hand to fire off another spell at them, "Fire Lance!" the warrior shouted. Two large projectiles made of flame erupted from his hands and came soaring towards them. Virgil launched his scythe at the flames. Soul Reaver whirled through the air, slicing through the Death Dealer's spell, destroying it in the process, the flames falling harmlessly to the ground before dying out. Soul Reaver slammed into the warrior's upraised weapon, he used his Devil Arms to block the scythe from cutting him down. Virgil and Tucker raced to him, Virgil didn't need to hold onto his weapon to fight with it, using his mind Virgil moved the scythe attacking the Nephilim who desperately tried to parry the incoming blows. Virgil clenched his left fist, black flames spreading from his black Devil Arms symbol, he swung at the warrior striking his shoulder. Virgil's hand ached with pain; the Death Dealer's armor was too thick to fight with bare fists.

Tucker sprinted with his polearm aimed at the enemy Nephilim, who was too preoccupied with Virgil's scythe flying around him, he didn't block the attack. Tucker rammed the point of his blade through warrior's armor, sinking it into the enemy's flesh. The Death Dealer grunted in pain, and lashed out with a strong kick, knocking Tucker down, his javelin went with him, and was ripped from the warrior's chest plate. Virgil's scythe came flying back into his hand and he rounded on the Nephilim, he was skilled, more so than many of the warrior's Virgil had faced so far. But Virgil was a Seraphim Nephilim, he'd battled Arch Demons, Fallen Eidolons, and even his fellow Seraphs, this man would not be the end for him! Virgil's blade locked with the warrior's, Virgil broke from the hold, bringing his scythe around for another swing, this time the warrior's block barely caught the sickle blade. The Death Dealer's axe buckled under the pressure from Virgil's scythe. Virgil pushed against the warrior with all his might, the warrior's blade was shoved aside, and the scythe sank into his shoulder. The Nephilim screamed in pain as the flames burned away his aura. Virgil ripped the scythe out, and spun around letting out a yell as he swung the scythe at the impaired Nephilim. Soul Reaver glided through the warrior's armor slicing open his midsection, the Death Dealer fell backwards to the ground, defeated.

Homer and Damian, were battling the apparent leader of the small squad of Death Dealers. He was clad in battle armor like the others, but while most warriors wore helmets to obscure their faces, this one did not. He had a fierce and determined look on his face, battling both Homer and Damian, he somehow managed to not only repel their attacks but fought back with a startling ferocity. Damian struck out a left hook with his gauntlet Devil Arms, that the warrior blocked, followed by a few jabs with his right fist. The warrior's sword strained against Damian's gauntlet Devil Arms, he deflected Damian's blow to the side, Damian moved forward carried by the weight of his momentum. The Death Dealer swung his blade, slicing Damian across the back as he stumbled past him. Damian cried out in pain, the wound was deep, but not lethal. Homer rounded on the warrior using his mace Devil Arms. He relentlessly tried to land a blow, the warrior's blade blocking every strike. Homer's Devil Arms became locked with the Death Dealer's, the Death Dealer broke the parry, and in a devastating riposte, he shoved his sword deep into Homer's stomach.

"HOMER!" Tucker and Virgil screamed.

Homer gasped open mouthed, in shock, his Devil Arms falling from his grip, fading in a flash of light before it hit the ground. The Death Dealer met Homer's eyes, a satisfied grin creeping up on his face. He removed his blade from Homer's flesh and shoved him. Homer fell to the dirt.

Virgil opened his wings and propelled himself forward like a rocket, screaming at the top of his lungs. The other Death Dealer, who had been fighting Trent, rammed into Virgil knocking him out of the air, into the ground. Virgil went rolling but quickly jumped to his feet. The Death Dealer had wounded Damian's brother who lay on the ground clutching his body in agony.

"Out of my way," Virgil spat through clenched teeth his eyes narrowed.

"I won't let you overwhelm Master Armis," the Death Dealer told Virgil with an angry and determined glare. "I promised the Gatekeeper I would protect him! I won't fail!"

"Your friend is a dead man!" Virgil screamed charging the Death Dealer.

The warrior fought with incredible skill, almost knocking Soul Reaver out of Virgil's hand the first time their weapons clashed. Virgil didn't have time to waste, every second Homer lay bleeding, Virgil's chances of being able to save his life diminished. Virgil summoned Ragnorak shouting its name the Holy Blade quickly came to his right hand. The Death Dealer was taken back for a spilt second, his confidence shaken by the sight of the most powerful Devil Arms. Virgil concentrated steadying his focus with Ragnorak, feeling its power course through him. Virgil ran forward using both his Devil Arms in tandem. He pushed the warrior back, precious seconds ticked by as they battled. Tucker joined Damian in fighting the warrior who'd severely wounded Homer. Virgil's scythe locked with the warrior's Devil Arms, Virgil moved his right arm back and thrust his sword forward with as much strength as he could muster. Ragnorak pierced the warrior's armor, he grunted and his strength weakened, Virgil knocked him back, and used Soul Reaver to end him.

Tucker was slashed across the chest with the Death Dealer's Devil Arms. He fell to the ground, clutching his arm against his wound. Virgil screamed in panic, racing to his friend's side. Damian valiantly battled the warrior, the two locked in a battle to the death.

Virgil stabbed his weapons into the ground. "Cura!" Virgil commanded the spell draining its cost from Virgil. The spell flew from Virgil's hand to cover Tucker and Homer. Tucker and Virgil anxiously looked on at Homer as the spell went to work closing his wound rapidly. When the spell faded he still had a wound, though its circumference had shrunk by two thirds, and it was no longer as deep. Homer wasn't breathing. Virgil checked for a pulse at his neck, he didn't feel anything.

"You can heal him right?" Tucker asked Virgil. "You can save him!" Tucker shouted.

"I," Virgil's breathing began to race, panic setting in, "I don't know," he said feeling overwhelmed tears coming to his eyes. This can't be happening; this isn't my life!

"Try!" Tucker said grabbing the front of Virgil's clothing. "You're supposed to be some legendary hero, save him!" Tucker demanded.

"He's gone," Virgil said looking into Tucker's eyes, "My spells can only repair the body, it can't bring someone back from the dead."

"NO!" Tucker said shoving Virgil back. "You bastard! This is all your fault!" Tucker screamed at Virgil. Tucker knelt by his best friend, sobbing, holding Homer's lifeless body in his arms.

Virgil grabbed both his Devil Arms taking them firmly in hand. He couldn't save Homer, he was already gone, but Damian, he was still alive and battling for his life! Virgil choked back his emotions, he didn't have time to fall apart. Damian had helped saved countless lives by betraying his fraternity tonight, Virgil needed to protect him. Damian slammed his metal fist into the Death Dealer's face, who stumbled back from the power of the blow, the Nephilim's nose was smashed. Damian came at him again before he could recover, the Death Dealer raised his Devil Arms to shield himself. Damian used one fist to deflect the weapon, and the other smashed into his face again, the Death Dealer's eyes rolled in his skull. The Death Dealer fell back to the ground stunned, Damian began to pummel the warrior's face, screaming his fury out. Blood sprayed across Damian's gauntlets and onto his face, as he beat the Death Dealer to death.

"NO!" A blood curdling scream rang out. Virgil spun around alarmed. Standing not far off was the Gatekeeper, freshly emerged from a spiraling black portal in full battle armor complete with a helmet. A Chaos Devil Arms was in their hand, a powerful gunblade. Virgil had met the Gatekeeper, the First Lieutenant of the Death Dealers, on several occasions, and had

even battled the warrior briefly at the Tournament of the Chalice. The Gatekeeper leapt back into

the portal, and it instantly closed and disappeared. A new portal opened up right behind Damian

and the Gatekeeper emerged, the dark portal closing.

"DAMIAN!" Virgil cried out spreading his wings and flying as fast as he could.

Before Damian could turn around the Gatekeeper thrust its sword through Damian's

back, the blade coming out through his chest where his heart was. Damian gasped in shock, the

Gatekeeper savagely threw him across the ground, Damian was dead before his body came to a

stop.

The Gatekeeper knelt down, cradling the slain Death Dealer in its hands. "Armis," The

Gatekeeper cried, "Brother, NO!" The warrior screamed in pain.

Virgil was almost upon the Gatekeeper his eyes blazing with rage like molten lava, he

would rip the Gatekeeper apart! The Gatekeeper turned its attention to Virgil raising its gunblade

at him, the weapon transformed into a demonic gun and a blast of energy fired off at Virgil.

Virgil veered hard to the left, narrowly dodging the blast, he flew straight at the warrior who'd

taken his friend's life. Virgil swung out with Ragnorak, the warrior's gunblade transformed back

into a sword catching the strike. The Gatekeeper strained against Virgil's momentum, and Virgil

knocked the warrior back. Virgil stabbed Ragnorak down to skewer the warrior. The Gatekeeper

fell back into the earth, a portal opening beneath, they disappeared through it before Virgil's

sword could touch them. The portal closed and Ragnorak sunk into the ground, where the

warrior had been, not a second earlier.

Virgil turned to face the Fifth Seraph, who appeared several yards away. "You killed my friend!" Virgil screamed in rage.

"He killed my brother!" The Gatekeeper yelled back.

"He deserved to die!" Virgil spat. "Your evil brother killed my brother Homer!" he shouted.

"My brother was NOT evil!" the Gatekeeper screamed angrily. "He was a kind, and loving boy, he shouldn't have been here in the first place!"

"All Death Dealers are evil," Virgil told his fellow Seraph his face twisting into a revolting sneer. "You know nothing of what it means to love, to feel. You're all heartless killing machines, cutting down innocent children and people who didn't even have the ability to defend themselves!"

"I've never ONCE killed an innocent," the Gatekeeper told Virgil defiantly, "I still have my morals! Yes, I've fought Paladins, perhaps even killed a few from the wounds I inflicted. But when I fight it is not to kill, just to defend myself. I have no interest in taking the lives of others, but I have no choice but to follow Diablos," the warrior said sadly.

"There is always a choice!" Virgil screamed. "A choice to do what is right, or what is wrong! Your Death Dealers swept across this campus killing everything that moved, THAT IS A CHOICE! You bastards could have stormed the Omega house for the Chalice, that's what you're after. Instead your troops delighted in the slaying of students and their families, was that part of your order as well?" Virgil asked so angry his whole body was shaking.

"We have no choice!" The Gatekeeper yelled. "We are slaves of Diablos, his will is law, defying him is under penalty of death!"

"Perhaps death is better than being a murderous puppet," Virgil spat back at the Gatekeeper. "I would never bow to his will! I would choose death over killing children! You are weak!"

The Gatekeeper hung its head, "I am done arguing with you Redeemer," the Gatekeeper said. "I will take my brother's body and be gone from this place."

Virgil quickly moved to stand over the slain Death Dealer's body, Ragnorak and Soul Reaver held tightly in his grip. "You're not going anywhere!" Virgil told the warrior. "You're too dangerous. If you leave now, you'll surely murder thousands more in the future, innocents and Paladins alike. That, I cannot allow," Virgil said assuming a fighting stance.

"I don't want to fight you," the Gatekeeper told Virgil looking up to stare at him.

"No?" Virgil asked. He lowered his scythe so the flames were close to the Gatekeeper's dead brother. "Perhaps you'll have more motivation if I torch your brother's corpse," Virgil taunted.

"You wouldn't," the Gatekeeper said hesitantly, "You're not like that!" The Gatekeeper shouted.

"I've watched three men I loved as family, get cut down by Death Dealers today," Virgil said hurting so much inside he felt like screaming at the top of his lungs until he couldn't anymore. "You'd be surprised what I'm capable of," Virgil said darkly.

"You think you're strong enough to defeat me?" The Gatekeeper asked. "I've seen you in action, you're powerful, but lack proper technique and skill. You're no match for me," the warrior told him. "I don't want to hurt you, but I will if I must. Now move aside, let me take my brother's body, and I swear I will leave this campus, never to return."

"No," Virgil said coldly. "You don't deserve that, not after what you did to Damian," Virgil forced out through clenched teeth. "I will avenge my friend, and all the people who were killed today! Your death will be a blessing for all mankind!" Virgil shouted.

"You bastard," the Gatekeeper said clenching its fist. "Where is your compassion? I thought you were better than this!"

Virgil laughed, "You don't know me! And I owe you nothing! You kill my friend in front of me, and expect me to just, play nice? You're insane!" Virgil screamed.

"I tire of this pointless banter," the Gatekeeper said a portal opening behind the warrior. The Gatekeeper stepped through and vanished along with the spiraling vortex of dark energy. Virgil spun around ready for the Gatekeeper's attack.

"Virgil!" Tucker yelled from across the way, still kneeling next to Homer's body.

Virgil looked up in time to see a blast of energy from the Gatekeeper's gunblade barreling at him. Virgil swung Soul Reaver, his scythe connecting with the attack just in time, destroying the incoming blast. The Gatekeeper dive bombed Virgil slashing at him with the Chaos gunblade. Virgil let go of Soul Reaver using his mind to move it. He blocked the warrior's sword with his own, using the scythe to strike at the warrior. The Gatekeeper landed on the ground, and charged Virgil, attacking with overwhelming fierceness. The Gatekeeper was unbelievably agile, Virgil could do little more than parry the incoming slashes and stabs, he didn't have time to attack.

The gunblade was coming in too fast, Virgil felt overwhelmed his skin starting to sweat, he kept getting stabbed, blood flowing from his wounds, with each cut his limbs grew weaker. The Gatekeeper was toying with him, fear reflected in his eyes for the Gatekeeper to see. If not for the healing effects of Ragnorak, Virgil doubted he'd still be standing. The gunblade reached past his guard, cutting him horizontally where his neck meets his collarbone. A few more inches, and his neck could have been ripped apart! Virgil edged away from the warrior taking several healthy steps backs.

"Where are you running to?" The Gatekeeper demanded falling backwards, but instead of slamming into the ground a portal had appeared, and they fell through. A portal opened up behind Virgil and the Gatekeeper bolted out like at the start of a race, striking with the gunblade to kill. The gunblade stabbed his chest once more, lower this time on his right side. Several deeper cuts were created as the gunblade reached through Virgil's Devil Arms, hitting him four more times. Virgil screamed in anger releasing power from his weapons, energy blasting out from both of them, the Gatekeeper leapt back gaining distance. Virgil struggled to stay on his feet, his wounds were deep, the golden veil that surrounded him seemed to fade, his vision was swaying. *Hang in there!* His inner judge yelled, the persona that came into his conscious mind when he Ascended. *Hold onto Ragnorak, it will heal our wounds!* Virgil's wounds were gradually diminishing, the cut at his collarbone was a minute at most from being a closed angry red line.

"The Holy Blade is the only reason you're a half way decent challenge," the Gatekeeper snidely mocked him. "The constant Veil spell that you have cloaking you guides my gunblade to miss its target. The Regen spell is what makes you such a good punching bag," they added poignantly.

"You haven't begun to see what I'm capable," Virgil shouted readying his Devil Arms.

The Gatekeeper leapt into the air flying on ebony wings of darkness, Virgil flew out to meet them head on. The Gatekeeper was higher in altitude as they came close, the warrior lazily fell from the sky its gunblade aimed out transforming into a large demonic gun. The barrel filled with energy discharging with a powerful blast. Virgil veered to the left, and the Devil Arms fired again, Virgil found himself dancing through the sky, avoiding volley of energy arrows that rained down. The Gatekeeper was lithe like a ballerina, its movements fluid, and purposeful. The gunblade in this form was similar to Louie's bow, but its energy blasts were exponentially more destructive than his arrows. And Louie's bow didn't transform into a sword at the whim of its master. A blast caught Virgil in the right arm, it exploded, and Virgil was knocked from the air by the force, falling to the ground. Virgil managed to recover before he ate dirt, and beat both of his wings with renewed force climbing back up into the sky. This warrior needed to be shown that he couldn't be pushed around!

A portal opened up right in Virgil's trajectory, the Gatekeeper flew out almost colliding with him. The Gatekeeper screamed and surged forward slashing out with its saber from the gunblade. Virgil was cut deep across his waist. The Gatekeeper flew into a portal as it passed Virgil, it surged from a portal below Virgil reaching out and slashing at him again. Virgil used his wings to try and dodge the incoming blows. The Gatekeeper became a swirling tempest, jumping from one portal to another, relentlessly assaulting Virgil. Slash after stab, deep lacerations cut across all parts of his body. At last his strength gave out, his body was sliced all over, his wounds were too severe, and Virgil plummeted to the ground, crashing into the sand near the playground. Blood oozed out from all over his body, running into the sand. Virgil coughed hard, he couldn't take much more of this. He had to end things quickly, or he'd be cut to pieces!

The Gatekeeper landed near Virgil. "Have you had enough? To continue this demonstration is madness, there is nothing to be gained in beating down a clearly inferior opponent," the warrior mocked him.

Virgil laughed, "What do you expect me to do, lay down and die?" Virgil struggled to his feet, grinding his teeth, the pain was excruciating.

"No," the Gatekeeper said sadly, "I'll take my brother, and I will leave."

Virgil considered the offer, he needed to get to the Omega house to check on his mother, and Lambda class, along with all the brothers who had stayed to guard their home. "How can I trust that you will keep your word? That you'll leave campus peacefully," Virgil asked the Gatekeeper.

"Because it is the truth," the Gatekeeper told Virgil.

Virgil shook his head, "I can't trust you," he said knowing it was true.

The Gatekeeper became angry almost growling at Virgil, "You stupid, immature, LITTLE BOY!" the warrior shouted and then sprinted towards Virgil. Virgil gripped Ragnorak's handle tightly feeling its power pulse in his fingers like a heartbeat. Virgil closed his eyes and took a deep breath reaching out feeling with his aura, the Gatekeeper jumped into a portal. Virgil saw the portal, like he saw his aura, he could *feel* it. The portal closed behind the warrior. Virgil couldn't let the Gatekeeper cut him apart by bursting through portals all around him. He listened with his mind and spirit. A ripple to the east of the sphere of gold light that surrounded him, he swung Ragnorak towards it, a wave of Creation energy cutting through the air. A portal opened and the Gatekeeper surged forth, Virgil's energy wave slammed into the armored knight, and they were flung back into the portal as it closed. Virgil swung Ragnorak around looking about wildly, he'd definitely got a good hit in, though this was a Seraph, one older than he was. Which meant they had more time to train and master their Devil Arms. Virgil closed his eyes again feeling and sensing past his aura, behind him! Virgil barely had time to spin around, he swung his sword and a wave of Creation energy swam from its surface. The Gatekeeper emerged and was engulfed by the blast, the warrior rolled across the ground.

Virgil ran to the warrior using Soul Reaver like a flail, he beat the scythe upon the armored surface. The Gatekeeper grunted, struggling to stand swinging the gunblade, catching the scythe's next attack. The warrior shoved against Virgil and they both slid back.

"I don't have to put up with this," the Gatekeeper told Virgil, "I'm out of here." A portal opened behind the warrior.

"NO!" Virgil shouted angry. He would not let this warrior get away with the wrongs that had been committed. Someone had to pay for all this death, and the Gatekeeper was at fault for the assault on Bay Valley. Ragnorak's blade had filled while he had battled, Virgil closed his eyes and lifted Ragnorak into the air. "Howling Blade!" Virgil shouted. Ragnorak howled in response, as if the Devil Arms had a mouth. The blade began to hum with power, the inside filling with so much light it began to leak out of the sword, Ragnorak was shaking his hand now! Virgil could feel the ripple of distortion, right where the fallen body of the Gatekeeper's younger brother lay. The portal came into existence; Virgil didn't have any more time.

"Judgment Bolt!" Virgil shouted and Ragnorak's Soul Scream was unleashed, the beam of energy crackled like a ray of lightning. The Gatekeeper emerged from the portal, immediately aware of the impending doom. They turned back to the portal to evade Ragnorak's power. The bolt of light hit the Gatekeeper in the chest, they were picked up and flung backwards, their limbs being thrown about, the sound of bones breaking. Virgil spread his wings and flew to his enemy's side. The Gatekeeper was badly wounded, the warrior was on its side, its helmet almost knocked off its face.

"I have one final question for you before you meet your end," Virgil told the Gatekeeper. "What has Sethos done with Amari?" he asked impatiently betraying his concern. The Gatekeeper lay silent. "Answer me!" Virgil demanded. When the Seraph would not answer, Virgil lowered Ragnorak's blade to their throat and kicked them onto their back. The helmet was barely on anymore, Virgil could see the Gatekeeper's face. It was nothing like what he'd expected, he was thinking someone along the lines of Sethos or Rasler, but they looked more like TK or Selene. Virgil ripped the helmet away, his mouth falling open, and his eyebrows furrowing together in anger.

"Amari?" Virgil asked her almost choking on the words that had once made his heart leap. She wouldn't meet his gaze she stared ahead, past his legs. "YOU BETRAYED ME!" Virgil bellowed the veins on the sides of his neck popping out. "LOOK AT ME!"

Amariana turned the full weight of her dark green eyes on his sapphire ones, they stayed still, staring deeply into each other. Virgil had felt so close to her, he'd felt things for her, that he'd never felt in his entire life. The woman whom he had spent the last few months with, had become his best friend. He cared for her, like he cared for himself. She'd felt so…safe, so warm. The person he looked at now, was a stranger. Virgil's eyes began to fill with tears and Amari broke eye contact first. Her eyes were a deep wellspring of emotions unspoken, agony, fear, and regret.

"Say something," Virgil demanded clenching his fists.

"What is there to say?!" Amariana snapped. "From here on out you'll never believe me anyways. Words are pointless," she said sadly shutting down, and shutting Virgil out.

"You knew who I was from the first time we met this fall," Virgil whispered, everything making sense to him. "Because we'd met before, when you released the Arch Demon from that tree in the woods! You were tricking me the whole time!" Virgil said gritting his teeth. "You made me think you…," Virgil turned away. Amariana rose to her feet taking a shaky breath. "What was it all for Amari?" Virgil asked her. "Getting close to me, getting me to trust you. It was for the Chalice wasn't it? For today?" Virgil asked suddenly feeling sick. "You made me think you were my girlfriend, so I could be lured away from campus when the Betas 'kidnapped' you!" Virgil screamed. "Knowing full well, the Death Dealers that came in my absence would kill all those people!" Virgil was enraged shouting at the top of his lungs. "What kind of monster are you!"

"NO!" Amari shouted in protest. "It wasn't like that! In the beginning, I was supposed to see if I could steal the Chalice from the Omega house, without the need for a battle. That is why I got close to you," Amariana's words were sour, tinged with embarrassment. "I was only able to walk onto Omega grounds because you invited me in," she pointed out. "But even then, trying to reach the Chalice and remain undetected, soon became impossible. I wasn't able to reach it, even with my ability. It became clear the only way to destroy it, was to destroy the house around it," she told Virgil.

Virgil looked into Amari's fiery beautiful green eyes, "What about us?" He asked her. "Why did you make me think…you loved me?" his words were strong. He needed to know the answer, his mind was racing, he felt like he was going insane, replaying over every conversation they'd ever had, new perspective given to her actions and behaviors.

"Virgil," Amari said her words cracking with emotion. "I, I," tears came to her eyes, she turned away from Virgil walking to her brother. Virgil chased after her, his Devil Arms disappearing from his hand, her gunblade fell away in a shimmer of dark light. He grabbed her shoulders, and turned her to face him.

"Tell me," he demanded. "You owe me, Amari. I have to know, what we had, was it ever real? Did you ever really care for me? Or was it all just a show, from a talented actress, dressed like a sorority girl, with the heart of a Death Dealer," his words were stinging and bitter.

"You don't know my heart," Amari snapped back with attitude, "Don't pretend to understand me! In the beginning, it was an act. I was doing as I was instructed by Lucifer, the First God General," Amari rambled, obviously uncomfortable. "I had a dorm on campus, I slept there on occasion, and would often warp home to give report on how the operation was going." Virgil's stomach felt acidic, he hated what he was hearing, and yet it was all stuff he needed to know or he'd go crazy. "But then I started pledging for the Alpha sisters," Amari said leaning back motioning with an arm, "It was…fun! More fun than I could ever remember having. Everyone is so, close, they care about each other. I met the Omegas…and you. I came here knowing that the Paladins are my enemy, and that the Upsilon Delta Chapter was our enemy number one. But what I saw, it wasn't what I'd been told," Amari said looking off forlornly.

"What did you think it would be like?" Virgil demanded. "That we were all a bunch of blood hungry wolves, looking to start a war?"

"No," Amari shrugged, "But everyone talks down humans, and Paladins so much, that once it's all you hear, the culture becomes all you know," she pointed out. "None of you were what I had expected, you weren't what I expected," she said sadly. Amari stopped, she really looked at Virgil, like she used to, and for a moment, Virgil could see in her face, the woman that he had fallen for. "Even when I was cold to you, you never stopped being kind," she said softly staring deep into his eyes. "I've lived in the Ever After since I was fourteen, I was living on the streets at thirteen. Most of the people I met, were cold, cruel, and selfish. That didn't change moving to the Ever After. When I arrived, I thought I would be spending time with my father. Instead I was immediately trained to be a warrior, and beat down until I fought back. Most people in this world, they don't really care about each other, just what they believe people think of them. It is all about appearance, fake social interactions, no real empathy or compassion," Amari told him looking down. "I was alone for so long. But then, my brother Armis, came to the Ever After," she said her face lighting up, her full pouty lips breaking into a large grin, her teeth showing. "He was four years younger than me, we had different mothers, but were sired by the same father. We instantly connected as neither of us had family, we started living together, and we loved each other. For the both of us, it was a piece of happiness," her words went bitter and she looked down at her dead brother's body.

"Who is your father?" Virgil asked her.

"The Fourth God General, Beelzebub," Amari told Virgil. "My mother was human, and she died giving birth to me. Armis was the first real family, I'd had since my grandma died. I loved him, and I'd forgotten what it was like to love someone else," she said not meeting Virgil's eyes.

"If you really cared about me, why didn't you tell me you were a Seraph?" Virgil fired back crossing his arms over his chest his eyebrows flaring in anger.

"I was scared!" Amari cried out tears coming to her eyes. "Things happened so fast, one minute I was spying on the Redeemer, and keeping tabs on the Chalice. And the next I was friends with Blair, and TK, and Selene. I enjoyed spending time with you, you made me feel like nothing else in the world mattered, you made me feel so special. Days with you turned into weeks, and soon I found myself feeling that this was my real life, and the one in the Ever After was my double life. After the semi-formal, after we spent the night together, I knew I had to tell you. I tried so many times, last night before we," Amari's words trailed off and both of their faces flushed. Virgil couldn't believe that was just last night, it felt like a lifetime ago.

Amari looked at Virgil, "I had just found out Sethos' plans for today, I wanted to tell you, I wanted to warn you! To admit my faults, and beg you to forgive me! So that we could run away somewhere, and spend the rest of our days together, just you and I," Amari said breathlessly. Her words came out like she'd walked through this conversation in her head relentlessly.

"So why didn't you?" Virgil shrugged his shoulders.

"I chickened out, it was always my responsibility to initiate the conversation, I'm the one who deceived you," Amari owned a defeated look coming on her face. "And I was so scared that you'd tell me you hated me, and that you'd turn your back on me, before I had a chance to explain myself."

Virgil could yell and scream, and argue about every little hurt, but that wouldn't accomplish anything. They stood so close to each other, but Virgil had never felt so distant from her. Amari had become the person Virgil felt closer to than anyone in the world. He'd felt comfortable being himself with her, saying what he had on his mind without feeling like he had to sensor his thoughts. Now, things couldn't feel so different. How had two people who had once had so much to share, so much love to give, reach an impasse where a chasm had opened up between them, devoid of compromise, nullifying any hope of surmounting its depths. Virgil looked at her right hand, the black Devil Arms symbol was so foreign.

"You always had a blue symbol," Virgil remarked.

"I was wearing a glove, spelled with an illusion," Amari explained. Virgil nodded, he'd worn a similar glove over the summer on his first trip to Alexandros.

"Ms. Morgan, she knew you were wearing a glove," Virgil said aloud, "That's why she was distrustful of you." It was all starting to make sense. There had been so many little things, he'd never pieced it all together before.

Virgil didn't know what else to ask, what else to say, he didn't want to know anymore. "Where do we go from here?" Virgil asked Amari.

"I don't know," she replied the wind picking up a piece of her dark wavy hair, twisting it in the breeze. Virgil had loved moving his fingers through her soft long locks, he clenched his hands at his sides, that was something that would never happen again. So many things that he'd enjoyed about Amari would never happen again. "I don't want to fight you Virgil," Amari said honestly. "I'm sorry for all that you've lost today."

"Your brother," Virgil paused, he had watched as he ruthlessly slayed Homer. "I'm sorry for your loss as well," he managed to tell her. "Amari, I loved you," Virgil said looking at her, "A part of me always will perhaps. However, knowing you deceived me, and lied to me from the beginning of everything…you betrayed me, Amari!" Virgil was shaking he was so upset. "And I don't know if I can ever forgive you for that," Virgil didn't want tears to come to his face but they did anyways. Is this what all relationships brought at the end? A painful, soul crushing blow, that brought you to the edge of your confidence in your own identity? "Even if I could forgive you…I don't know, if I can ever forget," Virgil looked Amari full on. "The memory of you stabbing Damian through the back, it is too much to handle," he admitted.

"He was pummeling my little brother's skull!" Amari shouted. "What would you have done! In that instant it didn't matter who was killing Armis, they were already dead," she told him coldly.

Virgil seethed at her words, his temper flaring, "I wanted to kill you earlier, until I saw your face underneath the armor. I wanted you to die for all the pain you'd brought this place! And now," Virgil shook his head laughing like a madman, "I think seeing who you really were, cut me deeper than anything ever has," Virgil admitted to Amari having clear insight into his feelings in that instant.

His words wounded Amari and she recoiled from him, going over to her brother. Virgil turned away from her as well seeing Tucker, he'd almost forgotten he was there. Virgil locked eyes with him, and his brother saw the pain raging on inside Virgil. Virgil ran over to him. Damian's fraternity brother was close by, knelt next to Damian.

"You both need to get inside one of these buildings and stay there until this mess is over," Virgil advised.

"I can hide in the bathroom," Tucker suggested to Virgil, "What about you?" he asked concerned.

"I have to go check on everyone at the Omega house," Virgil replied, "And it'll be easier without having to worry about you, got it?" he asked sternly.

"Gotcha," Tucker nodded and they shared a quick hug, knowing they may never see each other again. Lightning crashed down from the sky in the direction of the Omega house. Virgil immediately went on high alert, more spells seemed to crash down from above, something was happening!

"It is Sethos," Amari's words cut through, cold, and fearful. "He's attacking the Omega house!" she yelled. "He'll destroy the fraternity house along with everything in it!"

"My mother is in there!" Virgil shouted starting to run his wings opening.

"Wait!" Amari yelled and Virgil turned towards her. "Please don't go!" She said fiercely. "Sethos will destroy you! He's the most powerful of the Seven Seraphs, and he relishes in death and destruction. You aren't strong enough to stand against him!" Amari warned.

"The people I love most in this world are at that house!" Virgil shouted. "I won't let my friends and my mother be killed because I was too scared to fight for them!"

"If you go, he will make you submit to him and join the Death Dealers, or kill you for rejecting him," Amari pleaded.

"I am not afraid of the Harbinger!" Virgil shouted in Amari's face. "Anyone who tries to take them from me will face the wrath of Ragnorak! I am an Omega of the Upsilon Delta Chapter, of the Paladins! It is my duty to defend the Chalice of Immortals from the Death Dealers!"

"Virgil," Amari's words were sweet, like they'd been when she'd whispered his name at night while they lay next to each other. She reached out touching Virgil's arm gently. He shrugged her hand off like it was venomous spider.

"You don't get to speak to me like that anymore," he said shaking his head. It was too painful.

"Please," Amari asked once more, "Listen to me, I don't want you to die!" she shouted.

"You no longer have any impact over the decisions I make with my life," Virgil said coldly to Amari. "You're a Death Dealer, and I'm a Paladin," Virgil walked away from Amari and spread his wings. He turned his head back to her, and met her gaze one final time, his beautiful Amari, the woman who'd stolen his heart. "The next time we meet, will be as enemies," Virgil's words were cold and deadly serious. "I will avenge the murder of my friend Damian, even if that means cutting down the Gatekeeper, Amariana!" he shouted.

Virgil took to the sky summoning Ragnorak to his hand with a bolt of light. "Take me to the Omega house!" Virgil commanded and the Holy Blade surged forward, pulling Virgil along like a shooting star.

"Goodbye Virgil," Amari whispered and stepped through a portal with her brother in her arms.

# Chapter 24 Ultima Weapon

Meanwhile, as Virgil fought with the Gatekeeper Amariana, the future of the Omegas was in peril. Sethos, the Fourth Seraph, approached the gates of the Omega house with a squad of a dozen Death Dealers. Sethos was garbed in the traditional Death Dealer armor, distinguishable from the others with a regal design, and a lavish cape to assert his superiority. Sethos blasted down the gates with a simple spell plucked from his massive aura, fortunately they didn't make it far into the grounds, they ran into the barrier protecting the house. Sethos could not see the Omega house, though he knew it was there, the barrier's power gave the illusion that there was nothing to his naked eye. An unseen force pushed against them, preventing them from walking any further.

"Your spells cannot protect you Omegas!" Sethos yelled. "Ultima Weapon!" Sethos commanded. The Chaos Devil Arms on his hand flared to life, dark energy billowed out as smoke extending from his palm, shaping into an enormous weapon. Sethos' sword was unlike any Devil Arms in existence, the blade was thick and so massive it would have taken several people to lift it in anyone else's hands. The edge around the blade was pure white and translucent, the same material as Ragnorak's blade. Sethos slashed at the barrier with his Devil Arms, the sword collided with the invisible wall, and energy crackled along the blade, the barrier was made tangible to their eyes. Sethos stepped back and his soldiers released a volley of spells at the barrier, it weakened under each one.

"The barrier won't hold forever," Sethos told his men and they continued to assault the barrier. "I have no need for prisoners. Kill them all."

In retaliation the Omegas inside, along with a few Paladins from the Capital, stormed out of their home, to fend off Sethos and his troops! Gabriel led the warriors, with Lambda and most of the older brothers, including the three Chapter Advisors, Ramuh, Ifrit, and Ezekiel. There were still parents, including Sue, waiting in fear in the fraternity house, their sons, and brothers leaving to defend them. The Paladins ran to the edge of the barrier, their large open yard giving them plenty of room to maneuver.

They charged the Harbinger and his men running past the safety of the barrier, and a bloody battle erupted! Both sides quickly lost numbers, the Death Dealers with Sethos were outnumbered, and their forces dwindled to eight, then five, then three. The Omegas and fellow Paladins from the capital were cut down without mercy, some suffering severe wounds, left to lay in the grass, their lives hanging in the balance.

Soon it was just Sethos against the Omegas, they were getting hits on him, but Sethos never seemed to stagger. Each hit only seemed to make him smile more, laugh harder, his eyes were wild, he was a man unhinged with power. Wielding Ultima Weapon with impudence he swung the large sword knocking two or three men over at a time with its tremendous reach. The brothers had a hard time getting close to him due to his weapon's elongated blade, and one blow from that sword…people weren't getting back up.

"Give it up you prick!" Zender demanded. "You're outmanned fourteen to one, with plenty of reinforcements from Alexandros on their way. You're not getting in our home!" Zender shouted.

"Inferior filth!" Sethos spat clenching his non-Devil Arms hand. "What makes you think, even a thousand of you, would have the power to end me!" Sethos screamed. Sethos leapt into the air, his dark wings stretching out, he slammed down striking Ultima Weapon into the ground with tremendous force. A sphere of dark energy erupted from the point of impact spreading out with the speed of light. All the brothers were thrown into the air; the force of impact was like being at the center of a bomb's detonation. They struggled to get up, some of them were knocked unconscious. Ultima Weapon was a Devil Arms unlike anything the brothers had faced, they couldn't hope to match its power.

"I won't die here!" Magnus yelled standing up, raising Tempest Staff to the sky, a massive thunderstorm began to gather. "Shine Plasma!" Magnus commanded, and a barrage of purple lightning strikes shot down slamming into the earth around Sethos. The spell damaged Sethos, but he never faltered, the powerful spell doing little more than slowing his gait.

"Aeroga!" Master Ramuh shouted to the sky and a windstorm engulfed Sethos, a funnel snaking down and tearing everything up from the ground in a small contained sphere around the Harbinger. Sethos was thrown to the ground when the spell subsided, brothers began sending volleys of spells at him, he got to his feet without hesitation.

Sethos yelled, he spread his wings and shot into the air, dive bombing the group of brothers. Sethos swung at them with Ultima Weapon, Professor Ramuh was slashed across his chest, hard, he fell to the ground, unable to rise as his life blood poured out his gaping wound exposing his organs and bones. Professor Ifrit howled in anger, the flaming gauntlets on his hands blazing to life as he charged the young Commander of the Death Dealers. Zender, Landon, Tarek, and Gabriel joined Professor Ifrit, racing towards Sethos. Sethos spun his massive sword around him knocking over the brothers that approached deep bleeding wounds their reward for challenging him. Benson, Buck, Thiago, and Jagger charged him next, his eyes danced with delight as he dealt out powerful strikes, sending them all to the ground.

Zane, the youngest brother present, ran forward diving into a roll under a sword swipe that was aimed at his neck. Within striking distance Zane spun his lance and began stabbing at Sethos, Sethos slashed forward, and Zane nimbly dodged the sword's reach once more by rolling underneath. Zane gripped his wind lance tightly, surging forward with incredible speed and force, he plunged it into Sethos.

Sethos was surprised, his eyes widening as the metal sank into his flesh, "You're quite skilled for one so young," Sethos spoke with true admiration to Zane.

"You're an overconfident asshole!" Zane retorted. Sethos gripped the lance sending dark energy racing down its shaft, zapping Zane off his feet. Sethos swayed then grew steady, his almost immortal constitution holding strong. Zane got to his feet, his weapon materializing back in hand, and raced at Sethos. Sethos stabbed Ultima Weapon, Zane dodged the blow, jabbing his lance at Sethos. His blade was bloodied red, with Sethos' blood, Zane was one of the only brothers who'd managed to actually make him bleed. Zane was nimble on his feet; his speed was the only thing keeping him alive.

Sethos closed his eyes, seeing with his aura, "I sense that you will become a great Nephilim one day. Your power will grow while others plateau, and you will rise to be a leader among the Paladins," Sethos opened his eyes right as Zane was coming in for his next attack. Sethos struck out his sword stabbing Zane through the chest, Ultima Weapon had come out the other side. "However, now your future holds nothing," Sethos delightfully told Zane, as he gasped his last breaths. "Because you were blinded by the arrogance of your youth, and challenged a foe ever your greater," Sethos coldly whispered to Zane, the last words he heard. Sethos ripped Ultima Weapon from his body. Zane fell back into the grass, gone from the world, forever. Sethos turned his attention to the enraged Omegas that surged towards him.

"YOU MONSTER!" Vahn screamed using Furybrand he made his attempt to strike Sethos down. All the men left standing charged Sethos at once from all sides. The brothers as one began to stab, slash, strike, and pummel Sethos who was unable to stop all of them as he was surrounded. Sethos did his best to strike those he could reach, knocking over two brothers at a time. Soon his armor was coated in blood. The perimeter of Ultima Weapon's blade had subtly changed from the stark white it was when first summoned, to a blue-black hue.

"Stand back you fools!" Sethos shouted, "Ruinaga!" A sphere of dark light shot out from his hand to hover above him, it opened up, expanding into a massive globe of energy, everyone it touched was lifted off their feet. The light imploded and shot outwards knocking down every warrior except Sethos.

Sethos walked towards to Gabriel, who was still struggling to stand from the aftermath of Sethos' powerful spell. "You disappoint me Gabriel," Sethos said to the warrior below him. "I was hoping you might finally be the one strong enough to give me a challenge. It appears your reputation is cheap talk. Pitiful, I expected more!" Sethos leapt into the air, his greedy eyes leering at Gabriel, and he brought Ultima Weapon down with startling force.

"NO!" a chorus of voices rang out as they were powerless to intervene. Gabriel watched as Ultima Weapon came down to spear him through like it had Zane.

"GABRIEL!" Ezekiel screamed throwing himself at Sethos, and unto his sword.

"EZEKIEL!" Gabriel howled in horror as his older brother, Ezekiel, sacrificed himself to protect him.

"Pathetic, giving one's life, for thy brother," Sethos shook his head removing his weapon from Ezekiel's body, he stepped back. Ezekiel fell to the grass, life leaving his body

"Ezekiel!" Gabriel yelled hysterically grabbing his brother sobbing. Gabriel rose to his feet, LionsHeart radiating light from his hand. "AHHH!" Gabriel screamed charging Sethos, fighting his massive Chaos sword with his Earth longsword.

"Gabriel!" the other brothers shouted. Professor Ifrit, Brody, Vahn, Tarek, Jagger, Spencer, and Magnus joined him in battle. Sethos welcomed the warriors, enjoying being outnumbered. With a swing of his sword, he slashed Spencer and Jagger, both fell to the ground their lacerations too deep to get back up. Magnus caught the next blow with his staff, Ultima Weapon slid down the staff, slicing off Magnus' non-Devil Arms hand. Magnus screamed as he stumbled back staring at his wrist as it gushed blood, his hand on the ground.

Gabriel wouldn't go down, he fought with a motivation greater than he'd ever known. He wanted to kill Sethos, for no other reason than to see the blood run from his body, and watch the light leave his eyes. "You're mine Sethos!" Gabriel told him as their Devil Arms clashed in a battle of strength, skill, and power.

"You can't kill me!" Sethos taunted him. "When will I be challenged? Have I not waited long enough to taste my true power!" Sethos screamed into the night. "Must I rip my own body apart to touch the face of the Creator!" he shouted. Brody and Professor Ifrit came at Sethos, he cut them both down with one swing, they fell clutching their wounds, struggling for life, their Devil Arms fading.

"I'm the last face you're ever going to see you freak!" Gabriel answered Sethos reaching past his guard and slicing his blade clean across Sethos' midsection. Sethos grunted falling to one knee clutching his sword, firmly planted in the ground. The outer rim of Ultima Weapon's blade was filling up becoming a dark black purplish color.

"As I wander closer to death's shadow," Sethos chanted cryptically, "Ultima Weapon's true power begins to unfold." Sethos grabbed his blade, and stood up, swinging it towards Gabriel and the other brothers. A wave of Chaos energy swam from his sword barreling over all of them leveling everyone flat on the ground. The brothers were severely wounded, some barely clinging to life.

Sethos walked slowly, asking the group, "Whose death blood will Ultima Weapon drink next?" Gabriel was writhing on the ground in immense pain; the wave of darkness had washed over him like napalm, everyone it had touched was in agony, in too much pain to stand. No one was uninjured, who had the strength left to stand against Sethos? Sethos looked to Gabriel, a cruel glean lighting his eyes, he walked towards him. Vahn struggled to his feet, taking every ounce of strength he had to stumble in front of Gabriel, blocking him from Sethos. Furybrand firmly in his hand poised for combat. "You?" Sethos asked swinging Ultima Weapon around to point to Vahn. "Step aside, you're only prolonging his inevitable demise."

"I won't let you take Gabriel from us! For my brothers!" Vahn cried out willing to give his life in the defense of his best friend!

Virgil came racing across the sky, the Omega house just coming into view. Virgil saw Sethos approaching Vahn, the macabre scene that sprawled out before him was sickening. So many people lay slain, some were still breathing and holding onto life. Virgil's mind couldn't take it all in, it was too much to process! He saw his brothers, ripped to pieces, Virgil immediately felt like he was going into shock, Zane was gored through! Agustin didn't look like he was breathing!

"Die for your brothers Paladin!" Sethos shouted at Vahn swinging his sword a wave of darkness swam towards him.

"VAHN!" Virgil yelled his focus narrowing in. Ragnorak radiated with power and Virgil swung his blade towards Sethos, a wave of golden energy crashed to the ground, cutting in front of Vahn, absorbing the blast of darkness. Sethos took a step back twirling his massive weapon he looked to the sky, watching as Virgil streamed through the air to meet him. Virgil landed in front of his Big, shielding him with his body.

"Redeemer," Sethos taunted Virgil. "I had thought you were going to let me kill every one of your brothers," he chuckled. "I'm delighted you decided to join us. Perhaps now I will have an adversary worth facing." Sethos eyes' gleamed with a dark hunger and he stared Virgil down.

"Begone from this place, Harbinger," Virgil beseeched him.

"No," Sethos shook his head, "This fight won't be over until the Chalice is destroyed, and even then...I don't want the fight to be over," Sethos said with sneer. "I've been waiting for this moment since I first began to master Ultima Weapon, I needed an opponent who is worthy. Wielder of the Blade of Life, against the Sword of Death," Sethos whispered almost seductively to Virgil. Sethos reached out to Virgil, "Help me achieve my potential, help me to embrace our fate, and release Diablos from his prison!"

"I won't help you accomplish anything!" Virgil yelled at Sethos. "You're insane! A rabid, wild animal that's killed to the point where it needs to be taken out."

"You'll give me what I want in the end," Sethos said rising into the air on his ebony wings.

Virgil spread his wings and raced to meet Sethos, Ragnorak extended out as Ultima Weapon came into range. The two warriors collided, and their swords clashed. Virgil screamed as he struggled against Sethos' godlike Devil Arms. Ultima Weapon had a purple-black hue in the glass like edge of its massive surface. Ragnorak's beautiful blade buckled under Ultima Weapon, Virgil broke the dead lock, and began to fly away, Sethos coming up like a bullet on his flank. Sethos swung his massive blade when he got within range, Virgil had no choice but to meet the attack with Ragnorak. The two Devil Arms grinded against each other, sparks of energy spraying. A screeching sound, that reminded Virgil of nails on a chalk board, filled the air. Was that…Ragnorak? It sounded…scared? Virgil was flung down, he used his wings to save himself from crashing, and landed in the Omega's yard, a healthy distance from any of his brothers.

"Why do you run Virgil?" Sethos asked him. "Is it because Ragnorak is afraid?" Virgil stared dumbfounded. "That wasn't my Devil Arms crying out in fear," Sethos laughed. "Perhaps it does not have faith in its wielder?" Sethos asked mockingly. Sethos' wings lifted his feet to barely hover above the ground, he zipped across the space between him and Virgil. A portion of Sethos' blade slashed Virgil across the chest, Virgil barely managed to deflect most of the blow. Sethos quickly moved back on his wings, then surged forward once more. Virgil raised Ragnorak in defense, Virgil was slammed so hard, he was knocked across the ground. Virgil struggled to his feet, blood dripping from his body, he was badly wounded, Ragnorak's power would heal him, very gradually, he needed time.

"Is this the power of the Redeemer?" Sethos asked angry. "You're not giving me your all!"

"What do you want from me!" Virgil yelled at him getting to his feet, he was so tired, the fight with Amariana had exhausted him. He didn't have much more to give.

"Your best Redeemer, fighting at your peak, no holding back," Sethos spoke with rapid speech his eyes lit with a battle lust. "I want to see your power at its fullest!" Sethos cried.

Virgil didn't feel like he had much fight left in him. His aura was weakened, the Optimum extinguished of spare energy, Sethos was clearly beyond his skill level. Getting hit with Ultima Weapon was akin to getting hit by a car, Virgil's arms felt shaky thinking about blocking his sword again, he couldn't hope to last against him.

"Get out of here Virgil!" Vahn yelled from across the blood-stained grass. "He'll kill you!"

"You're no match for him!" Professor Ifrit said struggling to stand from his injuries.

"If you won't fight me, then perhaps they will," Sethos suggested with a devilish grin.

"I'm willing!" Virgil yelled slicing Ragnorak through the air in a show of force.

Sethos extended his hand out to Vahn, dark lightning shot out from his Devil Arms symbol, Vahn was knocked off his feet. He lay on the ground, body convulsing with pain, he screamed, the smell of his burning flesh filled the night air.

"STOP!" Virgil screamed the dark Devil Arms on his left-hand blazing to life.

"Now you're getting fired up!" Sethos laughed and the energy stopped flowing from his hand. "Darkness is your true power; I can sense it. Chaos is strong within you, do not ignore its power," Sethos advised Virgil. "You're angry right now, you hate me, don't you? This mortal is your friend; you'd die for him, wouldn't you?" he asked already knowing the answers. Vahn lay on the ground steam rising from his body.

"Leave my friends alone!" Virgil yelled.

"No," Sethos smiled, dark energy flowing out from his hand, zapping Vahn again, who screamed from the excruciating pain.

"KNOCK IT OFF!" Virgil screamed feeling his power surge. Both his symbols flared with energy, leaking out of his hands, *let me help!* His Godhood called out to him.

"You're at your strongest, defending others," Sethos nodded understanding the secret to Virgil's abilities. "Pitiful," he sneered.

Virgil knew if he didn't try to kill Sethos, he would murder everyone Virgil loved, and take joy in it. I don't use this power lightly, Virgil thought, but I don't stand a chance without it! "Prepare to face the Light!" Virgil yelled at Sethos. Virgil Ascended and the power of his Inner Judge came out. Virgil's eyes glowed gold, his aura expanded, his power radiating out. Virgil could feel the presence in his mind of his immortal self, his spirit given conscious form. *Take him!* Virgil shot forward like a bullet, his senses heightened, he stabbed Ragnorak at Sethos. The sound of Ultima Weapon swinging through the air was ominous, Virgil summoned Soul Reaver to his left hand, and used it to catch the Ultimate Chaos Devil Arms. Virgil stabbed Ragnorak through Sethos chest, penetrating his armor.

"No fair!" Sethos laughed, high on the pain of his wounds. "You have two Devil Arms!" he smirked. Sethos pushed himself, *into* Virgil's sword, and kicked Virgil hard in the stomach. Virgil stumbled back, the wind knocked out of his lungs, his Devil Arms firmly in his hands, he stood back to his full height. Virgil surged forward, using the ground like a trampoline with the power of his wings, he leapt up, and struck down on Sethos. Soul Reaver spun around with blinding speed, using both of his Devil Arms, and his heightened reflexes and strength, Virgil began to overpower his opponent. Virgil blocked Ultima Weapon with Ragnorak, and sent Soul

Reaver spinning through the air slashing his exposed back. The more strikes Virgil got in, the more confident he became, Ragnorak was starting to fill up with golden light, when it was full he could release its Soul Scream again.

"We were supposed to be brothers, you and I," Sethos said staring into Virgil's eyes.

"In what Hel did you dream that nightmare?" Virgil asked.

"The Harbinger and the Reaver, the sons of Lucifer and Raphael, an unstoppable force," Sethos whispered nostalgically to Virgil.

"I'm the Redeemer, not the Reaver!" Virgil proclaimed.

"Now you are," Sethos shrugged, "But even gods have fallen from the Light, and turned to the Dark. You are a mere mortal, no more infallible than they are!" Sethos protested. "Someone has twisted your fate! You were supposed to be a leader of the Death Dealers! A knight that stood by your fathers' side, the Devil's Reaver." Sethos declared. "That is how I've come to understand it."

"There are possible futures for everyone," Virgil explained to Sethos, "Each of us, make decisions every day. Choices that begin to shape who we are. The kind of company we keep, THAT is how our futures are shaped," Virgil spoke passionately. "People are what matter. The people you love. My only possible future, from here until the end of time, is to stand by the people that I love, and fight for the things that matter most to me!"

"You're boring," Sethos decided talking to himself out loud, "The Light must have dulled your sense of fun. Soul Reaver's true power is being tempered by your Will. Give into its

Darkness, Virgil," Sethos told him fervently. "And you will know a power you've never known with the Light," he whispered.

Virgil looked at Soul Reaver, it was a curse, rather than a weapon to defend himself. Virgil didn't want something like this, something that could lead him astray, it was becoming his greatest fear…releasing Soul Reaver's power one day, and not being able to turn it off. "I choose to limit Soul Reaver's influence, because that's not the kind of man I want to be," Virgil spat at Sethos. "I don't want to be someone who gives into his anger and hatred, to become blinded by prejudice and intolerance, and trample on the rights and freedoms of his fellow people in turn!"

"We're not running for office you moron," Sethos spoke condescending to Virgil. "You're the Redeemer, the Sixth Seraph. One of the most powerful demi Judges that will ever exist. You are a God among mortals, we do not answer to the masses, the masses answer to us," Sethos smiled.

"LEAVE!" Virgil demanded tired of his superior, and manic temperament.

"I'm not leaving," Sethos firmly asserted, "If you want me gone you'll have to kill me."

Chills went down Virgil's spine, Sethos meant it. Virgil raced forward using Soul Reaver to strike out and Ragnorak to follow up. Sethos never faltered, his strength only increasing as the battle wore on. Virgil beat Sethos back, cutting his thighs with Soul Reaver twice, Ragnorak collided with Ultima Weapon! Sethos was slashed in his chest as he couldn't restrain both the scythe and the sword, Sethos spun around almost losing his balance.

Sethos suffered severe wounds, he was bleeding profusely, his Devil Arms wasn't healing him, like Virgil's did. He stumbled, backing away from Virgil, for the first time showing a crack in his immortal exterior. "We're getting there," Sethos told him, "I've never felt more powerful," he admitted happily. Virgil noticed for the first time Sethos' Devil Arms was changing color…why? Did he have a Soul Scream? Was it charging, just like Virgil's? Virgil's blood began to pump a little faster, time was not on his side, something was happening, and if he couldn't figure it out…

"Finish him!" a dying voice cried out from the battlefield, it was frater Agustin. "He's too dangerous for mercy!" He yelled his last words his chest ceasing the struggle to breath.

"AHHHHHHHH!" Virgil roared sailing on his wings for a collision with Sethos. Virgil savagely ripped into Sethos with Ragnorak, swinging Soul Reaver around to finish him, when Ultima Weapon caught the scythe. Virgil's arms strained against the power of his blade, his veins popping out along his skin, his arms shaking…had Sethos' Devil Arms grown stronger? The scythe was flung away sailing behind them, Virgil had enough time to start running backwards before Ultima Weapon came flying at him, Ragnorak caught the end of the blade, Chaos and Creation energy crackled along their blades. Virgil was forced back, the momentum behind Sethos' swing was almost unbearable to sustain, the sword WAS getting stronger!

"Have you figured it out?" Sethos asked. "The secret to my power?"

Virgil needed to either finish him, or get him to leave, this little dance would end badly the longer it continued. "For the Omegas!" Virgil cried out raising his sword into the air. "Howling Blade!" Virgil commanded and Ragnorak began to scream. Virgil flew at Sethos once more, using all his strength and speed, Virgil slashed Ragnorak with devastating power and accuracy, Sethos stumbled back, his flesh being sliced into ribbons, the blows knocking him to his knees. Virgil released a few waves of Creation energy from Ragnorak, Sethos was powerless but to guard, and take the blast. "Judgment Bolt!" Virgil yelled and Ragnorak screamed releasing

458

its powerful beam of light, that destroyed and damaged all things dark or malevolent in its path. Sethos was shot through the brick wall surrounding their yard, and into the woods.

Virgil ran over to the many wounded, Vahn, Gabriel, Tarek, Professor Ramuh, and Magnus were laying in the same area. Everyone was in pretty rough shape, Vahn and Gabriel couldn't stand, most were laying on their backs, waiting for it to be over, for help, or mercy. "Cura!" Virgil commanded his aura couldn't take much more. The spell launched out connecting with Magnus, Gabriel, and Professor Ramuh, they looked some of the worst. "Cura!" Virgil commanded again using what precious little energy he had left in his body. Three more clouds of healing energy wisped out, seeking the next three most wounded. Virgil didn't have enough energy to save everyone, but he'd made a difference.

"You fool!" Professor Ramuh told Virgil. "Go finish the Harbinger, NOW!" he commanded. "He must die! He is growing too powerful!"

"Magnus looked like he was slipping, and you didn't look much better," Virgil cried out. "I thought Sethos was taken care of!"

"We need to get everyone inside!" Zender said leaning on his polearm for support. "If he comes back, we can't afford to be sitting ducks!"

Virgil looked in the direction that Sethos had disappeared, he needed to finish things once and for all…

"What is that?" Landon asked pointing towards their broken wall. It looked like a glowing purple lightsaber, but nothing as cool as that existed in this reality, unfortunately. Sethos slowly walked back into view from the darkness of night, that had engulfed their home and battlefield.

"I should thank you Redeemer," Sethos gloated happily. "You really have made this a most memorable experience for me." Ultima Weapon was transformed. It was still the massive hulking sword as wide as two people, but the outer layer of the blade was glowing black and purple, energy rippled inside like how Ragnorak just was. Virgil looked down at Ragnorak, it was once again a diamond like substance, no gold energy inside. It needed to recharge. "Have you heard of Ultima Weapon before? Do you know why I am called the Harbinger of Destruction?" Sethos asked Virgil. "When I am at my physical peak, my blade is weak, and no stronger than the average Devil Arms among any of these commoners," Sethos proclaimed. "But the closer I approach death; the stronger Ultima Weapon becomes. I couldn't send out waves of energy like you can, not until I'd taken enough damage. And until now, I've never unlocked its hidden power!" Sethos' was consumed with it, his eyes dancing wildly, he was close to death, and yet was overflowing with more destructive energy than any Nephilim before him. "I needed an opponent strong enough to bring me to the brink of death, yet too foolish to outright destroy me," Sethos laughed.

"I'll finish you, right here, right now!" Virgil commanded Soul Reaver to fly back to his hand, both of his Devil Arms flaring to life.

"Gladly!" Sethos agreed. "I wish to test out Ultima's capabilities. Come Sword of Death, Greatest of all Chaos Devil Arms, show your Master your true power!" Sethos cried raising his glowing black blade into the air. Ultima Weapon let out a howl, it was deeper than Ragnorak's tone, more…sinister, and hateful. There was a hunger in its voice, the desire to drink up the world, an insatiable thirst to destroy everything! No wonder Sethos had been paired up with this Devil Arms, they both relished in death and utter devastation of life.

Sethos brought his blade crashing down in front of him, a wave of darkness ten feet high flowed out from the Devil Arms barreling across the ground towards Virgil. Virgil gripped the handle of his sword tightly, a pulse emanating from the blade. Virgil swung Ragnorak forward and a wave of Creation energy swam out to protect him. The forces collided, the energy from Ultima Weapon thundered into Ragnorak's, the dark energy quickly overwhelmed the other, and what was left of the dark wave came forward running through Virgil carrying him backwards. Virgil's Ascended state fell away, he couldn't keep it active any longer. Virgil fell to the ground, feeling weak and exposed. Virgil couldn't breathe, his whole body ached, and tremors ran along his arms and legs. Ultima Weapon was too powerful! Ragnorak's attack couldn't even stop it! Sethos continued walking towards Virgil.

"You know, I'm still willing to forgive you, after all this," Sethos told Virgil nodding his head. "I did kind of start things between us," he nodded sounding guilty and almost regretful. "I'm willing to move on from the past if you are, and we can start over as comrades," Sethos smiled happily.

"Haven't you listened to a word I've said!" Virgil yelled forcing his body to sit up. "I could never join you! Not after what you've done to this place, these people, these families! Your traitor cousin, Malachi, died tonight because of you! I've seen what happens to those loyal to you. And Amariana, the Gatekeeper," earning gasps from his brothers. "They were your pawns to make sure tonight went exactly like this? Am I right?" Virgil asked.

"This operation has been in motion since the Chalice was moved here," Sethos told Virgil. "Diablos is inpatient and will not wait to have his essence released from that Chalice!" Sethos told him. Sethos paused and smiled wickedly, "So…you know about your hot little piece of ass?"

"Shut up!" Virgil yelled angrily.

"You sure do!" Sethos laughed. "You actually thought Amariana loved you?" Sethos mocked him. "My father ordered the Gatekeeper to spy on you, to find out what you knew, and to bring you over to our side," Sethos explained.

"Amariana is my enemy, as are all who pledge their allegiance to the Demon God, Diablos," Virgil objected.

"You didn't kill her after finding out?" Sethos was surprised, "You're too soft. You need to get more hate in your heart before you'll be truly ready to join me. Your training in Chaos needs to be tempered," Sethos instructed. "I can show you," Sethos spoke with passion. "Power beyond containing, enough to control or destroy whomever you wish," Sethos said excitedly.

"No," Virgil firmly reiterated, "Never, never Harbinger. I will never stand at your side, while I am in control of my own mind, my own fate, my own destiny!" Virgil shouted.

"Then this conflict is at an end. It is time to achieve my destiny, and do what I came to accomplish," Sethos stepped up to the barrier blocking him from walking closer to the Omega manor.

"Get him away from the barrier!" Professor Ramuh urged, his complexion ghostly from blood loss. Several brothers got to their feet, Devil Arms drawn, and went after Sethos.

"You're no match for Ultima Weapon!" Sethos cried and swung his blade towards the approaching warriors. A wave of darkness, the size of a school bus, shot forward with destructive force, knocking all of them down, if they were lucky, they'd survive.

"Now I can finally unleash my Devil Arms TRUE power!" Sethos declared with a smile. He'd waited his whole life to use this power, the Ultimate spell in the universe, more destructive than any other magical incantation. The spell could destroy anything, anyone, similar to an atomic bomb going off...

"Behold the most powerful Chaos spell!" Sethos cried out. "Let it be known that Sethos, the Harbinger of Destruction, son of Lucifer, Lord of the Fallen, was the being to harness the forbidden power. ULTIMA!"

A mushroom cloud of dark purple and black energy rose up from the ground consuming the entire Omega house. It expanded out, reaching several meters past the house stretching towards the brothers, Virgil, and Sethos. Then the sphere of dark energy rippled and stopped growing, the sound of a bomb exploding resounded outwards from the cloud and everything inside was destroyed. The mushroom cloud imploded, and the energy blasted open the contained dark purple energy.

"MOM!" Virgil screamed running towards the mansion, the power of the blast throwing his body into the air like a rag doll. The blast radius of Ultima created a deep and ugly crater where the spell had been cast. Everything that had been in its circumference was gone, nothing was left except a massive hole in the ground, where the proud and mighty Omega mansion once stood. The red brick walls surrounding their complex were blown away from the force released by the spell. There was nothing left of their beloved home or the family members who'd been inside...

# Chapter 25 The Edge of Darkness

Virgil's world was shattered. He was a crumpled heap in the grass, thrown back to where the gates of the Omega house used to exist, because nothing of their home existed anymore. Virgil couldn't stop himself from breaking down, tears freely flowed from his eyes, so many people had been inside, parents, siblings, MOM! Virgil's mother had stayed behind, too concerned for him to leave!

"MOM!" Virgil cried out in vain struggling to get up. Ragnorak was lying next to him in the grass, along with Soul Reaver. Virgil grabbed Ragnorak, its golden sphere of light surrounding him, and beginning to heal his broken body. Virgil got to his feet staring out at where the smoking crater now existed. "MOM!" Virgil screamed running to the edge. Nothing, there was nothing there, what could have survived?

Virgil turned around, still bodies of Death Dealers, Paladins, and brothers littered the yard. Sethos stood proud of his handiwork looking on at the massive destruction with awe, Virgil's eyes narrowed into a scathing glare. "YOU!" Virgil accused, "You killed her! You killed my mother!" Virgil cried.

"Did you not feel that? Diablos' power was unleashed," Sethos whispered looking off.

"YOU'RE DEAD!" Virgil screamed. Virgil brought his scythe to his hand with a thought, the dark flames spreading up his arm.

"You still want to fight?" Sethos asked in disbelief. "Playing with you has lost its appeal, I must return to the Ever After. I can't rest on the laurels of my success! No doubt Lilith and the God Generals will want to hear all about the operation's triumph," Sethos boasted to Virgil turning from him to leave.

"You took everything from me! I HATE YOU!" Virgil screamed.

Virgil ran at Sethos jumping into the air so his wings could propel him faster. Virgil's Devil Arms slammed against Ultima Weapon, the massive sword not budging against Virgil's assault. Sethos blasted Virgil back with a wave of darkness, Virgil released a burst of light from Ragnorak, it managed to block some, but the rest came crashing over him like a massive wave in the ocean, he fell to the ground, too much pain coursing through his system.

"Now you're just being rude!" Sethos shouted getting angry. "And after we had such a nice time bonding," Sethos sneered at Virgil. "You have no one to blame but yourself Redeemer! I couldn't have cast Ultima, if you hadn't brought me so close to death! You killed your own mother," Sethos insulted Virgil.

"I'LL KILL YOU!" Virgil leapt up and like a wild animal, anger consuming his thoughts and rational thinking, the flames of Soul Reaver reached out to cover his entire body. This had never happened when he wielded Ragnorak, once the dark flames covered its Devil Arms symbol, Ragnorak flashed, disappearing. Only a shimmer of gold light was left behind, it fell to the ground, fading from existence. He couldn't wield the Holy Blade with Soul Reaver like this. Covered in flaming body armor, Soul Reaver's flames rising high along his blade and body, Virgil flew forward to fight Sethos once more. Virgil managed to cleanly dodge the first blast of energy, and tear into Sethos when he got close, tearing open a large section of his armor with the scythe. Sethos thrust out his other fist, punching at Virgil's deadly body, a sphere of energy pushed Virgil back. Sethos arm was burned in the process, he held it to his side in searing agony he howled.

"You'll pay for that one Redeemer!" Sethos yelled narrowing his eyes. "I've gone easy on you, as a favor to your father, but I don't care for your attitude. I might as well try out Ultima once more before I go, see how it does against a single opponent, versus a well spelled fortress," Sethos clenched his burnt hand into a fist, Ultima Weapon radiating power.

"You can't possibly take anymore," Virgil forced out through clenched teeth, his tone demonic. "Doc, Homer, Damian, Zane, all those families, OUR families, MY MOTHER!" Virgil screamed at the tops of his lungs, feeling them hurt as he bellowed.

"You haven't begun to know suffering," Sethos smiled sadistically, like he'd be pleased to be the tour guide. "Allow me to instruct you on the power of Darkness!" Sethos raised his Devil Arms in the air, and it howled a sinister, evil, and hungry cry.

Virgil grinded his teeth narrowing his eyes in hatred, the flames along his skin cradling his anger and contempt. Virgil had never known such hatred, all he wanted was to cause pain, to tear Sethos apart, and delight in watching him die. Virgil had never had such dark thoughts, it went against everything he thought he was, who he considered himself to be. Virgil felt a power bubbling below the surface inside him, different from Ascending. Ascending was like feeling conscious control of his spirit, in turn harnessing complete awareness and function over his brain and body, pushing himself to superhuman levels. This power…was foreign, it didn't come from within himself, it came from within his Devil Arms. A wellspring of power, HIS for the taking! But the power wanted control, unlike when he Ascended which was a union, a partnership, the price for this great power, was dominion. It would not share control of his body, it wanted it all. Virgil wanted Sethos to pay! At all costs! Nothing else mattered anymore…

"I'll show you the power of Darkness!" Virgil declared in a demonic tone. Focusing on the power he'd tried so hard to contain within himself, he embraced it. Virgil began to hover off the ground, his pitch-black eyes narrowing in focus as power cascaded all around him. Virgil raised his left hand outstretched to the heavens, Soul Reaver spinning around above his hand eerily.

"Virgil don't do this!" Vahn begged running towards his Little Brother.

Gabriel and Tarek grabbed their best friend, "He's too dangerous!" Tarek cried out.

"Virgil!" Vahn screamed. "You're more than the Darkness! Don't let it control you!"

Soul Reaver whispered dark unsettling thoughts into his mind, the words bubbled to his lips. "Hellfire," Virgil whispered to Soul Reaver. Soul Reaver howled its Soul Scream, its voice deeper than Ultima Weapon's, wilder, more sadistic. Columns of fire like tornado funnels burst out from the ground, three, four, five, they began to weave around Virgil. This power hadn't cost him a drop of power from his aura. The fire wanted to be used by him, it hungered for his command, to do his bidding. The fire was responding to his thoughts, and it wanted to burn everything Virgil wanted it to burn. Virgil felt the massive columns of fire dancing around him, following the mental image in his mind, his to control.

"Destroy the Harbinger!" Virgil commanded. Soul Reaver flew forth and the columns of fire followed.

"Ultima Weapon!" Sethos cried out its power surging out from the blade. The first column of fire descended on him, twisting like a snake, it slammed into the ground, a massive twister! The rest of the columns striking right after! The energy from Ultima Weapon surged out, fighting back the dark fire, struggling against the gathering strength. More columns erupted around Virgil, the width of large trees. They snaked up to gently glide past him, before savagely flying forward to destroy for their master. The fire kept coming, Virgil simply wanted more, needed more to accomplish his desires, and the earth responded.

Sethos began screaming, the flames had formed a cocoon around him, that was slowly gathering in, Ultima Weapon was releasing a protective blast of power, but was buckling under the unending might of the indomitable power of nature. Soul Reaver glided back to Virgil, hovering in the air before him, twisting around. Virgil hadn't taken his eyes off of Sethos, he wanted to watch him burn, and wouldn't rest until he had. He felt so good at that moment, he didn't know why he hadn't used this power sooner. It felt GOOD to hate, it felt GREAT to punish the one who had hurt him. The euphoric high was almost numbing, Virgil's perception of things had dialed down, narrowing to killing Sethos. He couldn't really think past that, he couldn't feel much of anything either, which he was thankful for. Virgil never wanted to have to feel pain like he had moments ago, ever again. There was no reason to go back to that.

Virgil slowly clenched his left fist together, the twisting almost living funnels of fire, that sprung from the bowels of the planet's mantle, grew tighter around Sethos, mimicking Virgil's movements. Virgil's ears buzzed; it was annoying. He slowly turned his head to the right, staring up at him from fifteen feet down on the broken and burnt grounds of the Omega fraternity, was Vahn, yelling his heart out.

"Virgil listen to me!" Vahn pleaded. "I know you want Sethos dead, we all want him to pay for what he's done! But this isn't the way!"

"Vahn let's go!" Gabriel demanded. "It's too dangerous! We need to get some distance from them!"

Vahn lavished Furybrand to his hand swinging in Gabriel's direction, "I'm not leaving without Virgil!" He told his pledge brother with a tone that left no room for arguing. Vahn was willing to die trying to bring Virgil back from the brink of the abyss, Vahn just prayed his Lil hadn't jumped over its enticing edge...

"Virgil please, let me in!" Vahn demanded a column of fire twisting up from the ground not ten feet from where he was standing, the heat was uncomfortably intense on his skin. The flaming tornado reached forward to leech onto Sethos, who was almost consumed. "Let me help you Lil! I know you're hurting, we all are! I need you to know, you don't have to face this pain alone!" Vahn yelled. "I'm here Virgil!"

Virgil's eyes narrowed at Vahn, he extended his right hand towards him, he was distracting Virgil. *Kill him, kill them all,* a dark voice whispered. *Every, last, one.* Virgil needed to finish his goal, he just wanted him to go away. Fire began to gather in Virgil's palm.

"Vahn get the hell out of there!" Magnus demanded. A tourniquet had been placed at the stub where his hand had been, he was ghost white, too weak to even materialize his staff into his Devil Arms hand.

"Virgil your mother is dead!" Vahn screamed at the top of his lungs. "Sue Pitcher was destroyed with the Omega house, Brody's sister, Benson's father, Lamar's grandmother, and countless others!" At the mention of his mother's name Virgil hesitated, the flames that surrounded him dying down slightly. Mom? Pain too unbearable to handle came to him, Virgil wasn't strong enough to cope with this, the fire was easier, it felt better. Virgil's eyes narrowed, the fire spiraled out of his hand, dancing through the air, snaking towards Vahn. More fire erupted from bellow the ground, heading towards Sethos, the gathering of fire was larger than the Omega house had been, and was beginning to touch the trees surrounding them.

"YOUR MOTHER IS DEAD VIRGIL, DEAD! YOU WILL NEVER SEE HER AGAIN!" Vahn bellowed as loud as he could, going for shock rather than reason. "AND I AM SORRY MY BROTHER!" Tears streamed down his face. "FOR NOT BEING ABLE TO KEEP THE BAD THINGS AWAY FROM OUR HOME! FOR NOT KEEPING MY PROMISE TO YOU, THAT I'D KEEP HER SAFE!"

Virgil began shaking the words made it to his ears, he could hear him…Vahn.

"I KNOW YOU'RE IN PAIN," Vahn sobbed, "BUT YOU'RE NOT ALONE VIRGIL! I'M RIGHT HERE! THE DARKNESS MAY FEEL GOOD, THE NUMBNESS MAY FEEL GREAT! BUT PAIN IS WHAT MAKES YOU HUMAN! IT'S THE THING THAT ALLOWS YOU TO BE EMPATHETIC TOWARDS OTHERS, SHARING AND UNDERSTANDING THAT PAIN, AND HELPING OTHERS TO GET THROUGH IT! DON'T GO WHERE I CAN'T FOLLOW VIRGIL! DON'T LEAVE ME BROTHER!"

The fire racing towards Vahn died before it reached him. Virgil slowly descended to the ground, the black flames surrounding him subsiding.

"Lean on me," Vahn whispered, "That's what I'm here for brother."

Soul Reaver didn't want to release its hold, even with Virgil now in control of his own mind, the Devil Arms had control of his body and refused to relinquish control.

"I love you so much Virgil, I'm sorry, I don't know what to do besides hug you," Vahn poured his heart out to him slowly approaching him.

A tear trembled down Virgil's face, a Devil never cries. To cry is to feel, Soul Reaver's hold was broken. The scythe disappeared in a cloud of smoke, and the fire that grew from the earth, twisted back down into the massively deep holes they'd tunneled up from. Vahn embraced Virgil, who began sobbing uncontrollably.

"I lost her!" Virgil cried out. "She's gone, she's gone," he told himself. Virgil knew this was his fault, everything. The Chalice, all of the deaths, Amariana, Sethos…he'd brought this upon Bay Valley, upon the Omegas. Virgil knew others would feel the same. But none of that really mattered to Virgil, he felt so numb from all the death. His mother was gone, his world had ended. Nothing really mattered anymore…

"I'm so sorry," Vahn whispered holding onto him fiercely. The rest of the fraternity, those who were conscious and alive, slowly came towards them.

"We should finish the Harbinger now!" Professor Ifrit declared. "We can't allow our tragedy to be reenacted by this foul ingrate!" he yelled.

"I'LL DO IT!" Gabriel thundered fiercely. "His life belongs to me," his words were uncharacteristically cold and ruthless.

Gabriel and the others approached the smoldering body of Sethos, his Devil Arms weapon had disappeared, only the dark mark on his hand remained. Gabriel screamed into the night charging the still body of Sethos. A loud crack filled the night air, like the sky had broken open, a figure glided down to the ground, landing next to Sethos' body.

"His life belongs to ME," Lucifer thundered back at Gabriel. Lucifer tucked his large black wings on his back. The Fallen Judge stood close to eight feet tall, his very presence was stifling, his aura was so powerful within its sphere of influence, moving became impossible.

Lucifer's aura was larger than any being Virgil had ever met, and it had a commanding authority, one that did not tolerate disobedience. This was THE Lucifer, the guy from all the stories, some people get him confused with The Devil, which is actually Diablos. Lucifer is the most infamous Fallen of them all, his power and presence reflected his authority as Commander in Chief of the Fallen.

"You're not taking him anywhere!" Gabriel shouted running into Lucifer's aura he immediately went still, his body frozen in place.

"Mortal," Lucifer spoke dangerously, "Your grossly over familiar tone is a good way to lose a head. Choose your next words carefully, a half breed does not make demands of a GOD!" Lucifer's voice thundered down and everyone who heard was forced down closer to the ground, like an invisible thousand-pound weight had dropped their shoulders.

Virgil was a wreck. He didn't know if he had it in him to fight, Lucifer was more than anything he was ready for, he just wanted to go to sleep, and not wake up. This couldn't be his life; he didn't want this life.

"Redeemer," Lucifer called out. Virgil raised his attention, meeting the gaze of the mighty immortal. "You did this to my son?" Lucifer asked his face was calm and collected, but his golden eyes, betrayed his irritation.

"He killed my mother," Virgil said, he didn't know what else to say. He looked down; he was finding it hard to care about this. Nothing mattered anymore…

"You need to be taught a lesson about obedience," Lucifer warned Virgil, "Its time you took your proper place in the Ever After, your allegiance to the Paladins will no longer be tolerated."

"Piss off!" Virgil screamed. "I don't give a shit about anything! My mother is DEAD!" Virgil screamed. "LEAVE ME ALONE!"

Lucifer narrowed his eyes, "Omega Weapon!" Lucifer commanded, a katana, three times as long as the average and twice as thick came to his hand. The brothers who had the strength to stand all reacted as one drawing their Devil Arms. "I will be spoken to with more respect than that, mortal," Lucifer scolded Virgil coldly.

Virgil didn't respond, he had nothing more to say. He didn't summon his Devil Arms, he didn't want to touch Soul Reaver, and he doubted Ragnorak would come to his aide, he honestly didn't want to touch it either. He was tired of the fighting, using his Devil Arms was what had gotten him here, they'd brought nothing but disaster and ruin to his life. Virgil cursed them both, regretting having ever fallen into this life. He didn't want to wield them anymore.

"Virgil snap out of it!" Magnus demanded. "We need you!"

"Virgil?" Vahn asked.

Virgil felt so numb, he didn't want to talk anymore, so he didn't.

Lucifer spread his wings and bolted across the sky towards Virgil. Virgil didn't run, he didn't turn his back, he slowly tilted his head to watch. The sky sounded like it was being ripped apart! Raphael, Third God General, burst forth racing through the sky. Raphael drew a regal and powerful lance into existence, he slammed into Lucifer crossing blades with him.

"Still your hand!" Raphael commanded.

"I'll not take orders from you!" Lucifer shouted breaking contact, he flew back to make another dive for Virgil.

"I won't let you take my son!" Raphael yelled. "If you seek to harm him, I'll be standing in your way!" Raphael fiercely asserted.

"You dare defy me!" Lucifer shouted. "Stand down Raphael!"

Raphael came to land near Virgil, standing protectively in front of him. Lucifer landed a healthy distance in front of them both.

"We have what we wanted," Raphael told Lucifer. "The Chalice is destroyed, and Diablos will be more than pleased. Let us return to the Ever After," Raphael suggested.

"Your son," Lucifer said coldly.

"What of him?" Raphael asked defiantly.

"He needs to pledge his loyalty, or suffer the consequences," Lucifer said flatly.

"He is shattered right now," Raphael insisted, "He needs time to recover from his loss. Forcing him over to our side now, would only break his mind," Raphael explained. "Better to wait till he comes willingly. I have seen it."

"And what if he never comes willingly?" Lucifer asked.

"Let Diablos decide how much time he should have," Raphael insisted.

"One year," Lucifer declared, "If Virgil does not come to our side by then, we'll take him by force, or end him." Lucifer lowered his guard his sword losing its corporeal form. He walked over to his son. "I have no interest in crossing blades with you in front of this rabble," Lucifer picked up his son's unconscious body, miraculously he was still alive. He did not love his son like a normal father loved their child. His son was more like property, and disrespecting his property was disrespecting him. Lucifer turned to give Raphael a blank stare.

Raphael nodded and turned to Virgil, "I'm sorry for your loss," Raphael spoke like he meant it, he walked up to Virgil and embraced him. "You will always have a family, and a home, as long as I live," Raphael whispered into his ear. Raphael then walked over to stand with Lucifer.

"Let us be off," Lucifer said sounding bored.

"Goodbye Virgil," Raphael called out to him with a sad smile. The three of them slowly lifted into the air, the sound of the sky ripping apart rent the air, and they disappeared.

They were left in silence, their world shattered. The brothers who had survived, didn't know what to do, too many were lost, the ones who survived were forever changed. Sirens descended on Bay Valley, the second wave of rescue workers, only this time Death Dealers weren't there to take them out. Word spread quickly that the Death Dealers had left. The explosion at Bay Valley and subsequent fire storm, which could be seen from the distance, drew in brothers and friends from campus. Dante, Birdy, everyone from campus started arriving, they slowed down to a crawl as they approached the ravaged ground, standing open mouthed, their house was gone.

"What the hell happened?" Dante screamed running up to everyone with a group of brothers.

"Where's my grandmother?" Lamar asked.

"Where's Agustin?" Troy asked looking for his best friend.

No one answered any of them, the bodies were everywhere. A few brothers began going around, people were crying. Reinforcements from Alexandros showed up, they were too late.

They gathered their dead, and went about helping to start with the cover up, shaping the presentation of what had happened at the University to the American public. Something this big wasn't going to be polished over. The Paladins had powerful connections and worked with their contacts to make the cover story as credible as possible.

Bay Valley's Chapter of Betas were shut down by the Paladins. Malachi's relationship and secret alliance with Sethos was revealed, and their Chapter was labeled as terrorists by the Paladin government. Maybe someday the Betas would be welcomed back to Bay Valley. Though those brothers seeking to reestablish their Charter would have to prove to Alexandros that they were loyal to the Paladins.

The aftermath of the attack had profound effects. Campus had been damaged, hundreds dead, more injured. The massacre became a national news story. Officially it was being labeled a terrorist attack, a bomb was set off at the Omega house, and campus was stormed by a group of militants wielding blades and explosives. The Paladins did their part to shape the story, though a tragedy of this scope was hard to conceal details. Classes were canceled for the next week, they'd be having finals, and the professors were just skipping over material. The students and families of Bay Valley were traumatized; the whole community was grieving. There were campus vigils, speakers, and therapists came in to help the students and parents process.

The brothers had lost more than most, besides their home, countless brothers had fallen. Gabriel's brother, Ezekiel, Louie's Big Benson, Doc, Agustin, Zane, and Homer. The brothers that lived had to deal with the insurmountable loss before them. Virgil had lost his friend Damian, who had died selflessly protecting the people of Bay Valley. Virgil was numb, and tuned out from the world around him. He'd lost countless friends, though something that cut just as deep, his girlfriend Amariana was actually a Death Dealer spy, and a Seraph, the Gatekeeper.

He'd met her twice before she came to Bay Valley, she'd just been in full battle armor, her face hidden behind her helmet. Virgil felt foolish, he'd been completely enamored with a woman who'd been playing him from the start. Virgil's mother…she'd died waiting for him, scared, worrying he'd never come back. He felt responsible for all the death, his own loss, all of it would have been avoided if he'd been a better person. If he'd not let his arrogance blind him, he'd have sat out of the Tournament, the Omegas wouldn't have won the Chalice, and he'd still have a mother. Now, he had no one. Virgil felt like his world had ended.

# Chapter 26 Some Losses Cut Too Deep

The brothers had to start looking for housing immediately. The semester still had a week to finish out after the temporary break, and the Winter Semester was only a month and a half away. People started grouping up, house and apartment shopping. Gabriel, Magnus, Tarek, and Jagger found a house to rent fifteen minutes from Campus. Vahn, Brody, and Rowan found a house ten minutes in the other direction. Nolan took it upon himself to find a townhome apartment for Louie, Nev, Virgil and himself. They were only signing a six-month lease, to get them through to the end of the school year. Everyone was upset over the loss of the Omega house, it had been more than their fraternity house, to many it had become their home. They lost everything they owned, Virgil didn't even have a change of clothes, as his were partially destroyed and filled with dirt and blood.

Blair took Virgil, and Birdy, they crashed on her couches. Louie crashed across the street at Tucker's place, he wanted to look after him. Following the loss of his best friend and roommate Homer, he'd become more introverted. Tucker was usually so lively, cracking jokes, and making everyone laugh. He walked around like a ghost, scarred by what he'd seen. Most brothers had the same haunted expression following that terrible night, some losses cut too deep...

The incident at Bay Valley was labeled an act of Terrorism, the organization behind the heinous day, had not yet been identified. Over a hundred people were lost, hundreds more were injured, funerals kept everyone busy. The days that followed, Virgil dwelled on thoughts of his friends, of Doc, Zane, Homer and Damian, friends he'd never see again. Benson, Agustin, Ezekiel, brothers whose lives were over; their stories had ended. The only time they'd be talked about was in old memories, there was no future, no more...anything for them.

Virgil was like a zombie, so disoriented, detached from his surroundings, he was being taken care of, and looked after by his friends. Blair went to a thrift shop and bought him a couple of cheap outfits. So many of the brothers were suffering, some brother's parents didn't want them in the fraternity anymore, some brothers didn't really feel like being in the fraternity anymore. Morale was at the lowest Virgil had ever witnessed, and a large share of the animosity was being channeled towards Virgil. For the first time since he had become a part of the Omegas, he felt like an outsider with his brothers. When he would see them by chance, they skirted his attention. There wasn't a house for them to congregate anymore. Brothers were working on getting apartments, but it took time. Without a central location for them to talk, bond, and complete the business of the fraternity, a new and unknown social atmosphere was starting to be explored, life in a fraternity without a fraternity house.

Virgil was depressed, all he wanted was privacy, space, and isolation. He slept as much as he could, ten to twelve hours a day, his sleep schedule started to become erratic. Amariana, the woman who Virgil had fallen in love with, the person whom he had thought about night and day for months, she'd been spying on him. It still didn't feel real. Virgil had been proud for his mother to meet her too, he'd never 'brought a girl home' before. Sue had adored Amari; Virgil couldn't have been happier. But Sue…his mother was gone. He felt excruciating guilt over her death, agonizing over his mistakes, he knew the brothers blamed him for the loss of the Omega house, he did too. They'd never actually said those words, and Virgil didn't dare bring it up. Of course his best friends stuck faithfully by his side, Louie, Birdy, Dante, and Blair they were sullen from the events as well, everyone was more quiet than usual, deep in thought.

Gabriel and his family took Ezekiel's death hard. Gabriel overnight had become a changed man. Less humorous, more serious, less playful, more stern, less friendly, more cold.

He'd been hardened by his loss, deep within his heart he harbored hatred for Sethos, and desired vengeance on the man who had killed his brother. Virgil hadn't talked to Gabriel since everything….TK spoke with Virgil briefly, they ran into each other on campus, and took a walk so they could speak privately.

"He doesn't blame you," TK said seriously with conviction, "I know he cares about you. He's just…angry and hurt. He's hardened, death does that," TK hung her head. "He blames himself for his brother's death. His family is taking this hard, his other brothers and father are falling apart," TK got misty eyes. "I wish I could do more for him, for you," TK got quiet. "There's nothing you can say to someone who has suffered tremendous loss. What words have meaning? What speech can placate the scars?" TK hugged Virgil and they walked back to the others.

The funerals were hard to get through, Virgil had never been good at that sort of thing, all the depression, crying, it always brought him down to a very dark, very low place. The fraternity offered their plots, at Oak Park Cemetery, and funeral expenses for free, to any and all family who wanted, or needed them. Virgil accepted the generous offer for his mother, he invited her friends to come, her group of friends had their own get together, to share pictures and stories of their time with Sue Pitcher. So many unanswered questions, so many lies, stories, half-truths, the act started to become memorized, Virgil sank deeper into a blurry mess. It was easier not trying to process things alone right now. Virgil talked with families and relatives of the brothers that had come, so many were scared for the fraternity to be at Bay Valley.

Virgil was surprised by visitors at the funeral for his mother, Alexa, Sybil, and King Aseril Diamond had come to Bay City, to support everyone in this time of great tragedy. It was the first time Virgil had seen them without their wings. Their clothing was stylish and classy.

The Grand Prytanis certainly helped to ease the tension surrounding the fraternity, as the top guy in their organization he did his best, speaking with each family to help them sort things out, and try to come to an understanding. Doc's family were taking things among the best in the group, his mother was a strong woman, and though she mourned her son she had fight in her eyes. Gina was doing her best, socializing with her sisters, and the brothers, she'd become a little sister to most of the Omegas overnight. Alexa gave Virgil a giant hug, squeezing him tight when they first saw each other.

"Hang in there," Alexa whispered to him. Virgil didn't mean to react so strongly, he started crying and fell into Alexa's arms, sobbing uncontrollably. You expect to outlive your parents, but no one plans on being an orphan as a teenager. Virgil still had ten months before he turned twenty; he was an adult now though, there were no parents to lean on anymore. Virgil collected himself, and sat down smiling at Alexa, he realized that he did have family still. Friends are the family you choose for yourself, and Virgil loved his friends like family. Sybil was so good with the people, she very slowly made her way through the crowd, meeting new faces, and genuinely inquiring as to people's health. She was the Grand Hypophetes after all. She was so busy Virgil didn't have a lot of time to talk with her. When they bumped into each other, she hugged him affectionately, with familiarity. Virgil got red in the cheeks, he never knew how to respond to her.

"Hang in there," Sybil whispered to him.

"Thank you for coming, Lady Diamond," Virgil told Sybil sincerely as they broke contact and she rubbed his shoulder, "I was so shocked when Alexa came running up to me!" Virgil laughed a little with a small smile.

"She would have come with or without us," Sybil sighed shrugging her shoulders, "She's been bound and determined to come visit you since…everything happened," Sybil put it gently looking Virgil in the eyes.

"She's a great friend," Virgil nodded.

"She considers you one of her only true friends," Sybil admitted looking down, almost embarrassed.

Virgil didn't know how to respond to statement like that, "Thank you, that's humbling," Virgil struggled at a loss for words. "Alexa means a lot to me, she's a dear friend," Virgil settled on.

Sybil stepped slightly closer, speaking softly, "I know things are going to be really hard for you, these next few months, the next year, or even your whole life, being the Redeemer. I'm so sorry you lost your mother, Virgil. I need you to know, that even if you don't have your…mother anymore, you are never alone Virgil," Sybil said passionately getting a little misty eyed. "The Creator, his infinite love, wisdom, and Light, are always within you, within your spirit. If ever you're feeling like the dark is clouding your heart, or your mind. Close your eyes, feel the world around you, and the light that is within you Virgil. Let it guide you," Sybil said passionately.

"Thank you," Virgil smiled at Sybil, she was wise beyond her years.

"You'll be coming to stay with us for the winter break," Sybil offered. "We'd love to have you for the holidays."

"Virgil!" Blair called out coming up to them, "How ya holding up buddy?"

"Take care Virgil, we'll talk more soon," Sybil smiled and walked on.

The evening of the funerals, the Grand Prytanis called together a small meeting at Professor Ramuh' house. Thankfully Professor Ramuh had not perished from his wounds in the battle. It was a modest mansion on Center Avenue, on the east side of Bay City. The property was under powerful protection wards. Professor Ramuh had to meet each new guest at the gate, to allow them access, past the barrier that surrounded his property. They met in a large living room parlor on the first floor. A small gathering of Omegas and Paladins from the Capital were present. The topic was the destruction of the Chalice of Immortals, and the actions of the Death Dealers, as well as their plans for the future. Once pleasantries had been exchanged, the Grand Prytanis called the room to order and took the floor.

"I gathered you here, to tell you something you should have been told long ago," Aseril said to the people present. "The Chalice of Immortals was more than a symbol, and token of our history. It was one of three Nethicite, powerful magicite containing Diablos' essence. When destroyed, Diablos regains a portion of his power, consciousness, and influence," Aseril told them.

"That's why the Death Dealers attacked campus?" Magnus was furious. "We were protecting a piece of Diablos' soul, or whatever it is? WHY WOULD YOU BRING THAT HERE!" Magnus screamed.

"It was tradition for the strongest Chapter to guard the Chalice," Aseril said meekly.

"We begged you to keep it!" Magnus recalled. "Gabriel and I told you we didn't feel safe taking it. We didn't know it held the Devil's soul," Magnus sank into his seat getting very quiet, and very scary.

"Why weren't we told?" Gabriel asked. "Why didn't the Paladins know about this?" he was angry as well.

"The Paladins have known since the day the Judges handed it to them. They kept it a secret, to protect everyone from the Chalice. Knowing what it held inside wouldn't have changed anything, that is why you weren't told," Aseril said to Gabriel, he sounded sincere.

"Did you see what could happen to us? To our families?" Gabriel asked staring Aseril down.

"No," Aseril said solemnly. "The future is never promised. Choices change the flow of fate, creating new futures, sometimes with little notice."

"What are we supposed to do?" Brody asked him. "How are we supposed to recover as a Chapter?" Brody yelled, he was visibly shaking.

"You move forward, and rebuild," Aseril said simply. "If you can't heal from the memories of war, then that is not to be shamed. There is no cowardice in settling into life with the humans, and stepping away from the Nephilim world," Aseril said this to the whole group. "You are all Nephilim yes, which means you are part human. The choice is yours," Aseril smiled. "We wish our brothers and sisters freedom to pursue happiness as they see it."

"The Capital is funding the rebuilding of the Omega house," Professor Ramuh told them. "The Chapter should be able to move into the new fraternity house, not next year, but the following fall."

"Two years!" Louie groaned. "We'll be going into our fourth year," Louie sulked in his spot.

"How are we supposed to do fraternity stuff?" Nigel asked angrily. "Like Brotherhoods and meetings?"

"Be thankful that we're getting a new house," Professor Ramuh told the men. "Some Chapters don't have fraternity houses. We'll survive."

"Thank you for your time," Aseril said to the room. "As for the Paladins, we'll continue to fight the Death Dealers, and protect humanity. Nothing about our mission has changed. In fact, our resolve has only strengthened. Diablos is now stirring in the Ever After. The Paladins must protect the last two pieces of Nethicite. If destroyed, Diablos will end our way of life, and that of every human on the planet. Every civilization will fall. Nature will decay, and the living things that make this world unique will perish." Aseril slammed his fist against his chest over his heart, "We are all that stand between this world, and the War of Ragnorak!" Aseril yelled. "Continue to fight by our side, rebuild your Chapter," Aseril looked out at the brother's faces with passion. "We need Upsilon Delta," Aseril told them. "There is something special about this Chapter, and it hasn't been lost. Your fallen brothers live on through you. Carry them with you, honor them by living the code of the Omega, Valor, Honor, Brotherhood," Aseril's words were heartfelt among the men.

Aseril didn't stay long, the brothers were saddened to hear Professor Ifrit was retiring at the end of this year. The battle with Sethos had taken too much out of him. Professor Ramuh was also retiring, the wounds inflicted on him had permanently disabled him, he was having a hard time getting around. With Ezekiel dead, they'd have no Chapter Advisors. Gabriel told the brothers he was working on a solution to their problem. The brothers used the time to heal and grieve. Classes weren't being suspended forever. Everyone had to concentrate on academics.

A week later, it was Sunday night. The brothers had elections for Jeweled Officers, it was time for the leadership of the Chapter to change hands. Magnus had reserved a room on the second floor of the science building, people started trickling in, they taped newspaper over the doors, and closed the windows. It felt strange having their meeting on campus, discussing secret fraternity business, away from the Omega house.

Virgil was running for Grammatues again. Troy was running against him. Gabriel became their new Prytanis. It was a natural fit, he had been the Social Chair, Hegemon, Epiprytanis, and now, the leader of the Chapter. Truth be told he'd always been the guy everyone followed. Nev was elected Epiprytanis after a long debate. Virgil didn't know if he'd get the position, Troy and him sat out in the hall for a long time. Virgil was guessing the brothers were talking about him, some were probably fighting hard to get Troy the position. Troy was a great brother, he deserved to be a Jeweled Officer the same as Virgil. Magnus came out into the hall after making them wait almost forty-five minutes.

"Brothers, welcome your new Grammateus, Virgil!" Magnus shouted. "Who is already our Grammateus," Magnus smirked as the room clapped for Virgil, as they did for everyone after the nominees were brought in, and the winner announced. "We thought he deserved a shot at having a full term. Congratulations Virgil, take your seat," Magnus motioned and Virgil nodded returning to running the speaker's list, and counting the votes.

"Good!" Jace joked as he got up out the seat. "It sucks doing your job!" Jace said to Virgil and took a seat back with the other brothers.

Nolan was elected the new Crysophylos much to everyone's delight, he made a vow to get the Chapter free money from the University's budget. Birdy became the new Histor, he impressed the brothers with a well-organized presentation, talking about all the Alumni relations that the Histor should be doing but wasn't. Hypophetes was the most brutal election, six brothers ran for the position. The top three contenders were Louie, Jagger, and Rowan. Virgil wished he could have run, though with everything that had happened, he knew he didn't stand a chance. Virgil made a case for Louie, as did some of the Rho class brothers. The older brothers backed Jagger, speaking to his experience, and pointing out the E-board was all younger guys, save for Gabriel so far. This point drove home the argument, helping Jagger win, much as it had helped Thiago in last year's election. Jagger was overjoyed at being elected, he smiled and got misty eyed. He wasn't an emotional guy.

"I'll make you guys proud you elected me," Jagger told his brothers with a large grin.

"Glad to have you on board," Gabriel grinned and bugged his pledge brother. "I needed another Lambda," he said to his friend.

Zender was reelected the Pylortes. He was so good at his position, which was great, because no one else wanted the job! Zender was the only one who ran, Jace at the last minute demanded Magnus let him run against him, so Zender just wasn't given the position. Jace made a joke, then said vote for Zender, that was his five-minute speech. Magnus got peeved, claiming Jace was just wasting their time. They quickly voted, it became a joke and broke up the tension of the long meeting. Virgil read aloud some of the ballots, half of them were for people not in their fraternity, some like Superman, or George Washington weren't very serious. Brody won the Hegemon position. Virgil had always seen him as such the goofy, prankster of the group, he hoped he could be serious as the Hegemon. Lax and loose Hegemon's made for pledges who didn't take the fraternity, or the traditions seriously. Sigma class would be pledging within a few months, brothers had mixed feelings. They needed more brothers after losing so many. Some were just not ready to get close to new people, thankfully they didn't start pledging till February, so there was time to mend those feelings.

Virgil passed his classes and had three weeks off from school. He didn't have his mom to go home to, or a fraternity house to spend time at. Virgil didn't see his friends as much, now that they were so spread out. Virgil needed the time, he was still hurting, his mother was on his mind every day. He hadn't used his Devil Arms since fighting Sethos, he knew he'd have to eventually, he just wished that day would never come. For the first time in his life, Virgil looked to the future, with uncertainty.

# Epilogue

At the center of the Ever After, was a giant scar that stretched far across the land. It was a massive crater that stretched for miles with nothing except in the very center. A shrine had been built there reminiscent of the Greek Parthenon. It towered into the sky looking more like a castle, full of towering columns, that cast deep shadows down through the center of the architecture. Inside the building was a large single room, at the head stood a large throne. An enormous humanoid stone statue rested on the throne, over fifty meters high. The statue had a single large black wing stretching out from its back. A smaller throne rested at the feet of the large statue, it was pure black. Sitting in the small throne was a cold woman, with long slick black hair, and demon red eyes. The four God Generals entered the sacred place of Chaos. The Doppelganger, Harbinger, and Gatekeeper were with them. The seven figures approached the two thrones. The woman looked out lazily at her commanders.

"You've done vell," Lilith's cold, voice commended them.

"It is always an honor to receive praise from a self-appointed overlord," Lucifer replied sweetly.

"Do not spoil such a joyous triumph," Lilith spat at Lucifer. "There are only two pieces left to destroy. Ve must focus on finding them as our highest priority." Lilith looked down at the Fallen and Seraphs. "Vhere is the Redeemer?" Lilith asked Lucifer. "You vere told to retrieve him. The Dark Lord vas expecting him to return vith you."

"I was going to bring him by force," Lucifer said angrily through clenched teeth. "Someone intervened," Lucifer looked towards Raphael.

"Raphael?" Lilith's voice left little tolerance for insubordination.

"I suggested that we wait," Raphael said confidently not letting Lilith affect his tone. "Virgil was shattered, to bring him here would have broken his mind."

"I gave Virgil a year," Lucifer said to Lilith. "If he doesn't come to us by then, we take him, or kill him. We won't tolerate anything else," Lucifer finished and looked off.

Hrist stood close by Lucifer, the greatest swordsman to ever take up the art of warfare. Hrist had flowing golden locks, and a fierce beauty. She was a powerful warrior, the mightiest and most feared of the Judges, colder than Lilith, her only love in the world…her undying loyalty to Lucifer. Beezlebub had long white hair, he seemed disinterested, standing furthest away from the thrones, and furthest from the other Fallen. Raphael stood between the Seraphs and Lucifer. Sethos, and Rasler stood alert, their attention focused on Lilith. Amariana was clad in full battle armor, face obscured by a helmet, she stared off hiding in her own thoughts, used to being silent, you stayed out of trouble that way.

"You should have killed him," Hrist said cruelly.

"I tried to do as you commanded," Sethos told Lilith. "I fought till I was rendered bloody and burnt."

"I vouldn't have expected any less from our most faithful servant," Lilith praised Sethos. "I trust you above all others, save for my own children," Lilith smiled at Sethos, a twisted relationship had formed between the two.

"What is our next objective?" Raphael asked wishing to change the topic.

"Send Fallen to Alexandros and take the city," Lilith suggested. "Vith the Oracle ve'll know the locations of the last two Nethicite."

"Our people will suffer heavy casualties," Raphael shook his head. "We'll need those numbers for the greater battles ahead. We should exercise that as a last resort."

"You'll do as your told," Lilith snapped reaching for her mighty blade, gifted to her from Diablos. It could bring true death to any immortal, the Fallen had a healthy fear of her power. She was Diablos' first, and only Creation. Lilith was an immortal, and the most powerful sorceress the world had have known. "Retrieve the Oracle, bring that infidel here a bloody pulp if necessary," Lilith demanded. "But ve vant him alive!"

"That's not up to you!" Lucifer shouted angry with Lilith. "We aren't your spawn; we can't be ordered around like your servants!" Lucifer finished narrowing his eyes at the Demon Queen Mother. "You want him, send your children!"

"You know demons can't get through the barriers around their lands," Lilith shook her head. "Send your armies!"

Lucifer stood tall, pride was his greatest sin, he did not bow to Lilith. "We'll do as Diablos commands," Lucifer's words were steel.

"We serve Diablos, not you," Hrist added crossing her arms.

"I alone have heard his voice since the Dark Lord vas forced into slumber," Lilith said rising from her throne. She grabbed the dark blade that rested beside her chair. "I alone speak the vill of my Master!" Lilith screamed the group slipping slightly back.

"I CAN SPEAK FOR MYSELF," a voice thundered in the room. Everyone's faces fell in surprise, they'd had similar meetings over the course of the millennia they'd been trapped in the Ever After. Never had he joined them in conversation. Diablos' servants stared up, gazing upon

491

the magnificent horror in wonder, their eyes resting on the frozen body of the Demon God. He was still encased in stone, unable to move. His voice echoed out from his body now, his first words since his battle with the Creator. He'd regained a piece of his power, with the destruction of the Chalice.

The room fell to their knees before their leader. "What is thy bidding, my Lord?" Lucifer asked of Diablos.

Diablos' dark laughter echoed through the halls of The Throne of Diablos; the Demon God was awakening!

**About the author:**

Christiano Prime, born and raised in Michigan, by age 10 was an avid reader and developed a passion for storytelling. His dream since he was a child was to become an author and captivate readers' imaginations. When Christiano isn't playing RPG video games, or daydreaming about his next story, he is saving lives as a social worker/counselor in a hospital ER doing crisis interventions and mental health evaluations. Christiano dreams of the day he can live on the West coast and return to Michigan each year for its beautiful summers, and his three dads, two moms, and seven sisters.

This is the third of a seven-book series, the fourth novel is completed, and I'm currently seeking representation from a literary agent or a publishing company. If you liked this book and would like more like it, please rate my novel amazon.com/author/christianoprime and leave a review. Your support and feedback allow me to keep working hard on the next installment of the series. Thank you for taking the time to read my story, by doing so you've helped me fulfill a lifelong dream, and I couldn't be happier to share more! Those interested in being added to my mail list to receive information about upcoming releases send your email address to primechristiano@gmail.com.

www.ingramcontent.com/pod-product-compliance
Lightning Source LLC
Chambersburg PA
CBHW060212030726
47499CB00004B/1017